Ballet of Comedians

BALLET OF
COMEDIANS

---

a novel based on the life of

J. B. P. Molière

by

PETER ARNOTT

THE MACMILLAN COMPANY, NEW YORK, NEW YORK

COLLIER-MACMILLAN LIMITED, LONDON

The Macmillan Company
866 Third Avenue, New York, N.Y. 10022
Collier-Macmillan Canada Ltd., Toronto, Ontario

Library of Congress Catalog Card Number:
71-155272

First Printing

Printed in the United States of America

This book is dedicated to Nicholas Meyer
who has in every sense become
part of it

Ballet comique: Comique for the lovely, tranquil and happy conclusion by which it ends; by the quality of the personages involved, who are almost all gods and goddesses or other heroic persons. *Ballet* because it is a geometrical arrangement of numerous people dancing together under a diverse harmony of many instruments.

BEAUJOYEUX

CONTENTS

PART ONE

Entry and First Remove

THERE WAS SILENCE IN THE ROOM, and heat. There were
also seven people, but these for the moment were of secondary
importance. Heat and silence were tangible things, disputing
possession with the human occupants. The sun that every
August left Paris baked and sprawling had come early this
year. It burned through the leaded glass and etched diamonds
on the floor. On the lonely chair set opposite, a dock where the
prisoner awaited sentence, the young man fidgeted and wished
he could open the window. No use. The small impatience
brought the others' eyes upon him; you could hear eyes move
in this stillness. He sighed inwardly and resigned himself to the
unyielding discomfort of his father's chair. Not merely belonging
to his father, but made by his father; as were all the other chairs
in this room, this house; the couch in the corner, the carpet on
the floor where the sun smoldered, the hangings on the wall.
The house hung out the smell of horsehair, flock and feathers

like a sign of business. It was the smell in which the young man had been brought up. With which, finally, after twenty-one years, his long nose had become dissatisfied. The workshop smell of Jean Poquelin, Upholsterer to the King.

It was Jean who spoke first, denting the silence. His round face shone bright red. How much was heat and how much anger it was impossible to say. The closing of the window was a symbolic act: it signified that this was the most private of private business, family business, and that no signal from the outside world was to disturb the awful solemnity of the Poquelins in conclave. There was no denying, however, that it had its disadvantages. Poquelin the father considered it expedient to speak.

He had relished the silence and its powerful effect upon his son, but enough was enough. Aunt Jeanne was already looking queasy, and what his mother must be feeling he preferred not to think.

"My son," he said. "An actor."

He turned the phrase around his tongue. Disliking the taste, he spat it out.

"My son. An *actor*."

As though on cue, the waxworks in the other chairs sprang to simultaneous life. The young man ran a wary eye over them, wondering, without much hope, which way their favor would lie. How often he had seen these faces in the past. At births, marriages and deaths; at financial crises, now so happily rare; at the inauguration of new ventures and the signing of contracts. Like the choruses in the Greek plays he had learned to read among the Jesuits, they were omnipresent, verbose, platitudinous. Aunt Jeanne with the sniff and watery eyes, as stiff and stuffed in her rusty dress as one of his father's chairs. Fat Uncle Nicolas, belching in memory of lunch, with grease on his chin and business on his mind. No sympathy here. Grandmother Agnes, over seventy, too old to be of use but brought out periodically for effect. It had been impressed on her deaf ears that this was a solemn occasion, and she had her church face on: upright as a ramrod, parchment skin and beady eyes, hands shaking ever so slightly in her lap like old lace in a little breeze, her mind a hundred miles and fifty years away. Louis Cressé, his mother's brother. He had been in and out of the house constantly when his sister was alive; in the ten years since her death he had been seen less often, and only came now on occasions like this. Like Jean and Nicolas Poquelin he was an upholsterer. In the name of Heaven, thought the young man, is there nothing in the world besides upholstery?

The sixth was the unknown quantity. The young man eyed him speculatively, and caught a quick glance in return. This was a member of the family he hardly knew. From his father's side, a cousin. Like the rest, he represented a long-standing family profession, but a different one. Michel Mazuel was a musician, like his father and his father before him. But where they had been mere instrumentalists, Michel had risen to higher things. He was a composer with a court appointment, one of that select, insecure band that catered to the royal pleasures and trusted that the shifts of fashion would never rob them of their livelihood. Not that Michel's face revealed any anxiety. It was fine drawn, delicate, with lashes long enough to be a woman's. In this hot room, this stuffy shrine of commerce, he stood out like a lily in a herb garden. As the young man looked at him, the lid flickered on the quick brown eye. A wink? A sign of favor? He dared not look again for fear he might betray himself. He so desperately needed support. From his brothers and sisters—and he saw them in his mind's eye, on the landing outside with ears pressed to the door—there could come no help whatever. Girls had no voice in such affairs, and the boys had their own interests at heart. Brother Jean might help me, he thought bitterly. If I'm allowed to go the way I want, he'll succeed to the royal appointment. But Jean was too afraid of his father even to serve his own advantage in the case.

A saving notion struck him. If Cousin Michel Mazuel was here, it could only be because he had been summoned. And who could have invited him but his father? Was Jean Poquelin then not totally prejudiced? Was he prepared to make at least a small concession to the right of free choice? Another look at the turkeycock face and hope sank again. One violinist against a whole battery of upholsterers.

Silence fled when the family came to life, and the heat was forgotten. They reasserted their dominion of the room by speaking all at once. Uncle Nicolas fired his heavy guns from the corner. Aunt Jeanne kept up a rattle of light musketry, and even Grandmother exploded periodically. What she said had nothing to do with the matter in hand, but at least it was a noise.

Jean Poquelin cut them off with a gesture. The chorus hushed again and fixed their eyes on their leader. Armored in severity, he stepped forward to annihilate his victim.

"My son," he said. "An actor."

He considered. He had already said this. Time now for the body of the speech. His chorus waited, hands folded, mouths pursed, decently attentive.

Jean-Baptiste made himself as comfortable as he could and let the flood of domestic rhetoric wash over him. He did not need to hear the speech. He could foresee quite accurately the course that it would take, predict whole sentences and paragraphs. Also, he would rather not listen because on the whole he agreed with it. Father, as usual, spoke superb sense, even if he lacked oratorical finesse. The fledgeling dramatist reflected that he could have put it better himself.

But no exception could be taken to the content. First, what he was proposing to do was colossal stupidity. Agreed. There had been upholsterers on both sides of the family for generations. Jean Poquelin had risen to the summit of his profession. The royal appointment not only gave him the entrée to the palace but brought the aristocratic trade. No small thing, snapped Jean Poquelin. Even if (he sighed) the nobility was sometimes slow to pay its bills. In the rigid society of France in this year of Our Lord sixteen hundred and forty-three, where each echelon was separated from those above and below by impenetrable spikes of caste and protocol, Jean Poquelin had built himself a niche. In a land where all illumination descended from the King, he had come near enough to the eternal sun to warm his hands. And was it not appropriate that an eldest son should follow in his father's footsteps, as he had followed in his before him? Particularly when those footsteps led to so illustrious a place; when the son had already been given entrance to the court; when such enormous sums (the bitterness increased here) had been expended on his education, to fit him for the high position he would hold? Had he not gone to the same school as the Prince de Conti himself?

Yes, fretted Jean-Baptiste, if you can say you went to school with someone who had been a boarder when you had been a day-boy; who had a private tutor and a desk with a little gold railing round it; who had a staff of servants to keep away impertinences. Jean-Baptiste had been decently respectful to the Prince. This was proper and politic. He was a child of his time and knew how futures might depend on such coincidences and the right use made of them. The Prince de Conti had been civil in return; that is to say, he had looked on young Poquelin with no more disfavor than on others of his low rank and station. There were other schoolfellows whom Jean-Baptiste had liked far more, certain that his father would not approve of them. Chapelle, for instance, and that long-nosed fellow Cyrano, who was as Parisian as the rest of them but pretended to be Gascon because it sounded more romantic. He had been a wild one. Those satires he had written on the masters . . . Jean-Baptiste's lip twitched as memory took hold. Funny how those idiotic songs and stories stuck in the mind. If all went well he might be able to use some of them, some day. . . .

If all went well. His father, sensing a lack of proper attention, grew more vociferous. Stupidity was one thing. God made fools, and who was he to question the divine will? Though it seemed hard that He should have decided to make one of his eldest son. But illegality was something else. What Jean-Baptiste proposed was nothing short of criminal. Everyone knew that there was only one licensed troupe of actors—the company of the Hôtel de Bourgogne—who enjoyed the favor of the King. If he wanted to be an actor, which God forbid, the proper thing would be to seek employment with them. And if they would take a green young man with no training for the stage, no qualifications but a head full of dreamy nonsense, no respect for the value of money, then actors were even bigger fools than he took them for. But to start an opposition! To contract with a parcel of other untrained idiots—or worse—to rival the idols of Paris! He could hardly find words to express his shame and disgust. (I wish at least *that* were true, thought Jean-Baptiste, he seems to be finding a good many.) In short, if they did not find themselves in prison for bankruptcy, they would surely be there for flagrant violation of the Royal Charter.

Not so, thought Jean-Baptiste. I could fight him on that. He has only half a point. It was true that the Hôtel de Bourgogne had the only licensed company. Their privilege went back for centuries. So far, that people had grown a little tired of it. Eyewinking was customary. Those who started rival companies were never penalized . . . if they were any good. And if they were not, no penalty was necessary. Ignore them, and they would go away. Public disfavor would put them down as effectively as any law, and with less trouble. Was there not a theater near the Poquelins' own home which had faced the older company's displeasure? And was not the Marais now successfully established and attended by the court almost as much as the Bourgogne? Of course it was a cruel and capricious business. But there must be some luck, even in upholstery. In any case, there was no question of *his* being unsuccessful.

"And then," said Jean Poquelin, "there is a third matter." He assumed a peculiarly horrible and knowing expression, the face that fathers wear when talking of a son's love life. The female members of the family gazed at the ceiling and pretended deafness. Uncle Nicolas leaned forward, listening avidly. This was the part he had been waiting for.

"The matter of this . . . girl."

Jean-Baptiste jerked forward in his chair and barely stopped himself from rising in protest. No, it was unfair to bring her into it. Unfair but—he slumped back again—inevitable. They could forgive him an infatuation. They could not forgive his betraying the family for the stage. But it was still unfair to blame Madeleine. It could have been anybody else.

He had known who she was, of course, long before they ever talked. All the quarter knew the Béjarts. Joseph stood for everything his neighbors distrusted. True, he held a court appointment; though who did not, these days? And his was only in the Department of Forestry, which made him practically a gypsy. There were rumors of worse things. It was whispered that the Joseph of earlier days had been an actor. No one whispered louder than Joseph himself, who in his cups was wont to drop great names; and it had been remarked that these had more to do with tragedy than history. So Joseph tilted backwards on his stool, propped his great boots on the tavern table, spent more on drink than he could afford, and swaggered and boasted. Sometimes, when very drunk, he would close one eye, lay a finger to his nose, and call himself by a name not his own.

"A nobleman fallen on evil days," sighed the romantics.

"An actor," snorted the cynics, "and worse, a failed actor, who's played so many ranting parts he's forgotten who he is." And Joseph Béjart would chuckle evilly, call for another round and say nothing. Surely no way for a King's officer to behave.

What annoyed the censors most was his wife's indifference to her husband's behavior—and even more, to what people said about it. No one could have been more respectable than Marie Béjart. No breath of scandal had ever touched her name. Inventive as they were, her enemies could find no calumny to stick. Where her husband was florid, she was restrained. Where he went round half in, half out of uniform, his hair too long and his moustache untrimmed, his chins jostling one another over a dirty collar, Marie dressed demurely in gray and brown, and her linen was spotless. She always looked as though she were going to or coming from church. She usually was. Unfail-

ingly pious, she knelt at the altar every Sunday and feast day
with a selection of her sons and daughters; and as nothing
annoys the respectable more than one who is more so, their
fury knew no bounds.

With the Béjart children, at least, tongues could run riot.
To start with, there were eleven of them. Their father's children, clearly. Whether they were also their mother's was an
open question. There was, particularly, Madeleine. She had
been a noisy and precocious brat, running wild before she could
talk. Shopkeepers soon came to know and dread her bold gaze
framed in russet hair. She had her mother's self-control, her
father's love of the dramatic. No one could be wilder, when
wildness was in order; no one could as suddenly clap on the
mask and stand amid her shrieking playmates as sober as a
nun. She never stole, as far as anyone could find out. This also
set her apart from her brothers and sisters, who were clumsily
light-fingered. Madeleine did not need to steal. She was the best
bargainer in the quarter. In Paris, wailed the hucksters she
had beaten down, and who had now largely given up the
fight. They would sell at her price on condition that she did not
bargain before strangers and set a bad precedent in the neighborhood.

"With a face like that," said the prurient, "and her sense of
money, she needn't worry about the future." As usual, the
prurient were right. At nineteen Madeleine had contributed to
the family scandals by becoming a count's mistress. This was
normal, and expected. What antagonized the neighbors was the
birth of her child. A girl with any sense of shame would have
gone off to the country. Her mother should at least have had the
decency to display herself with her apron over her head, crying.
But Madeleine had the child right there, in her own house,
where it was promptly assimilated among her brothers and sisters; and the count her lover not only declared himself a proud
and happy father but gave the child a name and godparents.
Mother Marie went her usual pious way. Gossip bounced off
her back. With face unmoved, she was as regular at Mass as

ever. The honest burghers at last gave up in sheer exasperation. They did not mind the Béjarts being what they were. What annoyed them was that they admitted it.

Jean-Baptiste had seen Madeleine many times, alone or with the brothers who usually escorted her. They had never spoken. If he had any interest in the Béjarts at all, it was as a subject of table conversation. They were censored almost daily at his home, a divertissement in the long monotony of dinner. Like most people in the quarter, he had a repertoire of Béjart anec-dotes. He liked to tell them because he found he could dress them up and make them funny. The more familiar stories he could hide behind, and think his own thoughts while making obligatory conversation. They were like the weather, the doings of the King or the state of trade. Table talk. Slightly more interesting than the King, because nearer; more colorful than trade or weather.

It is disconcerting when a piece of table talk talks back. It happened to Jean-Baptiste one March afternoon, early. He was crossing the Pont-Neuf, forty years new, that bound the sprawl of Paris to the island at her heart. The sky was washed pale blue, white at the edges; there was still a threat of snow, and the wind bit cold across the Seine. On the bridge, the crowds gave warmth. The Pont-Neuf had been built for traffic. In their wisdom, the architects had left it void of shops or houses. No crazy tenements would crowd this bridge, no houses overhang the water suicidally, and crowd the passengers into a narrow path between. Wide sidewalks and a spacious carriageway, they said. Paris was growing and needed room to move.

That was the intention. But Paris, ever on display, saw an empty space and promptly occupied it. Near one end stood a pumphouse, drawing water from the Seine. Its builders had adorned it, in an unhappy moment, with figures of Christ and the woman of Samaria meeting at the well, and the people took this as divine dispensation to loiter. The peddlers and the ballad-mongers came. Orange-women cried "Portugal, Portugal!" And drums and trumpets sounded the coming of the clowns. It was a fair, a marketplace, and harassed drivers threw their hands up in disgust, and complained that things were as bad as ever.

Chestnut sellers did brisk business. Their braziers winked out signals of comfort to pedestrians in midcrossing, and Jean-Baptiste was glad to stop with the rest and burn his mouth on the hot, delicious offerings. He could afford to loiter. An errand to the fringes of the court had kept him busy all morning. Everything had been concluded with diplomacy, the customer was satisfied, his father would be pleased, and he could take the rest of the day for himself.

Speculating on what he might do with it, he was brusquely interrupted. He stepped into the shelter of a buttress to avoid a particularly vicious whiplash of the March wind. Someone cannoned into him from behind. He almost lost his balance. Chestnuts flew, and urchins scrambled for them. When he turned with a curse there was Madeleine.

She had her saint's face on, which spelled trouble. She looked as passionless and frozen as the moon, but burning eyes swam in the sea of tranquillity. Her hair frayed outwards, tortured by the wind; as she stood and looked at Jean-Baptiste, she might have been Medusa in the looking glass, a lovely russet monster who had turned herself to stone.

"Oaf," she said, "why don't you look where you're going?" To Jean-Baptiste, still smarting from lost dignity and chestnuts, this was unanswerable. He gave a half-bow, muttered something more or less polite and turned away from the offense.

"Come back here."

He walked on.

"Please."

For some reason, he came back.

"You're the Poquelin boy. Jean-Baptiste."

A statement, not a question. He could only nod again. She was looking at him strangely. For the first time he felt that she was at the disadvantage. Then something clicked inside her, and she made up her mind abruptly. Moving forward a step to bring her face to his, she said intently and with a curious passion, "Would you like to take me to the theater?"

Whatever he had been expecting it was not this. All his inclinations rose up in revolt. Girls did not ask men to take them to the theater. And what about his grand, free day? There were a thousand ways in which he could spend it. Well, a few, tried and trusted; reading, probably, from his favorite Romans in the books his mother had left him, by the big fire in the workshop; or, chillier but more private, under the eaves in his tiny room. Anyway, he hardly knew the girl. He matched her abruptness.

"Why don't you go by yourself?"

She made a face. The saint's mask slipped and the gamine peeped out from underneath.

"It isn't . . . respectable," she said, burlesquing the word. "Not that it worries me, as you well know, upholsterer's son." Jean-Baptiste blushed as he remembered some of the jokes he had made about her. "But it's a nuisance. The doorkeeper makes fun of you, and doesn't care whether he lets you in or not; and then the men paw you and . . . ugh!" Remembered afternoons screwed up her mouth in distaste and closed her eyes. It struck Jean-Baptiste for the first time that she was very pretty.

"From what they say," he retorted, prim, "you wouldn't mind."

"They say! They say!" He thought she was going to hit him. "All right. Sometimes, perhaps, I don't." What was she after? "But that's not what I go to the theater for. It bores me and I can't listen to the poetry."

She was a wistful child now, earnest and appealing. He was baffled by her changes. It was like conversing with six people, not one.

"I was supposed to meet a man. He was going to take me, but he . . . didn't come."

Jean-Baptiste wondered what bitterness had suddenly aged the face and lit the eyes again. Her hand tugged at his sleeve, appealing.

"Please, will you take me? It's nearly time, and there's nobody else, and you have a kind face, and I *almost* know you, and I wouldn't miss this for the world."

And without warning she burst into tears.

People were beginning to stare at them. They had blocked the way long enough. In the crowd Jean-Baptiste recognized a couple of people he knew. Their eyes bored into him, and he could already hear the rumors starting. There he was on the bridge with that Béjart hussy, making her cry in front of everybody. Don't know why, but I can guess, can't you?

"All right! I'll take you! Let's go."

Anything to get away from here. He could make some excuse, cast her off, when they reached a less public place. But she looked up at him with a face shiny with gratitude, and as if reading his thoughts clung to his arm with both of hers.

"Thank you. You're much nicer than I thought."

By the time he found a reply to this they were off the bridge and running over the cobbled streets.

"Where are we going? The Marais?"

"No, silly, the Bourgogne. Where else?"

Without much urging, she condescended to explain. This was the first performance of a new play, which was exciting enough. But it was not any new play. It was by Jean Rotrou, of whom even such an ignoramus as Jean-Baptiste must have heard. The ignoramus retorted indignantly that he had not merely heard of him but seen his work several times.

"Didn't think much of it, though. Wordy stuff."

This seemed likely to cause another explosion. Madeleine checked herself, however; she had realized that if she lost Jean-Baptiste her chances of finding another escort were nil. She contented herself with a long and highly technical critical defense. She spoke of Rotrou's power and dignity, of the subtle contrivances of his plots; of his skill in rhyme, and the demands he made upon his actors.

"He's . . . oh, he's a great man," she ended, smiling, her good humor restored by talking of her darling. "I was in love with him once. Many, many, many years ago. I used to send him verses, and he never replied. Oh, how awful they were!"

Jean-Baptiste was not used to poetic arguments conducted at running speed in a public street, but he could recognize professional authority when he heard it and was impressed in spite of himself.

"That was very interesting. You might have been an actress yourself."

"I have. Among other things." The trouble is, she thought, that people only remember the other things. It was the acting she remembered. Not the boredom, the drudgery, the humiliation. Not the things one had to do to win a playwright's notice, or attract the manager of a company. Only the joy of wearing a fine costume, stepping out onto the boards; of taking wings and flying, of entering another world. The plumes and chandeliers; the dignity and measure of the verse. It did not matter that the verse was soon spoken, and the small role of nurse or servant done. It did not matter that the chandeliers went out, and the dreariness of finding another part began again. They could always be relit, those candles.

They had reached the Hôtel de Bourgogne. Jean-Baptiste, fascinated in spite of himself, had forgotten to run away, and it was too late now. As they rounded the last corner, Madeleine gasped in horror. Rotrou appealed to many more beside herself. It was almost time for the three knocks to sound and the curtain to rise, and there was still a crowd in the street, fighting for places at the little ticket window.

"It's no use," said Jean-Baptiste, reasonably and with relief. "We'll never get in now. Look at them."

He had reckoned without Madeleine. The pressure left his arm, and he looked round to see where she had gone. She had squeezed into an alley, a crack between two houses. The shawl she wore against the cold March wind was off her shoulders, being rolled into a ball and stuffed—he blanched—under her dress.

"Come on," she hissed fiercely. "And if you don't play up I'll kill you." She would, too. They were in the crowd again, she using him as a battering ram and shield. In cold horror he heard what she was saying behind him.

"Have pity, messieurs, on a mother near her time. I can't stand too long on my feet. Oh, Jean-Baptiste, we never should have come. I think I'm going to faint!" She swayed dangerously, and the crowd around her opened.

The ticket taker took advantage of the diversion to reestablish his authority. "Let the lady through, you louts! Have you no manners?" The shouts of protest where Madeleine's stout shoe had found a toe or shin faded and gave way to sympathetic murmurs. The sea of faces parted, and Madeleine stood triumphant at the window. Behind her Jean Baptiste fumbled for money with his free hand. The crowd's antagonism was now turned on him.

"Great brute!" they were saying. "Fancy bringing the poor dear out in her condition!"

And, ominously,

"Hey! Isn't that old Poquelin's son?"

He blushed bright red, pulled his hat over his eyes and wished that the earth would swallow him up. Then the doors shut behind them and they groped their way through the candled twilight to a bench; away from one crowd and into another, the intent spectators at the Hôtel de Bourgogne.

It was still one of the sights of Paris. Critics might carp and mutter that the plays were old and the actresses older; the scenery might have come out of a monastery. But this was still the capital's most venerable theater. It basked in patronage. Dramatists were eager to write for it, for this was the surest way of reaching the royal ear. Audiences still flocked to it, for here was the distillation of all that was tried and true. Whatever the state of the performance, the plays were nearly always good. True, the Bourgogne was inclined to be old-fashioned. Even now, in this enlightened age, a play by old Hardy could still lumber out of its grave and putrefy upon the boards. But if you wanted surprises there were other theaters—the fly-by-nighters, full of modernisms and sensation. The good stuff, the real stuff, was here; and here, too, you could hear verse spoken as it ought to be, with full attention to the meter and sonority. A well-known tale told in a solemn chant. That's what tragedy should be.

The crowd was quieter now. The whistles and jolting subsided. On the stage they were lighting the candles: sparks flickered, a ring of flame ran round the chandelier, and with the perfection of ballet the lights were hoisted, bathing the stage in their glow, swinging ever so slightly in the breath of expectation. Jean-Baptiste clung desperately to the corner of the bench, silently cursed Madeleine sitting rapt beside him, and wished that he were dead.

The hush deepened. This time it was the prologue. He took center stage, magnificent in cloak and plumes; there was a roar from the benches, and a spatter of polite applause from the pinched loges behind. He advanced, bowed three times and postured. One eye rose ecstatic to heaven, frozen in poetic fervor, overwhelmed by the glory of the work he was about to describe. The other, under cover of his purple plumage, counted the house. Nothing to worry about today, thank heaven. Not that he had thought there would be. Rotrou would always pack them in. He swayed backwards, gestured grandly, and let the magic take hold.

"Really," said Jean-Baptiste, escorting a deflated Madeleine through the streets afterwards, "I'm very grateful to you." The time had passed more pleasantly than he expected. The initial discomfort had been forgotten. Only when a knee jabbed his spine, or a querulous attendant tripped on his foot in the aisle, had he remembered the place and the people. It was a moving play, one of which nobody could possibly disapprove. It was so moral, in fact, that he was surprised to find actors performing it. To begin with, it was a play about a saint. Nothing odd in that; saint plays had always been popular in Paris, and Jean-Baptiste had seen many himself: quaint survivals from the past, they still delighted the crowds at fairs and fêtes, though what appealed most now were the instruments of torture and streams of stage blood, not the inspiration and the message. A picturesque martyrdom would always draw a crowd. But Rotrou's play was not one of the vulgar sort. Its hero was Saint Genesius, the actors' patron. Genesius had been an actor himself once, in pagan Rome. The Emperor ordered him to burlesque the new and dangerous sect of Christianity on the stage. Genesius had performed an obscene mimicry of the rite of baptism, but in the middle of his mockery found grace. What began as parody ended in earnest. Genesius died by torture, a martyr to the faith he had once scorned.

This was the story that Rotrou had chosen to celebrate in five acts of singing verse. Roman history was enacted on the stage, dignifed by French decorum. The audience had seen the conversion and the martyrdom—or rather, heard about the martyrdom. Actually to show the death and suffering would have been the grossest breach of good taste. Buckets of blood were for the fairground. At the Bourgogne they were unspeakably vulgar.

Still, even without such spectacle the play had been convincing enough. The audience had muttered against the sneering Maximian and wept with the martyr's wife when she begged her husband to recant. True, there had been flaws. In a play like this, the Bourgogne style had been more blatant than usual. Montfleury was the chief offender. He gesticulated with a curious shaking motion, more like palsy than passion; before every big speech he took stage center, cleared his throat, quelled the other actors with a look and in general behaved like one of those singers from the new operas they were importing from Italy.

In spite of all this, and in spite of his initial hostility, Jean-Baptiste had been edified, and said so. He was a serious young man; sobriety had grown upon him by association; and he found this better than the usual run of plays. None of this stuff about love and battles. It was nearly as good as a sermon.

Curiously enough, it was Madeleine who was disappointed. She scuffed her heels in the dust as they picked their way home through the thickening light, and said so.

"I thought you liked Rotrou."

"I do. At least, I always have before. But this was different. It was a silly play. A traitor's play." She was incensed again. "Preaching against his kind. As if he were ashamed of belonging to the theater. If this goes on, there'll be no more theaters, only churches. And all the playwrights will turn preacher."

She was so upset that Jean-Baptiste felt ashamed of his own enjoyment and grew sorry for her. He remembered the little-girl eagerness with which she had looked forward to the afternoon. It was a pity she had been so disappointed.

"I'd like to take you to the theater again some day, if I may. Perhaps we can find something we both like."

They were nearly home. The lanterns were lit; it was time to hurry, if they did not want to be caught out in the dark.

Madeleine stopped at the turn of the street and looked at him. She smiled.

"You know," she said, "you're really not as stuffy as you look." She leaned forward and kissed him on the cheek. "Upholsterer's son!"

The rattle of her shoes and laugh faded away into the twilight.

And there, thought Jean-Baptiste, was the beginning of my downfall. At least, that's what the family would say. If only they knew how little she had to do with it.

They went to the theater often after that. The next time things went more smoothly. He was aware that he had behaved like a prig at their first meeting, and did his best to make amends. Madeleine, by the same token, was no longer a tartar. No one could have been more demure than she. They met, and continued to meet, in the angle of the Pont-Neuf where they had first collided. It was an arrangement that secretly appealed to him. He was sure his father would not approve of his seeing a Béjart.

They met two or three times a week to see a play together. He was continually impressed by Madeleine's knowledge. She knew everything about the stage. Not merely the gossip—who was whose mistress, who was new, who passé, who had paid how much to have a satire suppressed or a too promising rival stricken from the company. Everyone knew these things, and what they did not know, invented. But Madeleine knew the theater at work, the bone and muscle underneath the satin. She spoke to him of dramatic verse and showed him beauties he had missed. She showed him how an effective posture could disguise a poor line, and bad delivery ruin a good one. She began to take him behind the scenes and introduce him to actors, musicians, painters, managers. Her life in the quarter, the gossip life, was only a fraction of her real one. The air that nourished her stank with sweat and powder; her native heath was floored with planks and hedged with canvas.

Nor did they confine themselves to the Bourgogne, though Jean-Baptiste would have preferred it so. The nobility came here, after all, and it was no shame even for the son of the Upholsterer Royal to be seen in such a place. Other locales were less respectable; and he began to learn with dismay that Madeleine's passion knew no social boundaries. She took him to the tiny playhouses, struggling in shacks and tennis courts; to the gaudy booths in the marketplace, to the showmen at the fair. This was how they first quarreled.

In everything he saw and learned, the pattern of their first afternoon was repeated. As he grew more enthusiastic, she grew critical. He was like the neophyte drinker who has overcome his first distaste for wine and spends weeks in joyous intoxication. She stayed sober. What he applauded, she derided as pretentious. When the kings swaggered and the queens died, he was enraptured and she sarcastic. He laughed at her for her lack of wonder and accused her of snobbishness as she had once accused him. She was honestly baffled.

"I don't know. When I started going I liked everything too. You just had to put a man in costume and set him on a stage, and I was happy, just watching. But then you learn to listen. And so many of these things . . . they're like one of your sofas. Rip the cover off, and what is there? Old rags and horsehair. Feathers and dirty stuffing. No strength. No substance. It's difficult."

"What about Corneille? You like him."

They had just been to see *Le Cid* for the fourth time. A six-year-old sensation. Still being argued over, still setting the critics by the ears. A French play glorifying a Spanish hero—and this when France was at war with Spain! What a scandal that had been! And worse, the way the playwright thumbed his nose at every rule and standard so laboriously worked out by the academicians. The plot was nonsense, but the public loved it.

"That one, yes. There's meat there. Stuffing too," she defended herself hastily. "But there should be more like that."

What alarmed him most was her love for the comedians. Every theater had them. When the tragedy was over, their bouncing music started and they roared on with the afterpiece. Even the dignified Bourgogne employed them, and there were many who suffered through the tragedies for the sake of the clownish delights that followed. Jean-Baptiste found them insufferable. Gros-Guillaume, tight-waisted as an hourglass, flowing out above and below in stupendous fat. Turlupin, with face stiff as the scenery behind him and lips that scarcely moved when he drawled out his inanities. Gaultier-Garguille, the melancholic: the sadder he became, the more the audience roared. If he died on stage, thought Jean-Baptiste bitterly, they would become hysterical. Foolish faces, foolish names. No one knew their real ones, or cared. Their stage presences were all the people wanted: grotesque balloons to duck and float and buffet one another. And how the people laughed, the fools!

In the streets, the booth theaters thrown up like jetsam where the masses ebbed and flowed, it was worse. Here the mountebanks ran wild. Foreigners, most of them; Italians, doubly suspect. To think they had once been fashionable in Paris. But they had grown too wild, their mockery too caustic; they had given offense in high places and been banished by royal decree, but still came sneaking back. This is why the theater is despised, thought Jean-Baptiste. If they would only leave us our tragedies —he was already thinking "our"—how noble it would be, how fine.

It irritated him that Madeleine seemed to like these things. In fact, she preferred them. Often now she would be bored before a tragedy had run two acts and suggest an expedition to St. Germain, or Les Halles, where the clowns were. He tried to resist, but she was a forceful persuader. Without his realizing it, she had adopted him. Gossip spoke of her many men. If they existed he never saw them. How she spent the rest of her days he did not know and would not ask. He was content with what was his. They could be seen together like a betrothed couple, her hand resting lightly on his arm, their heads together, whispering. Love talk, thought the passersby, and so reported to his father. They would have been more shocked if they had known the two were arguing about plays and defending the rival merits of Arlecchino and Orestes.

Jean Poquelin heard the gossip, and his heart was troubled. A kindly father, he recognized that his son was grown and that such things should be expected. But a Béjart! However, there seemed to be no immediate danger. Jean-Baptiste had not turned notably dissolute. He still worked hard, and spent more time than ever reading in his room. No crisis loomed immediately in sight. Jean decided to watch, but say nothing.

He did not know that in the long evenings, when Jean-Baptiste removed himself from the family circle and went quietly to his room, he was writing a play.

A tragedy, of course. In five acts, as was regular; with a classical subject, as was appropriate. What else? He had pondered the matter deeply and decided on Julius Caesar. Here was a figure of unquestionable grandeur. And what a mass of promising material! The conquest of Gaul? No; better leave that out, it was unpatriotic. The crossing of the Rubicon? Difficult to stage. For the first time, Jean-Baptiste regretted that tragedy had become so refined. The delicacy of the day insisted that there be no vulgar show, no spectacle. None of the barbaric marching of armies, the slaughter, the violence, of the old plays. One day's action, and a single setting. Dramatic composition had been defined. The poet had to limit himself, and within these limits show as much sensitivity as possible. To take the minimum of matter and illuminate it with the maximum of art.

He decided, in the end, to deal with one event only, the day of Caesar's murder, and set the whole action in a room in Caesar's house. This would mean that the assassination could take place offstage—highly desirable. The murder would be the background. He could concentrate on the sufferings at home, the miseries and premonitions of the women. Actresses liked good parts. Who would play this, he wondered, when it was finished? In the story, Caesar's wife had a dream that her husband would be murdered. That would make a fine speech; vivid, almost daring. Too daring? No, such things were allowed. That play of Rotrou's he had admired so much—what was it called again?—had been full of dreams and visions.

But then there were the conspirators, Brutus, Cassius and the rest. They had to be in, they were important to the story. But how? If he set the play in Caesar's house, there was no way for them to meet. Unless . . . wait a moment . . . yes, that's it!

Act One, Scene Three. Enter Brutus and Cassius.

> CASSIUS: My lord, the emperor, has now departed.

Julius Caesar was not an emperor, though. No matter. Tragedy should be about emperors.

> My lord, the emperor has now departed.
> He goes to court. And should we, brokenhearted,
> Sit mute beneath his swelling tyranny?

"Swelling tyranny" was good. Impressive without being vulgar.

> Brutus, arise. 'Tis time that we were free.
> He takes our land, our living and our wives
> And leaves us nothing but our paltry lives;
> And these are nothing worth without the rest.
> Of all our remedies, this were the best:
> To take the tyrant's life, and in his stead
> Set up some other, or we live in dread.
>
> BRUTUS: You read me, Cassius, and speak my mind.
> If you misdoubted me, you were unkind.
> But do you wish my honor to debase?
> Why have you brought me to this hated place?

And here, thought Jean-Baptiste, crowing in anticipation, was the art of it.

> CASSIUS: His spies are out; there's no safe place in Rome.
> We may securely meet in Caesar's home.
> Here, tranquil, let us come to our decision,
> For Caesar's palace is above suspicion.

Corneille could hardly have done better. In fact, thought Jean-Baptiste, recalling those extraordinary incidents in *Le Cid*, Corneille had done a good deal worse.

The pile of manuscript grew thicker on his table. He hid it nightly, for fear the maid might discover it and report to his father. She could not read, but had the peasant's suspicion of the unusual. He came down bleary-eyed to breakfast after only two or three hours' sleep. Jean Poquelin was alarmed. In any other boy he would have suspected debauchery. In this case it was impossible. Jean was a watchful man, and after dark the house was barred so closely that a sigh could not get out. He wore the keys to bed, strung on a belt under his nightshirt. The shutters on the bedroom window had not been forced. He checked. No, Jean Baptiste clearly slept alone. But he did not check the closet where the manuscript was stored; and he could not open the shutters of the mind.

The Death of Julius Caesar was tied in a ribbon and presented to Madeleine with a pretty speech. There was a dedication to her on the title page, he proudly pointed out. She received it with appropriate surprise and gratitude, and promised to read it that night. Secretly Jean Baptiste was piqued. He thought she could have been more enthusiastic. For some days she had seemed abstracted. Something was preying on her mind. He brushed the thought away as unworthy. His own enthusiasm had made him oversensitive. She would be ecstatic when she read it. He slept well that night, and dreamed that his play was performed at the Hôtel de Bourgogne. Montfleury played the main part and the King came with all his court. They filled the theater with their applause, and created him First Playwright of France. His ears were still ringing with their plaudits when he woke; he came down to breakfast in a happy daze, and his father was delighted to see the color in his cheeks and the warmth in his eyes.

His first inkling that the day was awry came when he reached the appointed meeting place to find not one Béjart but three. Madeleine had brought brothers. He knew them vaguely as he had once known Madeleine, by report and calumny; fat Joseph with the easy laugh, who had inherited his father's disposition with his name; little Louis, the serious one, his mother's child, who had attracted small comment for a Béjart. He played the mask of Tragedy to his brother's Comedy; mouth turned up mouth turned down, and the sister in between, a blend of them, and able to be either at a whistle.

They greeted him warmly, even Louis. They were fussed and excited. They must all have read my play, thought Jean-Baptiste; she showed it to them, they love it, they've come to talk about it.

He took himself in hand, and asked the question.

"How did you like it?"

"Like what?"

The sky fell in.

"My play. My play, of course."

A curious noise from Joseph, stifled when his sister looked at him.

"We haven't time to talk about that now," said Madeleine. "There's something more important." She saw his face. "Even more important."

They surrounded him, his three Fates; and in that moment the thread of his life was spun and measured.

"Jean-Baptiste, we're going to start a theater!"

He had not realized how much talk it took to start a theater. In the wine shops over empty stoups, with the hostess grumbling noisily in the corner; in the street, with Louis finding new difficulties at every stride, and Joseph greasing them with his laugh; in the Béjart parlour, with the father out as usual at his drinking, and the mother banished upstairs, neither approving nor disapproving but silent as ever, thinking her thoughts. They talked about everything. Costumes and actors, plays and authors. Madeleine paraded the list of her connections. This friend would write a new play, that acquaintance allow them to revive an old one; familiar names ran lightly off her tongue till Jean-Baptiste, besotted with the glory of it all, imagined that he knew them too, and spoke of them as familiarly as she. He mentioned his own play from time to time, when there was a lull in the discussion, but Madeleine explained to him, with gentle reasonableness, why this was impossible.

"We have to start with names the people know. Authors

they know. An old company can afford new names. We can't."

New names, he thought resentfully. My father has a court appointment. But the thought of his father was such an overwhelming obstacle that it stopped his thoughts from running any further in that direction.

"All in good time," said Madeleine.

"All in good time," said Joseph and Louis, patting him on the back with the affection of old comrades.

And so he thought it would be. The second season, when the public, dazzled by their luster, would be ready to accept a new masterpiece.

They did not, he thought, talk enough about money. It was all about Art. But he was a merchant's son, and knew that money had a place in the scheme of things. His relatives could not be entirely wrong. But when he respectfully inquired how all this would be paid for, he was once again put down. Any venture, they explained to him, required a risk. Had he no faith? Paris was bored with the old actors, gasping for new talent. It was the time for youth. True, they lacked experience; vitality would see them through. But authors, he suggested timidly, expected to be paid. At least, so he had heard. And though they might find actors willing to work for nothing, landlords demanded rent for their property.

"We'll sign a note," said Madeleine. "We'll borrow it. And pay them back out of the first month's takings."

"The first fortnight!" said Louis.

"The first week!" roared Joseph.

And the meeting broke up in a blaze of euphoria.

He let this worry him less than it would usually have done, because other things weighed more heavily upon his mind. How to break this to his father? However much he planned; however much the others laughed down his objections; all things paled before this, the knowledge that without his father's permission he was powerless. He confided his fears to Madeleine and as usual—she had grown much softer with him now—she sympathized.

"It has to be done," she said, "and we need you, "Jean-Baptiste. Go and ask him. I'll wait for you outside."

So he had gone to seek an interview, like a customer explaining why he could not pay his bill. They had arranged a signal. If his father said yes, he would close the shutters of his room and open them again immediately. If no, he would leave them closed.

His father was a fair man. There were many things he admitted he could not understand, and he now regretfully included his son among them. After the initial shouting and bitterness, which sent the maid into hysterics and caused the youngest apprentice to run away to sea, he had slammed his own shutters, confusing Madeleine greatly, and brooded for the rest of the day while his family nibbled in terror at their dinner. Finally, emerging candle in hand like a portly archangel barring the gate of Paradise, he had announced the direst of portents. He would hold a family conference.

So this is what it had come to. Jean-Baptiste had been kept incommunicado in the house. He had smuggled notes to Madeleine through the maid, who had giggled salaciously, suspecting an amour; and Madeleine had come from time to time to wave furtive encouragement through the windows, until his father had sent the shopboy to tell her to go away. The day appointed had come. The relatives had brought their long, important faces to the door and rapped discreetly, as for a funeral. They had eaten heavily and greasily downstairs, and Jean-Baptiste, interrupted in his thoughts of suicide, had been summoned to postprandial judgment.

They were unanimous in condemning his infamy, but differed as to the cause. Aunt Jeanne said it was the monkeys. The ones carved round the Poquelin door, she explained, when her husband gaped at her stupidly. Everyone knew that monkeys stood for actors: nasty smelly things covered with vermin and eating any garbage they could find; aping their betters without mind or manners of their own. Oh, she was aware that clever people pooh-poohed such things; but she knew what she knew, and a child born under such an unpropitious sign could never grow up to be respectable. At this point she was put down by the head of the household himself, who pointed out—"with quite unnecessary gruffness," she told her husband later—that he had several other children born in the same house who were, God be thanked, respectable enough. Privately he resolved to have the carvings taken down.

Grandmother Agnes, with surprising clarity, announced that it was all the fault of these Italians in the government. Now that the old Cardinal was gone, God rest his soul, and this foreign upstart was advising the King in his place, wasn't it natural that boys should lose all sense of moral values and steal money from their fathers?

A chorus of angry whispers informed her that this was not the issue, and she subsided into silence again. She still whispered to herself from time to time and kept her beady eyes on Jean-Baptiste as if she suspected that at any moment he might sneak out with the family silver in his pockets. Cheated of his hope that his tormentors might turn against one another, he slumped in the hard chair and awaited decree, sentence and judgment.

Salvation came when he had stopped expecting it. The man in black pushed back his chair, coughed slightly as if calling an orchestra to attention, and asked permission—silkily, oh, so silkily—to speak. His voice eased into the hubbub like a thin man into a crowded room. There was something in him that commanded attention, even among the snarl of relatives in this stifling chamber. He had a way of speaking as if he were addressing not them, but some more illustrious figure in the room beyond. His eye fixed on a point some feet above their heads; his words rippled out in a musical cadence as the wig rippled over his sleek black shoulders, and he moved his slim white fingers slightly, conducting himself. In that company of honest and indignant tradesmen, he was a creature from the moon, remote and unapproachable.

First, he said, he would like to thank the family, and particularly his good friend Jean, for the honor they had shown him in allowing him to share their confidences this day. His tone belied the words, and made it clear that the honor was theirs; reluctantly, they believed him.

"And what is more, a day of such significance. Of crisis, dear friends, and decision. For what is more important than the beginning of a life? That is what we are faced with here. The beginning of a young man's life. You may tell me he has been alive these one-and-twenty years. I say no; he has merely existed. He has been protected in the nest. He has fed off the nourishment brought to him so plentifully by others. No, my friends. Life is work. Until we labor for ourselves, we do not begin to live. And here we have a young man who sees this clearly. He seeks to set out on his own; to find his work; to stand by himself. And while we may not all approve the work he wants to do, we must applaud his energy and good intentions."

The family, who had begun to feel nervous, relaxed again. These were unexceptionable sentiments.

What followed once more set them worrying.

He would venture to take exception, he went on, to certain remarks made by Aunt Jeanne—with the best of intentions, he was sure—about the connection between monkeys and actors. Not because he was enamored of actors. If Grandmother Agnes (a little bow in her direction) complained of Italians at the helm of government, he could tell them stories of Italian actors he had met . . . but these would not bear repeating in mixed company. (Disappointment.) No. He took issue with her words because he felt they cast a slur on the arts generally. The arts of which he was, in his humble way, proud to be a representative.

After a pause for contradiction, he went on. Surely Jean would admit that in all trades there were good and bad. Jean himself was a model of his profession, an upholsterer of sterling worth whose rigid principles and high devotion to his calling were an inspiration to all who knew him. But Jean himself would surely admit that his profession had its riffraff too. Scoundrels who cheated their customers with shoddy work, and asked outrageous prices for it; who did their best, without succeeding, to bring the honorable profession of upholstery into disrepute.

Jean was prevented with difficulty from naming five or six. Michel changed course without warning. Were not the arts a trade like any other? One which attracted good and bad? A way of life in which dignity, application and a sensible attention to the wishes of the customer would ensure a rapid rise to the top? He was a tradesman himself, and proud of it. The days of the wandering troubadour were past. Thanks to the late King, of glorious memory; thanks to Cardinal Richelieu, whom Grandmother Agnes so justly remembered; thanks to the present occupant of the throne, still young, still impressed, perhaps, by bad advisors—"but this is a secret among us; it would ruin me if they knew that I had spoken so of Mazarin"—the arts were an instrument of state, like politics and the law. Things were done with decent order now. No eccentricities, no dangerous experiments. We knew what good taste was, from the King, his court and his Academy. The artist worked by sure standards. By devotion to his calling and deference to his superiors, he could prove himself and rise.

Were not actors, he expostulated, warming to his theme, received now in the most elegant salons? Did not some of them have the ear of the King and the greatest nobles of his court? Were they not summoned to the palace to play for royalty and fed off golden plate? After all, what difference was there between Jean's profession and his own? One deals in velvet and brocade, the other in notes and instrumental noises. A customer asks him for a length of carpet; he measures, cuts and lays it down. A customer asks me for an interlude or a ballet; I fabricate it by rules no less strict than his, measure it off and perform it. A business contract, no more. Signed, sealed and delivered.

Jean-Baptiste was suddenly sickened by his voice and the metronomic beat of the too-white hands. No, he wanted to shout, it's not a business contract for so many words, so many sentiments of a certain size, wrapped and delivered in a pretty bundle. It's fire and passion and glory; it's fear and pity and outrage; it's the breath of life.

Prudence silenced him. That, and the feeling that he could not slip a word in edgeways. Nothing could interrupt that flow of silver eloquence.

The family sat hypnotized, slaves to the man's spell. In a few minutes he had cast the aura of the court upon them—an aura that Jean, in his backstairs visits supervised by glacial officials, had never felt. In their imaginations they rubbed shoulders with the great. They heard the violins tuning in the park, and saw the courtiers strolling in their finery among the placid deer; they saw young Jean-Baptiste (what a good boy he was, to choose so noble a profession) poised heroically upon a golden stage, uttering memorable verse in grave and measured tones.

After that, it was a formality. Jean-Baptiste was sent out of the room, stumbling over his brothers on the stairs—for they too had been hypnotized outside the door, and could not tear themselves away in time. In ten minutes he was summoned back to hear his father's blessing.

"I'm still not sure that I like it," rumbled Jean; "But if it's what you want to do, who am I to stand in the way of your advancement?" And he kissed him sloppily on both cheeks.

Jean-Baptiste said goodbye to his defender at the door.

"Thank you," he said. "But it's not like that, you know."

"I know what you're thinking," whispered Mazuel, "because I thought exactly the same, at your age. But you'll find out. Unfortunately."

And he passed elegantly, and a little sadly, into the outer darkness.

Jean-Baptiste ran to find Madeleine. She kissed him warmly, and the next day they went to see a lawyer. In spite of his feelings about Mazuel, Jean-Baptiste was enough of a Poquelin to be glad that things were businesslike at last. The contract was a formidable document, with every contingency, likely and unlikely, set out in detail. It stipulated whom they were going to employ, and who should have first choice of parts. Jean-

Baptiste was, among others. He had insisted on having this written in, to compensate for the failure to include his play. He was determined to make his mark early. No sense in waiting till next season for the glory. Once they saw how firm he was, the Béjarts had given in more easily than he would have expected. "Of course, you've had no training," said Joseph, stroking his moustache, "but who needs it? Youth is what we need. Youth, and fire, and new faces." This so suited his own ideas that he was more than happy to become a leading actor, and wait until next year to be a leading playwright.

There were other documents to sign too. The lease for the building—the sum involved still made him uncomfortable. Contracts with carpenters and timber merchants. With printers and painters. With actors, promising them salaries which Joseph swore were minute compared to the money they were bound to make, but which still seemed huge to him. His eyes were sore when he had finished. Like all well-bred boys he had been educated with a nod towards the Church and the law; he knew what he was reading, and insisted on reading every word. If any passage gave him difficulty, he wanted it explained to him. The Béjarts skimmed through and signed their names with a grand flourish. The supercilious clerks were annoyed with him by the time he had done and drummed a tattoo with their ebony rulers on the old oak table to match the ticking of the clock, while the sky grew dark outside.

The brothers wanted to go and drink to celebrate, but Madeleine said that she was too tired, and he walked back with her through the thickening dusk to her house. On the threshold she stood on tiptoe and kissed him for the first time full on the mouth. Her lips were soft and moist and smelt of garlic.

"I'm glad it's all over."

"Are you?" she said softly. "I hope you won't be sorry." Her red hair hung around her face, a flaming aureole in the lamplight. When he gently tried to pull himself away she clung to him with a new tenderness. The oak door, never latched, creaked open behind them. Before he could protest she had seized his hand and led him swiftly upstairs, treading on tip-toe, finger to her lips, past the door of her parents' room to her minuscule chamber in the attic. Jean-Baptiste, deprived of resistance and too much of a gentleman to object, followed her with surprise. This was not included in the contract. But after all, he reflected sleepily some time later, it was not entirely disagreeable.

She was surprisingly thick and muscular for a woman, and her smell was not pleasant. After it was over, as they lay in the great dumpy bed, he saw a louse crawl from behind her ear and explore the perimeter of her body until it lost itself some-where in the thicket of red hair under her arm. She did not seem to notice. Never mind, he thought. It was the duty of the artist to explore every sensation.

He pushed himself gently out of her sleeping embrace and let his mind run through the events of the day. Of course they could not help but make money. Even if they weren't good—which they were, which they were—it was impossible for them to fail. This was Paris, after all, and everyone went to the theater, it was almost a national duty. Look at the way people flocked to those fusty old things at the Bourgogne. The King went to plays, and what the King did, everyone did. It was his father, they had taught Jean-Baptiste in school, who had set all Paris writing, and wanted to make the city into another Athens. Well, that is what it would be. And he would be its Sophocles. And Madeleine—

He could not recall if Sophocles was ever married.

Would she expect him to sleep with her every night, he won-dered? It was interesting. Enjoyable, even. But too often would be tiresome. Did she realize it was his first time? She must have. It obviously wasn't hers. Everything they said about her must be true. He hoped that she had not been disappointed. Not that he was ignorant. Innocent, perhaps, but not ignorant. You could not grow up in a family as large as his without learning something. Or go to a school like his.

But was this really what the poets sang about? What Ovid

and Catullus wrote of at such extravagant length in those poems they would never let them read at school? What sent Lucretius mad?

He fell asleep dreaming of the theater.

In the room below, adrift in the billows of their great bed, Marie and her husband slept too. When Madeleine and Jean-Baptiste had first come creaking up the stairs, Marie had nudged her husband awake. Together they listened to the sounds above.

"Again!" grumbled the elder Joseph, cross at being woken from his vinous dreams. "Little bitch! Has she forgotten all the trouble she gave us last time? I'll throw the young puppy out."

Marie pulled him back as his feet flopped to the cold floor.

"Let her be. It's meant, this one. I've seen it coming for a long time. He's a nice boy, Jean-Baptiste. Good family, too. He might even marry her."

"That's likely, now."

"Why not? We had five years of it, before I was able to drag you in front of a priest!"

And, with a giggle that would have confounded the neighbors, the pious and proper Marie Béjart pulled her husband back into bed. He was not unhappy to be overruled.

To his considerable annoyance, Jean-Baptiste found that the first activity of his new life was to wait. With the best will in the world—and all the others were as anxious to begin as he—there were still more papers to be signed, and conveyances to be made, and moneys to be transferred, before the work could begin: all the pompous ritual, in fact, of the world he thought he had left behind for good. He filled in the time as he had always done at any critical moment in his life, by clearing out his room. It was a symbolic act, as it had always been: the removing of the lumber of the past, to make way for the furniture of the present. It was providential, he considered, that he should discover the diary at this particular point in time. At this catastrophe, to use the word as he had been taught in school, correctly, in the classical sense, meaning the turning point, the

change, the up or down. Of course it was providential. There
was no doubt about it. Jean-Baptiste believed, like practically
everybody else of his time, that everything was providential. A
man's life was ordered from the moment of his birth. And all
had their divinely appointed place in the scheme of things. It
was only a matter of waiting till the place was recognized. God
at the top of the pyramid, and then His saints and angels,
though he was not quite clear about their order. And then the
King, his nobles under him, and somewhere in the lower
regions, not quite at the base of the pyramid but far from its
summit, an insignificant integer labeled Jean-Baptiste Poquelin.
Though if pressed, he would have admitted to being not quite
clear about his order either.

It was not really a diary, of course. And he had not discovered
it, only rediscovered it. It was an old ledger, belonging to the
shop, that his father had thrown out because some muddle-
headed clerk had spilt ink all over it. Then he had second
thoughts and combined prudence with benevolence by making
a present of it to his son. He was never one to waste anything.

The ink stain was still there. It started on top and spread
down the side like a finger, insinuating itself between the pages
and probing the crevices that ran towards the spine. The book
must have cost a good sum of money once; and then it was
spoiled in a second, fit only for a child to amuse himself with.

It had a key, once, too, that sat in a great solid lock on the
ledger's face when it was not hanging over his father's equally
solid stomach. Jean-Baptiste had never had the key. Perhaps it
was still hanging there with the others. Perhaps Jean Poquelin
fingered it occasionally and wondered what it was for. But
then of course he would know. He always knew.

The ink stain was at least selective. It overran the middle of
the book but left a number of pages at the front untouched.
It was strange to look back at them, to browse through his
childhood scratchings. Everyone must begin a diary in the same
way. The first few days completely full. Everything he did and
thought and ate and drank, set out in minute detail and

atrociously misspelt. Then it started to taper off, to grow cursory. "Same as yesterday." "Same." "Same." Had his life really been so dull? It must have been.

One or two notes from school. One of them broken off halfway through a sentence, where the priest must have caught him. A sting of knuckles about that page. And then a rare day written up in full, the day he fell down chasing in the playground and cut his knee so badly.

He could still remember that without the diary.

It had been a very bad cut indeed. There was a big flap of skin hanging loose on his knee, and he bled like a pig. The master was upset, not because he had hurt himself but because he was messing the floor. He took him into a back room and tried to bandage it, but the flap of skin was in the way and he decided it would have to come off. He rummaged in his desk and found a knife. It was the same one, Jean-Baptiste believed, that he kept to cut his bread and cheese when he was cheating on fast days. It was old and blunt and dirty; he came at him holding it straight out in front, like a sword, and they must have heard the screaming in the town. He wept and kicked and yelled, the way he would have done with his own mother. She would have cut it too, in the end, but only after Jean-Baptiste had relented and let her get on with what he knew in his heart of hearts would have to be done. But at least she would have left him with the illusion of giving permission.

The priest had no time for any such nonsense. He boxed his ears to set his head ringing, knocked his hands away, and while the boy was still dazed sawed away at the hunk of flesh till it came off in his hand.

Jean-Baptiste had stopped crying. He didn't know whether at the pain or the indignity. But, looking back, he honestly believed that it was the first time in his life that he realized—that he truly realized—that people were able to do things to him that he did not like, and that he was unable to do a thing to prevent them.

Then the long monotony of empty pages. And after that

another bunch of virgin sheets, a new beginning. He started again to memorialize the most important day of his life. For there could be few people who acquired their first theater and their first mistress on the same day.

Once again father and son confronted each other in a little room. Once again the sun beat through the windows and made patterns on the floor. But this time the floor was stone, and the windows had bars to them, not glass.

"My son," said Jean Poquelin. "In prison."

Jean-Baptiste was tempted to reply that he was only in for debt, not murder, and that, judging from his observations, he was in good company. Some of the more fashionable figures of Paris were there. But the theater had taught him its first lesson, tact.

After all, what could he say? His father was right as usual. It had been a disaster from the beginning. They had opened grandly enough. Madeleine's friends had brought along their manuscripts, as promised. It became apparent, however, that her connections were a little rusty now. The poets who brought their compositions with such pomposity, and read them with such condescension in the candlelight, had been good writers once, the idols of the public some of them, whose names on the bills would guarantee a crowd. But the years had dimmed their luster, and the public had forgotten them. The big theaters no longer wanted them. Their affability was born of happiness to see their work performed again; their condescension came from fear, and from a desperate desire to impress.

And then the public. The capricious public. They had come in crowds for the first week or two. Joseph, totaling the receipts, had announced, as much to his surprise as anyone's, that the sum equaled his expectations. But the charm of new faces had worn thin. They complained that the theater was uncomfortable and draughty. They disliked having to come so far for a performance. (Unfair; it was practically in the center of Paris!) They thought the plays outmoded, the costumes cheap and the actors incompetent. Jean-Baptiste was wounded to his heart by this. He had not been *that* bad. He admitted that he still had much to learn. Madeleine had taught him how to stand and move; there was more in this than he suspected. His voice, he knew, was weak. He lacked the breath to pound out those tragic lines with the vigor they demanded. A long speech left him coughing (hiccuping, as one unruly member of the audience put it, that awful time they laughed him off the stage. Better not to think about that.) But he would improve. It was unfair to expect everything at once.

Louis was everywhere. He took the money at the door, swept out the theater, carried scenery, smiled at patrons, scowled at creditors and made himself useful in whatever way he could. His small size kept him off the stage; he was useless in anything but minor parts. As the season dragged its dreary length along, he found time hanging heavy on his hands. The chink of coins into his box grew rarer, and great gaps appeared on the benches. Jean-Baptiste one night gave his three knocks to signal the beginning of the play, and turned bitterly to Madeleine who was standing in the wings beside him.

"One knock," he said, "for every member of the audience." The patrons' faces were replaced by others, arrogant, peremptory. The names on the contracts they had so blithely signed appeared as real and forceful personalities, demanding with various degrees of rudeness that those contracts should be honored. In a panic meeting, the company agreed to take no salaries for themselves until the payments had been met. They borrowed more money. Marie Béjart, bless her, mortgaged her house to give them a month's respite.

Still no luck. The public continued to stay away; the cries for payment became angrier. Another meeting. What had gone wrong? How had they failed? It must be the plays. It must be the location. It could not possibly be their fault. And so they moved their theater. More money to be borrowed, more contracts to be signed; a new beginning, new scenery, new costumes. A new beginning and the same response. And then fate, feeling that it had tortured them long enough, delivered the *coup de grace*.

They were accustomed to walk back to the Béjart house together each day after the performance. Jean-Baptiste had made his home there. Once the charm of Mazuel's presence had worn off, the family had reverted to sullen disapproval. What was signed could not be undone; his father had to accept the bargain he had made. But there were mutterings when he came in at all hours; his food was often cold, his bed unmade; the business world pursued its sober way, and he was declared an outlaw. The Béjart house became first a refuge, then a permanent abode. His presence under Madeleine's roof and in her bed was accepted by the family as a matter of casual routine. This relieved him. Joseph, in the heroic parts he played upon the stage, regularly fulminated in rhyme against scoundrels suspected of tampering with the virtue of his sister or his wife. Jean-Baptiste was happy to discover that in this as in other ways the stage divorced itself from life. About his real sister Joseph could hardly have been less concerned.

In the large untidy room awash with babies (Jean-Baptiste had stopped trying to count the Béjart children) they sat down to complain about the fortunes of the day. Louis was usually late. He stayed behind after the others had removed their paint and gone home to sweep, tidy and lock up. When the clock showed an hour after his normal time and he had still not appeared, they thought it best to go and look for him. Paris was a strange place after dark. Players, who worked strange hours and made odd acquaintances, sometimes found themselves in trouble. The city was still talking about Jean de Magnon, a fierce and gaudy writer who had been found dead across the Seine one chilly dawn, stabbed, they said, by assassins hired by his wife. She was standing trial now, but nothing would come of it; the courts would consider the death of a playwright a divine judgment, brought on by irregular habits and loose living.

They did not want the same thing to happen to Louis, who was too young to take care of himself. He would have the money with him too—not much, but large enough to tempt some passing bully whose need was even greater. So Joseph and Madeleine went back to look for him. Jean-Baptiste closed his ears to the cry of children and tried to write a little. But he was drowning in fatigue, his fire had gone out. He was always so tired, these days. The heroic lines slipped mockingly away when his pen tried to capture them. *The Death of Julius Caesar* slept in a locked chest. When he looked at it, as he still did occasionally, he found himself in doubt. Was it as good as he once thought? No, that was treachery; of course he could write tragedy. If not, what was the point of this daily drudgery, the wrestles with creditors, the indecency of slapping paint on his face and strutting through a part someone else had written for the amusement of a handful of clods who had come in out of the rain? Fatigue was no excuse. He would be strong. He must write. He took the pen and a virgin sheet of paper and set to a fresh start.

He was still dozing over the blank sheet when Joseph and Madeleine returned. They burst in without ceremony, Madeleine's face ashen and Joseph's red with fury. Without a word, he hurried to the closet where the wine was kept, swallowed a huge draught and set the bottle down with a thump beside Jean-Baptiste.

"Take this. You'll need it."

Startled, bleary-eyed, he looked from one to the other. They had no one with them.

"What's the matter? Where's Louis? Has something. . . ."

"Show him," said Joseph, taking back the bottle.

Madeleine opened her hand, and a screw of paper fell upon the table. "Read for yourself."

With trembling fingers Jean-Baptiste spread out the pathetic, dreadful document and read, in straggling letters and mis-spelled, the proclamation of their doom.

"Pleese do not be angry with me I needed the money for

sumthing I wanted to do I will pay you back sum day the theater
is not for me I wish you all success your brother Louis."

"All the money!" shouted Joseph. "Not just today's! The
whole week's takings, the filthy little bastard!" He was working
hard at the bottle. "Wait till I find the dirty tyke. I'll break
every bone in his body."

"Find him?" said Madeleine. "In Paris?" Her frightening
calm was beginning to slip, but she spoke sense as usual. In
the warren of the city a boy could lose himself in five minutes.

"But there are bills due tomorrow," stammered Jean-Baptiste.
"He couldn't ... we won't ..."

He could, and had. Marie and her husband, drawn downstairs by the noise, joined in the expostulations. The younger
children cried, and Jean-Baptiste, strangely detached as though
this were happening to someone else on a planet a million miles
away, found himself caught up in a family conclave that was an
insane burlesque of those that had plagued him all his life. They
roared, wept, shouted. Joseph the father and Joseph the son got
desperately drunk, and cudgelled up from their befuddled
memories old play tags that had relevance to their present situation. Marie, ever practical, counted up their losses, balanced
them against their debts and revealed the totality of their ruin.
Only Madeleine said nothing. She sat with Jean-Baptiste on the
bumpy couch and stroked his hand. He could not tell whether
she was giving comfort or seeking it. It was long into the
morning before they got to bed, and even then only the two
Josephs slept.

Next day the vultures gathered. They had agreed, over
Joseph's protests, to say nothing of Louis' treachery, but merely
to plead inability to pay. They must keep some shred of honor.
"Anyway," said Madeleine, "who'd believe us? It's just the sort
of thing we might invent." So they watched in silence as the
world moved in upon their dream; as the bailiffs hauled the
costumes away, and stripped the theater of its furniture. They
bowed their heads when the landlord spat in their faces and

called them gutter-scum, a pack of filthy monkeys. They went without protest when the officer tapped them on the shoulders and led the men off to the debtors' cell.

Joseph flourished in prison. It was his element. His easy manner won him rapid friends. With the impoverished gentlemen he ingratiated himself by reciting his repertoire of tragic speeches. It amused them, though he did them badly enough, and with a drunken slurring of the syllables. There was always wine for Joseph. His cronies condescended to him, making a game of it, and adopted him as licensed buffoon. There was a club in prison, the Club of the Unfortunates, composed of younger sons who had run through a small inheritance or seedy noblemen who had spent their incomes on their backs, ruining themselves to keep up appearances. It was just a game for them. Someone would get them out. They all had friends, relations; there would be a little grumbling for form's sake, a few promises would have to be made, but in the end some more prominent connection would throw his money on the altar of family honor and release them. They formed a small court in prison, and Joseph was court jester.

Jean-Baptiste was not invited to join them. He had no wish to. Even in this squalor the social rules applied. He was a tradesman's son, a bourgeois; a traitor to his caste, a fool with money. They sneered at him, and he resented them as fashionable idiots who behaved and gossiped as if they were in a green park by the Seine, instead of locked up in a cell. What he resented most was their air of being under some sort of divine protection; their bland assurance that whatever happened to them was a temporary nuisance, and that the sun would soon smile on them again.

"And it will," he thought indignantly. "It will. They talk about having no money. But all they mean is that they'll have to sell a coach or dismiss a servant or two to pay back whoever bails them out. If they even bother to do that. When I say I have no money I mean it. Not a sou. No honest trade, no profession. I'm finished." He was convinced that his family had disowned him, and could expect nothing from the Béjarts but sympathy.

With the riffraff of the prison, and the jailors, Joseph was equally at home. He parodied the gentry to them, behind their backs. He drank and swore with them and told foul stories, of which he had an inexhaustible supply. He played dice with them, and usually won; he always had a few coins to jingle in his purse. Jean-Baptiste could not enter this world either. He grew solitary and morose, spending his days in what passed for a quiet corner of the room, trying to ignore what went on around him. His nights were sleepless with worry.

Once, near the beginning of his imprisonment, when he was still picking at threads of hope, he had caught Joseph in a rare moment alone and talked of future plans. What they might do if they ever got out. Where they might pick up a little money again and salvage what they could from the company. The provinces, perhaps. People were easier to please there, and living was cheaper. With Madeleine and Joseph and himself. . . .

But Joseph was in no mood to indulge pipe dreams. It was a bad day; he had lost money at cards, and had just been snubbed by one of the new friends with whom he was trying to ingratiate himself. And he had long since sized up Jean-Baptiste's position in prison and dismissed him as useless. The mask dropped, and a pig leered out of the wide, frank brown eyes.

"You snivelling little whey-faced fool. Do you think I'd have any more to do with you, after the mess you've landed us all in?" Louis' theft, he went on to explain with detailed brutality, had been of minuscule importance compared to Jean-Baptiste's contribution to the debacle. The theater had failed because it had been forced to carry him. Poquelin, an actor? "You walk across the stage," he roared, illustrating his words for the benefit of his growing audience, "like a club-footed water carrier. You read a line like an old horse whinnying for mercy in the knacker's yard. And you write with all the passion of a ninety-year-old nun making up her shopping list."

Here, to Jean-Baptiste's total confusion, he whirled round to the crowd and shouted, "You may not know it, gentlemen, but we have a great playwright in our midst. A new Corneille! A greater than Tristan! A shining light, destined for Parnassus! Let me declaim for you a passage from his play!" With deadly accuracy he began to recite from *The Death of Julius Caesar*, in a cultivated whine that showed up every false emphasis, pointed each forced rhyme; the sentiments became absurdity, the masterpiece on which he had labored so long and passionately was torn apart before his eyes, a grotesque, maimed, dismembered thing.

He must have learned it long ago, thought Jean-Baptiste. From the very beginning, when I showed it to Madeleine. They've been mocking it behind my back all this time.

Joseph finished his recitation amid loud applause, sketched a parody bow and turned back to his victim. "Do you want to know why we kept you with us, upholsterer's son? Do you want to know what made us so polite?" He snapped his pudgy fingers in his face. "Because in spite of all this trash you had one singular virtue. A good name. We needed one on our contracts. People would lend money to a Poquelin. Nobody in his right mind would trust a Béjart!"

Jean-Baptiste, mad with rage and humiliation, leapt on his tormentor. He was blind to the disparity of their strengths. He wanted only to gouge, to maim, to hurt, to do anything to drown the shame that burnt his body like a fever. Surprise gave him the first advantage. Joseph stumbled backwards over a loose flagstone and fell sprawling. Jean-Baptiste went down on top of him. His fingers tore at the dirty lace round Joseph's throat. A fat hand rose in protest and he sank his teeth into it. The warm taste of blood was the last thing he remembered.

He could still taste it when he came to. It was his own. They told him that two of Joseph's cronies had held him against a wall while his former partner made a bloody ruin of his face. It only stopped when the jailors, tiring of the fun and fearing trouble if he should die, tore Joseph away and flung his victim on a pile of straw.

He was ignored after that, and Joseph's rendering of *The Death of Julius Caesar*—the gestures marred by a bandaged hand—became the standard entertainment of the prison.

Madeleine paid her weekly visit a few days later, bringing a few coins and some food in a basket. He refused to see her, but she charmed her way in. He was crouching in his corner, his face still raw and throbbing, coughing through his broken teeth. The prison damp had caught him by the throat.

He would not look at her at first, but jerked his head away. Then, when she sat down in the filth beside him and stroked his hand, he began to talk against his will. Still without looking her in the face, he recounted everything that Joseph had said. The accumulated bitterness washed over her. All the anguish of the last few days, the mockery, the insults, the final infamy of hearing his work derided, beat against her ears. She heard him out in silence.

"And it's true, isn't it?" he said, looking at her for the first time. "You knew from the beginning."

She could not help him with a lie.

"Yes, it's true." Her voice came from a long way off. "We needed you, in the beginning, for just what Joseph said. Who were we? Nobodies. A drunken buffoon for a father; no hope, no steady work; the talk of the neighborhood." Her other hand came down and rested on his head. "You saved us from that. It seemed a fair bargain, at the time. Your name, our talents. Your dream, our need. It was our only chance."

"You might have told me. You might have been honest. Especially after—or were you part of the bargain too?"

"No." He did not need to look to feel her flush. "There are some things I do for myself. We started by using you. And I ended by . . . liking you, Jean-Baptiste."

She stroked his hair again and he pulled away. The sharp movement made him wince.

"No more of that. It's all finished. Find someone else to amuse yourself with."

She moved to him and held him by the shoulders, forcing him to look at her.

"Don't be a fool. Oh, you're right, I can't expect you to believe me. But stop being reasonable for a moment and listen to what I have to say. I'll know I tried, at least."

She tightened her grasp as he twisted, partly to avoid the disconcerting intentness of her eyes and partly from the pain.

"Everything Joseph said was true. Up to a point. But he wanted to hurt you, not help. He was right about your acting. When you started, you didn't know your right foot from your left. It was like teaching a child to walk and speak. We spent all our time trying to cover up for you. We tried to talk you into parts where you wouldn't do much damage. You still did a lot."

He was her victim now. She was hypnotizing him again.

"But what Joseph didn't tell you—oh, he would have done, I'm sure; he isn't really vicious, only spiteful sometimes—was that we watched you grow. You can talk all you like about art and rules and principles. But the only way to learn is to get up there in front of an audience and educate yourself in public. That's what you did. When you started you were making a fool of yourself. And us. But now . . . you'll never be a Montfleury, Jean-Baptiste. But you've the makings of an actor in you."

She rose, brushing the straw from her skirt.

"And there's one more thing, that you'll never be able to shake off however hard you try. You've been bitten. You've caught the disease. You can sit there now telling yourself that you hate me, you hate Joseph, you hate the theater. You think you can forget us all and go back to your father's ways. To a nice safe life. But you never can. For a year, perhaps. Then you'll start to smell the paint and powder again, and say a few lines before the mirror; and you'll write another play when you should be adding your accounts, and perhaps it will be better than the last one. And you'll come back, to me or someone else. To my sort of life. I hope it will be me, Jean-Baptiste. Because you need me. And I need you, a great deal more than I care to admit."

She bent and kissed him, and he heard her neat step crossing the flagstones and the clang of the door outside. As he sat in the vomit of his bitterness a small insurgent voice, Hope at the bottom of Pandora's box, whispered that she was right.

He never knew whether it was Madeleine who had persuaded his father to come, or if so, how she had worked the miracle. How much older he seemed. Quieter, too; less bombast, this time. As though the last had been only a dress rehearsal, and this was in earnest, the true crisis.

Father looked at son and saw the battered face, the torn clothes; smelt the cell-stench and heard the distant catcalls of the prisoners; but he saw something else in his son's eyes, and knew that things would never be the same between them again.

But Jean Poquelin was a stubborn man. He made one last attempt.

"I'll pay your debts," he said. "I have to. If it were up to me, I'd let you rot here for a year. You need a lesson. But I have some sense of my family obligations," bitterly, "even if you have none."

Jean-Baptiste hardly heard the rest of the expected harangue. His mind was in the country with Madeleine. She would be waiting, he was free to go. Many players had made their names there. They would not have a company of their own, of course. At least, not at first. But somebody would take them on. He was still personable, and Madeleine—well, Madeleine could do anything; she would help him and—he admitted ruefully— standards were lower in the country. He could conduct his education in peace there.

His father's voice broke in upon his thoughts. A document was being thrust at him.

"You might at least have the courtesy to pay attention. I said I'll pay your debts on condition that you sign this paper."

"What does it say, father?" He was not really interested. Anything so that he could leave.

"A promise that you will leave this foolish business. That you will have no more to do with the stage."

It was the best performance of his short career. He drew himself erect, the model of a noble youth whose honor has been impugned.

"A family should need no written contracts, Father." He looked him full in the face, his eyes brimming with trust, honesty and affection. "I give you my word of honor that the name of Poquelin will never be associated with the theater again."

Behind his back, his fingers uncrossed. It would be an easy matter to change his name.

It was not, after all, so easy. He could change his name, and did so, three or four times. But he could not change the sick feeling of failure in his stomach. While he was in prison, anything had seemed better to him. But now, as he and Madeleine stumbled through one humiliation after another, he could almost have wished that he was back in prison again. At least he had been safe there. Anonymous, enclosed, protected, caught up in a predetermined and unshakable routine in which you ate when the jailor pushed the food through the big barred door, slept when the sun went down, for you had no money, as others did, to buy candles, and, in time, learnt to stop worrying about anything else, for there was nothing that worrying could do. And prison had given him an excuse for his failure. If only the creditors had held off for a few more days, if only Louis had not run off with the money, then, then, we would have seen. . . . But the world outside was contemptuous of excuses. He stood on his own two feet again, and there was no one to blame but himself.

His father tried to find him, as he had known he would. Poquelin the elder was a respected man, his connections were wide; and when the word went out that he was anxious to retrieve his errant son, there were many prepared to put themselves out to look for him. Messengers came, friends, toadies, distant relatives, to persuade him to go back, to appeal to his good faith, to invoke the ties of family affection or threaten him, in the last resort, with the law. Jean-Baptiste ignored them all. To go back to his father now would have been a worse kind of prison, where the chains were those of anxious love and the food the price of slavery. He could face a brutal jailor, but not a kindly one. He could endure the callousness of a paid bully, who knew him only as a number, but not the look of hurt bewilderment in his father's eyes. If he was doomed to live his life as a failure, he would rather have no one to disappoint but himself.

And so he sent the messengers away, gently or roughly, depending on who they were, and on his own mood at the time. With each rejection he sent back a word of love, and an appeal not to try to move him again. For a while his father remained as obdurate as he, and though he changed his name again and again as they moved from place to place, the friends of the family still found him, and the appeals and threats still came. Then, as the months passed, they came less frequently, until at the end there was only a curt note, sent by a paid messenger and written in his father's most formal hand: "When I am dead, perhaps you will remember who I am. And who you are." He tore it up, and wept, and sat looking into the night sky, to where he imagined Paris to be.

They had traveled so much that he hardly knew where he was himself. In the first flush of enthusiasm at beginning again, at smelling the fresh air and dodging the familiar rumble of traffic in the city streets, he had never imagined that his fortune would take him so far from home. They only need go outside the city, he thought; to Vincennes, to Nanterre, to St. Denis, where no one would have heard of them, where they could live down their failure and make a fresh start. But apparently the world of the theater was as small as that of business. When they went to look for work, as soon as they mentioned their Paris company, there were winks and smiles and raised eyebrows, and sympathetic noises which meant polite refusal. If they hushed it up, as they soon learned to do, and said nothing of their previous ventures, they were told abruptly that there was no place for beginners, and that they should come back, in ten years' time, perhaps, when they had learned their trade.

"They're all failures themselves," said Madeleine, fiercely. "That's why they have no time for anyone else. They're all hanging round Paris trying to get in. Or trying to get back in. We have to start farther away."

So they put their small store of money together and took to the coach, to go north. They tried the old towns, Reims, Rouen. But it was damp and chilly there, and the people shuffled about their work with hanging heads and heavy eyes, and had no time for players. Madeleine and Jean-Baptiste found a few days' work in a sacred play that the cathedral was offering, because the honest citizens who should have given their labor free were suddenly sick, or did not have the time. They bargained for a few coins with a sour-faced cleric who finally, out of desperation and necessity, gave Madeleine the part of Mary of Magdala —"because of my name," she said—and Jean-Baptiste, to his great surprise, that of Jesus Christ. He was overjoyed with this, and thought that they had at last found a place where talent was recognized. But on the first day of rehearsals his spirits fell again when he realized that he was only to act as a substitute in the crucifixion scene. The speaking part was given to a portly burgher whose weight would have imperilled the Cross, even if his dignity had allowed him to hang from it. So Jean-Baptiste spent a number of painful days on his precarious perch, shivering in the damp air on the cathedral steps and registering an agony that was by no means feigned. Madeleine complained constantly that her role was an insult to her profession. There were no scripts, for the play had been performed in the same way, in the same place, from time immemorial, and all the people in Rouen, apparently, knew the lines by heart. The only copy was in the hands of an aged priest whose mind was on other things, and who stood muttering in the square and brandishing a large stick to show the actors where to go. The costumes and the scenery had come, apparently, from the Ark, and bore the marks of sweat, grime and overuse. An enormous pasteboard head was trundled out of the cathedral and propped in one corner to represent the mouth of Hell. When Jean-Baptiste was finally lowered from the Cross by inexpert hands that made the descent another crucifixion, he was thrust into a shaking canvas tomb where he found himself surrounded by devils in fantastic costumes and ferocious masks, waiting to bounce into view through Hell-mouth to the accompaniment of thunder, lightning and bursts of red fire. They were happy in their parts, for they knew well that the audience came to see them and nothing else.

And yet there was a certain shabby grandeur about it all. When the time for the performance finally arrived, when the rickety stands were erected round three sides of the square and the trumpeter called the citizens of Rouen to attend out of pious duty; when lamps and torches were lit along the roof of the cathedral, so that the carved saints and gargoyles stood out against the evening sky, and seemed to engage in flickering battle; when the townspeople climbed into their unfamiliar costumes and started to intone the old words whose meaning they had almost forgotten, and the choir of angels sang from the steps and the voice of God declaimed from an embrasure far above the people's heads, Jean-Baptiste was fascinated and caught up again in spite of himself. He watched the parade of the Old Testament from the back of the crowd, knowing that there were hours to go before *anno domini*; and he was so enraptured, even by the long line of the Prophets declaiming their parts with stiff and ridiculous gestures, that he was late in changing into his loincloth and crown of thorns. The priest snarled blasphemously at him as he raced to his position, and the Torturers, angry at being kept waiting, gave the ropes another stiff turn, and cracked his head against a cornice as they hoisted him aloft. His task done, he waited out the rest of the play inside Hell-mouth, peeping between the teeth to see the devils cavorting, cartwheeling and singeing one another with fireworks to send the crowd home in a holiday humor.

They left the following morning, when they had managed to prise their wages—less than they had been offered—out of the old priest, whose memory for a bargain was apparently as bad as his memory of the play.

"I'm glad to be rid of *that*," sighed Madeleine. "All these respectable citizens! Just because I was playing a whore didn't mean I am one." And she showed him where she had been pinched black and blue by several of the Twelve Apostles.

"This is no place for us, Jean-Baptiste. Let's go south. It's warmer there."

So they counted their money again, and followed the sun, carefully skirting the Paris that had too many memories for them, and looked for work in Tours, Limoges, Bordeaux. There was little to be had. Madeleine could usually summon up enough charm to be given a walk-on, or a small speaking part; and the name of Paris had a certain magic so far away, where nobody knew of their disaster. But the managers took one look at the gangling youth who accompanied her and threw up their hands in a contemptuous shrug; or let him read a few lines and laughed at him, saying that the stable boy could do it better. More often than not, while Madeleine walked the stage, Jean-Baptiste walked the streets, or picked up a few sous sweeping the courtyard or holding the patrons' horses. The longer this life went on, the lower his spirits sank. He was doomed. He was a proven failure. He was achieving nothing.

"Do you love me, Madeleine?"

She looked at him coolly.

"How can you ask such a question? Don't I live with you? Aren't I kind to you?"

"My father would have been kind to me."

"What do you want, then?"

"I want you to stop feeling sorry for me. Oh, do you think I don't know why you're here? Why you've tied yourself to me all these months? It was because your conscience hurt you, Madeleine. You thought you were responsible for . . . all this. For what happened in Paris. The theater breaking up. Everything. I don't want you to be sorry for me. I want you to love me for what I am. For what I can do. I want to be worthy. To make you proud of me. Not have you keeping me, consoling me."

"You want to do something, then. What can you do?"

All the frustration and resentment of the past months boiled up in him, and the angry tears ran from his eyes.

"Nothing. I can do nothing, do you understand? I can't walk across a stage. I can't speak an intelligible line. I can't write. Oh, I should never have come. I should have stayed in Paris, with my father. I probably wouldn't have been any good there, either. But at least I shouldn't have known it."

She bent over and kissed him very gently on the cheek.

"So you have learnt something, at least."

"What?"

"That you know nothing. That's a very big thing to learn, Jean-Baptiste."

"And now I know it, what?"

"That is the first thing to learn. The moment when you start learning. There was nothing I could do with you until this moment."

"I don't understand."

"In Paris, you were only playing at the theater. You had enthusiasm, yes. All the enthusiasm in the world. But so does every stage-struck boy who spends an afternoon at the playhouse and thinks he can do as well, or better. The ones who stick, the ones who make a success of it, are the ones who realize that it's impossible."

"What can I do now?"

"You can start again. I can teach you now, because you are offering yourself. Before, in Paris, you knew it all. You pretended to listen to what we all said to you, but it meant nothing, really. You went your own way, and made the same old mistakes. And when we corrected you, and tried to point out what you were doing wrong, you thought it was because we were jealous of you, or because we lacked sensibility. You couldn't learn from me, or Joseph—"

"Joseph!"

"Yes, Joseph. No, don't interrupt, or splutter and fly into a rage. You know it only makes you cough. I know Joseph has his faults. He's a cruel man, and a very selfish one. He thinks a good deal too much of himself, and hardly anything about others. But stop and think for a moment. When Joseph walks onto a stage, something happens. People stop talking and take notice. He has a sort of magic about him. Did that ever happen when you walked onto the stage?"

He grinned in spite of himself. "They talked louder."

"Exactly. And why do you think that was? Do you think Joseph was born with some sort of magic charm, some gift from the fairies at his christening that made this happen? It's nothing of the sort. It works for Joseph because he makes it work. Because he went through years of making mistakes, like you, and being honest enough to admit that he made them, which you've never done. Because he learnt how to count a pause to the fiftieth of a second, and how to crook his little finger, and when to raise his eyebrows, and when to talk loud and when to talk soft, and when to stand completely still. And he practised these things for hours and hours, until they entered into his soul and became part of him. You thought you could walk onto the stage and be an actor overnight, just because you had a good education, and could read books the rest of us couldn't begin to understand. Because you knew how to address a marquis, and make some sort of acceptable bow. And all the while you knew nothing. No wonder Joseph laughed at you. I was often tempted to do the same thing."

"But . . . in the prison . . . you told me I had talent. . . ."

"I know I did. And I meant it. Oh, I know I would have said anything to get you out of there. You were a dead man. I had to revive the corpse somehow. But I meant it, all the

same. You do have talent. There's something there, though I
doubt that anyone's ever seen it beside myself. But do you
think talent's enough? There are thousands of talented young
men in Paris, just like you, panting to get on the stage, ready
to desert their homes and families, just as you did, when they
smell a whiff of paint and powder. But talent's just the start
of it. We take that for granted, in our profession. You have to
take that talent, and work till you bleed."

"How can I learn, if no one will give me work?"

"I'll teach you. I can, now. We shall have lessons, every day.
Every hour that I'm not at the theater, or you're not drudging
to keep us both alive. We shall work so hard that you will
cry with pain, and beg me to stop. And you'll come to hate me,
Jean-Baptiste. But if you have in you what I think you have,
you won't stop working. You'll loathe me, and despise me, and
call me a tyrant. But it will be worth it, in the end."

"Will it be worth it?"

Her eyes flashed, and she cried to him, "You must never ask
that question! Because if you ask it, you're finished. You have
to believe, Jean-Baptiste. You have to know in your soul that it
is worth it." She knelt down, and buried her face in his lap.
"I've never been a religious person. If you asked me whether I
believed in God the Father and God the Son, I'd have to say
honestly that I didn't know. Sometimes I think I do. And then
sometimes I think it's all a fraud, like that charade we went
through at Rouen—all the lights, and the candles, and the
incense, and the people chanting, and the great solemn words,
and the smugness and laziness and hypocrisy behind it all. But
one thing I do know. I believe in the Holy Ghost, if that's what
they like to call it. There's not much in the world for people
like me. Or for people like you, either. I never had the chance
for an ordinary life. You did, and put it behind you. And I
don't know which of us is the worse off. But I believe that if
we work, and if we're faithful to what we want to do, we can
pass through all the hunger and the misery and the humiliation,

and touch heaven. Did I ever tell you about the first time I saw a play?"

"Never."

"Then I will now. Listen. I was very young. Scarcely eleven. And my family had never taken me before, because they said I was too young to go, I wouldn't understand. And then it was a holiday, a name day, or my father had come into a little money, I forget; and they took me. I can't remember the name of the play any more, or the theater, or the actors. I only remember that I sat there and it was like being in church. Or what they say being in church ought to be. I laughed, I cried, I shivered; I was outside of myself, I grew ten years older in those two hours. These people on stage were gods. The way they carried themselves, their language, their voices! They had fallen straight out of heaven, and I worshipped. When the play was over I ran away from my parents and hid backstage. I wanted to kiss their feet, these gods called actors, to touch the hems of their garments. I peeped into the dressingroom, and there they all were. Dirty, coarse, unshaven, passing a bottle around, and swearing about the audience. And one of them, the one who had played the king on stage, saw me, and grabbed at me. He had a great wart on the end of his chin, covered with red hairs. I can still see it. And I can still smell his sweat, and the wine on his breath. I ran away, and cried and cried. But even then I knew that this would have to be my life. And if this was what I would have to do, and these were the sort of people I should have to spend my days with, it was worth it, for the magic of those two hours. I've always believed that. And you must believe it too, or I have no time for you. We shall have to part, you and I. Do you believe it?"

And Jean-Baptiste answered, from the depths of his heart, "Yes. I believe it."

"Good. Then let us start work."

She was right. He did learn to hate her, because she gave him no rest. They would begin before the sun was up, when they could scarcely see across the room. This was good, she told him; he would have to make her see him with his voice. Though at first she let him speak no words, but made him recite the letters of the alphabet, like a child. When he complained about this, she told him:

"That is exactly what you are. A child who is learning to speak. For to speak properly on the stage, you must learn again from the beginning."

And she made him recite his letters over and over again, forcing him to spit out the consonants and dwell on the vowels, till every one was clear and precise. Then she would tell him to recite them like a man happy, or a man sad, or angry, or in pain. When he failed to please her, she would call out, across the dark room, "I cannot see you, Jean-Baptiste"; and he would have to begin again. In the daylight hours she taught him how to move—or rather, first, how to stand still, for this, she said, was the most important thing. "Few actors know how to stand on a stage," she said. "You must be relaxed, yet firm. If you fidget, the other actors will hate you. And if you stand like a ramrod, the audience will laugh at you." From there they went to walking, and bowing. He learnt a new grace that would never seem graceful in real life, but looked so on the stage; he learnt how much you had to exaggerate if the audience was to think it natural. And he learnt the elaborate and wholly unnatural movements that all tragic actors had to learn: how to throw up the hands when apostrophizing heaven, how to draw the back of his hand across his eyes in sorrow, how to throw out his arms to register astonishment or grief. When they returned to the voice again, he balked; for she insisted that he learn the sing-song tones fashionable at the Hôtel de Bourgogne, where the verse was chanted with a measured cadence never heard from other lips on this earth.

"It's ridiculous," he objected. "It's not natural. I never liked it when I heard them do it in Paris. No one ever spoke like that. I can't do it. I won't. You lose all the sense of the lines. Listen. This is how it should be read."

And he did it his way till she stopped him, mocking him.

"When you are a great, great man, Jean-Baptiste, and a hundred years old, then you can start reforming the stage. But this is how we speak tragedy. My way. I know there's some sense in what you say. But no one will ever listen to you. The voice in tragedy is like an instrument. What's natural about a violin, or a trumpet? They're wood and strings and brass, put together by man's hands. And why talk about sense? There's no sense in a note of music. But when you put the notes together, you get a lovely noise. And that's what people go to the theater to hear."

He gave in, as he always did, and read the lines her way, until she finally, grudgingly admitted that for the provinces at least, he would pass.

The next step was to let him try his wings, and get him an engagement. It was not easy. He was still a novice; he had no experience that he was prepared to admit. The weeks went by with no luck, and Madeleine saw him falling into his old despair again. Then, one day, she came back with her eyes shining, and a triumphant smile on her lips. She was playing at a small theater near the port. It was a shabby place, too close to the water for comfort. The smell of the wine casks on the Bordeaux quays hung heavy over it; the whole town reeked of wine, it was the city's lifeblood. The audience was a motley one, a few merchants with pretensions to culture, sailors who came to the theater to stare at the girls. The company was third-rate, and the manager paid her a pittance for the privilege of billing her as "the new actress from Paris." But it was work, her work, and it had kept her happy, while Jean-Baptiste earned enough at menial jobs to keep them in food.

"I've done it," she said. "I've been talking to the manager for weeks, trying to get him to give you a hearing. And I've finally done it. He wants to see you tomorrow. You must read these pieces for him."

He could hardly believe his ears; and, though he had been

waiting so long for such a chance, felt the old doubts attacking him again, and began to protest that he was not ready.

"Nonsense," she said. "If I say you are ready, you are. It's not the best place in the world to begin. But you have to start somewhere. And if they like you here—and they will, I promise you—you can go on somewhere else. Don't be afraid."

They read over the pieces together, all night. She rehearsed him in every word, every nuance, every gesture. He was so fatigued that he thought he would fall asleep on the stage; but when they left their lodging and walked the cobbled streets to the theater, he felt the excitement welling up inside him and promised himself he would do well, for Madeleine's sake.

The manager was a greasy man, sulky at being up so early in the day and clearly only too anxious to find an excuse to reject Jean-Baptiste so that he could get back to his bed. But there was nothing he could immediately object to. Jean-Baptiste had taken care to dress his best. He had on his new breeches, bought with money they had scraped together for just such an occasion. His hair was combed and his beard trimmed; there was a sprig of fresh lace at his throat. The manager—his name was Porchon, which suited him—finding nothing he could complain of at first sight, began to cast doubts on Jean-Baptiste's intentions. "You said you were bringing me an actor," he whined. "And you've brought me a young gentleman." He spat the word. "He looks very pretty. Does he have anything else besides nice manners?"

"You'll see," said Madeleine, not in the least discomposed. "He reads well, and he's a quick study."

"Oh God," said Porchon. "Don't tell me he's intelligent." He waddled up to Jean-Baptiste and circled him, fingers twitching as if they were tempted to feel the merchandise. "All actors are fools, boy, y'know that? If they weren't, they wouldn't be actors. And when I see an actor who isn't a fool, I say to myself, Porchon, you watch that fellow. He thinks he's too good for you. And that means trouble."

Jean-Baptiste flinched at his breath, but before he could say anything Madeleine interposed quickly:

"You needn't worry. You'll find him trustworthy and obedient. He'll do a good day's work and not complain."

Good God, thought Jean-Baptiste, does she have to talk about me as if I wasn't here? She might be selling a spaniel, or a horse. And, like a spaniel, his hackles began to rise. Madeleine's quick hand on his arm restrained him.

"Let him read, M. Porchon. You did promise."

"Oh, very well. It can't do any harm, I suppose. But make it quick. I haven't got all day to waste."

He squeezed himself onto a bench halfway back in the gloomy theater while Madeleine and her protegé climbed onto the stage. Jean-Baptiste thought he had never seen a sadder place. The scenery, still in place from the last night's performance, was torn and shabby. There was a great rent in the curtain from someone's careless manipulations with a broom. The chandeliers, if they had ever had any lusters, were devoid of them now. A small dog was relieving himself in one corner, and there was a gentle coo, coo of pigeons that had nested somewhere in the roof. A smell of neglect and decay, flavored with wine lees and cooking, washed over the whole theater, and the rumble of barrels from the streets outside could be plainly heard through the cracks in the boards, as the draymen unloaded their wagons to ship the precious claret to England.

"I can't do it," whispered Jean-Baptiste frantically. "This place feels like death. Are there no lights?"

"When you've been acting as long as I have," whispered Madeleine back, "you'll know that every theater looks like this in the morning. No, there are no lights. Do you think he'd waste a single candle-end on hearing a new actor? Go on, now. Don't disappoint me. Let him see you by your voice."

And with a light, soft kiss she was gone into the wings, leaving Jean-Baptiste alone in the center of the filthy stage. He stared gloomily at the cracks that marked the trapdoor, and wished that it might open and swallow him up.

Somehow, he started. He caught himself standing rigid, like a dragoon on guard, as Madeleine had called it, and forced himself to relax. His head came up as he caught a murmur of impatience from the huddled shadow that was Porchon. All right, he thought, in a burst of defiance, I'll show him. I'll be magnificent, and then laugh in his face and walk out of here. I'll take Madeleine with me. We'll find honest work. She shouldn't have to live in a hole like this.

The lines came to his tongue automatically, he had rehearsed them so often through the long night before. To calm his nerves, he let his mind run free. He pretended. He pretended he was standing on the stage of the Hôtel de Bourgogne—no, not the Hôtel, that was not grand enough; at court, yes, that was it, that was where he ought to be. And Porchon vanished and his place was taken by the King in all his glory, with the court around him nodding and smiling their gracious approval. He threw himself into the part with all the skill and energy he had learned so laboriously to acquire, his voice soaring through the approved ranges of the scale and, miraculously, not faltering, though often at the end of a line he felt himself nearly out of breath. His hands moved in spite of him, his body set itself into the attitudes hallowed by tradition. He knew, at this moment, the truth of what Madeleine had said to him so many times: "Do it, do it, do it, until you forget that you are doing it. And that is when you really do it."

The court, unable to restrain itself, forgot decorum and burst into rapturous applause. Even the footmen ranged between the gilt mirrors were moved; he could see the tears running down their cheeks. He moved into the closing lines of his last speech and capped them with a bow, holding the position while the King came forward to embrace him and grant him honors and a title. Outside, all Paris shouted for their new favorite.

Coo, coo, called the pigeons; and they were answered by a fat snore from the benches. Jean-Baptiste brought himself upright with a jerk. He was trembling in every limb, and he found to his surprise that his face was running with sweat. Madeleine came running from the wings, clapping her hands.

"You did it, you did it! Oh, Jean-Baptiste, I'm so proud of you!" He gestured towards the offensive noise.

"But he's asleep!"

"He always goes to sleep when he can't find anything to complain about. If he hadn't liked you, he would have had you off the stage after you'd said two lines. Let's wake him up."

The huddled figure moved and shrugged.

"He'll do. He's got a lot to learn, but he'll do." He still did not look at Jean-Baptiste. His finger jerked at Madeleine. "Come on."

"You have to stay?" asked Jean-Baptiste. "Why? We must go out to celebrate."

"Not yet. I have to see about your contract."

"I can see about that for myself. I'm a merchant's son, remember?"

"No, no. You must leave these things to me. You're still an innocent, Jean-Baptiste. He'd twist you round his little finger. Wait for me on the quay. I'll be with you in an hour." He protested, but she stopped him. "And besides, you must stop thinking of yourself as a merchant's son. That's what you were when you came in. You go out an actor."

Jean-Baptiste, as he swaggered out to inspect the shipping, reflected that he had rarely seen so charming a theater.

They dined that evening at an inn outside the town, on the banks of the Garonne, where the noises of the port were muffled and the only sounds to disturb their peace were the sunset cries of birds in the tall trees at the water's edge and the occasional call of a wherryman beating upriver. It was the perfect hour when nature smiled at what she had done that day, and began to think of rest. The air was fresh and cool after the ordered frenzy of the city, and they savored it, taking hours over their meal while Jean-Baptiste called for carafe after carafe of wine

It had been grown on the hills around them, and came to the table fresh and young and strong. Jean-Baptiste, ecstatically happy over the day's events and suddenly aware, after the weeks of work, that he was very tired, let it go to his head. But he did not care. If ever there was an evening when he could get drunk, it was this. He drank, and talked, and drank, and talked; he was a new man, the old despair and lethargy had been purged from him. He talked of their future, telling Madeleine of his imaginings on the stage that morning, and assuring her that they were not imaginings but real. That was how it would be for them, some day. And it would not be long. They would go to Paris again, they would play before the King. He had his start now; they would be rich and famous, they would never want again.

At the beginning, Madeleine was as happy as he. She drank to match him, pouring glass after glass, till he reflected that he had never seen her drink so much before. But then, he thought, she had a right to share his triumph too. There should be no rules, no restraint on this joyous night. But as the wine captured his nimble brain and whirled it to new heights of fantasy, it slowed her tongue and made her morose. As he painted his visions of a golden future she grew more and more silent, answering him, if at all, only with curt monosyllables, till at the end she was not even feigning interest. She turned her face to the water, and in the yellow light of the swinging lantern he could see a tear trickling down her cheek.

He reached across the table and patted her hand.

"What's the matter, Madeleine? Aren't you happy? Have I said something to upset you?"

"No. It's nothing. It's just that I can't bear to see you so smug."

"Smug? Don't I have a right to be? It worked, didn't it, just as you said? All I had to do was put my mind to it, work hard . . . you were right, I did hate you. I've never been bullied so unmercifully in my life. But it was worth it, oh, it was worth it.

As soon as he saw me, that fat old man, he knew I was an actor. I've done it, Madeleine. Work is all it takes. Work, and dedication. It's not playing now. It's real."

She looked him full in the face, and smiled wearily.

"Oh, you poor innocent. You think you know it all, don't you? You really think that's all it takes. You don't realize that everything has to be paid for."

"What are you talking about?"

"Nothing." She drew back quickly. "I'm sorry, Jean-Baptiste. I shouldn't have said that. Let's have more wine. Let's go on celebrating your triumph."

"No." He stopped her as she was about to call the potboy. He had sobered quickly, and his brain was miraculously clear. "I want to know. What do you mean, everything must be paid for?"

"Oh, let it alone. Enjoy yourself. Be happy. It wouldn't do you any good to know the things I know."

He was relentless, probing her. "No, you have to tell me. We should have no secrets, you and I. Was it something that happened? Something that happened today?"

She was silent, and he knew that he was right.

"That man. Porchon. It's something to do with him. Something's happened since this morning. You haven't been the same since we went to the theater."

"Leave me alone. Give me some more wine."

"What was it? Didn't he want to pay me?" A horrifying thought struck him. "Did you have to pay him? Is that the only way you could get him to take me?"

No answer.

"Yes, that's it! That's why you wouldn't let me stay to sign the contract! You bought me a place. The way my father would have bought me a place in a business. It wasn't me at all, was it? I did nothing. It was all you. Being kind to me. Not wanting to see me hurt. So nothing's different. I'm back where I was before."

"Why go on like this? You're only hurting yourself. I should have said nothing. It was the wine. I was stupid. Leave it alone, Jean-Baptiste. Let's go home to bed."

"But what did you pay him with? That's what I can't understand. We have nothing. How could you—"

And then he saw her weeping face, and knew.

"You slept with him, didn't you? In that filthy theater, after I was gone. You let him paw you, and roll on you, and make love to you!"

"Yes, yes! If you want to know, I did! Now are you satisfied?"

He jumped to his feet. A glass shattered somewhere in the dark, and the bench fell on the flagstones behind him. Somewhere in the night a bird called, a low mocking noise.

He slapped her on the face, so hard that she staggered back and almost fell. "You filthy stinking whore!"

"It was for you, Jean-Baptiste! It was for you!"

"You think that makes it better? What sort of a man do you think I am? Oh, you were right, weren't you? I was so proud of myself this morning, I thought I'd done it all. And now look what you've made me. I was an actor this morning. Now I'm a pimp. A man who lives off his women."

Her red hair spun in the moonlight and she slapped him back, so viciously that his lip bled.

"You silly little fool! So your pride's hurt. Listen to me for minute. Do you think I enjoyed it? Do you think I liked having that pig do what he did to me?"

"Probably. The voice is an instrument, you used to tell me, for people to play on. Your body's an instrument, too, isn't it, Madeleine? How many people have played on that?"

"Insult me all you want. I only did it for you."

"Do you think that makes it any better? Do you think I wanted you to do this for me? I'd have starved in the gutter first. What sort of man do you think I am?"

"A good man. A man who's grown up, fast. A kind man, a talented man. A loving man, when you remember to be, and aren't thinking too much about yourself."

"Loving! I thought you loved me!"

"I do, my dear, I do. If I hadn't, I would never have done it. Not if you were the best actor in the world."

"A funny kind of love."

"The best kind. The only kind. The love that gives itself, and isn't ashamed to be hurt, or humiliated, as long as it's for you. No, listen. All those things I told you before were true. About the life we have to lead, you and I. About the theater, and how glorious it is, and how sordid. You touched the glory this morning. I really saw it in you, for the first time. You have to learn to live with the rest of it."

"Some glory! A job bought with your body!"

"No. If it makes you feel any better, you got the job yourself. I had nothing to do with that. I could have been the Queen of Sheba and Helen of Troy rolled into one, and he wouldn't have taken you for my sake. I was the price for seeing you. For giving you the first chance. You did the rest yourself."

"I'm going back to kill him—"

She leapt at him. "Are you mad? Now that I've done it, you're going to throw it away?"

"You don't expect me to work there after this?"

"You have to! If you don't, I'll never see you, never speak to you again. You'll have this on your conscience for the rest of your life—and you'll never have another chance like this, never. You remember when we started I told you that you had to believe in what you were doing. That you had to know what you really wanted and let nothing stand in your way. Well, this is what you have to do now. You hate what I've done. You hate me, for the moment, because you can't understand what I've done. But use it! Use it! And then you may have your dreams, and Paris, and the King, and all the rest."

"You're ruthless, aren't you?"

She smiled ruefully.

"Ruthless? I don't know. Perhaps I am. I used to be, for my own sake. Now I am for yours. Let's just say that I have learnt the value of things. As you will, too, in time."

There was a long silence before Jean-Baptiste answered.

"Very well. I'll do as you say. Because I do want these things. Because you've taught me to want them. But remember, in the future. If I ever seem ruthless—if I ever hurt you, because of our work, because of the theater, because of these things we want—then remember that this, too, was one of the things you taught me."

They went home together along the road to Bordeaux. And though in time he came to forgive her, or thought he did, and though they slept together again and called each other by affectionate names, it was as if, from that moment, a sheet of glass lay between them, so thin that they could feel the warmth of each other's bodies, but not the beating of each other's hearts.

PART TWO

Interlude of Maskers

THERE WERE TWO INNS IN UZÈS, one cramped, pestilent
and malodorous, the other sprawling and with some shabby
pretensions to grandeur. They lived in the smaller but drank
at the larger, for appearances' sake. In the lazy time of the
afternoon they kicked their heels on the bench outside, waiting
for the coach to bring Madeleine back from Paris. She had
made the journey more frequently since her father died. Jean-
Baptiste had accompanied her to the funeral; it was a memory
he did not care to dwell on, the first time he had seen Marie
Béjart upset. Together—he had clung to the scraps of his
legal training as a harlot keeps her first communion dress—
they had gone through the chaos of Joseph's papers, adding
up the widow's assets.

"Debts," said Marie bitterly, "all debts. Not a sou to bless
ourselves with." And the famous composure had vanished in
vituperation and tears. The neighbors would have enjoyed that.

The happy-go-lucky life was all very well, he thought. He had come to love the Béjarts like the adopted son he practically was, relishing their hand-to-mouth cheerfulness as a contrast to the rigors of his own upbringing, where no one was ever in want but every penny had to be accounted for. But what happened when the bubble burst? It all came down to money in the end. Perhaps he was grown up. The first sign of maturity was when you realized that money was important.

By the next day the family had reformed ranks. Marie had resumed her public face and Madeleine, as the eldest daughter, became the family provider. Joseph had wandered off into the great unknown; rumor said he was in prison again. Of Louis no one had heard a word. But there were still mouths to be fed and appearances to be kept up. The greater part of Madeleine's earnings now went to her mother. Jean-Baptiste contributed. It was a small return for Marie's help. If she no longer owned her own house, it was his fault.

It was something, at least, that he could help now. He stretched and yawned. Would the coach never come? The sun of the Midi had filled him out and ripened him. He was larger, more confident. It was not a bad life. For the last few years they had been paying their way. Provence was not Paris, and the dull farmers who came to gape through two hours of heroics never understood the half of what they saw. But they came in sufficient numbers to put food into the players' mouths and clothes on their backs. Not that there was any left over.

As if with deliberate irony, the voice of the proprietress broke in upon his thoughts.

"More wine, Monsieur Molière?"

She stood meaningfully in the doorway, rubbing her fingers on her apron and glaring at the tankards which had stood empty for a good half-hour.

He answered without hesitation to the new name now, though it had taken time to get used to it. It was a good name, distinguished but not ostentatious. He had found it by lanternlight in a rainstorm, painted in straggling letters on a crossroads sign, pointing the way to some godforsaken village he knew not where. As the coach grumbled on, bursting with its load of weary players, the syllables had jogged through his head. By the end of the journey he had adopted it and made it his own. It had no echo of Poquelin, his father would not be embarrassed. Though the old man could be under no illusions as to what his son was doing. To his surprise, he realized he did not care.

Strange. A year ago it would have torn his heart to have admitted, even to himself, that he no longer needed or cared for his father's love. He was able to be dispassionate about it now. It was strange, he thought, that the most natural of relationships should also be the most artificial. Because his father had made him, in an accident, a spasm of the flesh, probably not caring, possibly not even knowing what he did, in the eyes of the world they were bound together for all time. It did not matter what he was, or what he made of himself. He could become a cardinal, or a drunken sot rolling in the gutter, and it would still make no difference. He would still be his son.

The last time he was in Paris, on Madeleine's business, he had walked by himself in the park. It was a beautiful September day, gray-blue and still; the tall trees shivered occasionally as autumn walked over summer's grave. In their gilt birdcage at the end of the walk, the King's musicians were playing. They played exquisitely, and the ripe sun sent little ripples of shadow across them as they sat serenely on their stools and bowed away. A precious moment, like a breathing tapestry. Molière had sat down on the grass to listen to them. By his side were two women with a baby. It was jerking itself down the path, grinning and drooling, tripping over its skirts every so often and making those grunting sounds that doting parents take for language. The two women were deaf to everything else. The heavenly host might have been playing in that park, and they would have taken no notice. On the one side, the highest and most perfect art, the consummate expression of God in man, his creative mind. On the other the most common, lumpish, formless work of nature, something that happened a million times a day without design or premeditation. And this is what the women preferred.

And that was how it was, Molière thought, between his father and himself. His father never really cared what he did. It was just the same when he was first at school, and used to bring home some blotched, sprawling piece of writing that had as much likeness to decent script as man's first pawings in the primordial mud, when he learnt that those strange protuberances on his hands were tools that he could poke with. And yet his father would praise them to the skies, as if they had been the tablets handed down from Mount Sinai. He knew, even then, that he hardly looked at them.

So it had been between them ever since. Even those things his father claimed to abominate he approved of in his heart because they were done by him. To Molière's knowledge, his father had never seen one of his plays, or even read one. He had never even seen him act. If he did, the old man would be stern enough to his face, and then go off boasting, in a deprecating way, to his cronies about his wild son who had run off to be an actor—"but a damned good actor, don't you know? Fit to play before the King! And he will too, one of these days, you mark my words!"

Why could he not be judged by what he did, rather than by what he was? Why could not his father forget Jean-Baptiste the son and remember only Molière the playwright? "By your works are ye judged." If only that were really true.

At least his father prized hard work. Surely he could judge him in that respect without prejudice one way or the other. For surely no human being had ever worked so hard. Up at dawn to study the promptbooks and prepare for the day's rehearsal. Meet the company to put them through new business and polish the old. The constant worry and the nagging care.

"More wine, Monsieur Molière?" The landlady again, insistent. He raised an eyebrow at Robichaud, who played the serious young men, kept accounts and, by common consent, carried the company purse. In answer came a tiny, rueful shake of the head.

"Thank you, no. The wine is excellent, but we've had enough. The coach is late," he added, by way of apology.

"Never anything else, in Uzès."

She waddled to the table and wiped it portentously.

"That will be all, my good woman. We told you that we needed nothing more."

This from Marie du Parc, on his other flank, who could always be relied upon to say the wrong thing. He sometimes wondered why they kept her. In any company she would have seemed affected. In a troupe such as theirs her pretensions were ridiculous. Despising her given name, she insisted on being addressed as the Marquise. This was nothing new. It was common among players to feign descent from the nobility, as though their roles had eaten into their brains the way the paint soaked into the pores of their faces. Her trouble was that she believed it.

He rose in haste to forestall the landlady's wrath.

"Let's take a stroll round the square."

"Round the square!" the Marquise mimicked. "The summit of excitement in this dreary place!"

She slipped her arm through his nevertheless, and they sauntered off with Robichaud following at a discreet distance.

For all her airs, it would be difficult to let her go. She was too good an actress. So good, perhaps, because she never stopped. Every day for her was one continuous performance. A fair part of the night, too.

What would Madeleine have to say about that? It was not his fault. Women found him attractive, he could not help knowing it. If it had been left to him, he could have honey-talked that old cow at the inn into letting them sit until the coach arrived. Not that he had any illusions about the Marquise's interest. She went where the money was, or in default of money the influence. It was a compliment in its way. She had held off for a few months, not for any want of approaches—she was beautiful enough in a big-boned way—but biding her time, to see where she might attach herself with most advantage. Perhaps she had been frightened of Madeleine a little, too. It was not until Madeleine had been away two weeks that he had come back to his lodgings aching from rehearsal to find the Marquise established in his bed. She had bestowed herself on him like an accolade.

Lord, how the woman chattered. As if she were parading through some elegant salon, not tripping on the cobbles of a grubby southern town. He wished with all his heart that Madeleine did not need to go away so often. He would be less vulnerable to this sort of thing.

They made three circuits of the square, on each occasion making a detour round the inn; the landlady was moved to comment on players in general, and Molière's troupe in particular, whenever they hove into view. The coach came in at last with a flare and a flurry, pretending that it was punctual and everyone else early. Its arrival was the signal for work to stop. Doors and windows were thrown open, tools flung down with a clatter, tankards left half empty on the table; the good folk of Uzès swarmed into the square, shouting cheerful obscenities to the driver and cossetting the horses, exclaiming over them as if they were unheard of marvels from some fairy place. As indeed they almost were; the weekly coach was Uzès' one precarious link with civilization.

Madeleine disembarked crumpled and cross, and they ran to meet her. She had brought back little presents for them from Paris—a book for Molière, a pair of gloves for Robichaud, even a tiny painted fan for the Marquise. She cooed over it, and made a great show of kissing Madeleine on the cheek.

"But what are you doing here? Aren't you playing today?" she scolded.

Molière and Robichaud exchanged shamefaced glances.

"We had to cancel. The usual reason. The Italians."

"Italians!" said Madeleine. "Controlling the government, ruling the church, ruining the stage. The country's turning into an Italian colony."

They were silent, for it was a well-worn theme, the one subject on which the company found itself in unanimity. For years the Italian comedians had been infiltrating France. They occupied the Paris stages, till the authorities threw them out; they swarmed over the South; they were ribald, irrepressible and—worst offense of all—popular.

In Provence, Molière's company had been constantly running into them. They traveled like gypsies, these Italians, here one day and gone the next, setting up their platforms wherever they could find a crowd to play to and a sou to drop into a hat. Shopkeepers and farmers loved them for bringing light into lives whose peak of excitement, normally, was Sunday mass. There was some resentment, too. They tended to be neglectful in money matters, and would move on leaving bills unpaid and scores unsettled. Usually they would send scouts into the town a day or two ahead, to sniff out local gossip and work it into their shows. Many a local worthy had stamped out in a rage after seeing himself burlesqued on their stage. But they were adored by the people as much as they were mistrusted by the shop-keepers and the magistrates. They gave them a rare chance to laugh at their betters. And so they were ineradicable; in addition, they were cautious. They never visited the same place too often in succession. Waiting till official indignation had died down, and resentment had been forgotten amid the pressing concerns of the olive market or the price of pigs, they would appear without warning, perform the same gay mockeries and as quickly vanish. Every chance meeting with them—and there had been too many—had meant financial disaster for the Molière company.

"They came in yesterday," explained Molière, "and they're going to perform this afternoon. Why fight them? You know what always happens."

The Marquise, with her Tragic Muse voice, was properly incensed.

"People have no taste any more. We offer them the glories of Corneille! Tristan! Pradon! Molière!" she added just in time. "And they prefer these monkeys, these gibbering clowns. With a public like this, it's a wonder we get any audiences at all."

"It's easy enough to understand," said Molière. He had faced the problem often enough to have no illusions. "They come to us as they go to church. Because they think it's the proper thing to do. They sit through a tragedy and don't understand a quarter of it. But it makes them think they have good taste. They come to us out of duty. They go to the Italians for amusement."

The beating of a drum brought an awareness in the crowd and reminded the players that the enemy was at the gates. The coach, having exhausted its novelty, was abandoned for gaudier pleasures. People began to stream off purposefully in the direction of the noise, the driver among them. Soon only a grumbling ostler was left, soliloquizing blasphemously about the fate that made him work while all his mates kept holiday.

"Well," said Molière, "how shall we spend our enforced leisure?"

"Let's go and see them."

They looked at Madeleine as if she had gone mad. It was as though a priest had leaned down from the pulpit and suggested holding a Black Mass.

"Why not? I've had a long hot day, and I'm in the mood to enjoy myself. And you must allow them some virtues. Wouldn't it be good if we could draw crowds like that?"

Surveying the deserted square, Molière was forced to agree with her. The same drum beating to announce the Molière troupe in tragedy would scarcely have rippled the surface.

So they went to spy out the opposition, consciously slumming. The Marquise, loudest in her protests, was overridden. She only accompanied them because she did not want to leave Molière alone too long with Madeleine. Picking up her skirts as she walked, she gave the appearance of one about to be contaminated by unmentionable filth.

It was a short walk; there was not much of Uzès. It was a town that had looked upon the seventeenth century, shrugged with Provençal nonchalance, and turned its back. Its streets had remained unchanged since the Crusades. Huddled on the grudging hillside, it was seen by the approaching traveler as a gray, crumbling excrescence on the sun-baked fields. A mean town, Uzès, and tightfisted by necessity; it clung to the slope as if afraid that Fate might one day step on its fingers.

On the south side, in the shadow of the church, some long-dead civic fathers with delusions of grandeur had constructed a pretense at a terrace. It could be reached by any of the winding streets; no street in Uzès led straight anywhere. The flagstones gaped with weeds, those that were left of them; the rest had been carried off by dour farmers who saw no reason why good masonry should be wasted in decoration and smuggled off their plunder in the night to build a wall or pigsty. A gap-toothed balustrade looked down upon the hill. Against it the Italians had built their stage.

"Easier for them to get away, if they're arrested," snorted the Marquise, "which is more than likely. Really, Madeleine, what a place to bring us to!"

Indeed, the stage was poor enough. A few boards on a shaky trestle, and a paint-daubed sheet behind. Round one corner, where the sheet did not stretch far enough, one of the actresses could be seen dressing. The spectacle made the male part of Uzès whistle, but incensed the Marquise all the more. Molière, in spite of himself, felt a sneaking sympathy. He knew what it was like to make do.

A dwarf was taking money at the corner, simultaneously pumping a pedal to bang the drum. His foot kept rhythm with his conversation. He had a joke or a remark for everyone, in bad French spiced with some outlandish dialect. All courtesy to those who extended their money promptly, he had a sharp eye for those who tried to slip in without paying. His face purpled, and he stopped them in their tracks with a torrent of vituperative Italian. It needed no translation. The malefactors, ashamed, crept back with money in their fists, and pretended they had not noticed him.

Molière's money was waved away grandly. The dwarf bowed like an arching cat, his head level with Molière's knee. "No indeed, *signore*. The courtesy of the profession. We take no money from our fellows." Molière was half flattered at being recognized, half indignant at being classed with a pack of vagabonds. The dwarf, abandoning his drum for a moment, offered to lead them to prime seats in the front row, but this was too much for the Marquise. Having made the supreme sacrifice of coming, she wanted to remain as far from the offense as possible. The dwarf bowed and twinkled again, but said something between his teeth that amused Madeleine; she knew the language. They compromised by seating themselves on the fringe of the crowd, perched on the stone wall which threatened to crumble at any moment and precipitate them into the gardens below, where water from a wooden conduit trickled grudgingly into a cask and the drip, drip, drip beat a measure to the murmurs of the crowd above.

By this time the terrace was seething, and the three began to regret their snobbishness. They were in real danger of being dislodged. A sun-black snorting peasant pillowed himself on Madeleine's legs. His heavy wife, seeking a safe enclosure for her basket, butted it agonizingly against Molière's shin. The Marquise, on his other side, paled perceptibly and shut her eyes, pretending to be somewhere else. She was abruptly recalled to reality. Out of the basket came a pair of beady eyes and a sinuous neck, belonging to a goose in a temper. Perhaps it was a stagestruck bird, annoyed at being cheated of a view; perhaps it merely disliked tragediennes in general and the Marquise in particular. It inspected her calf with a malevolent eye, stretched out its beak and nipped. Her scream for once was pure nature and no art. On stage, it would have done honor to the death of princes. In the present hubbub it passed unnoticed. She rose in panic; the farmer's wife roundly cursed her for disturbing the basket and she sat down. They were trapped. It was impossible to go forward or get out.

The Marquise turned even paler, and pawed at Molière. "Put your arm round me, darling. I'm terrified I might fall." She turned the full intensity of her tragic gaze on the water-butt below, as if it was a group of conspirators huddled round the steps of the Capitol.

The endearment was not wasted on Madeleine. Molière felt her stiffen as the Marquise rubbed insistently against him. Damned women. But what could a gentleman do? Sighing inwardly, he gave the desired assistance.

A final rattle, and the drum fell still. A squeak of trumpets, and the audience did likewise. Not a murmur now. Only heavy breathing, and the smell of sweat, garlic and cheap wine as the people leaned forward in their benches determined not to miss a word.

"Look at them," whispered Molière. "It always works. Even here. Idiots gaping at mountebanks. But the magic's still there."

He wasted his breath. Madeleine was leaning forward herself, as rapt as those around her. The Marquise, having made her point, had gone back to pretending that she was not there.

The sheet quivered, stuck and, with a wrench, parted. A preposterous figure bounded onto the stage. His face was masked and wrinkled in brown leather. A huge hump bestrode his back, and a broadsword of lath swung loosely from his belt. From the flamboyant hat that obscured his eyes, a motheaten plume hung halfway down his back.

He turned a double somersault and bowed. It was clear that he was among friends. "Brighella!" roared the audience with one voice; and he acknowledged the greeting with a gesture of the fingers of one hand not ordinarily used in polite society.

"The same to you!" roared the audience.

"Disgusting!" muttered the Marquise.

"Sssh!" said Madeleine.

Brighella pirouetted to a standstill and drew himself upright. One hand swept back the plume which had contrived to wind

itself round his neck. The other drew the sword jerkily from its
scabbard. It stuck. With a shrug of pained remonstrance, as
though he were the victim of some diabolical plot, he crossed
one leg over it to pull it free. Sword, hat, plume and man
went down in a tangle. When he rose, the sword had somehow
twisted itself behind his back and stuck out between his legs
like an enormous phallus. At least that was how it seemed to
the audience, who commented noisily on the fact between bouts
of hysteria. Brighella pantomimed his surprise that they should
suspect him of any such lewd intention. This only set them off
again.

At last, when he had gathered his accoutrements together
and extricated his sword (which turned out, to no one's surprise, to be broken) he advanced to the front of the stage,
signaled for silence, put a finger to his nose and stared up at
heaven.

> "How swift the evening shadow veils the sky.
> 'Tis time for us to meet, my love and I;
> For by her promise she will be here soon
> To plight our troth beneath the silver moo-oo-oon."

He bellowed out the last word like a cow in labor, provoking
more expert comment from the audience.

There was further doggerel of the same sort, interrupted by
the entrance of an equally fantastic personage. This one was
dressed like a soldier. His helmet was balanced precariously on
his nose, from which it slipped frequently to blind him. From
his boots—each wide enough at the top to admit another leg
beside his own—protruded enough daggers, swords and pistols
to stock an armory. His belt jangled with more of the same.
A short cloak flared behind him; he had a starched ruff, Spanish
style, a red nose, and a moustache a yard wide.

"The Captain!" shouted the audience in joyful recognition.
He gave them a long, contemptuous gaze, turned his back on
them, hitched up his tunic and farted.

"I'll never forgive you for this," muttered the Marquise.

The Captain, having acknowledged his public, turned his attention to Brighella. Laying down the lid of a giant soup tureen which served him for a shield, he reached into his paunch and produced a bladder, with which he proceeded to thwack his colleague unmercifully.

"Spare me! Spare me!" howled the unfortunate. "What have I done?"

"Done, you rascal?" Thwack. "*Nombre de Dios*! Taken money from these poor people under false pretenses! They came here expecting to see a comedy. *Estrada di Seville*! And here you are giving them a tragedy!"

"But *capitano mio*, invincible warrior, scourge of Mahomet, conqueror of Troy, commander of the Uzès civic guard," chattered Brighella, scrambling between his legs as the bladder flailed the air around him, "this is no ordinary day. Look! Don't you see our distinguished company?"

And to Molière's total horror he pointed across the audience to where he sat between the two girls. He saw now why the dwarf had urged them to the seat of honor in front. The Marquise, misguided in her snobbery, had placed them in an even more vulnerable position. They sat head and shoulders above the crowd, isolated in a sea of jeering faces. He prayed devoutly that the balustrade might crumble. Even the water-butt was preferable to this.

Brighella and the Captain bowed deeply towards them, sweeping the ground with their hats. "*Vida breve*, my friend, you're right!" roared the Captain, twirling his moustache until it came off in his hand. "What unspeakable joy! What fantastic honor! But, *sueno di madre*, they are not going?" For Molière had fought his way to his feet, and was looking desperately for an exit.

On the stage, Brighella threatened to commit suicide if they departed. From behind, Madeleine tugged him back to his seat.

"You can't go now! You'd never live it down. You have to stay, and pretend you're enjoying it."

Brighella, reassured, recited another tragic speech, juggling three oranges the while. The Captain, entering into the spirit of the thing, suggested that they should fight a duel. "They always have duels in tragedies, don't they, *senorita*?" he bellowed to the Marquise, who sent a mute appealing glance to heaven.

The duel took place, with predictable results. The Captain caught his foot in his helmet and lost his breeches. Brighella, punctured by a lucky blow, paused for a swallow of wine, which promptly squirted out through holes in his costume. When the Captain staggered back against the screen, some person unseen crowned him with a chamberpot. Finally Brighella found a blunderbuss and fired it, causing the Captain to expire in a shower of confetti. Brighella read a funeral oration over him in dog-Latin, and two white-faced zanies dragged him out, his bottom scraping on the floor.

After this the plot, such as it was, began to evolve. There were, it appeared, two fathers and two sons, of whom Brighella was one. His father was a crotchety old man in red, who lived in perpetual anxiety for his moneybags. These he hid in various remote corners of his person—his slippers, the seat of his breeches, his stocking-cap. Brighella, in need of money for some fell purpose of his own, always knew by instinct where it was to be found. He took the slippers off to be heeled, and was almost off the stage with them when the old man remembered the purse in the toe. He pretended to be a statue, on which the old man hung his cap. He persuaded him to look through a telescope while he picked his pockets. The father pointed the telescope erratically towards the sky. "No, no!" cried Brighella. "The stars are over there!" And once again Molière and his companions found themselves the objects of unwelcome attention.

The other father was rotund and dressed in black. His specialty was Latin orations, into which he would launch himself on the slightest pretext only to be stopped by a blow from a large stuffed fish (which Brighella, by some mystery of his art, had acquired) or from the omnipresent bladder. His main function in the play was to be knocked down. At every running exit from the stage the father in black was sure to be coming in. He fell with a resounding thump, emphasized by the bass drum backstage, and was not allowed to rise again until several people had walked over him.

Interwoven with this nonsense, as Molière recognized with increasing dismay, was a devilishly clever parody of the tragedy they were currently performing. How could the Italians have done it? They must have had spies in the audience; ingenious spies, too, with memories that could record every turn of phrase and plot. Brighella, when he was not pouring water down his father's neck or pretending, for indecipherable reasons, to be a horse, would utter singsong speeches in a nasal voice, pounding out the rhymes with as much gusto as he brandished his bladder. He seemed to be having trouble with his voice. He stammered a great deal, and from time to time would stop outright, taking several breaths before uttering the final explosive syllable. Once he fell to such wheezing and coughing that it took the efforts of both fathers, the Captain (miraculously revived) and several buckets of water to set the couplets staggering on their random course.

The Marquise for some reason found this funny. She laughed for the first time, so long and loud that Molière asked her what the devil she was sniggering at.

"Don't you see, darling?" she said, squeezing his arm affectionately; "It's you!"

He pushed her off so hard that she almost toppled over. Yes, it was clever, no doubt of that. Clever, cheap, vicious and insulting. And all these turnip-fed idiots who snored through his magnificent lines; look at them now, laughing fit to burst. He remembered Joseph mocking him in prison, and his fury grew.

The Marquise, in revenge or self-defense, was now affecting to enjoy the performance hugely. I wish the goose would come back, thought Molière.

The afternoon wore on, and the preposterous plot strangled itself in its own convolutions. Brighella finally fought, stole and bullied his way to his lady love. Seizing a guitar, he serenaded her beneath her window. A coy rose fluttered down (followed, foreseeably, by the pot) and the lady herself made an appearance. She minced on stiltlike heels. Her head jerked like an automaton. Her face was varnished and her painted eyebrows lost themselves beneath her wig. A limp white handkerchief, in best tragic style, dangled from her hand. She ignored Brighella, who was rolling on his back with delight, and stared at the audience with hauteur.

"Ugh!" she simpered, handkerchief to nose. "How you *smell*!" This time it was Madeleine who laughed.

"Don't you see, darling?" she mimicked across Molière's bowed shoulders. "It's you!"

The debacle was complete.

The show ground to an end amid tumultuous applause. The crowd departed, with remembered laughter to carry them through the dreariness of everyday. So hedged in were the three that, by the time they were able to escape, the little stage was almost down and the actors nowhere to be seen. In the excitement of the afternoon they had said things about the mayor and local clergy that might more prudently have been left unspoken. It was as well to be out of sight before someone remembered. Molière was thirsting for revenge, implacable. Not that the others had the energy or interest to soothe him. They glowered at each other; the air was thick with promise of storms. He told the two glaciers that had been Madeleine and the Marquise to make their own way home, and set out to find the perpetrator of the insult. If anyone had asked him what he intended to do when he found him, he would have had no clear answer. To track down Brighella was his only thought. A duel was vaguely in his mind, but duels could not be fought with vagabonds. Besides, to judge from his agility on the stage, Brighella was probably the better swordsman. A whipping? Inelegant. A demand for an apology? Inadequate. What, then?

He neither knew nor cared. He wanted only to confront the author of his shame.

The moronic boy who was the sole representative of the troupe left on the terrace stopped loading planks on mule-back long enough to answer his questions. Yes, he knew who Brighella was; who did not? It was Adriano Geloso, the leader of the company. Where might he be found? Well, that was another matter. The boy had wit enough—or, more probably, the suspicion had been beaten into him by his employers—to fear that Molière might be an unpaid creditor. To him, a red-faced man demanding his master's whereabouts could mean only one thing. A couple of coins loosened his tongue, however, and Molière followed his pointing finger across the fields, leaving his informant scratching his head beside the patient mule and wondering with oafish cunning how to explain away his breach of trust.

He walked so long without a sight of anyone that he began to suspect the boy was more intelligent than he looked, and had deliberately sent him in the wrong direction. As he was about to give up and retrace his steps, he saw smoke rising from behind a clump of trees. A few more paces and a clutch of caravans came into view, drawn up round a fading fire. This was evidently the nearest the players dared camp to town. There was nobody in sight. The horses munched mournfully on the thin grass, and gazed at him with hopeless eyes. A half-filled bucket stood before the fire. Only a few garish blankets drying on a line, and a costume hung across an open door, confirmed that this was the place that he was seeking.

The players had probably gone to drink their profits in a village nearby, where there would be less risk of their running into somebody they had offended. He passed from one caravan to another, wrinkling his nose at their squalor, scenting lice in the costumes and filth on the floor. Not a soul inside. He was about to return home in disgust when, in the last caravan he tried, he found a wrinkled old man, bent double in the half-light, stitching at a costume.

He looked up as Molière stood silhouetted in the doorway.

"The *signore* wished something?"

Nervous, thought Molière. Expecting a dun.

"I'm looking for Adriano Geloso," he said in his brusquest tone. "The master of the company."

"I am sorry, *signore*. Adriano Geloso sees no one."

"He'll see me." He brushed a small dog from the bench inside the door and sat down. The old man shrugged, and went back to his sewing. Minutes passed. Completing his task, the old man bit the thread, laid his work carefully aside and broke the silence.

"The *signore* has some business?"

"None of yours."

"You are angry, perhaps, about our play?"

Molière was startled. He had not thought he had been recognized.

"Of course. What else do you expect?"

"Angry at what you saw, or what it made you see?"

Surprise made him bluster.

"What are you talking about?"

"We have many, *signore*, who come like you. Hurt, angry, insulted . . . and perhaps with some reason. But I always tell them they should be flattered."

"Flattered? To be made a laughingstock by a pack of beggars?" The dog was trying to seduce his ankle. He kicked it off, and it crept whining into a corner.

"Of course." The old man picked up another costume from the pile beside him. "If people take the trouble to make fun of you, you must be an important man. With a nobody, who bothers?" The French was liquid and seductive on his Italian tongue. "But a man of mark, a man the people know . . . ah, that's a worthy target. Every king once had his jester, *signore*. Better perhaps if they still did, eh? We are the jesters now. We laugh, show you yourselves in a distorting glass, make fun. But what harm? None in the world. A cure, rather. You are angry now. But you will go home, the anger will pass. And you will see some good in us, perhaps. Maybe even thank us."

Damn him, thought Molière, there's something in what he says. To be known, to be important enough to be made fun of. . . . "Confound your smooth Italian tongue. You can't get round me. Where's Geloso?"

The old man shrugged again, abandoning without regret a plea too well rehearsed, too often spoken. He continued stitching though it was now quite dark. The dog snuffed around in the pile beside him, and wet unconcernedly into a discarded mask.

"What would you do if you found him?"

"Thrash him within an inch of his life."

"I do not think, *signore*, that you are the sort of man who could thrash Adriano Geloso."

Molière pressed his back against the wall. You heard strange tales of these Italians. A cord round the neck, a stiletto sliding out of the dark. . . .

"And even if you were, would that help? We have shown you as you are. You are an actor; you have strengths and weaknesses. No one is perfect. Few are even tolerable. But it takes time to learn that. It took me many, many years."

"I don't care so much about myself," said Molière, lying a little. "It's what we're doing that I care about. We spend weeks here trying to show the people something good, and true, and holy. Yes, holy. And you come along with your cheap tricks and ruin us. We'll have to leave. They'll never take us seriously again."

"Cheap tricks? You think what we do is easy?" The old man's voice crackled out of the darkness. "Listen to me, my friend. All's fair in love and war. We take our targets where we find them. If you're as good as you think you are, they won't laugh at you for long. What worries you is that you're afraid you're only as good as we think you are."

He reached into some recess of the caravan and produced three balls. He juggled with them. "You think this is easy? Catch!"

They came spinning out of the air towards him. He grabbed at them. One flew through the open door and lost itself in the pool of dark beyond. One struck his shoulder, bounced back and hit the dog, who ran out yelping. The third, by some miracle, stuck in his hand.

"You call what we do cheap and easy," chattered the old man. "It took me ten years to perfect that. Could you do it? Or this?"

He turned a double somersault and struck an attitude at Molière's feet. The costume he had been stitching dropped to the floor. It had a false hump.

"You!" stammered Molière. "You're Geloso! You're Brighella!"

"I am."

"Then I know one thing about you at any rate."

"What is that?"

"That you're a coward. Why did you say Geloso never saw anyone?"

The old man came close, and put his face to his.

"Does that answer your question, *signore*? For the last ten years, I have been completely blind."

In his confusion, he hardly knew how he got out of the caravan. As he stumbled in a tangle of ropes by ember-light, the old man's voice floated over his head, sepulchral, disembodied.

"One last word of advice, *signore*. When you get back to the path, turn left, not right. You may be interested in what you see."

And, when he was almost out of earshot:

"Do not be too discouraged. When I began, I would have dropped the third ball, too."

He realized he still held it in his hand.

When he reached the path he stood uncertain for a moment, then turned left as the old man had directed. In a little clearing on the far side of the encampment were the other players. They were not drinking; they were busy. By the light of a torch stuck into the ground, they were rehearsing the play they had performed that afternoon. He watched them for an hour as they went back again and again over a piece of business that was still not perfect; they were still absorbed when he slunk away ashamed. It was a relief to discover, when he finally got back to his lodging, that the promised storm, if it had not cleared the air, had cleared his bed. Neither Madeleine nor the Marquise was in evidence. He rolled between the sheets and slept like a drunken man.

He told himself it was at Madeleine's insistence that he began to write the silly things. She had turned cool and professional; hurt in her dignity, she was abandoning him to the Marquise. It was an adequate revenge. The woman's chatter was insufferable, her pretensions outrageous. He began to devise excuses to avoid her, to have a few hours to himself. Madeleine had put the matter to him reasonably, and used the one unanswerable argument, money.

"If these Italian idiocies make the people come, we ought to be doing them too. We can't spend our whole lives in the provinces. We must get back to Paris some time, and that needs money."

And so she played on his vanity, asking him to sacrifice himself for the good of the group. It was an easier victory than she expected. The challenge tossed to him by the blind Italian stuck in his mind. If he can do it, he grumbled, I can; a man who cultivated the higher forms ought to be able to stoop to the lower.

It was thus that he wrote *Scaramouche Beside Himself*, despising it because it came so easily. Used to laboring long hours balancing rhymes and wrapping noble sentiments in carefully calculated syllables, he was suspicious of a play that flowed onto the page like water from a pipe, fully formed, already grown, with hardly an erasure or a change of thought. It was a simple subject. Scaramouche, the servant, had ideas above his station. He was in love with two grand ladies; pursuing each, he was rebuffed by them in turn. Finally he found true happiness with the little servant girl who had adored him in silence all the time. The sketchy plot was filled out with stolen tricks. If the Italians could mock him, he could take from them. No juggling. There was no one in the company to do it. But the falls, the clowning, the knockabout . . . if I'm going to demean my Muse, he thought, I might as well go the whole way.

His company, sated with heroics, received the play with joy, and began rehearsal before the ink was dry on the page. On one thing Molière was adamant. He would not act in it. They pleaded with him; no use. He was firm. There was a point beyond which he would not go. If this was what they needed to get back to Paris, it was his duty to write it. Make a fool of himself on the stage he would not.

They cast the play without difficulty, except for Scaramouche himself. At last, in desperation, they gave it to Garcin, their youngest member. He had not been with them long. His chief function was to walk on with the leading characters and engage them in conversation; after act three he rarely appeared, and had never taken a leading role in his life.

In comedy, out of his safe, anonymous routine, he was unimaginably dreadful. Molière, lured to a rehearsal by threat of disaster, watched with growing melancholy from a corner. Garcin had no grace, no style, no sense of timing, little memory. He plodded around the stage with furtive desperation, as though looking for somewhere to hide. Madeleine and the Marquise, as the two great ladies, were both superb—Madeleine because this kind of brittle gaiety came easily to her, the Marquise because she insisted on playing in the tragic vein, which gave a demented grandeur to the part. She was playing a parody of herself. She'll be marvelous, thought Molière, as long as she never finds out what she's doing.

But between them where the hero should have been, slunk Garcin, a walking gulf, stumbling over feet and lines with equal maladroitness. He was worse than a nonentity.

"You have to do something," whispered Madeleine in a pause between scenes, while the actors mopped their brows and Garcin edged off to hide himself in shame. "We daren't go on like this."

"What can I do?" said Molière, ignoring the hinted appeal. "He's the only one we have."

Garcin came back, the grumbling company resumed their places, and the rehearsal proceeded on its jagged way. Miserably conscious of his inadequacy, Garcin stumbled in the middle of a big speech he had known the last time through. His mind went blank, his face red; he stood staring at the floor hoping it would swallow him up.

Molière raged, entreated, cajoled. No use. He was furious. Stupid though they were, they were still his lines. Was the product of his pen to be disgraced by an ignoramus? They started the speech from the beginning. This time the lines were right, but Garcin forgot the move. Two vital pieces of business were ignored.

"Idiot!" screamed Molière, losing all patience. "Come here and sit down, if you can do that without falling over your feet!" Garcin was pushed onto a bench by no gentle hands, and Molière stood fuming in his place. "Now watch me. It couldn't be easier. When she says 'And which of us would you prefer?' you turn to her like this. And then you move upstage—head erect, fool, no one's trying to steal your shoes—and take the big speech from here. You're trying to woo her, not send her to sleep. And you have all these fine phrases that you've got out of books; and you get them all wrong, but you don't *know* you're getting them wrong. They all sound magnificent to you. You can't understand why she's laughing, you've got to be completely sure of yourself, right through the speech. You're blind. You're blinkered by your own conceit. You only see the image of the self you want to be. Listen. Like this."

And he went through the speech, line by line, pointing it as it should be pointed, boasting, strutting, pausing where his intuition told him that the laughs should come. He was lost in it.

He forgot that he was merely instructing a stupid actor; forgot the women in their practice clothes, and the chairs that stood where scenery should be. He saw only Scaramouche, arrogant, cocksure, inflating himself like a pigskin for his inamorata to puncture.

It was magnificent. The rest of the company, sick to death of the speech on Garcin's stuttering lips, heard it as for the first time. They stopped their gossip and grumbling and crowded forward. Catching fire from their interest, Molière preened and postured. The words that had dropped from his pen so easily had new meaning now. He caught the hardness under their facility: he grasped the desperation of a man who thinks himself in love, who is not so much convincing the adored one as persuading himself. Carried by the surge of his own performance he topped the speech with a pirouette, and then, with a mental bow to the Italian, deliberately stumbled. Whack, down he fell. He had stolen Madeleine's thunder, but it did not seem to matter; instead of waiting for her to puncture his pretensions he had accomplished the deflation himself.

He sat on the stage blinking, returning slowly to reality. He remembered what he was supposed to be doing. "There!" he bellowed into the auditorium. "That's what I want! Do it that way!"

But Garcin had gone. Unable to endure so spectacular a demonstration of his own inadequacy, he had fled to his lodgings. They found him later rigidly drunk with the bottle still clasped between his hands; he never played anything but hero's friend again.

Molière hardly noticed his absence. All he heard was the applause. His colleagues were beside themselves. Professional offhandedness was forgotten. They surged round him, laughing, clapping, slapping him on the back; they hauled him to his feet and carried him offstage in triumph.

"It was wonderful! You have to do it, Molière!"

"The Italians couldn't have done better!"

"You have to play the part yourself!"

"If you don't, we'll give up the theater and sell fish for a living!" And when Madeleine came towards him, eyes shining, to add her appeal to theirs, he was lost. It would, he told himself, have been stupid and pompous to refuse.

She came back to his bed that night. On the whole it had been worth it.

Once committed, Molière flung himself into his new work with a masochistic glee. In his heart he despised what he was doing. But to escape this dreary round of provincial performance, to earn his way back to Paris where the wise and witty were, the people who knew what good theater was . . . for this, he would have done anything. After all, he thought, there are many writers who take other trades to support themselves. At least I'm still working in the theater.

What gave him concern, however, was that he now had little time for his serious writing. There was a constant demand for new pieces. Each member of the company wanted something to show off his particular talents, and though he continued to write them easily the mechanics of putting pen to paper filled the few hours left over from rehearsal. He wanted to write for posterity; instead he found himself writing for Madeleine, and Robichaud, and the Marquise, capturing their foibles on paper, using their strengths, glossing their weaknesses, evolving characters his company could present because they were the people they were playing. Even writing parts for himself. He had a new, cynical eye for his own deficiencies; or perhaps his eyes had simply been opened. He made a comic valet of himself, a man who wheezed when he became excited; whose clumsiness of body betrayed his moments of high passion.

The pile of scripts grew. They seemed to be endless. For every one finished the company demanded another. They were piled high on his rickety table; they flowed onto the floor and over the trundle bed on which he caught his few hours' sleep; they filled the trunk which sat beneath his window. There was no escape from them. *The Doctor in Love, Scaramouche at Sea, Brighella Takes A Wife, The Flying Doctor.* He even found, or told himself that he had found, some artistic satisfaction in writing these things, though he would never have admitted it, particularly to Madeleine. She would never have said "I told you so." She had too much tact for that. But he would never give her the pleasure of knowing that she knew him better than he knew himself.

The satisfaction was that these little plays reaffirmed his sense of order, which circumstances seemed more and more concerned to shake. But the hierarchy now was different. He had believed, once, that the King was God's appointed representative on earth. Now he knew that it was the artist, the writer. In his little room, at his desk, when it was not cluttered with Madeleine's clothes, he ordered and arranged all things. To each character his appointed destiny. They fell in love, they fell down, they fought, they conquered, they laughed, they cried, they sorrowed, they repented. And above all they were all tidy, these creatures of his. Not entirely his; they had been the Italians' once, but he had made them his; he was their godfather. Each followed the path laid down for them, not just by him but by tradition. If that was the right word, though Molière was beginning to think that there was a law behind these things which he was beginning to sense, instead of merely transmitting. His characters moved in their appointed paths like the stars in their spheres; and he, the artist, self-contained, all-sufficient, sat in the center and gave them motion. He took from the world what he needed and gave back what he thought good.

As he scratched away by the sputtering candle, he thought with a quarter of his mind about the great tragedies that he would write as soon as he had time. Not *The Death of Julius Caesar* now. That had been a juvenile folly, better forgotten. The new play would be truly great. *Orestes.* As soon as he had the time.

They needed more plays than ever because since his fall from grace their audiences had notably increased. They still sat dully through the tragedies, hardly comprehending, rarely applauding. Molière insisted on performing his old favorites, however. They had to keep in practice for the return to Paris; he himself had to perfect the tragic style whose weakness he was curing by mockery in his comedies. But it was the comedies the people came for. And came back for—two, three, four times. The company was making money. Not enough to get them back to Paris, yet. They all realized how costly this would be. To operate in the capital they would need a patron. The more illustrious their sponsor, the greater their chances of success. Finding such a one was no problem. Great men were interested in the arts. They had to be; the King had set the fashion. But to gain access to him was another matter. Palms had to be greased, bribes circulated throughout Maecenas' household. Money to the tailor, so that they could cut a figure in society. No man, in this Paris, could expect to be successful unless he looked as if he already were. Money to the porter, to gain admittance to the lord's levées. Money to the flunkeys inside, to ensure that they would be placed prominently where the eye of favor would light upon them, and not pushed behind the scores who had their own favors to ask, their own petitions to present. Money to the bodyservants, to be forewarned when authority was in a benign or testy mood. Money to the secretary, to have their scripts read; more, to have them read favorably. Money, probably, to the great man's mistress, for a word in his ear at some delicately propitious time. And in the end, when they had passed through all this—it might take months—Apollo might, only might, bend his elegantly bewigged head and graciously allow the performance to take place, never dreaming that he was on auction to the highest bidder and that his favors had been bought and paid for.

For such a siege they were not yet ready. It would come in time, if they saved diligently. For the present they lived a little better and ate more regularly. They traveled less often and in greater comfort, for they now stayed longer at one place and, when they moved on, could afford a private coach. They grew into a family. Like all families they bickered, but the worst rancor was forgotten. Molière and Madeleine presided as father and mother. They made love less often now, relaxing into the cosiness of early middle age. Molière himself was looked on with growing respect because of the sacrifices they all knew he was making. And he was a worker, no one could deny that. The long years of practice were making themselves felt. He was less stiff on stage now. His voice rang true in tragedy, though still tending to crack on the downfall of a cadence. In comedy, where he threw aside decorum—for after all, the rules did not matter in this silly business—he was positively agile. In secret, the taunts of the blind man still murmuring in his head, he practised juggling. He was now adept with two oranges. The third would take a little longer.

The Marquise still paid him occasional visits, when he was not busy with his writing, but with Madeleine's full knowledge and dispensation. Madeleine was queen, the Marquise licensed concubine, and Madeleine waived her rights with amiable frequency. Molière, in decency, had to make time for the two of them. If I took as many mistresses as King Louis, he thought, I'd never have time to write a play, let alone govern a country.

To this ménage Robichaud played eldest son. He gave advice when needed and withheld it when it was not wanted. He was grave and studious, good at his books; the family was proud of him. Daily he struggled with the accounts, regarding every debit balance as a personal demon to be vanquished. His pages were masterpieces of calligraphy, every item neatly filed and documented. So much in, so much out; this for candles, lace and wigs, that for paint and lumber; so much for the hire of halls, for criers to announce the play, for coaches. So much for food, so much for rooms, so much—not nearly enough—for the Paris fund. He took pride in his work. The others had no real concern for money, though they talked about it constantly. But that was understandable, they were artists. He asked only to be among these magic people, to share a little of the grandeur and the glamor, to enjoy the laughter and applause, though he contributed so little to creating it. No actor he. He could turn a pretty enough speech when the need arose, but people approved of him on stage because he looked like the honest son every merchant in the audience would have liked to have. Molière often argued that they should exchange fathers. "Mine would love to have you; and yours is probably so disappointed that you threw yourself away on a pack of players that he might just as well have me."

One day Robichaud came running to Madeleine and Molière as happy as a child bringing home a prize from school. They had never seen him so excited. In his hand was a letter, an edict rather, written in great script on thick paper, sealed and stamped with a coat of arms.

"Read it!" he shouted. "It's an invitation! A command! The Prince de Conti is holding a fête, and wants us to appear!"

"The Prince de Conti!" They could hardly believe it, though it had been clear for some time that their audiences were improving in quality as well as quantity. A great man's servants might sometimes appear, haughty and invariably late, having sent some menial to hold their places. From time to time a country squire might come, dressed in the Paris fashions of five years ago, and insisting on a separate seat in the middle of the hall as if he were King Louis himself. But the Prince de Conti! This was another matter. He was a truly great man, and close to the King. If all went well—if he condescended to like them—

The Marquise voiced the unspoken thoughts of them all.

"If we succeed," she said, "it means Paris."

A reverent hush, followed by pandemonium. Actors going crazy, slapping Robichaud on the back, dancing with Madeleine, bellowing appropriate quotations as actors will; there comes a time in every actor's life when he knows an apt quotation for everything.

Moliére held up a hand. They fell silent, listening to their father.

"No time to lose. The fête is only two days off."

How peremptory great men were. How could they possibly be ready in two days?

"We have to plan. Make decisions. Rehearse. We must be perfect. Which play shall it be?"

"Corneille's *Nicomedes*," said Garcin, putting on his serious face. "That's a grand play. And safe." They knew what he meant. After his fall from grace with *Le Cid*, when all the critics clamored about his ears, Corneille had turned respectable. No more experiments. No more excesses of violence and passion. Restrained and elegant dramas. A little on the pompous side, but universally approved.

"An excellent choice," said Molière. "You show good taste." Garcin beamed, and shot an Italian grimace to the little apprentice in the corner, who giggled and was promptly cuffed into silence. "But a little heavy, don't you think, for a celebration? We need something lighter, more romantic. Magnon's *Titus*, perhaps. That's a grand play for a festival. Lots of speeches about love. Disguises. Yes, let's do *Titus*."

Robichaud coughed apologetically. "I'm afraid we have no choice. You haven't finished the letter."

He gave it to them and they scanned it anxiously, most of them picking their way uncertainly through the flourishes and curlicues of the script.

Molière gave a gasp of dismay. "He wants a comedy! A comedy! Have even the nobility no taste?"

And then he read further and was dumbfounded. The Prince had asked specifically for *The Doctor in Love*. The most trivial of his hasty farces. A nonsensical thing that he had scribbled in an hour because they needed a new play for Avignon that week.

The uproar began again, and over it could be heard the Marquise's sniff. "I begin," she said, "to despair of my class." And she stamped off to her room in dudgeon. *The Doctor in Love* had only a small part for her.

They could talk as much as they liked, but there was nothing to be done. The farce it had to be. Madeleine and Robichaud took charge, ignoring Molière's grumblings. Bills went up outside announcing that there would be no performance that day or the next. They pulled out tattered scripts, feverishly recalled their lines and rehearsed. And again. And again. Madeleine was adamant.

"There must be no slips. No slackness. No improvising." This to Robichaud, who was notorious for putting things into the script that the author had never written. "This is no barn-yard performance. Whatever we think of the play, we must do it with all the polish we can."

So they polished the play into the small hours, and after that set up polishing the equipment. A sleepy ostler was dragged out of bed and coach and horses hired. "I hope the Prince pays for them," said Robichaud. The brasses and harness were rubbed till they shone. Robichaud and Garcin hung festoons and banners from the roof. The Marquise, brought by threat of dismissal from her dignified retirement, was set to ironing costumes. Molière curled wigs. Madeleine did everything, laughing, scolding, keeping them awake and in a tolerable humor by promises that this would ensure them Paris.

"Please the Prince," she said, "and the world is at our feet. The Prince's château is the back door to Versailles."

The next day, the day of the fête, they set off in great form. The horses trotted proudly, the banners fluttered in the breeze, the actors forgot their fatigue in happy anticipation. But when they had traveled only a few miles, the first hot, heavy drops of rain began to fall. Within minutes they were driving through a torrent. The summer storm, spilling on the hot and gasping earth, raised clouds of steam enough to make them think they were entering Hell. The road became a marsh. As the coach swayed and wallowed their careful labor of the night was destroyed. Plumes dangled limply, the bunting slipped and frayed under the clutching fingers of the rain. The downpour caught the drum which, for lack of room, was hung behind, and played a funereal tattoo. Rain leaked through the roof ("I'll have something to say about that tomorrow morning," thought Robichaud) and took the curl out of the wigs that Molière had worked on so laboriously. It was a damp and sorry party that drove through the great iron gates and up the avenue to the pillared door.

The sound of music, soggy through the trees, revived their spirits somewhat. Even the horses pricked up their ears and put on a better show, bringing them with a dash and a clatter to the wide stone steps. Pavilions could be seen here and there through the dripping foliage, with a scattering of servants outside and the promise of gaiety within. The Prince could control the weather.

"After all," said Madeleine, cheering them up, "it's what we look like on the stage that matters. The costumes are dry, at least." They were indeed; they had sat on them to make sure. But even the Prince had no protection against cold. Molière, who had been in great houses before, and the Marquise, who had not, both wondered why the nobility should choose to live in iceboxes. The lobby was a cavern of the winds. Draughts clutched them, and the cold crept into their bones. Their feet froze to the floor. There was not a stove in sight; the contemptuous footman who had left them there had pretended ignorance of their existence, and given them strict instructions not to move.

It was the best part of an hour before he returned, accompanied by a tall, thin, balding man with a flick of a moustache, his eyes harassed and darting, constantly looking over his shoulder as if in fear of missing a command. He announced himself as the Prince's secretary, demanded their names and checked them against a much-thumbed list produced from a veritable library that he carried on his person.

They stood damp and impatient, forced to await his pleasure. Water trickled dismally down Molière's leg and into the top of his boot. He felt like death.

The little man checked the list twice with excruciating care. Three times. The footman stood smirking in the background. Finally the secretary raised his head.

"There seems to have been some mistake. There's no provision for you here. All the entertainers have arrived. The Italian comedians are performing now."

Death himself could not have delivered his message with such callous unconcern. They raged. They stormed. They expostulated. Robichaud produced the letter from the warmth of his wallet and waved it in the secretary's face. He shrugged helplessly.

"I assure you, it's no fault of mine. The Prince must have forgotten. Such a busy day, such a great occasion. . . . Great men have their little failings. You must accept that."

As the rest of us have to, his eyes added. As I have to, every minute of my life. His whole demeanor was a testimony to the capriciousness of princes.

"But our money!" babbled Robichaud. He was beside himself. "We must be paid. We've lost two performances in the town."

The secretary shrugged again wearily. "I know nothing about such things. I am the Prince's secretary, not his steward. But how can you expect to be paid when you don't perform?"

The grinning footman was convulsed with glee.

For Molière and Madeleine the money was the least important thing. It was their hope that had been stolen, not their wages. Paris had suddenly receded beyond the furthest limits of the ocean.

The secretary had had enough of them. Turning to the footman, he snapped "Show these people out." But as the flunkey moved to obey, reluctant to lose his sport, Madeleine stood in front of him, legs astride, eyes flaming fire.

"We won't go. This is an insult. We demand to see the Prince."

A shadow fell across the hall, and a voice cut through the air, making the cold room colder. If they had not shivered before they did so now. On the landing above them, lit by an aureole of candles and peering down into the gloom, stood a man, a demigod. He was magnificent in silk and ruffles; his beard fondled his chin, his wig fell sleek upon his shoulders; a hero from Greek fable, whose hands, tensed upon the banisters in anger, might have been gloved, so smooth and white were they.

A laughing girl hung on his arm. Behind him was a priest, wrinkled and malicious, a jackal to his lion. There were others in the angle of the stairs, peeping from the shadows, hardly less wonderfully dressed, curious at this impertinence, these strangers from another planet.

"Demand? Only the King demands to see the Prince de Conti," said the fabulous being. "And that not often. Throw these people out. If they won't go, have them whipped."

The sneering footman, miraculously multiplied, moved out into the lobby. Behind, the great door swung open. The drabness waited to engulf them again. The others were already slinking out, cowed, frightened, incapable of further protest. But Molière's anger gave him a voice. Surely not his own; it seemed to come from a million miles away. He stepped forward into the center of the hall, framed by faces leering or frightened. It was a play, and this his audience; he had to conquer it somehow.

"I would have thought," he said with a bow, "that the Prince would have been more glad to see an old schoolfellow."

Madeleine ran forward with a cry. "You fool! He'll have you thrashed!" The others stood in amazement, disbelieving what they had heard, seeing their world crumble about them, hearing already the churning of the galleys. Their leader had lost his mind.

But the Prince was already halfway down the stairs.

"What the devil! Who are you?"

Prince and player confronted each other. A hand was raised to strike. Molière sank onto one knee.

"Jean-Baptiste Poquelin, if your highness will permit. (I am sorry, father; it was forced from me.) I had the honor of attending the same school as your highness. Your desk was in the front row, in the center. I sat on a bench in the right hand corner, at the back."

The fine hand seized his chin and jerked him to his feet. The noble, bloodshot eyes looked into his. An oath resounded through the room, pertaining to some part of God's anatomy, which made the girl titter and the priest cross himself when he thought no one was looking.

"Poquelin! Yes, I remember you. You were a grinning little devil. What do you want of me?"

"I am the leader of this troupe, your highness. We had a letter, in your name, inviting us to play here before you today. And now your people say they have not heard of us. They try to drive us from your door like beggars."

The letter was produced and read. The Prince shook his head over it.

"This is my lady's doing. If I read everything that was sent out in my name, Jean Poquelin, I would never have time for . . . other things." He glanced up the stairs, but the laughing girl was gone. He was anxious to follow her.

"Well, there has been a mistake. I suppose you want to be paid? Here." A lazy flick of his wrist, and a purse went sliding across the floor.

"But your highness, our performance . . ."

"Do not annoy me, little man. We have enough performers here. And there's the worst." His voice and stabbing finger caught the priest and sent him cowering back into the shadows. "What can players want but money? There it is. Take it, and your leave."

And he was gone through the door, his retinue trailing after him. Their laughter echoed through the park; the rain, still falling relentlessly, seemed to part above their heads. Nothing could harm these golden people.

The purse lay on the floor. It was a long time before even Robichaud could bring himself to pick it up. The secretary, with a parting glance of reproach at it, as one more proof of the caprices of the great, scurried upstairs on other urgent business. Picking up their bundles, the players prepared wearily to depart.

"Great princes! Great princes!" said Molière bitterly, swinging his pack onto his shoulders. "We're nothing to them. We ask for a chance to perform. To show our art. And they throw us money."

The others crowded round him nervously, trying to quiet him. It was hardly treasonable talk; treason could not come from one so low. But it might still earn them a whipping, if the Prince heard.

"All is vanity," cried a voice as if in reinforcement from the stairway. "But the mighty shall be humbled and their pomp brought low. All is dust before the Lord."

It was the priest, alone, forgotten. He detached himself from the wall and shuffled down the stairs towards them. His nails were long and dirty, his face lined with privation. A stained cassock clothed him, and he wiped his nose upon his sleeve. God in this house lived less well than Mammon.

They did not know what to do with this unexpected, unwelcome ally. The company nodded to him sadly and resumed the drift towards the door.

"I wish the Princess had interceded for us," said Madeleine, nodding timidly towards the park where the laughing girl had gone. "She was a beautiful lady. And it was she who invited us. She could have been kinder, I think."

The priest's eyes gleamed with mingled prurience and anger, and he laughed at their naiveté.

"That was not the Princess."

"No?"

"A whore! A fornicator! She shall be damned too; and with her all who pander to the weaknesses of princes. Out, you players! Devil's toys! Ministers of hellfire!"

With a ferocity that surpassed anything they had yet experienced in this house he ran at them, flailing with his arms. They brushed him off and ran themselves, only anxious to leave a place where so many people, for so many reasons, did not like them. But they were still not to escape. A servant ran to catch Molière's arm as he was climbing into the coach.

"Sir! If you would come with me a moment? The Princess desires to speak with you."

Molière looked at Madeleine. Sir! This was something different. He glared into the servant's face, expecting mockery, but found only studied respect. He did not know that the man had been threatened with whipping if he abused the players. He turned to the others, already packed into the coach.

"Drive off, and wait for me by the park gates. I shall walk back to the road. Let me talk to the Princess, since she is so *kind* as to want to see me. Perhaps there is better news here."

And he followed the servant down a corridor into a tiny parlor.

The lady sitting in the high-backed chair was not like the laughing girl on the stairs. Her face was angular, and mottled where the pox had marked her. Her dress, of rich stuff, was still simply cut. Her eyes, Molière noted with surprise, were raw with weeping. Two maids-in-waiting whispered on a couch in the corner. She dismissed them with a gesture, as Molière entered and bowed low.

"Monsieur Molière," she said, "my people tell me you have been neglected in this house, forgotten and insulted. I sent for you to tell you I am sorry."

He began to stammer—the voice that he had found before the Prince had gone again, and left him his own—that no apologies were necessary from so great a lady. But she went on without hearing.

"It was I who saw your performance, one night at Carcassonne. I was with friends. We went as a masquerade. You would not have known me."

He would not indeed, but remembered the occasion now. There had been four or five of them giggling behind masks and fans. They had insisted on sitting at the back; an escapade, an adventure, a nervous game. The company had speculated on their identity between scenes. Obviously gentry, but how great, nobody knew. At the end they all applauded, particularly the tall lady in the red vizard. This one here.

"I saw your play and enjoyed it. It seemed to me that you had done an admirable thing. Taken the Italian vivacity and graced it with our language. You write well, Monsieur Molière."

He blinked. Such compliments for such trivial stuff? He wondered if he should mention his tragedy. Perhaps not. He spoke instead of their disappointment. Their longing for Paris. Their need to be seen.

"It was I who suggested to my husband that you should be invited here. He agreed. He knew about that letter. Perhaps he found it more convenient to forget. He prefers to forget . . . many things."

She rose. The interview was over.

"I only wished to say, Monsieur, that I prefer to keep my word even if the Prince does not. About today I can do nothing. This fête is in honor of my lord's birthday. You will return a year from now, I promise you. And next time you will perform."

She swept out, with a look in her eyes that boded no good for the laughing girl.

Another year, thought Molière. Well, they could endure it. What was one more after so many?

He was humming as he walked back through the rain to join his friends by the lodge gate.

There was a new Béjart in the company. This was nothing strange. Molière often teased Madeleine about it, saying that the troupe had become an annex to the family—"to hold all those you don't have room for at home." They turned up from time to time, brothers, cousins, more remote relatives; they stayed for a while, acting and working at odd jobs, and then left, according to their natures. Even Joseph reappeared, sublimely unconscious of ever having given offense, greeting Molière like a brother and creating such an aura of successful accomplishment that, when he reminisced about the Paris days, one wondered that the Hôtel de Bourgogne had ever managed to survive the competition. Molière remained cold for a while, but Madeleine brought him round, and it was not in his nature to bear a grudge for long. Joseph in his better moods was irresistible, and Molière owed him something after all. *The Death of Julius Caesar* had been impossible. But the new one; that would be a masterpiece. If he ever had time to finish it.

About Louis there was no news. He was rumored to have left the country. Someone had seen him, it was said, in England, at the port of Bristol. This was upsetting, if true. France and England, always at loggerheads, now eyed each other with increasing distrust. The French were wary of a nation that had recently so defied God's order as to execute their king. In Paris the exiled royalty was constantly plotting and scheming, to raise armies, to raise money. But King Louis would not risk open war. He had not loved his brother England so much as to pit French soldiers against Cromwell's iron men for the younger Charles's sake. He was content to host them at his court, allow them a pittance and occasionally marry them off. Most of them by now had abandoned all real hope of going back. It was all talk; something to do when the violins had been stilled and the last wine poured. In their secret hearts many preferred Paris. It was gay here, and a nobleman was treated with proper respect. Life, even without lands or money, was more than tolerable. There were many ways for impoverished gentility to survive on credit.

Some of the English actors had come over with them, following their only public. There was no play-acting in England anymore. Life there was one long Sabbath, and the English had always been so dreary about their religion. Things were managed better in France, where the priests and the world lived on excellent terms, and the King was seen by many as head of the Church in France as he was of all things else. And he was not a man to let religion interfere with his pleasures.

Some of these English actors formed companies, and toured plays through the provinces when Paris had tired of them. Their scripts had mostly been left behind—burned, probably, by order of the Commonwealth as the devil's work—but they patched the plays together from the parts they had by heart, filling the gaps with limping imagination. Molière had seen one such play, a piece admired in England, the players boasted. But even allowing for their execrable French, it was a tawdry thing. A play about a prince whose father had been killed by his uncle, and who spent some two hours making up his mind what to do about it. There was much shouting and running about, and people dying in every other scene. A comic old man had himself stabbed through a curtain. Molière rather liked him, because he reminded him of the doctor in his own plays, all wagging beard and prosy orations. But he had no time for the prince himself, or his faithful friend, or the queen, who was played by a man—barbarous custom; it had almost disappeared in France. There was no shape, no order, no rhyme and little reason; a welter of scenes, any one of which would have served a French playwright for a whole tragedy. And philosophizing one minute and clowning the next, so that you never knew whether you were watching a tragedy or a comedy, and might as well have been in two theaters at once. And the violence! Screaming and dying, and a ghost, and duel after duel: stuff for a puppet show, not the stage. If the English really enjoyed such nonsense, they deserved their present government. The audience shared his opinion, booed the ghost, tossed money at the unrepentant usurper, and offered grotesque and physically impossible suggestions to the prince when he wondered audibly about his next course of action. They went back to Paris in disgrace.

This year's new Béjart was a girl, a minx, a little beauty. It was impossible to guess her age. Molière thought she was eleven, Garcin and the apprentices, who debated the matter lewdly, sixteen. Armande smiled and refused to tell. Her cherub's face had eyes as black and old as sin. When pressed she stuck out her tongue and said "That's a woman's secret. Go ask my sister Madeleine." But Madeleine was equally uncommunicative, and turned off questions no less forcefully, if with greater dignity.

Madeleine herself was growing like her mother, and had assumed her habits. No one seeing her offstage would have taken her for a player. She was always quiet and decorous; the fleck of early gray in her hair made her look older than she was, and in the streets she passed for a justice's wife or the spouse of some complacent merchant. On the stage, and in bed, she was wild, gay, abandoned. Off it, she was a nun.

Molière trusted her absolutely, and every day leaned more upon her judgment. He still resented her insistence on his writing comedies, but acknowledged the necessity. He recognized, too, the wisdom of her reasons when she argued that anything worth writing was worth writing well, and that these farces, in their way, were as demanding as the tragedies he craved. He would read his plays to her in the evenings, and she would listen gravely, suggesting a modification here, a change of phrase there, to bring the laugh in earlier or make a cleaner exit. They rarely argued, for they shared the gift of simultaneously translating dialogue into movement, of seeing the actors strut between the written lines. It became a game with him, to make the play as perfect as he could, to deny his higher self and devote his art to trivia. Only when his pen ran away with him and the tragic muse temporarily took control did she seriously object.

"You mustn't make your people too real. The comic things hurt, then. When Scaramouche gets a sword through his breast we laugh because we know the sword's a dummy. But once you let them think the sword might just possibly be real . . . it becomes too painful to think about."

He argued on the contrary that even comedy should provide more than empty laughter. "I know we have to leave them happy; but can't we leave them thinking a little too?" It became a long and amiable wrangle between them. She rationed him severely, allowing him only one or two moral sentiments to a play, and insisting that they be well wrapped in laughter, but she yielded enough to let the characters touch ordinary humanity at times. And Molière found, paradoxically, that after he had allowed his clowns to be human for a while, the richer the laughter would be. The clowns developed feelings and the crusty old men a heart; the inevitable scapegrace son, predictably cheating his father of his money, reflected sometimes that what he was doing was not entirely honorable, and lamented the failure in their relationship which had brought him to this state. Molière let the mask slip sometimes, and showed the human being beneath; he made capital of the difference between what people were and what they seemed.

And it seemed to him, looking at the world around him, that the mask was not entirely confined to the Italian comedies. It was not simply a limp, wrinkled thing of cloth or leather. It was universal. Look at Madeleine, and the saintly air she put on in public, to impress those who, in spite of the King's public protection of their art, still looked on actresses as prostitutes or worse. Look at Joseph, who could be so charming when he tried, and a brute when the mask slipped. Look at Armande, who concealed heaven knows what devilment under that childish exterior, and whose eyes were like windows onto another person, infinitely older, infinitely knowing.

Armande followed him like a kitten, adorable, adoring. She hung on his every word. She asked him, respectfully, to teach her, and he did so; another hour gone from every day, but it was worth it. She flourished under his tuition. Like all Béjarts, she was naturally suited for the stage. So deft and delicate were her movements that she seemed to float across the floor, supported by no physical agency—certainly by nothing so gross as human legs. Her voice was high but pleasant, never shrill; it could cascade into laughter or swoop upon a song without a second's hesitation. She spoke Molière's lines as though each word was a jewel to be held up and examined for its individual perfection. He wished he could write more for her.

The women of the company, of course, hated her. It was only

this that prevented him from giving her bigger parts. The Marquise flatly refused to set foot on the stage with her if she were doing anything other than the smallest maidservant's role. "The girl's impossible," she barked. "There am I, pouring out my heart downstage, and who do you think is watching me? Nobody! They only have eyes for that chit primping herself behind me. She never stands still."

Molière had to admit that she was partly right. The Marquise's mature charms were no match for Armande's young freshness. When they were playing together, when the Marquise had her opponent under her eye, she had enough technique to keep the attention of the audience on her. She went at it with such malice that every scene between them became a pitched battle, with the audience's regard as the prize. The Marquise was merciless. She discarded the careful work of Molière's rehearsals and plotted every move like a chess game, forcing Armande, more often than not, to turn away from the audience. She would appropriate whole stretches of dialogue, leaving her with an occasional "Yes, madame." She would sometimes deliberately throw her a wrong cue, leaving her floundering, and then, with a sickening graciousness, flash an apologetic smile at the audience and resume in such a way that the lapse seemed to be Armande's fault. And for the next few moments her whole behavior would radiate a deep professional concern, assuring the spectators that she would do her best in spite of the appalling weaknesses of this person she was forced to act with.

Armande had her own defenses. She was powerless against the Marquise when they were together, for the older woman had years of experience behind her and was as tricky as a fox. When the Marquise was soliloquizing, however, and Armande's function was merely to dress the stage, she would set to work. There was never anything that one could put one's finger on. She was too clever for that. It would be something slight, almost imperceptible, that would have passed for an accident in the eyes of those who did not know what she was doing.

A curl would fall across her face and she would blow it away —"for even an insignificant actress like myself, monsieur, must present a comely appearance to the spectators, must she not? It would be insulting to stand there with my hair disordered, like a kitchenmaid." Or she would be wearing a ring to flash in the candlelight when she so far forgot herself as to twist her hand to and fro. "But I swear to you, Monsieur Molière, the candle must have been moved. Last night there was no light in that corner of the stage at all. And you cannot expect me to stand like a dummy through that long, long speech."

As she grew surer of herself and of her audience her boldness increased. When they played in one place for any length of time—which they were doing more and more now, for their fame had grown, and people traveled to see them—the spectators would realize what was going on and return nightly to watch the battle of wits. It was like a play within a play to see them. Molière was furious, for they threw his lines out of joint and reduced his carefully constructed scenes to chaos. But he could no more control them than he could have stopped two wildcats fighting in a sack. Robichaud took a more optimistic view. "Let them have their heads. The public loves it. We're making more money than we ever have before." Molière was compelled to agree, though he felt that the company was growing rich at the cost of his peace of mind.

A crisis came one night. The Marquise, delivering one of her best speeches to the audience, cossetting each syllable with her rich voice and displaying to the best advantage the amplitude of her voluptuous body, was delighted to find the audience reacting more enthusiastically than they had ever done before. She beamed approval on them and redoubled her efforts. They chuckled. They roared. They applauded. She was a fantastic success. Then, as the speech proceeded and the audience approached hysteria, it began to dawn even on her that something was not right. The lines were surely not that funny. In fact she had just delivered a fairly serious passage, and the laughter continued unabated. Fear tickled the nape of her neck;

it grew upon her that something was going on behind her back that she ought to know about. Yielding to panic she whirled round, and there, upstage, was Armande, mouthing the lines simultaneously and mimicking her gestures with the precise shade of overemphasis that made them grotesque. For once, the Marquise lost her self-control. A long shrill scream of anguish escaped her lips. She flew at Armande, calling her names which no self-respecting Marquise should have heard, boxed her ears and fled crying from the stage. Armande, unperturbed, stepped down to the footlights. She winked at the audience.

"Alas, my beloved mistress is unwell. But ladies of a certain age are subject to these indispositions . . . so I hear. So that my friends in the audience may not be disappointed, I shall play the part as best I can."

Picking up the fan that the Marquise had abandoned in her flight, she finished the speech and the scene with flawless precision. If Molière had tried to stop the play they would have lynched him. What could he do? The Marquise, having fainted twice, was lying on her bed sobbing her heart out. Her anguish redoubled when she heard the curtain come down on tumultuous applause.

The Marquise was adamant, Armande penitent, Madeleine scolding, Robichaud secretly approving, and Molière at a loss to know what to do. His company had suddenly turned into a pack of howling Bacchantes.

"Either that slut goes," said the Marquise, "or I do."

Nothing would move her.

Armande, as usual, had a story ready.

"Monsieur Molière, I know it was wrong of me. I am deeply sorry. A plump tear trembled in the corner of her eye. On any other day it would have wrung their hearts. "But to suggest I would do such a thing deliberately! I was carried away. You know how hard I have worked, monsieur. How I long for the day when I shall be thought worthy of such parts as Madame la Marquise now plays with such genius."

A snort from the Marquise, unappeased.

"And as I stood there on the stage, monsieur, I began to dream that the day had come, and that I was standing there with all eyes on me," continued the unabashed little liar, "speaking your wonderful lines, monsieur. With so strong an attraction, is it any wonder that the dream became a half reality? And then, when my senior so far forgot herself as to leave the stage in the middle of the performance—something you have impressed on us, monsieur, that we must never, never do, whatever the provocation—what could I do but carry on, and try my humble best to substitute for her? The audience is king. We had to finish the play somehow. If I have offended, I am sorry. But believe me my fault came from excess of zeal."

Her voice, her tears, her head bowed in penitence, would have moved Gabriel to sheathe his sword on the day of judgment. But the Marquise was no angel. She screamed with renewed fury, and a stream of gutter invective poured from her lips which deposed her forever from the ranks of the aristocracy.

After several acrimonious, head-aching hours they worked out a compromise. Armande, as punishment, was to be banished from the stage for a month. The Marquise demanded three, but Robichaud, who knew to a sou how much each player was worth at the money-taker's wicket, argued forcefully against her. After this Armande would be permitted to return, but never in the same plays as the Marquise. Fair enough, thought Molière, I'll be able to write bigger parts for her now. They're both too good to lose. In fact, far from being punished—the month's absence was nothing—she had done well out of the whole sordid business. In one blow, she had established herself as the Marquise's equal. A sudden suspicion shot across his mind. Had this been her intention all along? Had she gambled on his wanting to keep her and used the Marquise to force the issue? He gave her a long, hard look, but she returned his glance with such tremulous, appealing innocence that he dismissed the thought as unworthy. A naughty child, no more.

But as she grew, what an actress she would make. And what a beauty.

Armande accepted her discipline with suspicious docility. Molière was surprised. He would have expected her to sulk. Instead, she gave herself to rehearsals more heartily than ever, in spite of the fact that for another thirty days her labors would bear no fruit upon the stage. When formal rehearsals were over she would spend hours in private practice, strengthening her voice, perfecting her walk. Even the Marquise, who knew a professional when she saw one, grew magnanimous, though not so much as to offer to teach her. That remained Molière's job. He taught her all he had learned so arduously, and grew to know his own art better, because teaching forced him to think and consider; to recapitulate what he had come to do by instinct and look for the reasons behind it. Another happy outcome of the contretemps was that the Marquise and Madeleine became better friends. There was a bond between them now; instead of merely tolerating each other, they were united by a common enemy.

For Madeleine, curiously enough, had no sympathy for her sister. She had been one of the loudest to insist that she should go. "I should never have brought her here," she said bitterly. "She's a nuisance. A distraction. She's set the whole company quarreling. And she's plaguing the life out of you."

Not so, he argued. It was true he seemed to be spending more time with Armande than with anyone else. But he gave the hours willingly, and they were well spent. Armande was growing visibly as an actress. There was no doubt that she would be magnificent. He teased Madeleine gently. Could she be jealous of her own sister? And of such a child? Someone had to be a father to her, and it might as well be he.

"She's using you," said Madeleine, "and you're too big a fool to see."

He was surprised. It was unlike her to be so harsh. Try as he would, he could not wheedle her out of this mood. On the subject of Armande she was intransigent. He insisted, in his turn, that the girl must not leave. She was too valuable a property. So they agreed to differ, and rarely spoke of the matter again; though it remained a sore point between them, a fissure in the wall of their partnership and their affection.

They still had their evenings together. That at least had not changed. After the day's work was over, now that she had no performances to engross her, Armande vanished. He had no idea what she was doing. At first she had tried to join them in their writing sessions, but the elder sister had firmly resisted. She had no intention of sharing their few hours together with a third party. So Armande, submitting reluctantly, was left to her own devices. Molière suspected that she slipped out in front and joined the audience. It was against company etiquette, but so be it. Watching was a way of learning. She would be all the better for it in the end. He performed with greater vivacity himself, imagining that she was watching him and wanting to make the best possible example; and as he strolled back with Madeleine to their lodging he caught himself wondering what Armande had thought of him.

It was not until the month was nearly up that he found out how Armande spent her evenings. Madeleine was away on one of her regular trips to Paris, and he was at a loose end. She would be gone even longer this time. Her mother, whose business sense was diminishing as she grew older, had made a disastrous mistake in leasing some property. It would take time, money and lawyers to sort it out. Molière had come to rely so heavily on Madeleine's encouragement that without her he could not write. The new comedy lay neglected on the table; the spark was gone. His characters hung suspended in mid-scene, begging him to resolve their difficulties and send them spinning into fresh patterns on their antic way. He could not help them. Everything he wrote was tired, stale, banal. In desperation he exhumed the tragedy from the depths of his trunk and tried to work on that. Impossible. Rereading what he had written months—or was it years?—before, he found himself appalled. Could he have written this stuff? It was worse than his comedies.

The rhymes were forced, the sentiments pretentious, the characters posturing idiots. He rammed it back among his other papers and forgot it. Sleep? Too early for that. Accustomed to work into the small hours, he could not rest now if he tried. He knew that he would only lie there tossing, the day's events spinning in his brain, the elusive hope for the future: for the year was passing in spite of them, the Prince de Conti's fête grew closer, they had to hope and plan for that. At last, to shake his mood, he decided to go back to the theater. On the stage, alone in the dark, he would say a few speeches, perfect a piece of business that continued to elude him, that was still not exactly right. He was a different person there. The cares of the day vanished as soon as he stepped into the magic circle. He would adopt his fictitious personage. It would be better company than his real one.

The theater was dark and shuttered, an empty shell. Life went out of it when the actors departed. We are gods, he thought, we create life and remove it; a new birth and a new dying every day. Perhaps that was why actors were ageless. They had so many lives to enjoy.

He struggled with the lock on the heavy door, and it swung open with a creak. Taking the lantern from the hook, he lit it, and pulled the door shut behind him to avoid disturbance by late revelers or an inquisitive watchman. By the meager light he picked his way through the empty benches. It was sordid, when the magic had departed. Orange peel littering the floor. Playbills, crumpled and discarded. A fan. A single shoe, a woman's. Whose? Why only one? Had the lady hobbled home uncaring? She must have been strangely excited by the play. As his artist's mind recorded and imagined, his managerial conscience deplored. The theater should never have been left in such a state. It was Robichaud's job—one of his many—to sweep and leave all tidy. He would have a word with him in the morning.

Then something frightened him, so that he almost dropped the lantern. A creak, a rustle, a furtive mutter. From behind the stage. Thieves, he thought with dismay. Not that there was any money in the theater now. They were punctilious about that, remembering past disaster.

But the costumes were valuable. Heaven knew they cost enough. They would fetch a good price from any merchant not too careful about the origin of his goods. Enough to make it worth a robber's while. What should he do? Try to stop them? It dawned on him that he was not a brave man. Run for help? By the time he got back the thieves might be gone; and in any case the watchman was senile and decrepit, with barely enough voice to announce what o'clock it was. Even if he could be found—he preferred to do his watching from the back room of a tavern—he would be worse than useless here. No, it had to be faced. Drawing his cloak around him to hood the lantern, he crossed the stage on tiptoe, muttering an imprecation against creaky boards, and praying, at the same time, that the thieves might escape before he reached them.

The noise was coming from the dank little cubbyhole back-stage which doubled as storage space and greenroom. It had been given a tattered dignity by the addition of a couch, a wobbling table and two chairs, which lived here when they were not needed on stage. The players liked it; it was smelly, mean and uncomfortable, but it was the nearest thing they had to a home. Gritting his teeth, Molière waited for a moment outside the door. The soft noise continued. A rustle of fabric. A muffled laugh. Yes, they must be at the costumes. Plucking up his courage, he flung wide the door and raised his lantern to illuminate the room.

It was not thieves. He wished devoutly that it had been. He would rather have faced the most redoubtable brigand than this. On the couch, happily entwined, lay Armande and Robichaud. Her clothes lay mingled with his haphazardly across the floor. She was as naked as the day she was born, and comporting herself in a manner which showed that, whatever her age, her interests were entirely adult.

Molière had never been so angry. White-faced, head slumped

in shame, Robichaud bore the brunt of his fury. Molière spared him nothing, no insult, no reproach. A boy he had taken from the streets, to whom he had given food and shelter. He had been a father to him, and this was his reward. This shameful breach of trust. Rutting like an animal, a gypsy in the gutters, an Italian. And as if this were not enough, to debauch an innocent child. He was to leave the company at once. If Molière had his way, he would have gone to the gallows.

The last was too much for Robichaud to take. He reared up, a whipped dog fighting back.

"All right, I'm going. I wouldn't stay here now for ten times my wages. But don't talk to me about innocent children. Do you want to know what your little pet is like?"

His voice was rough and ugly. The practised actor's ring had gone. It was a wounded man speaking.

"She's been after me ever since she got here. I didn't take any notice at first, out of respect for you. But I wasn't the only one. Every man in the company's had her, this little innocent child. And half the audience as well, I swear. Ask Garcin. Ask the apprentices. Ask..."

He stopped as Molière's hand cracked across his face. Blood spurted from his nose. He dropped his eyes again, beaten.

"Take your clothes," said Molière, in a stifled voice he could not recognize, "and get out of here. If you ever come near me again I'll strangle you."

He picked up Robichaud's doublet, boots and breeches from the jumble on the floor and hurled them at him. The boy did not wait to put them on. Naked as he was, he ran out into the night.

Molière turned to Armande.

"Those things he said about you. Tell me they are not true. Tell me."

He did not need to go on. The Circe who had turned a quiet bookkeeper into a grunting swine was transformed herself. The innocent child became a sullen, spitting whore.

"Of course it's true. I'm fifteen years old. A woman, not a

child. Why shouldn't I do the things that women do? That Madeleine does? And that old hag who calls herself an actress?"

She opened her arms and the circle of the lamplight embraced her.

"Is this a child's body, Monsieur Molière? Won't you try for yourself?"

He backed away from the horror, reaching for the door behind him, following Robichaud in panic flight.

"You've wanted me long enough, haven't you?" she called after him, a Lilith mocking. "You've wanted to. That's why you were so angry with Robichaud. Because he did, and you didn't dare."

He slammed the door in her face, and blotted out the offense.

How he got back to his room he never knew. His head was splitting, his mind a tumult of half-formed thoughts. How could she do this? Madeleine had been right, the girl should never have come. Oh, Madeleine, where are you now? If only you were here to help me. While he had treated her as a daughter, a precious toy, she had been mocking him. All the company knew what she was. Everybody but him. The pieces fitted into a pattern now. The hints, the whispers, the half-heard innuendoes—things he had dismissed as actors' gossip, or the Marquise disseminating her spite.

And though he fought the knowledge, his greatest anguish was that she was right. He had wanted her, this adopted daughter, this child. He knew it now with stark clarity, had known it from the moment when she spread out her arms and offered herself to him. Curse these Béjarts! Was there some family witchery that made them all know him better than he knew himself? Was this his mask? Was he, who was so adept at penetrating the pretensions of others, fooled by his own disguise? Did the benevolent protector, the kindly employer, conceal a grinning satyr underneath?

One thing he knew. He could not stay here and face her again. He would go away for a while, it did not matter where. By the time he came back she would be gone, Madeleine would be home again, things would be as they were. He picked up an armful of clothes at random, a cloak, a book or two, an old coat; he stuffed some money into his pockets without bothering to count it or wondering what Robichaud would say when he found the takings did not balance in the morning. Robichaud? There was no Robichaud, he was gone too; his world was falling apart. Let them all look after themselves, he could do no more for them. He wanted only to be away from this accursed place.

He ran into the sleeping streets, not caring that the clatter on the stairs aroused protests from behind locked doors or that he left his own room wide open for any passerby to enter. Into the dark he went, along the dusty road and through the trees, deaf to everything but his own thoughts. He walked for hours, days, years, he did not know. The peasants rising by the light of dawn and going out into their fields gave him good morning when he passed, and then drew back as they saw his drawn face and staring eyes, and heard him mumbling to himself. They touched their foreheads, crossed themselves and muttered to their friends "A madman."

He stopped in the first town he came to, flung himself into a tavern and began to drink. The crude wine warmed his body and eased his mind. He stayed in a corner all day, drinking, while the townsfolk wondered about him, and the host, who cared only for his money, carried flagon after flagon to his table. The rough drink on an empty stomach made him vomit in the end, and his hand could no longer raise the tankard to his lips. They threw him out, jeering at him. He slept in the gutter that night. Next morning, shaken awake, he moved on, sick and aching, to the next village, the next tavern. Days passed in which he never knew where he was. He slept in straw when he could, on the grass or stones when he could not. His clothes were filthy, stinking of stale wine and vomit. His beard was lank and unshaven; he looked like death. At last, when his money had run out, they threw him into the town jail, in a stinking cell full of whores and pickpockets who baited him and feigned great reverence when he babbled that he was an upholsterer, son of a man who had a court appointment. In the morning they dragged him out and moved him on. His legs could scarcely carry him. He shook with weakness, with hunger and fever. He was forced to rest several times on the road. When the lamps of the next town beckoned him, it was already quite dark. His fingers, groping in his purse, found one small coin remaining. Enough for a final gulp of wine at least. After that, the devil could do what he liked with him.

By good fortune, the great door of the inn stood open. He could not have opened it himself, or even have summoned up the strength to pull the bell-chain hanging outside. He stood swaying on the threshold as the light and noise ravaged his senses. It was a gay place, with the scent of money in it, and fine wine, and fat meat, and good eating; not like the rat-holes he had drunk in on the way. Soldiers patronized it. There seemed to be a whole army spread about the room, laughing, shouting, legs splayed across the floor to trip the maids into their laps. Their hats shook with plumes, their great boots thumped, their red faces shone with animal good spirits. The sight should have cheered Molière, for, strangely for a peace-loving man, he had always been fond of soldiers. Not the death and the killing; the thought of hurting people made him sick. But he had always enjoyed watching soldiers in peacetime. Whenever a troop had come marching into the town where his company was playing, he had run like a child to see them. It did not happen often. They had been away from Paris so long that they had almost forgotten that such beings existed. Life was peaceful in the south. Men tended their grapes and olives, chopped their wood, repaired their houses before the winds came. But occasionally a group would come through on maneuvers, and it was as good as a play to watch them. Molière thought sometimes that this must be the perfect life. To know exactly what you had to do. To receive orders and carry them out, and know that your only choice, your only possibility of independence, was whether you carried them out well or badly everything else being taken out of your hands. To have an absolute and rigid chain of command. To be a defined person, secure in your relationships with those around you, because they were ordained by military law, which was as good as holy writ. A man could surely be happy in such a case. He would have time to think and be himself.

But that was how the old Molière thought. The Molière who still believed that there was an order in things, and that a man who had found his place could be sufficient unto himself. It seemed to him now, as he gazed on the ranks of flushed faces, that all the soldiers he had known had been brutes or idiots. Several of the troop were packed into a booth beside the door, listening to a ribald story told by a civilian and interrupting with their own bawdry. Molière squeezed onto the end of the bench, not caring that his neighbor shrank from him in disgust and bristled his moustaches angrily. The civilian stopped in mid-anecdote and stared at him. He was a fat man, with his paunch wedged awkwardly between bench and table. He had a double chin, fleshy lips and a Roman nose down which sweat trickled in a steady stream into his tankard. He continued to stare at Molière, and a look of bewilderment crossed his face.

The host fought his way across the floor, indignant at the intrusion, protecting his patrons.

"Out!"

"Wine!" he muttered. "I want wine. I can pay." He fumbled in his purse for the last coin and pushed it across the table. The host looked at it, spat on it and swept it contemptuously to the floor.

"That wouldn't buy you the dregs from the barrel here! Where do you think you are? This is a good house. Out! We don't serve your kind here."

A meaty hand shot out and seized Molière by the collar. He tried to resist, but the strength had seeped out of him. He was suddenly very cold, in spite of the fire in the room and the warmth of bodies. Helpless, he let himself be muscled to the door. In his delirium the host's face loomed up before his own, scarlet, gap-toothed and of enormous size, like Hell-mouth in one of the old plays. But there were two of them; no, four; and the candles overhead spun like comets, the floor reeled, and he went crashing down to it in darkness, falling, falling. Just before the night closed over him he saw the fat man jump to his feet and push the soldiers aside, uttering some kind of protest; and he thought he heard his name.

For a long while he saw and heard nothing. When he awoke, he was in bed. The sheets lay crisp and cool against his chin. There was something warm and heavy covering his feet. When he felt down for it—he could not raise his head—he thought it must be a cloak, until it put out a warm tongue and licked his hand.

The tiny noise brought an answering grunt from across the room. A shadow fell over the bed. Rumpled, unshaven, grinning, the fat man looked down at him.

"Awake, eh? About time."

Molière gazed dumbly up at him. He did not know where he was or what to say.

"Let's have a look at you."

Fingers descended like five plump cushions on his forehead, settled for a moment and were gone.

"Well, the fever's left you, at any rate. Let's see, now. Are you hungry?"

As his senses slowly returned, Molière realized that he was very hungry indeed. He had eaten no food since . . . he could not remember. The stale aftertaste of bad wine still hung in his mouth.

"A little soup. I have some ready."

The fat man was gone again briefly and returned with bowl and spoon. With surprising gentleness, like a nurse with a sick child, he hoisted Molière up on the pillow, tucked an enormous handkerchief under his chin, and began to feed him with the spoon.

The soup was thick and greasy, and made him retch at first;

but he kept some of it down, and discovered that he had power in his tongue again.

"May I have some water?"

And, a little later,

"How did I get here?"

A jolly laugh.

"I brought you, Monsieur Molière. No, no more," as Molière reached for the spoon again. "Little by little. You're a very weak man."

Molière was so surprised that he dropped the spoon. A rivulet of soup ran down the bedcover, but the fat man wiped it off with his sleeve and did not seem to mind.

"I don't know you. How do you know my name?"

"You're talking to an old admirer. I've seen you many times. No, don't talk. Bad for you. Sleep is what you need. Lots of it. And then more food. Time for talking by and by."

And Molière found, as he slipped back into oblivion, that sleep was most welcome.

He slept much during the next few days. Sometimes he awoke to find the fat man gone. Never for long, however. The stairs would creak to herald his return, the dog would lift up his nose and snuffle, and he would come panting through the door with some new tidbit to tempt his patient's appetite. In his absence, Molière learned the geography of the room. A small window, with trees and birds outside, A fireplace where the logs burnt constantly. A bulging bookcase. A great wing chair, where his host presumably slept, for there was no other bed or couch in the room. It was clean but untidy. The fat man had a habit of dropping things when he had finished with them, wherever he happened to be, so that the worn but decent carpet had islands of books upon it, peninsulas of plates and slippers, and the continental mass of the fat dog, who seemed immobile, only lifting his eyes from time to time to stare at the stranger in the bed.

As his strength came back he ate and talked more. The fat

man, it appeared, had traveled widely in the south, and had come across Molière's company frequently. He was complimentary. Molière's plays, he said, had a quality of their own. Something for everyone there. Slapstick for the peasants—"not that there's anything wrong in slapstick, Heaven knows; when the old man gets water poured down his breeches I nearly wet mine. But you've got something else. Something for a man to get his teeth into."

Molière was flattered, but self-assertive enough by now to argue that this was not his real work. This was only bread-and-butter writing. When they had enough money, they would go to Paris, and he could write his tragedies. Except that I can never go back now, he thought. The company probably thinks I'm dead; they've broken up, dispersed. All that's over.

"My God!" snorted the fat man, tears of laughter rolling down his cheeks, "a rival! Out of my bed at once, you impostor!"

Seeing the anguish on Molière's face, he hastened to assure him he was only joking.

"Do you write tragedies?" asked Molière.

"I do. At least, I try to," he replied, a shadow falling over his face. "Well, they'll perform them some day. I have friends."

He looked at Molière doubtfully.

"Would you like to hear some?"

Assured that he would, he rummaged in the bookcase, and found a torn, dog-eared manuscript. "This is one I started long ago. I've rewritten it four times, and it's still no good. But there are some parts I like. It's called *Medea*."

He had a dreadful reading voice. All the worst eccentricities of the most mediocre actors were there. He was evidently fascinated by them, to have studied them so assiduously. His voice swooped and plummeted; it strained the French language into grotesque and unnatural syllables, hooting in moments of passion, whistling like a kettle at times of stress. But in spite of this, the beauty of the verse came out. Molière listened half-entranced, half-appalled. The assurance of the man! The way

his thought was shaped like intricate machinery, each part lock-
ing with the next, not a word wasted. And his easy use of
rhyme, so dextrous that it had passed before you noticed it.
The clean simplicity of it all: no rant, no bombast, but a com-
plex tune played on a simple reed.

Not theater, though. Actors could never play this. There was
no action; it was all in the mind. A lyric poem written for a
single voice in a small room. Not for the great spaces of the
stage. He grew more and more depressed, and when his companion had finished lay back on his pillow and groaned.

"You don't like it?"

"It's superb. Magnificent. I can't begin to tell you how good
it is. I wish I could write like that." This was sincere, at least.
If only he had his own invention and his friend's gift of
words. What a combination that would be! "I've been trying to
write as simply as that for fifteen years. And my lines aren't
worth the inkblots on your paper. Even though," his professional sense reasserted itself, "you read very badly."

His host was flattered and amused.

"I only want to write them, not act them. But don't be
discouraged. It takes time to say things simply. So you really
like it, eh?"

He was as happy as a schoolboy. He looked sly, and rubbed
his finger on his nose.

"I'll tell you a secret. You've always wanted to write stuff like
this, well, I'd give my heart to write a comedy like you. But
I can't. Don't have the knack. I can see what's wrong with
people, what makes them go astray . . . but I don't have the
trick of making it funny, like you. All my people turn out to
be so solemn. But I'll write my comedy one day, and you'll
write your tragedy. And we'll play them on the same bill, and
have all Paris by the ears."

But Molière had gone back to sleep.

As his strength came back he began to seek diversion while
his host was absent, and started to read again. The journey to
the bookshelf looked too far, so he groped in the pocket of his

old coat that lay on the chair beside him, and discovered the books he had brought with him in his flight. One, he found, was his old friend Lucretius, the tattered copy he had had since he was a schoolboy. He had no memory of having selected it. Had his unconscious mind made the choice? Lucretius was a man who knew his, Molière's, mind. A man who, like him, knew the awful passion of love and its power to derange. A man who sensed the emptiness of things, and saw no evil in a gentle death.

When his host returned and saw what he was reading, he took the book firmly away from him and hid it.

"You don't want to read that. Gloomy stuff. Full of dead man's talk."

"You know Lucretius?"

"Lord, yes. All the old Romans. Had to read them when I was a boy. They wanted me to be a priest."

"They wanted me to be an upholsterer."

And they laughed together.

The fat man ransacked his shelves for happier things. Rabelais, and the drinking songs of Villon, and the latest comedies from Paris.

They read together at night with the dog making three; Molière's trained voice, faltering when the pain in his chest caught him short, and the fat man's robust one.

They grew in comradeship. When Molière was on his feet again the fat man took him out to dine. They spent an evening in the tavern where they had first met, drinking deep. Not the drinking of desperation now; the satisfactory, ruminative drinking of companionship when wine spun words upon the tongue and broke down barriers. Molière found himself telling of Madeleine and Armande; of the company he had abandoned; of the wreckage of his hopes and plans, and how he would have to start again from the beginning. The telling eased his mind as though his friend had indeed been a priest and they were meeting at confession, not across a tavern table.

After hearing the story, the fat man pursed his lips and took more wine.

"The trouble with you, my friend, is that you had a respectable upbringing."

"So did you, by your own account."

"I know I did, but I rose above it. Your parents—who I have no doubt were good, honest, respectable and extremely dull people—taught you to believe in God, and put the fear of the devil in you. So you see yourself, in your conceited way, fought over by the pair of them. And when you catch yourself in a vice, or even thinking of one, or assuming that, in some circumstances or other, you might be guilty of one . . . well, you think that the devil's winning, and you go in fear of your immortal soul."

He leaned back and looked solemn.

"That's too simple, my friend. You have the mind of an adolescent boy in a grown man's body. Don't you see that thinking like that reduces you to the status of a rope in a tug of war?"

He leaned across the table and tapped Molière's forehead with his finger.

"It's all in there, my friend. That's where the battle is. Not outside. To see that you could be weak, to contemplate something that would demean your true nature, to have what you probably still call sinful thoughts . . . that's natural. Who doesn't? Remember your mythology. Even the gods, the gods of high Olympus, the arbiters of man's destiny, the judges of right and avengers of wrong . . . they had their temptations, too. We're only men, after all. The desire to err is human. What's important is how far you succeed in mastering it. How you stop the thoughts from becoming action. You know what? I'd like to write a play, some day, which will have no action in it at all. It will be five acts about a man making up his mind."

As Molière looked unconvinced, he went on:

"Your situation, now. You really know what you ought to do, don't you? What's the most important thing in the world?"

"The work. Getting back to Paris. Writing."

"Then go back, find your company. They'll forgive you. Work till you drop. It's a cure for everything. You'll forget the girl. You know what she is now. Write more plays. You'll get her out of your mind easily enough."

And Molière, nodding soberly, agreed.

His friend had to go back to Paris. They had one glorious farewell carousal, reciting heroic speeches till the others threatened to throw them out, and sang songs until cockcrow. The fat man put Molière into a coach already paid for, and dropped a purse into his lap.

"No, don't thank me. A courtesy among artists. Nothing more. Work hard."

As the coach drew off, an awful thought struck Molière. He stuck his head out of the window.

"I've been living off your kindness for weeks," he yelled, "and I don't even know your name!"

"Jean!" shouted the other, his voice almost drowned as the coach rattled under the archway. "Jean Racine! See you in Paris, Molière!"

It was a short journey back, the easy way; but by the time he arrived his head was miraculously clear from the last fumes of the night's drinking, and he knew exactly what it was he had to do. Apologize to the company, if they were still there. Dismiss Armande, if she was still there; though it was unthinkable that she would be. She was a distraction, an ignoble byway to lead him from the path of greatness. Jean had recommended that he study his mythology. Very well then. His would be the choice of Hercules. Work, much work; for the Prince de Conti's fête would soon be upon them, and glory lay beyond. He would be a dedicated man.

It was early Sunday morning. The streets were quiet, and the people had not yet stirred for first Mass. He walked to his old lodging, hardly expecting that it would have been kept for him. Up the stairs to the familiar door. His name was still scrawled upon it. No change. All was as he had left it, except that his things had been tidied.

And in the chair beside the window was a figure. A woman. Madeleine had come home! He ran to her, crying his joy; and as she turned to him he saw that it was not Madeleine; and yet it was, but Madeleine grown young again. She stood and reached out her arms to him.

"I have been waiting for you," said Armande "every night since you went away."

In the second before her lips met his, he knew that what he had to do was of no purpose, now. It was what he wanted to do that mattered, and no god, no devil, no philosopher would stop him.

He was besotted with her. She gave him a joy he had never known with Madeleine, or the few others; she gave him back his youth again. In the years of touring, the grind of writing, rehearsing, playing, the daily anxiety of finding money, middle age had come upon him unawares. Armande blew the years away. The mingling of their bodies infused him with her freshness, her vitality. He could hardly bear to be away from her. He would have let the company go hang, forgotten Paris, forgotten everything but her. If memories of Madeleine arose to trouble him he shrugged them off, finding in Armande all that her sister had given him, something she had never given him. There was witchcraft in the child. She fastened onto him and sucked his blood, replacing it with hers. He was her creature.

He was deathly tired. Added to the fatigue of his working day were the increasing demands made upon his body. He no longer resisted them; he looked forward to their lovemaking more eagerly than he would admit even to himself, wallowing in his degradation. The first coupling, on the night of his return, had shocked and shamed him by its brute ferocity. He had never dreamed that the act which seemed such a dreary exercise when done with Madeleine could turn him into a panting animal, pawing her young flesh and bruising it, biting at her nipples till she screamed in pain, prying with his fingers and his tongue into the secret places of her body, tasting her, taking her. And she had led him on while pretending to resist; behind each whimper, every whispered no, lay an invitation to some new experiment, some new exploration, luring him to spill his seed between her breasts, her fingers, the warm ovals of her buttocks. He slept at last, his body and his senses numbed, exhausted. When he woke hours later—at what time in the morning he neither knew nor cared—she was sitting curled up in a corner of the bed, sucking her finger like a wistful child, speculatively watching him; and when she saw his eyelids flicker she put her hands on him again.

He had resisted her that time. It was the last time. He had staggered to his feet and dressed himself haphazardly, muttering something about seeing the company and going back to work. When he left the room she was still sitting up in bed, smiling, knowing. She did not try to stop him. She did not need to.

For the next day, and half the day after, he avoided her. He did not need to make excuses, there was much to do. The company received him back with cries of joy. There were no questions, no speculations on the reasons for his absence. This surprised him, till he found out that it had all been Armande's doing. She was as shrewd an organizer as her sister. When he had disappeared, she had given out that he had been called away on urgent business connected with their fortunes, and that there was no knowing when he would be back; she had kept the company together by hinting at his displeasure and the promise of great things to come. And they, poor fools, had believed her, and trusted in him. It was with some surprise that he realized he was a god to them, and they accepted such eccentricities unquestioningly.

Armande had even entered into a temporary alliance with the Marquise, to run rehearsals and revive as many of their plays as they could without their leading actor. The public grumbled, but continued to attend; the actresses, more scintillating than ever, drew them back. With Molière's return the alliance was shattered. The Marquise resumed her distance, hinting, slandering, and muttering darkly of treachery. But she could do nothing; the company accepted Armande's new eminence, as they had Molière's disappearance, without question. Robichaud had gone forever, fled into the night, no one knew where. There was no other witness of that dismal evening. If the others wondered, as they must have done, what would happen when Madeleine came back, they kept their speculations to themselves.

When Madeleine came back.

He tried to push the problem from his mind, telling himself that it was all over now, the madness had passed, he had cured himself of the fever by succumbing to it and letting it do its worst. When Madeleine came back, Armande would cease to trouble him; she would resume her place in the background and be the dutiful younger sister again. Life would be serene; life would be for work again, as it should be.

Armande, the sphinx, could read his mind as well as devour his body. She knew his reticence, and it piqued her. It was something new to her experience. She had been used to the earthy and unambiguous advances of boys her own age, to the breeches dropped gruntingly in the barnyard, to the hand up her skirt in a dark alley. For a day she let him alone, and then set about devising new ways to provoke him. They had been rehearsing, with Molière being very distant and professional with her, hardly talking to her at all except for a brief word of praise or instruction. It went well; the actors were reinvigorated by his presence, and worked uncomplainingly long past their usual time. Dismissed at last, they went off hungrily and with mutual congratulations to eat. Molière, left alone, sat happily for a moment on the stage, tired, but decently tired, safe in the old enclosure of routine. Then there came a soft footfall behind him. It was Armande, still in her costume and clutching at his,

tugging at the drawstring of his breeches, undraping Scaramouche and showing Molière. "It's all right," she whispered
eagerly, "there's nothing to be frightened of. Come where you
belong, inside me." And when he still held back she laughed
her tinkling laugh and said "Pretend, then. You're so good at
pretending. Make love to me as Scaramouche, not Molière."
And he did, seizing on this pretext to preserve his decency,
telling himself that it was not he doing these things but another,
that he could still stand aloof and be impartial, even as his
hand ruffed up her petticoats and her tongue flickered in his
ear, murmuring obscenities, speaking his cues to do those for-
bidden, delightful things.

They always made love in costume after this. She forced
him to it, knowing full well that it compounded his sense of
guilt and bound him to her more closely. They would enact
the famous lovers of history, improvising verses in which she
proved as facile as he: Titus and Berenice, Theseus and Hip-
polyta, Bacchus and Ariadne. His urgency grew irresistible. He
still could not bring himself to make the advances, but at a
hint from her he was ready; and she was never slow to hint.

She controlled his time. When she beckoned, he came running. He asked himself why and found no answer. In his saner
moments he knew she was coarse and disagreeable, that all the
slanders about her had been true. His room was a pigsty. It had
not been cleaned or tidied since the day he came back. Armande
was a slut. It was her habit to walk half naked round the room,
scratching herself. She deliberately waited to relieve herself till
he was there, so that he would be forced to watch her pissing
in the pot. When he remonstrated with her, she laughed and
told him that two people in love were as one. That such things
were pleasant and natural, not sordid and disgusting. That
nothing should be hidden.

There was nothing he could hide from her. He had given up
making entries in his diary, because she read them; it had been
a treasury of his thoughts before, of words and phrases stored

away against future use. But even this was denied him now. His mind was not his own.

She seduced him from the theater one afternoon, when they should have been rehearsing. He protested limply but in vain, knowing that she only did it to show her power. She would not be denied, but made some excuse for him to the company, and hurried him back to his lodging, while the actors looked after them knowingly and muttered that their leader was taking too much recreation. Once in the room she was all innocence, announcing that today they would play the parts of Samson and Delilah, brandishing a pair of scissors that she had secreted from the wardrobe and proclaiming that she was about to cut his hair. When he protested laughingly, claiming that he had little enough already, she dropped the mask of innocence and smiled a lascivious smile.

"I didn't mean to take it from your head." She lowered her hand, and pointed with the scissors at him. "I want a trophy, Molière." She advanced on him, and, suddenly repelled, he pushed her off; in the tussle that followed she nicked his thigh, so that when he eventually succumbed and she pulled him down on top of her, the blood ran down between their legs upon the floor.

This was how Madeleine found them when she came back unannounced, and thrust herself into the room without knocking. No, it was unfair to complain of that; it was her room, too, they had never stood on ceremony. She stood in the doorway, looking down at them. Molière saw the momentary terror in Armande's eyes, and he jerked himself off her to perceive his doom. He opened his mouth to speak, but no sound came out. It would have made no difference. Madeleine ignored him. Reaching across his body, bedraggled and travel-stained as she was, she dragged Armande to her feet. They stood glaring at each other, the older like a Fury come to judgment, the younger naked and defiant, but so alike that Armande might have been looking at herself, aged. Then, without a word, they began to fight. Armande was quick and vicious, squirming like an eel and using her sharp teeth to bite. Madeleine was big-boned, with the strength that came from years of labor, and bore down on her savagely, delivering great ringing slaps with right and left hand in turn, aiming for the face, the belly, the breasts. The room was tiny, and their struggles brought a mirror crashing down from the wall. Armande trod on it, and the floor was blotched with her blood.

Molière crawled from the floor in some vain hope of stopping them. He could have as well stopped an avalanche. He was naked, impotent, ridiculous. They both ignored him, he might as well have not been in the room. Forward and backward they swayed while the voices of their neighbors, disturbed from their siesta, sounded from the stairs. Then Madeleine had an arm round Armande's waist, the other round her throat. A sound came at last, but it was only a croak, as if he were the one who was being strangled; he thought she was about to kill her. Then, as suddenly, the tension slackened. Madeleine dropped her arms and groped, like a blind person, for a chair. Armande slipped from her grasp onto the bed. The room was full of the sound of their panting.

After what seemed like ages, Madeleine rose again. She looked round the room as if seeing it for the first time, and, moving slowly and painfully, began to pick things up, to rearrange the counterpane, sweep away the broken glass with clumsy fingers, and restore the lodging to some semblance of order. She looked at Armande, still nursing her wounds on the bed.

"Help me."

They were the first words she had spoken since she entered the room.

To Molière's astonishment, Armande did what she was told. The two women did not look at each other or speak, but went about their task, moving with slow, careful steps, avoiding each other, avoiding Molière until the last debris had been cleared away and the last spot of blood washed from the wooden floor. Then Madeleine nodded towards the door.

"Get out."

Armande went out without a backward glance. This is a day of miracles, thought Molière.

"Aren't you going to say anything?"

She turned to look at him. Her face was wiped clean of expression.

"You should be in rehearsal."

"Is that all you're going to say?"

She gestured towards the door.

"I've said it."

And then, as suddenly as the violence, came the tears. "Why did you do it? Is this all I mean to you? The others I could put up with. I always have. I knew they meant nothing to you. But Armande! Is this your way to hurt me? Did you hate me so much?"

He stammered. "We . . . I . . . . meant to tell you. You took us by surprise. It was your fault, bursting in like this."

"You knew I was coming. You knew I'd be here today. And this was the welcome you arranged for me."

Surprise made him indignant.

"Of course I didn't know. How could I? All these weeks away, and not a word from you. Do you expect me to live like a monk while you're gone? We're not husband and wife, Madeleine. Am I supposed to sit around here keeping house, until you condescend to show your face again?"

"I wrote to you," she said tonelessly, "three times. You never answered. I sent a letter by the coach last week, to tell you I was coming back today." He raised a hand in protest, but she stopped him. "Don't tell me you never had it. When there was no one to meet me, I asked at the inn if the letter had come. It had. I went to the theater, and there was no one there. I came here."

He did not, could not answer. There was nothing he could

say. He had received no letters. Armande must have intercepted them, destroyed them. She had known all along that Madeleine would be back today. That was the reason for this afternoon, then; not lust, but policy. Armande had forced things to a head, because she knew that he would never dare.

"I can't stay here now. You must know that." Her hands were busy with her costume, brushing, smoothing, tidying. "I'll make my way back to Paris. I can find work there somehow. You can obviously do without me."

"I can't. We can't. The theater, the company . . . doesn't that mean anything to you?"

"The theater! The company!" she mimicked bitterly. "Is that all you think about?" Her eyes returned to the bed. "No. Obviously it isn't. It's my own fault. I've brought it on myself, I suppose. I used you once. I admitted it. But if you think I spent these years with you . . . if you think everything I did was for the company, you're mad. I thought I meant something to you. I thought you needed me, a little."

"Armande—"

"Armande! Armande! Is that all you can think about? You fool, you don't know what you're doing. You can tell me I used you, and I admit it. But you use people, Molière. You suck them dry, and throw them away. People don't mean anything to you. It's all your work, your writing, the theater . . . but you've bitten off more than you can chew with her. She'll use you, the way she has others. She'll chew the flesh off your bones and spit you out. Then you'll know, perhaps, how I feel."

"But how will you live? Let me give you money at least. There's little enough, but half of it is yours."

She stopped him with a grimace of derision.

"Am I your whore? I'll take no money from you. Keep it, Molière. Keep it for your new whore. You'll need it, every penny."

"At least," said Molière, stung to anger at last, "it will stay in the family."

She turned so white he thought she was about to faint. She

gave him one last desperate look. Then the door slammed behind her and she was gone.

It was Armande, paradoxically, who made him work. After Madeleine had come and gone, a strange sort of serenity had grown up between them, as if they had passed through the crisis of some disease together and were recuperating on the other side. Armande's demands on his manhood were less importunate. She still summoned him from time to time, like a spoilt lady calling her poodle dog, and, God knew, he was glad enough to go. But this was only to remind him of her power. For the most part she was docile, even affectionate; they lived together like a respectable married couple. And, husband-like, Molière grew jealous. When Armande displayed her charms on the stage the manager in him applauded but the lover looked askance. But her public behavior was impeccable. She laughed him out of his suspicions and was as cautious of her reputation as any marriageable virgin under her chaperone's eye. When they were offstage together she sat demurely by his side, answering the others only when spoken to and saving all her attention for him. When he sat alone making up the accounts—for the burden had fallen on him after Robichaud's defection—she came to him whenever time allowed, smoothed his brow and talked happily about how well things were going. Whatever faults she may have had in the past—the faults of youth, thought Molière, my fault for not guarding her properly—she had turned her back on such things. If he had borrowed from her youth, she had adopted his sobriety.

Things were, as she said, in good order. Their weeks together were peaceably busy; living, working together by each other's side, seeing the company grow in confidence and hearing the cash box filled and refilled nightly. They were working doubly hard, for the Prince de Conti's fête was almost on them. This time there would be no error, for the Princess had promised; the golden gates would open. And if the old goats and young lechers came to the plays more for Armande than for the verse

—and particularly a dazzling young man who came three or four times a week, sat regularly in the front row and could not take his eyes off her—so much the better. The hopeless admiration and yearning that poured from the audience onto the stage was a tribute to his triumph, taste and prowess.

The day had come, the last rehearsal had been held, the troupe was ready to depart. *The Doctor in Love* was polished like a gem, improved with each new reading. The company had been trained to the last flicker of an eyebrow. Molière had welcomed the year's grace, once he had been forced to accept it. It gave him time to revise and strengthen. The roles now fitted the company like fine clothes, and Armande, in Madeleine's old part, gave the piece her own lightness. Once again they hired a coach, decked it out and set off in fine array. But this time the sun was shining. It was a dreaming June day with a little breeze to puff the plumes and bunting and make the horses lift their heads and snort with pleasure. All was perfection. Their success was assured, their spirits high. Even the Marquise so far forgot herself as to smile naturally and call Armande "my dear."

They drew up at the towering lodge gates, and waited for the servants to open them. Ten minutes. Fifteen. Twenty. The company grew restive, and the Marquise fell to grumbling again. Garcin blew an impertinent salute on his trumpet. "That'll fetch them!" But no response, and not a soul in sight. Finally Molière jumped down with a curse.

"The louts! We must be the last to arrive. They've deserted their posts, and slunk off to see the fun."

He signaled to the apprentices, and together they swung the gates open. The hinges squeaked and groaned. A whisp of ivy had twined through the scrollwork, and Molière tugged it off with an impatient hand. "Let's drive through!" he shouted. "It looks as though we'll have to announce ourselves!"

The Marquise was moved to comment on the lax discipline of great houses. Molière argued that on such a day a little license was permissible but as he looked around him he was forced to admit that she was right. The lawns, immaculate on their last visit, were straggling and overgrown with weeds. The symmetry of trees was gone. Some had been cut down. Those remaining were shapeless and unpruned, their branches drooping with melancholy down to earth as if they did not like what they saw and would happily return to the womb again. No water played from the fountains. The carved fish mouths puckered in a silent whistle, and dead leaves filled the basins. Against the bushes stood an upturned barrow and an abandoned rake, as if the gardener, appalled by the hopelessness of his task, had gone off in disgust.

And over it all, a noise. Molière heard it first, and signaled for the horses to be reined in. The actors stopped their bickering, and listened. When they heard, they shivered.

A bell. No music, but a bell. It tolled from the chapel at the rear of the great house. At every stroke, the mansion died a little.

"A death," muttered Garcin, crossing himself. "I wish we'd never seen the cursed place. No fête. Not a chance for us, now."

"Who is it?" said the Marquise. She was on the verge of hysterics. "Who's dead?"

No one answered. They knew who was dead. They all were.

Armande shuddered, and dug her fingers into Molière's arm. "Let's go away. We can do nothing now."

Gently he disengaged himself.

"No. I shall go in. If it is the Prince who's dead, I shall pay him my respects, for his wife's sake. If it is the Princess . . . then for my own sake, I can do no less."

He got down, and walked towards the portico alone. The others watched in silence.

On the cold marble floor that had twice seen the ruin of their hopes he looked around for some assistance. Were they all dead here? The house was as deserted as the garden. Had the plague struck? Was that the reason for this emptiness? But as the panic seized him and he turned to run, there was a footfall on the stairs. He turned, and his first feeling was of relief. It was not the Prince who was dead, for there he was, in costume for some masquerade. Nor the Princess, for here she came, out of the shadows behind him. But where were the laughing girls, the golden men? Just the two of them, and a third behind there, in the darkness. A masquerade, he told himself again. Some perverse whim of the Prince's. To give a fête and dress it as a funeral. Stranger things had been heard of in Paris.

He stepped forward, coughed and bowed. If this was their game, he could play it as well as they. The Prince stopped and frowned.

His voice came hoarse and tetchy from the depths of his cowl.

"Who is it? Who's there?"

As he came down into the light, Molière gasped. If this was a masquerade, it was a grim one; and it had been going on for some time. The Prince's face was lined and gray. His beard was as straggling as his lawns. His eyes were querulous and bloodshot, and he peered about him impatiently.

"Who are you, man? What do you want? You have no business here. I have no time. No time." His fingers twitched automatically as he spoke. They spun a rosary.

"We . . . I . . . it is the players, your highness," stammered Molière. "We were summoned here. By your lady. For your birthday."

"Birthday?" muttered the Prince. "Is it my birthday? It may be, I suppose. I take no notice of such things."

"What is earthly time?" intoned the third figure from the top of the stairs. "What is a single year but a grain on the sands of eternity?"

"Right. Quite right," muttered the Prince. Could this be the shining hero—whining, appeasing, currying favor from a priest? "We must think of eternity. We must prepare ourselves. What is life for, but to repent of having been born?"

"There is no fête," said Molière. It was not a question.

"There is no fête," said the priest above him, "nor will there be again." He pushed past the Prince, jostling him aside like a scullion. "The Prince has seen the error of his ways. He is above such frivolity now. He thinks only of repentance and salvation."

Would that bell never be still?

Molière and the priest confronted each other. The Prince's magnificence had not been lost; it was the priest who had it now. His hair was curled and his sleeves silken; the stained and threadbare cassock was replaced by rich brocade. A gold ring sparkled on his finger.

"And you. You lice, you caterpillars, that corrupt great men and pander to their weaknesses. For you there can be no salvation, though you repent from now till doomsday. Players! Devil's instruments! For you the hellfire and the stinking pit!"

He would have gone on, but a whisper from the stairs distracted him and made him jerk his head round sharply. The Princess was saying something in her husband's ear. He shook her off, but she insisted, and for a moment the lined face softened and the old proud glow came into the haunted eyes.

"Father, perhaps we should not be harsh. The Church tells us to show charity. Give him money and send him away."

The priest rounded on him, and he slunk back like a naughty child.

"Charity! Charity is for the deserving, my son. Mother Church does not bid us abet the sinners in their wickedness. What have they deserved but whipping and the galleys? Give the word, and I will have it done."

"No. Do not punish them. Only send them away." The flash of spirit had faded again. He was tired, anxious only to be rid of them.

The priest turned back to Molière, triumph burning in his sallow face. "You heard the Prince's order? Take your rabble and leave. If you are seen on this estate again, you will feel chains."

The Prince and Princess stood behind him, awaiting his pleasure.

"Let us go, my son and daughter. We are late for Mass. And then there is business to be seen to. The further gifts of land that you intend to make to Mother Church."

His fingers played unconsciously with the golden ring as the three of them went through the door. As they passed Molière, the Princess raised her head and looked at him. She gave a tiny, imperceptible shrug and was gone.

"And they say news travels quickly in the country."

Molière whirled round. It was the secretary, the scrubby, ginger man. "You mean to say you heard nothing of this?"

"Not a word. How long has it been going on?"

"Almost a year. Since the last time you were here." The secretary spoke with bitterness. "He's had these religious fits before, but they never lasted. One day, two days . . . a little fasting between feasts, more to clear the palate than for any other reason. There were always people to jolly him out of them. But this time . . ."

"What happened?"

"There was a death. A favorite child. The priest was at his ear the whole time. Telling him it was God's judgment on his sinful life. And he listened. The Prince grew weaker, the priest stronger . . . the Prince was ill, too. It all helped. And now look at this." His gesture showed the bare walls, the patches where tapestries had been, the empty sconces, the niches barren of their statues. "All swallowed up in the coffers of the Church, or the priest's belly." And he was suddenly blasphemous about the clergy in general, and this member of it in particular.

"Are you staying?"

"For what? There's no work for me to do now. The priest manages everything. He hates me because I was against him. Tried to persuade the Prince to use some moderation, not let everything go . . . but who ever listens to me!" He was blaspheming again. "And now where can I go? No work, no money; I can read and write, I can add figures, but there are thousands like me. It will be years before I find a place."

Molière was moved to sympathy and help. Perhaps something could be saved from this blighted place.

"Come to work for us. We need someone to do the things you do. Our last man . . . left. We can't pay much, but you'll be happier there than here."

The secretary looked at him dumbfounded. A tear started from his eye and hung upon his scrubby moustache.

"You mean it?"

"We'll try each other out at any rate. Come. Let's go back to the coach."

The ginger man's name was La Grange. He was to be Molière's devoted friend and servant till the day he died.

They went back to touring. They had to, but the life was out of them. Before, the drudgery of moving from town to town, from one tatterdemalion hall to another, had an end and purpose. This was now snatched from them and—such is human perversity—they began to blame Molière for what had happened. They all but accused him of misleading them, of offering false promises. In vain he protested that this was not his fault. The Marquise became impossible, giving only a sketch of a performance. The younger actors missed rehearsals, forgot their lines and tried to fill the gaps with horseplay on the stage. Twice they were booed. Audiences began to fall off again. Each night the cash box felt lighter.

Armande turned shrewish again. The kitten grew claws. He could find no peace of mind now, either at home or in the theater. At work, she pretended to be engrossed in rehearsals, and would not speak to him. In the privacy of their room—which seemed more meager and confining than ever—she spoke far too much. Why had he put all his eggs in one basket? Had years of writing about people taught him nothing about the way they think and behave? There were other avenues he could have tried, other prospective patrons. But to pin all his faith in one man, who was notoriously unstable—particularly after the disappointment they had had the first time! That was the height of folly, and she would never forgive him.

To punish him, she made herself even more enticing on the stage. She was the one bright thing in the dreary evening, but he hated what she was doing. She played deliberately for every man in the audience: posturing suggestively, reading a lasciviousness into his lines when he had intended none, leaning out to expose her breasts. When he complained, she defended herself indignantly.

"Someone has to do something. The others aren't acting any more. They're nothing but dummies standing on the stage. Why shouldn't I show myself? I'm a woman, aren't I? If that's the only thing these oafs enjoy, let's give it to them. There's nothing I wouldn't do to get out of these dreary provinces. Nothing!"

Her expression made her meaning amply clear, and the coarseness of her voice so reminded him of that awful night in the greenroom that he struck her.

As she taunted him, he grew more and more suspicious. He found excuses to surprise her when she was supposed to be alone. She always was, and jeered at him. There was no proof that she was being unfaithful, nothing he could put his finger on. But he found himself on stage watching the audience instead of concentrating on his part, scanning the faces of the men present, wondering which it was she favored, and how they were finding opportunities to meet. He was particularly suspicious of one: the dazzling young man he had seen so often before the fiasco, the one who had come regularly to their performances. He reappeared, in town after town; he must be following them. Following her.

The thought festered in his mind. The admirer was obviously rich. His clothes were of the finest, his beard sleekly trimmed; he carried himself with the assurance that only money or high birth could give, and stood out from the surrounding rustics like an illuminated letter in a script. When he was there, Molière tormented himself by trying to read his thoughts. When he was not, he was no less miserable wondering where he was, and what he was planning. And when he was not there on the

days Armande did not play—it was at this point that the
suspicions grew intolerable, and made him physically ill.

He made up his mind to follow the young man, and track
him down. At least he could find out who he was. Perhaps make
him confess what he wanted. Thrash him, drive him out, scare
him away. One night, when the man was present, he had an early
exit. He stripped off makeup and costume, wrapping himself in
an inconspicuous cloak. Instead of appearing with the company
at the end to acknowledge the applause (not that it was worth
acknowledging, these days) he slipped round to the public door,
making some excuse about a headache, and waited till the audience came out. The young man was alone, as always. He strode
along the street in his arrogant way, and Molière followed
from a distance, expecting him to turn in at the inn. He went
past it, and kept on walking, past the last houses into the fields
beyond.

An assignation, thought Molière. He's going to meet
Armande. His heart thumped so loudly he could have sworn
his quarry would have heard it.

The young man stopped, at last, by a dry well on the fringes
of the town. No one ever came here, except for children playing.
The ideal spot, thought Molière, for what they have to do. And
what I have to do.

Glancing round, the young man gave a low soft whistle.
Molière ducked behind a tree. He had not been seen. The whistle
again, and an answer. A girl appeared among the bushes on the
far side. Armande. She must have left early too, and run like
the wind, to be here so soon. How eager, thought Molière.
How desperate she must be.

The young man drew Armande into an embrace. Molière
could stand no more. The blood rushed to his head; he went
berserk. He forgot that his opponent probably had twice his
strength, and a sword as well, while he went empty-handed. He
only thought of hurting, and revenge. With a bound, he was on
to him. He came from behind, so that the gallant rolled over at
the unexpected blow. Armande leaped away and screamed as

the two fought desperately, snarling and clutching at each other's throats.

It was a short fight. Molière's advantage was only momentary. He was tired and clumsy, sick with worry and fatigue. His opponent was as lissom as a snake—in full possession of his youth and strength. And for all his pampered appearance, he knew every trick of rough fighting. Molière found himself being hurt in unexpected places, wrestling a man with six arms, and teeth no less effective than a sword. He was blinded, throttled: gasping for breath he managed to struggle to his feet, and was threshing wildly when a fist came out of nowhere, met his jaw and sent him into blackness.

When he came to, he was propped against a tree, and Armande and her lover were looking down at him. The taste of blood was in his mouth, and his face was puffed and aching. He wondered if his nose were broken, and decided that it was not worth the pain of finding out.

Armande was furious.

"A new part for you to play, master actor! The jealous husband avenging his wife's honor! How do you feel now? A pity that it doesn't work out as neatly as in the plays!"

The young man stopped her with a hand on her arm. He looked at her with anger, and then at Molière with what, he realized with surprise, was compassion.

"That's enough. It was stupid to let this go so far. Tell him, Armande. I wish to God we'd done so at the beginning."

"I'll tell him," she snapped. "Listen to me, and be ashamed of yourself. Is there any law that says a woman may not meet her own brother?"

"Brother!"

"Louis, Monsieur Molière."

The young man knelt beside him, and his face suddenly became familiar. "And now I have two things to ask your pardon for."

The whole story came out later, when they were back at the lodging. Armande, sulkily repentant, dressed Molière's bruises while Louis straddled a chair and talked. Defying the precepts of the moralists, he had thrived on stolen money. After he had abandoned them in Paris, he had made his way by devious routes to Marseilles, stealing where he could, working where he had to. A ship sailing for Turkish waters had taken him on as crew. He was lucky, for the ship's master was not too dishonest, and had allowed his sailors to invest their own money in the venture. He had come back by way of Genoa to France with his capital substantially increased. It was impossible for him to settle down. The wanderlust had gripped him. He had gone to England, which he hated but found immensely profitable. For some time he had acted as a secret courier between Royalists in the West Country and the exiles on the continent, carrying messages for them, for a price, and negotiating for the sale of jewelry and plate which could not be revealed in England for fear of confiscation, but which had to be converted into money to assist the Royalist cause. On each of these he had received a fat commission, often considerably larger, he cheerfully admitted, than his employers recognized. It had been a dangerous life, but he had relished it. At the end, he was almost captured by the Commonwealth forces. Forestalling them, he contracted to sell all the information he had. "I invented most of it," he said, unblushing. Then he had come back to Paris, and invested his money with the inside knowledge given him by years of intrigue and his intimate connection with the ports of Europe.

"But why all this secrecy?" demanded Molière, "If you wanted to see us, why not tell us who you were?"

Louis was curiously reluctant to admit this. Molière deduced eventually that he had suffered from a rare fit of conscience. He had gone back to his mother and Madeleine in Paris. ("She sends her regards, by the way.") They had told him where the troupe was likely to be, and he had come down, partly out of curiosity, partly from a real desire to make amends. There was the additional attraction of meeting a sister he had never seen. But once there, he had been unable to face a meeting with Molière—

"I was scared of you," he admitted. "I kept seeing the two of us as we were in Paris. You a strapping young man, me a scrubby boy. And I couldn't help thinking you'd put me over your knee and wallop me, for running off like that." He smiled a coarse, impudent smile. "Needn't have worried, though, need I?"

Eventually, he had sent a note to Armande. Molière was delighted to learn that she had been outraged at first, refusing to believe that this handsome fellow was her brother, and suspecting him of being a gallant with an unusually inventive approach. But he had convinced her, and continued to follow the company at a safe distance, meeting Armande in secret whenever he could.

Molière was overcome with remorse. How could he ever have suspected her? He squeezed the hand that was bandaging his cheek and got a squeeze in return.

It had been Armande, apparently, who had dissuaded him from revealing himself. After the great disappointment, with the company at sixes and sevens, she was afraid that Molière would be in no mood to welcome back the prodigal. She had urged him to wait awhile, until things improved and Molière was in a better mood. And it gave her a childish pleasure to have a secret brother. Particularly one who was so grand and handsome. It was like a story from a play.

"I kept telling her you wouldn't mind," drawled Louis, "particularly when you know what I'm here for. But she wouldn't have it."

"What are you here for?"

"I want to come back to the theater again. I always enjoyed it, see. Never had such a good time as when we were running that ramshackle old barn in Paris. But I wanted some money, too. I wasn't going to be poor all my life. And it was obvious I wasn't going to make any there."

Molière winced.

"But I've had my fun, and done what I wanted. So I came down to look you over. You know what? You're good." He jerked his thumb at his sister. "She's marvelous. You got a good thing there. And you're not so bad yourself. Of course, there's a lot you've got to do. A couple of people up there on the stage tonight would have been better off sweeping up behind the horses. And those costumes! They've been in the wars, all right. But we can make a going thing of it, if we work a bit."

Annoyed by the "we," by the arrogant dismissal of his years of labor, Molière was stung into curtness.

"You must be out of your mind. There's nothing here for you anymore. Look at yourself. Look at us. We've gone our different ways. You have your world now, and I have mine. You know you'd soon get tired of us again. Stick it for a few weeks, and then be off on some ship somewhere. It's dull here in the country."

Louis' eyes widened. He put his thumb in his mouth, and made a popping noise, winking at his sister.

"All right, all right. I deserve that, I suppose. But you don't see what I'm getting at."

"What?"

He got up impatiently and strode across the room, fingers hitched in his belt.

"I told you, I'm a fairly rich man. Not" . . . he went on hastily, "that I've got a bottomless purse, or anything like that. But I've got enough, and I know a good gamble when I see one. More than that, I know people." His face creased with the memory of the intrigues of the past years. "Yes, I reckon I can say I know people. So what do you say?"

"What do I say to what?"

"Are you stupid? I must have hit you harder than I thought. I'm telling you that I can get you back to Paris. If you want to go, that is."

But Armande and Molière were already ecstatically in each other's arms.

PART THREE

Triumph

I⊤ WAS RIDICULOUS that he could not concentrate. For years he had trained himself to shut his mind to distractions: to ignore the whispers from the pit, the champing of jaws from the gallery, the all-too-audible comments of people who came to the theater to gossip with their friends, transact business, arrange an assignation, anything but to hear a play. Before, he had succeeded. He could narrow his world to a strip of bare boards and exclude the crowd half-lighted on the other side, not caring how many they were, or whether they liked the play or not. It was La Grange's job to worry about things like that. He assumed a role as another man might don a cape and hood. It blocked his ears and narrowed his vision.

And now, at this crucial moment, when his life and that of those around him depended on his concentration, he was conscious only of the fly droning in the windowpane, and of the heavy-eyed, young-old man nodding opposite. It was ridiculous.

It made a difference, of course, that the glass the fly was desecrating was a window of the Louvre. And that the sleepy man, who had now stopped yawning to scratch his ear, was the King.

Louis—their Louis, not the one opposite—had succeeded beyond their wildest expectations. He knew almost everyone. Those he did not, he made it his business to cultivate. He had spun a web of connections that covered Paris, bribing, bullying, cajoling, persuading. He knew his limitations, of course. There were regions into which he did not venture. None of the illustrious personages ranged on uncomfortable chairs around the room had ever heard of Louis Béjart. They would have been mortally offended if told the truth: that they were here watching a troupe of second-rate provincial actors in an outmoded tragedy because of the enterprise of a former pirate and reformed spy. Louis had dealt with the lesser men, and matched Parisian evasiveness with tricks of his own. He did not circulate in the salons. It was the backstairs that knew the confident tread of his feet, the stewards' cubbyholes and secretaries' offices that rang to the brag of his voice. Sometimes he talked so long that they agreed to take up his cause just to be rid of him. Impervious to hints and deaf to insults, he never seemed to grow hoarse or pause for breath. Constantly he touted this unknown company in which he had an interest. After an hour of this, they would have signed anything, agreed to anything, simply to have peace and quiet. After one of these visits he would come back to Molière and Armande bubbling with malicious joy.

"They're too subtle, these Parisians. Overfed, overbred, over-refined. They're always on the lookout for the rapier. Walk in with a cudgel, and you knock them flat."

And he would slap his thigh and roar with laughter at the stupidity of his fellow men, before strutting off to his next visit.

Sometimes these encounters were more sinister. These were the meetings with men he had known before, in other ways. Nothing would actually be said, but implications hovered in the air. A light allusion to a letter that had once been carried between persons who, officially, had no knowledge of each other. How many secrets these great houses hid! And what a pity if some of them came out! Or Louis would compliment his host on his fine clothes and tasteful furnishings, and remark wistfully on how much money such things must have cost; and his host, who remembered all too well where the money had come from, would turn pale, grow suddenly effusive and express great interest in this new troupe of actors. Yes, of course, by Louis' account they well deserved to be seen in Paris. There must be something he could do? He had no influence himself, of course, but a word in his lord's ear, at the right time. . . . They would part with mutual expressions of respect, and the victim would shut the door firmly behind him, mopping his brow and thankful that he had got off so easily. Louis, on his part, would come home more circumspectly from such visits, looking carefully into archways before he passed through them, mixing with the crowd, and tending to be suspicious of sudden movements.

Or, if all else failed, money changed hands. Louis paid grudgingly, not because he lacked the means, but because he knew too well that money did not bind a man. A critic who allowed his opinion to be bought might forget his bargain as quickly as he had sold his standards. Happily, men who made their living out of literature always seemed to be in need of money. The vague promise of favors to come kept them faithful. Those who reneged were carefully noted down in a list that Louis always carried with him. They would pay for it, by and by.

All this had taken time. Louis, stating bluntly that he was not going to throw his money away, had insisted that they work their way back to Paris. The company had grumbled at this. When their new benefactor had been announced, they had immediately seen themselves stepping into golden coaches and driving to the King's front door. Louis had rudely squashed all such pretensions.

"You'll go back the way you came," he said. "By the sweat

of your brows. I'll need all the money I've got to get you going in Paris. And I want to make one thing clear. I'm not giving anything away. This is an investment and I want a good return on it."

The actors had been indignant at this, talking deploringly about this crude man who expected them to sell their souls for money. Molière shrugged at Louis apologetically. They had forgotten that they had been doing nothing else for the last fifteen years. And for far less money than Louis would get them, if all went well. La Grange, on the other hand, was delighted. His prim disposition was shocked by Louis' language. Used to the elaborate circumventions of the Prince's court, he could not easily reconcile himself to a man who saw things as they were, and said them straight out. But he approved of Louis' sound financial sense, and his insistence that everything should be regulated to the last sou. Louis, in turn, approved of La Grange, though he made fun of him behind his back.

"He talks like a nervous turkey," he said, "but he keeps his accounts straight. Give me a fellow like that any time. The finer a man talks, the surer you can be that he's trying to cover up something." La Grange's accounts, indeed, were meticulous. After years of adapting to the caprices of the nobility, he had no difficulty in dealing with actors' temperaments. He found they were more than willing to leave the administration to him, so long as they could shout and rage and weep and declaim at their pleasure, off stage as well as on.

"Children," he said. "Children, every one of them."

And he beamed with particular fondness on his favorite children, Armande and Molière, who in their lightness of heart were behaving as if they had been married the day before.

It was a happy company that entered Paris. The nearer they drew to the capital, the more it exercised its charm upon them. All the rancor was forgotten. Molière was their hero again; they saw him as their savior, approved of his shrewdness in acquiring so useful a connection, and lavished praise on him which should have been given to Louis. But Molière was there, and Louis was not; he was always in Paris, attending to their business.

They entered quietly, but in happy apprehension. The glory, promised Molière, would come later. The glory, snorted Louis, might never come at all, if X did not talk to Y, and Z continued to forget the little favor Louis had done him a year ago. They dispersed into lodgings, meeting only to rehearse. Molière made no attempt to see his father, and avoided any place where his family might be. So far as he knew, they thought him dead. Time enough to resurrect himself when he was successful. Joseph, on the contrary, stalked through his old haunts like his father's image, boasting of their triumphs in the south, and hinting of the great house they would select for their Paris opening. The Hôtel de Bourgogne? Nonsense. We have no time for such riffraff. No, what we have in mind is a select performance before discerning patrons. He dropped names like chaff, rising higher and higher through the social echelons.

"Perhaps—you never know—a certain party in the Louvre is interested in us. Nothing like starting at the top!" When the news came that they actually were to perform before the King, Joseph was totally deflated. He sat staring into his wine and muttering, "Whoever would have believed it. That young scamp Louis! Whoever would have believed it."

It had not, after all, been as difficult as Louis had feared. Paris was a city with a thirst for novelty, and there had been too little these last few years. The actors had all been seen, the plays all been heard. A new company, fresh from the provinces. Ridiculous, of course, but they might have something to offer. Stranger things had happened. At least it would be a change. The King, when word had filtered through the infinite convolutions of palace gossip to his ear, had been languidly pleased to promise his patronage. After all, he was his country's arbiter of the arts. If these people were as good as they were said to be, it was appropriate that he should be the first to discover them. It would be unseemly for any other patron to boast of a find that had escaped the notice of his sovereign.

And if they were bad—which was more than likely, for when did actors ever tell the truth about themselves?—he would have exercised the charity which was a monarch's duty and prerogative. In the last resort, it would give the court something to talk about. That was always desirable. Particularly now, with his advisors being so tiresome about the need for him to marry. Yes, on the whole it was a good idea.

So the royal fiat went forth. The company was overwhelmed, elated and apprehensive in turn. What should they offer? The monarch was more permissive than his subjects. Unlike the Princess de Conti, he made no stipulations. But this only increased their problems. Every play in their repertory was exhaustively discussed. For once, without jealousy. Success had unified the company. They were a family again. It was no longer a question of who would show to the best advantage, but of how their individual talents could best be welded into a brilliant, coruscating whole. Something that would so dazzle the King that their reputations would be assured for evermore. If they failed . . . but no one thought of failure. The Marquise found herself deferring to Armande. Armande respectfully consulted Molière. Louis and La Grange sat side by side and watched, for they had no part in such talk. La Grange never ceased wondering at how these flighty, unstable people could talk hard sense when there was serious work to be done; and Louis compared the Molière he saw now, mature, knowledgeable, assured, with the stage-struck boy who had embarrassed them so often when they last played in Paris together.

Molière, for his part, consulted Madeleine. For one of the joys of this adventure was that it had restored her to the circle.

For weeks he had been praying secretly that she might return. Sunk in the country, it had been easy to tell himself he did not miss her; caught in the familiar rut, he could delude himself that he no longer needed her advice. There was peace between Armande and himself now. If she still occasionally flaunted her power, he could affect to ignore it. But she rarely did. The return to Paris had brought her what she wanted.

She had no need, yet, to torment him further. But in this happy crisis, he realized how much he had been accustomed to rely on Madeleine's judgment. She would have told them unerringly what to do She would have advised, and they would have accepted. But Madeleine was gone. She had too much pride to come back. And he had too much humanity to ask her.

She came back. She walked into the middle of a rehearsal, pale and defiant, and stood by the wall, watching, not like an old colleague returning to her accustomed place but like a beggar at the feast who expects to be thrown out each moment. Molière did not see her at first. He was in the center of things as usual, reading two parts at once, prompting Armande through a difficult scene. Then he noticed that the actors around him were falling silent. Armande's voice trailed off in the middle of a line. All eyes had turned to the far side of the room, where she stood waiting to be spoken to, and then back to him.

Nervousness, eagerness made him gruff.

"Madeleine. So you spared the time to visit us."

She flushed, but ignored the sarcasm. Crossing to the center of the room, she took off her bonnet and laid it on the table.

"I would like to come back, Molière. If you will have me."

"Of course we'll have you!" shouted Garcin. "Welcome home, Madeleine! It's never been the same since you left!"

"Welcome home!" "Welcome home!" The actors crowded round her, now the spell was broken, shaking her hand, kissing her cheek, voicing their pleasure. Molière was ignored. He strode across to Louis, who was standing with his mouth open, and shook him by the shoulder.

"Did you do this?"

"I didn't! I swear I didn't! I had no idea where she was. I would have, though, if I could. The gods are on your side, Molière. This is all you needed." And he went across to add his congratulations to the rest.

Molière caught sight of Armande's face, and knew it was time to assert himself.

"Ladies and gentlemen, this is not a circus. We are here

for rehearsal, not for conversation. You are all excused for ten minutes. You too, Armande," he added, as she pouted and looked mutinous. "No, Louis, you must stay. And La Grange. This is a matter of business."

The last remark appeased Armande somewhat, and she went out with the others. He knew her ears would not be far from the door. Molière and Madeleine were left face to face, while the other two men retired into discreet corners, like seconds at a duel, to await the outcome.

"Well?"

"I told you. I want to come back."

"What makes you think I want you to come back?"

"I was afraid you would not. But I had to ask, none the less." She fidgeted, tracing the line of the floorboard with her foot. He noticed with a shock that her shoes were scuffed and broken. The rest of her dress was in keeping. Her skirt, though neat, was carefully patched, and she wore no ornaments; her face was thinner than he remembered it, and the bonnet she had dropped on the table was long out of style.

"Believe me, I did not want to come. You know me well enough to know that I'd try anything before exposing myself to this humiliation." Her voice broke, and she turned away, avoiding his eyes. "Well, I did try anything. You don't know what it's been like, Molière, these last months. It's all very well for you. You had your work, the company. But it's hard for a woman, all alone. I've been away from Paris too long. They've all forgotten me now. And I'm not a girl any longer. The theater is all I know. I should have realized that. I was a fool to go away. You have a right to your life. All I'm asking is that you give me back mine."

She looked into his face, pleading, with the tears beginning to flow. "Take me back. That's all I'm asking. For old time's sake. If I ever meant anything to you, have pity on me now. Not to act, if you don't think I'm good enough. I'll wash for you, sew for you, anything I can do to make myself useful and earn a little money to keep myself alive. Believe me, I wouldn't ask you if there were anybody else. If you ever had a kind thought for me, do this."

He was shocked, horrified. Had Madeleine, the proud, imperious Madeleine, come to this? Was it his fault?

"I offered you money," he muttered, ashamed.

"I know you did. I was a fool not to take it. I don't ask it now. I want to earn my keep. Just a small wage, and a job."

It was true. He had been cruel, unjust. He should have made her stay, explained to her. Or at least sent the money after her. Well, now he could be generous. Redeem himself. For courtesy's sake, he glanced at La Grange and Louis, but knew, without looking, the approval in their eyes.

"Of course you shall come back. And not to sew or sweep or do our laundry. We need you in the company again. We need your head, Madeleine, and your talent. I can't tell you how happy this has made me."

He bent forward to kiss her cheek, but she moved away. "No. I would not like Armande to misunderstand. If I come back to you, it must be strictly professional. Agreed?"

"Agreed. But . . . I shall have to explain things to Armande."

"Don't worry about Armande," said Louis. "Leave her to me. I'll explain things to my dear sister." He left the room to do so, and apparently explained things with some success, for when Armande returned with the rest of the company, although her cheeks were red and her eyes smouldering, she came to embrace Madeleine with the rest, and the two of them exchanged frigid but eminently polite kisses.

And so the group was reconstituted. Madeleine fitted happily into the company, and the bloom came back to her cheeks. Never by word or sign did she give any indication that she and Molière had ever been more than business partners. With the Marquise she was friendly, as among equals, and with Molière and Armande scrupulously polite. Molière relaxed when the days passed without any sign of trouble, and congratulated himself on his generosity and perspicacity. Louis swore, in private, that Molière had the luck of the devil; and even

Armande's suspicions abated to the point where she was playful with her elder sister again, and things were almost as they had been in the old days. They were all glad to have her. She worked as hard as anyone, and gave good advice when it was needed. The coming trial pulled them all together.

On one thing Molière was adamant. Their offering would be a tragedy. Louis tried half-heartedly to dissuade him. He had only seen them in comedy, and it was on this that he had staked his money. How did he know what they could do in anything else? But the others supported Molière. The comedies had been splendid in the provinces. Molière had done brilliantly with them. Perhaps one day, when they were established in Paris and he could draw on his observations of city life, he might start writing them again. But for the court, anything but tragedy was unthinkable. "To perform one of those rustic farces at court" intoned the Marquise, "would be like serving cold bacon off gold plate." Louis had to admit that they knew what they were talking about.

A tragedy, then, but which? Molière wanted *Nicomedes*, and the others thought he was right. It was the play they had originally intended for the Prince de Conti, and the same reasons held good in Paris. It was respectable; it was established; it had good parts for most of them. They had performed it often enough in Lyons, Avignon and all those other places; they could devote their time in the capital to polishing. *Nicomedes* it was, by general consent.

Which just goes to show, thought Molière, distracted by the fly again, how wrong intelligent people could be. It was not that they were bad. There was nothing slipshod in their performance, no grotesque errors that the satirists could seize on. They were well-trained people doing an adequate job of work. Adequate. That was the curse of it. Damn adequacy! There were any number of competent companies fighting for the ear of the King, trying desperately for the favor that would earn them residence. Next week another troupe would stand in their place, making the same plea, giving the same uninspired per formance. Adequacy was not enough. They had to make these jaded people sit up and take notice; they had to slap them in the face with a performance that would make them forget all plays they had ever seen before.

True, it had started badly enough. That was inevitable, thought Molière. The court must be used to it. There were so many hazards before the performance even began. The arrival, punctual to the second, at the private portal; the fuss and ceremony; being escorted along miles of corridors, through a maze of rooms, into the chambers reserved for them to dress in; most of all, the unaccustomed attentions, for King Louis, if nothing else, was civil to his entertainers, and ordered them to be well treated. And then the formal bow before the court: one show acknowledging another. Anybody would be nervous.

Molière wore a calm face for the sake of the others, but inwardly was as panic-stricken as they. His hands were so sweaty that when he gave the three knocks for the play to begin the cane slipped and rapped out a fourth. *"Four* knocks!" he heard the King whisper. "Is this play to be so much better than usual, then?" The court had tittered sycophantically, and the Marquise kicked Molière on the shin.

It was inevitable, too, that their positioning and movement should be less well-schooled than usual, for they were playing to only one seat in the room. The King sat in the center, properly aloof. The rest were arrayed at a decent distance behind him, whispering behind their hands and condescending. They did not matter. What the King thought, they would think. What he said, they would say.

Though there was one other seat that mattered—to Molière, if to no one else. In a corner, half behind a pillar, admitted as a signal act of grace to this august company, sat Montfleury, the leading actor of the Hôtel de Bourgogne. He came regularly to these soirées. He had a right to be there; he was king too, in his own domain, and like any ruler came quickly on the scent of a possible usurper. Grave and imposing, fully wigged and regally erect, he let no nuance of movement escape his eye, and checked off in his head every cadence of a part he had played a thousand times.

Madeleine had been indignant when she saw him.

"As if it weren't enough to try to please the King!" she whispered to Molière between scenes. "We have to please him, too."

"Try not to please him, you mean," said the Marquise knowingly. "If he likes us, we're failures. If he looks worried, we're a success. He hates competition."

Molière, stealing a glance across the room, had seen without pleasure Montfleury's face relax into a smile. No competition for him here. Damn him, thought Molière, he's tolerating us.

The salon was full of smells. Paint and powder, sweet and cloying, both the courtiers' and their own. Sourer smells of sweat and unwashed bodies. Not only from the actors. The aristocracy of France bathed no more frequently than the farmers of Uzès. The acrid smell of a candle that had guttered and gone out. A footman stepped forward to relight it. His movement brought Molière back to himself with a jerk. Just in time; Madeleine had stopped speaking, and it was his cue. The audience looked at him enquiringly. It suddenly occurred to him that they must know the play backwards. Why hadn't they thought of that? Why hadn't they chosen something else? Louis Béjart had been right, though he was not there to say, "I told you so." Only those with parts to play had been admitted. To their chagrin, Louis and La Grange had been kept outside, and were kicking their heels in the courtyard.

In the flurry his mind went blank. He improvised a line, and saw Montfleury raise his eyebrows reprovingly. This only disconcerted him more, and he stumbled again. Madeleine, sensing his predicament, threw him a cue which brought him back to the text. But at the same time Joseph, more nervous than anyone, prompted from the wings in a voice of thunder. A ripple of amusement passed through the court, and the King smiled. At least, thought Molière, we've stopped him yawning. He fell into the rhythm of the speech again, but the lapse had upset him, and he galloped through the words, forgetting the long hours in which he had taught himself to speak slowly and distinctly. His voice was going. There was a dull ache in his chest, his voice broke before the end of a line. Somewhere in the audience a woman said, with cruel clarity, "He hiccups, that little man!" And the laughter came again.

Ruination. One act still to go, and the play in chaos. What kept the audience in their seats? Why did the King not have the sense and mercy to rise? But no, they kept their places and gossiped through the pause. Not like a theater audience at all. Like a mob of ancient Rome, intent upon some butchery.

A hurried conference in the anteroom. Molière devastated, full of apologies. Madeleine efficient and reassuring. Armande —where was Armande? Her part was finished, she had no entrance in the fifth act. But it was against all etiquette to leave. Better this way, though. She would not see his shame.

Out before the torturers again. Joseph and Madeleine were superb, but the play was lost. The better they were, the worse Molière became. They covered up for him as best they could. Joseph even took one of his long speeches and, by twisting the words, made it sound plausible in his own mouth. It would have been effective if the whole audience had not known exactly what they were doing. Around the walls, the candles threw distorted shadows on the lords' and ladies' faces. They were no longer serenely disdainful. They looked like gargoyles, the sculpted heads of fiends. Molière, gasping, floundering, remembering a line here and a movement there, felt as though he were performing in Hell, and that every error would send him one circle lower down.

It petered to its miserable end. The actors, wan, bedraggled, (still no Armande—where was she?) stood to receive their smattering of barely polite applause. The King began to rise, and the court sighed with relief. For both sides the torture was over. In due order of precedence the company filed through the door. First in the anteroom, Molière looked wildly for some way of escape. He could not bear to look Madeleine in the face. And where was Madeleine, anyway? Had she deserted, like Armande? The others were now in the room with him, too limp to do anything except throw themselves onto stools and start to wipe off their paint. Where was Madeleine? Was that her voice? What was she doing there, still standing on the stage?

"Most illustrious majesty; my lords, ladies and gentlemen; what you have seen tonight has been a poor thing, we know . . ."

She must have lost her mind. However bad it was, you never apologized. Not even to the King. You did your best, and went away. If your best was not good enough, so much the worse. Did Madeleine think she had to grovel before these people?

"To bring our humble troupe to Paris; to perform a tragedy which you have all seen done by the great Montfleury himself . . ."

A little curtsey in the tragedian's direction. How he loved it! He was positively beaming. Molière groaned. This was getting worse and worse. Why could she not leave them to their shame? Let them slink back to the hayricks and the barnyards where they belonged.

"We wished to show you, however, that even in the country there are those who aspire to the dignity of Paris; who set their eyes on what is being done here, and do their humble best to emulate it."

A ripple of applause at this. Unexceptional sentiments, particularly from an actress. This woman knew her place. Not bad-looking, either.

"And now . . ."

Molière nearly fainted at what he heard next. She had gone insane.

". . . by way of tribute to the grace, the nobility, the intellect that has deigned to watch our efforts, we beg your indulgence for a short while more. We give you a country farce: a poor thing, but at least it will be new to you. It is called *The Doctor in Love*."

She stood with head bowed, awaiting the response. There was a pause. The court was restive. Sit through more of this? Louis harrumphed once or twice and picked his nose. Well, you never knew. It would do his nobles good to sit still for a little longer. Teach them patience. He flapped a languid hand.

"We will see the comedy."

The court forced its bodies into chairs again, and its faces into smiles. Madeleine curtseyed and walked off the stage with as much aplomb as if the tragedy had been a huge success and the King had gone down on his knees for an encore.

Molière forced his way through the other players towards her.

"Lunatic! Play a thing like that here? We can't do it! They wouldn't sit still for two seconds!"

She seized his shoulders.

"It's our only chance. We should have known that from the beginning. We can't compete with Paris on its own ground. Look at Montfleury, purring like a cat. He's head and shoulders above us, and he knows it. But the comedies are ours and ours alone. You made them. We lived them. Paris has never seen anything like them. We have to go out there and say this is us, this is what we do. They can judge us on that, and I'll accept it. But to let them condemn us because we aren't pale copies of what they already have . . . that would be the real insult."

"But we can't go on like this! We haven't rehearsed it since we've been in Paris! The last performance was months ago!" He was almost sobbing. "Another tragedy! A scene from a tragedy! We can redeem ourselves with that!"

"If I go out there and announce another tragedy they'll boo me off the stage. It's the *Doctor* or nothing."

"We're not ready."

"That's nonsense. You've given it a thousand times. You could play it in your sleep, all of you." Her eyes ran round the room. "The whole cast is here. Quick! Take off those stupid plumes. That silly armour! Get out there and show them what you really are!"

"But Armande's missing," he protested, even while his fingers obeyed her instructions. "She's vanished. Nobody knows where she is. We can't do it without her."

"I can do it," snapped Madeleine, pulling his cloak from him and clapping his own battered hat on his head. "I used to play Armande's part. Or had you forgotten?"

The voices rose impatiently outside, and a page appeared at the door to ogle the half-undressed actresses and ask if they were ready.

"You are," snapped Madeleine to Molière," and the rest of us will be, by the time we're called. Out you go." Her gaze wilted the rest of the company. "Listen for your cues. I don't care if you have to go on with your shirt tails flapping. Just go on."

As Molière raised his hands in one last protest she gave him a shove that sent him cannoning out of the door.

He staggered backwards, tripped over the page's foot and fell. Instinct and the memory of innumerable stage falls taught him to save himself at the last second. He landed adroitly and painlessly, legs splayed out, and skidded to a halt before the King. His face still wore the surprise of Madeleine's attack. The court roared at the sight of this ridiculous little man who had just made such a fool of himself in tragedy and was now determined to do it again. A flick of the King's finger, and the laughter stopped short. Their faces watched him. He had seen the same look, cruel, calculating, on the faces in the bullrings of the south.

Deliberately he prolonged the pause as long as he dared, fighting to regain his self-control. The anger seeped away from him, and he met ice with ice. These people, he thought dispassionately, as though seeing them for the first time, who are they? They dress in fine clothes, pride themselves on their taste and refinement; but at heart they're animals. No better than the rabble we played to in the south. They treat me like a performing animal. Well, I'll treat them like peasants.

And, rising to his feet, he prepared to insult them elaborately in three acts.

What he gave them was, had they only realized it, pure peasant fare. He treated his noble audience with contempt. He assumed nothing, expected nothing. He wiped from mind the fact that these were the cream of France, in whom all taste, all knowledge, all discernment was centered. On their languid painted faces he drew the gaping mouths of the yokels of Vienne and Carcassonne, Nimes and Alès; all the tricks he knew to wring laughter from the ignorant and uncomprehending he performed. Shamelessly, he hammered jokes home that a Parisian would have let go with a lift of the eyebrows, a passing allusion. He bellowed out the puns, staring defiantly at the audience as if daring them not to understand. Every farce trick learned in fifteen years of barnstorming he included now. A savage joy possessed him. He would show them what he thought of them.

In fact he could have given no other sort of performance had he tried. It was ingrained in him, he could not change it. And there were other things to think about. He had forgotten, when Madeleine so peremptorily announced the farce, how much the play depended on properties. Had she forgotten, too, or had she swept it from her mind? It doesn't affect her, he thought bitterly. He was the one who was bothered by it.

So he let his performance become automatic. The familiar words poured without prompting from his tongue. His body fell instinctively into the old routines, the familiar postures, as though he were a puppet with some invisible divinity pulling the strings. His mind raced ahead to anticipate what was missing and devise some means of supplying it. He played the doctor of the title, and the first scene was a long soliloquy in which he prepared for his daily visits. His doctor was, of course, a quack. When he wrote the play he had pandered to the countryman's suspicion of the learned. How they hated doctors, these peasants! They disliked their gravity and their Latin; they were alarmed by the fact that something which seemed to hurt a great deal could be dismissed as trivial, while a symptom that hardly mattered—a cough, a lump where no lump ought to be—was viewed with shakings of the head and dire predictions. Most of the countrymen he knew would do anything to avoid a doctor. Once you let him in the house, they thought, you might as well start ringing the funeral bell. And on the whole the rustics were right. Most of the doctors he knew were charlatans. They would promise the earth, and sell the patient a bottle of green water.

His doctor was such a one. As he arranged his bottles and phials, his picks and probes and the other sinister apparatus of his art, he smacked his lips over the people he would examine, and the tricks he would use to convince the healthy that they were in need of his ministrations. This man was a woodcutter, spent all his time in the open air and could fell a tree in half the normal time? Dangerous, that, very dangerous; for it was well known to science that the vital fluids of the body were drawn into whatever limbs were used most, weakening the others. Yes, you may have magnificent arms and shoulders, young man; what muscles, to be sure! But look to your legs! No pain there, no weakening? They stagger a little, when you drink too much? Aha! A bad sign, that, a very bad sign; for wine exaggerates the body's natural virtues and defects, and makes it easy for a trained man to see where the dangers lie. Drink this bottle of medicine, which I will sell you for only forty pistoles; give up drinking; and you will find that your legs never weaken again.

This man was eighty years old, the grandfather of sixteen bouncing children, and had never had a day's illness in his life? Bad, very bad; for was it not proved as long ago as Aristotle that each body must, in the natural course of things, succumb to several diseases in a lifetime? And he had suffered none so far? Then the next ten years would be crucial, and he might well expect to die. But, if he drank this potion regularly and lived a moderate and cautious life, perhaps the worst might be prevented, in spite of eighty years of neglect. The price? It did seem high, perhaps, but desperate cases called for expensive cures.

A mother with a child that was fat and rosy, bouncing, growing, taking all its nourishment? Dear, dear, dear. Watch out, my good woman; not for the child but for yourself. Thales of Miletus, a close friend of the Pope and the Sibyl of Cumae, had propounded that the bodies of mother and child were inextricably knit, even after birth, and exercised a planetary attraction on each other. As one waxed, the other waned. If the child grows up healthy and strong, as there seems to be every fear that it will do, you will find yourself weakening. You won't notice it at first, perhaps, but there are certain unmistakable signs, like the hair turning gray, and a refusal in the body to lift such heavy weights any longer; but by the grace of God I have a remedy for that. Drink this elixir (sixty pistoles) and I can almost guarantee you another fifty years.

Each speech was accompanied by a bottle, each bottle by a speech. Here, he had no bottles. They were not even in Paris. The players had dumped them all in an abandoned barn, assuming that they would never need them again. The scripts had been abandoned, too. There was an old trunk full of them somewhere; whoever found them was welcome to them. And now how desperately he needed these things. But no one could have foreseen that Madeleine would lose her mind.

Well, if he had no bottles, he would invent them. He would see them in his mind, and make the audience see them too. His fingers traced their imaginary outlines in the air. He conjured up their weight, substance, color. This one was green, this red. Could they see it? He could. He could almost hear the clink as he set them next to one another in the make-believe case.

This was not the worst of it. There was no furniture either. Who needed such humdrum things as chairs and tables in tragedy? None had been provided. So when the script called for him to sit down, he sat. His body scooped a chair out of the air. Heedless of the unaccustomed strain in his legs and back, he made them feel the seat, the arms; with a feat of balance that surprised himself, he even contrived to cross his legs.

They did not laugh, of course. Not a ripple of amusement disturbed the audience as the speech wound to its end. So much the worse for them. He had not expected them to. At least they were quiet. They had to be, at the King's command. He only hoped they realised what he was doing to them.

As the play proceeded, the intricacies of his make-believe involved him totally. The audience, his failure, his predicament, were forgotten. The next scene was an easy one, and gave him time to think ahead. Garcin came in, as the servant of a wealthy bourgeois household. His master's daughter was sick. She had no appetite; she could not sleep, had lost all interest in the world. Could the worthy doctor help?

The worthy doctor could, and would. He put on his cloak and hat, and made ready to hurry forth. There was some traditional horseplay with the medical bag here. He tossed it to Garcin, and Garcin, indignant at being asked to carry it, tossed it back. They made a game out of it, which continued as long as the audience was laughing. Over the years they had become adept, perfecting every variation of throw and riposte. Here, alas, with no bag, it would have to be cut. Molière was just about to exit when Garcin, turning away from the audience, caught his eye. He gave a slight, imperceptible wink. An invitation, a sign that he was ready and would play up. Well, thought Molière, what have I to lose? He picked up the imaginary bag, grunted at its heaviness, and tossed it. Garcin responded perfectly. He waited the proper time, and then received it in his arms. You could almost hear the smack of leather as it landed. A look of comic pain spread over his face. He tossed it back. Molière put out one hand and fielded it before it hit the floor. The bulk of it spun him round, and his hat fell over his eyes. He threw it again. Garcin caught it and returned it, high this time; they both stood and watched it pirouetting to the ceiling. Every eye in the audience watched it too. It came down, predictably, on Molière's head. Enough of this, he thought. Miming pain and outraged dignity, he booted Garcin through the door and made his exit, returning sheepishly to free his cloak which had somehow got caught on the latch.

End of Act One. This was where the applause usually came. Well, never mind. Now the action moved to the bedroom of the sick daughter. Her parents were in a state of desperation. The girl (Madeleine, every bit as good as Armande) responded to nothing. It was impossible to mime the bed. Madeleine, for all her talents, could not levitate herself. So she, too, sat on an imaginary chair, which seemed as solid as Molière's own. When he entered, he barked his shins on it.

The doctor was overcome. He had never seen a patient as beautiful as Madeleine. Stricken with love, he played with her hand while her parents' backs were turned. After years spent in inventing maladies, he was faced with one he could not recognize or cure. Frantically, he consulted his medical books. It would take time, but he would do it; he would devote himself to her cause, and stay by her side day and night.

Her sickness too, as it turned out, was caused by love. But not for him. For a young suitor whom her parents had rejected. But the suitor (Joseph) was an ingenious young man. With Garcin's help, he drugged Molière and eloped with the girl, who revived miraculously as soon as her lover appeared. Garcin, in girl's clothes, dropped a veil over his face and pretended to be asleep. Molière, waking and desperate, tried every remedy in his bag. From time to time he renewed his less medical ministrations. But the patient seemed to be succumbing to some sort of epilepsy. When he tickled her under the chin, a fist shot out and clipped him on the jaw. When he whispered suggestively into her ear, a well-shod foot caught him on the shin. At last the patient's struggles quietened, and he lifted the veil. There sat Garcin, eyes crossed, face contorted into a simpering moue of adoration.

"Marry me," he shrieked at the doctor, leaping into his arms.

"Witchcraft!" cried the doctor, "a changeling!"

"Treachery," cried the parents, appearing at the crucial moment. And the play ended in a chase, with Molière being thumped unmercifully and Garcin, by some mysterious means coming out on the side of law and order, doing most of the thumping.

The play's tag-line bounced against a wall of silence. They pulled themselves together, got to their feet, adjusted their dishevelled clothes and bowed. Heads high, Molière first, they left the room.

"They've got what they asked for. Pack your things," he ordered. "We're leaving."

And then a great braying laugh came from the man in the lonely chair. He threw back his head and kicked out his legs; he laughed so heartily his wig fell awry. It was the signal for pandemonium to break loose. They laughed, stamped, applauded. Had they gone berserk? Even Montfleury had forgotten his dignity and was hooting like a madman.

The little page came running back. "What are you waiting for? Come out, and take your bows again! They want you."

Molière was flabbergasted.

"But they can't like it! They never laughed! Not once!"

The page gave him a look of disdain. These ignorant provincials, who did not know the first thing about the ways of court.

"Nobody laughs until the King laughs. And His Majesty always reserves judgment till the end." He tugged at Molière's sleeve.

"Come on, for God's sake."

And they found themselves dragged on to the stage again, slapped on the back, punched, pummelled, surrounded by laughing faces. A group of courtiers surrounded Madeleine, another the Marquise, who loved it. Molière was seized unceremoniously and brought before the King. He was still wiping the tears from his eyes.

"Well done! Well done!" A fat finger wagged reprovingly.

"But it's naughty of you to make a fool of your King. Putting on that dull tragedy first, to make your comedy funnier. But you are forgiven. It was well worth it in the end."

Without turning his head or raising his voice, and addressing no one in particular, he said "See them well fed and wined. And give them a theater."

The celebration went on well into the night. Louis and La Grange, keeping their vigil in the courtyard outside, were convinced they must have been arrested.

How simple it all was, when you were a king. To make and unmake, do and undo; to bestow a theater like a bag of comfits, erase the years of struggle and fatigue, obliterate them with a word, a gesture. It was true, as they rapidly discovered, that the generosity was tempered with prudence. Or, as La Grange surmised, the generosity was the King's, and the prudence was his ministers'. They had their theater, but had to pay for it; nor was it wholly theirs. In the documents that were presented the following morning it was stipulated that they should share with the company already in residence. An Italian company, said Madeleine, we never shake them off. And Molière smiled ruefully and wondered how long it would be before they were edged out by the next newcomers to catch the royal ear. They had to fight still, to stay where they were.

But this was in the future. For the moment the elation was general, and almost complete. It even caused them to forget Armande's defection. She returned just as the signing was finished, tousled, pouch-eyed and unrepentant. The others were inclined to forgive and forget. Not Molière. He pulled her off into another room and questioned her angrily. Where had she been? Why, kidnaped, she replied, tossing her head defiantly. As she had made her last exit in the Corneille some young men from the court, bored and half-drunk, had seized her at the door. They had insisted that she accompany them on a tour of the palace. And she had gone? Of course. How could she refuse? Why had she not cried out? What? Before the King? Before the whole court? And interrupt the performance? The

youths had known she would not dare, that was what had
made them so bold. How was she to know there would be a
second play? It had not been planned, no one had warned her.
Anyway, it had all turned out for the best. Madeleine was
much better in those country farces than she.

By this time Madeleine had joined the argument, and it was
uncertain whether she or Molière would strike her first.

And where had she spent the night? With these same bold
young gentlemen, no doubt? Her eyes shone with a virtuous
indignation that would have convinced him had he not seen the
same look regularly on the stage. Of course not. She had finally
escaped from her hosts, found the company gone, and rather
than walk back through the streets alone at night had slept in
the house of an honest and elderly lady, a friend of the family
who lived down by the river not far from the palace. She could
take him there, if he disbelieved her. Or was he determined to
play the jealous lover again? Let him remember what had happened last time! Ask Madeleine! She would tell him that there
was such a friend. Madeleine, when pressed, conceded as much,
and agreed that she lived where Armande said. It might very
well be true.

Molière did not believe a word of it. But as he opened his
mouth to remonstrate, he felt suddenly very tired, and realized,
to his surprise, that he did not care. This girl, this pert, red-
faced, protesting thing, was she really his mistress? Did it
matter? Nothing mattered now, except that they were in Paris.
They had come home at last. He looked at Armande as if she
were a stranger. Paris had changed her, or him. She belonged
to the old life. He could do without her now.

But the manager was stronger than the lover. How she had
spent the night was her business and his, and for his part he
was happy to let her go. Yes, he could do without her now. It
was as if he had been ill for a long time, and recovered. His
body, even now, had a need for her; he knew this, but could
still look at her dispassionately, as one who had betrayed not
him, but betrayed the work. He would miss her. But there were

other, more important things he had forgotten. Now he was remembering them again.

She saw the change in his face, and it stopped her. For the first time in their relationship she was frightened of him. He spoke slowly, carefully, picking his words.

"How you choose to spend your time is your business. I do not believe what you tell me. It does not matter. I once thought I would kill myself if you were false to me. How foolish that seems now. You are nothing. I am nothing, compared to what we have done here, my friends and I. But deserting the performance . . . that is company business. If the years have taught me anything, it is that we exist only as a group. We have learnt and suffered together. That is what matters. Together we are strong. We must survive together, or die.

"I am not speaking to you as a lover, Armande. It is the manager who speaks to you now. What you have done to me, I do not care about. What you have done to us all, I care about deeply. You have offended the company. Then let the company judge you."

She spat at him. "Am I a child? Do you think you can still call me to order, as you did when I insulted the Marquise? Are you going to put me on trial? See if I care! Yes, I was with men last night. Why else do you think I came? Did you think I was willing to be an actress all my life? No, I'm worth more than that. I deserve better. Paris was what I wanted. The court, the life of fashion; to know men who counted in the world, to make my way here, yes, to sell my body to them if you like, but for what it was worth. I'm tired of being poor, Molière. Tired of the work and the drudgery. I want to live now, while I'm still young. Not to waste my best years, and then come crawling for sympathy, like her." With a jerk of her thumb she indicated Madeleine. "But I had no way of getting here except through you. Why else do you think I put up with you all this time? With an old man who spends most of his time wishing he was still a virgin? Do you think I enjoyed what I did with you? I hated it. I loathed the touch of your fingers on my flesh. But you are not the only stubborn one. That was what I had to do, and I did it. So do not think you can chastise me now. You still need me. And I am going to do as I please."

To judge from his face, Molière had not heard a word. He looked around at the assembled company. "Ladies and gentlemen, some punishment is called for here. With your permission, I will propose that Armande does not act with us for a month."

A month. Yes, they hastily agreed, with his cold eye on them. It was only just. Such disobedience merited no less.

She hissed an obscenity. "Is this all you have to say to me?"

When he made no answer, she turned away abruptly, and made for the door, her heels stabbing the carpet. "Very well. If that's the way you want it. Do without me for a month, if you can. It will be your loss, not mine. Do without me for a year, if you think that you are able. Or two, or three. If you send me away now, I won't come back till you come begging on your knees for me to return. And perhaps not even then."

"You fool," said Molière. "You silly little fool. I know you better than that. You will do the begging, not I."

"We'll see. I swear I'll never come back till you ask me."

"And I swear I will never ask you."

With a whisk of skirts and a slam of the door she was gone.

Molière sat looking after her, trying to summon up jealousy, indignation, resentment, all the things a man in his position ought to feel. As usual, his own emotions betrayed him. He felt only an emptiness. He could have said the words, but they would have been hollow; he could have uttered them convincingly and made Armande cringe, cry or come running to his arms, but it would have been a part like any other part, no more. Had he become callous, or simply clear-sighted? He saw her now for exactly what she was: a shrill girl, worldly wise beyond her years. He knew when she would raise her hands in expostulation and when the tears would start to flow; he knew every inflection of her voice and every posture of her body, for all these things he had taught her himself. A part of his life was over, but he saw its passing with no more sadness than he would have had from laying aside a well-read book that had suddenly grown tedious. The only thing that rankled in his mind was the knowledge that, in one respect at least, she had told the truth. She was too good an actress to lose. They would be hard put to it to go on without her. But she needed them, too, and had enough self-interest to see it. A battle of endurance, then. Let them see who would come running first.

All the same, it would be lonely without her. He looked round for consolation from Madeleine, but she had gone out long ago, with the others.

But loneliness was a rich man's luxury. There were things to be done immediately if they were to profit from the King's approval. Word-of-mouth had wings in Paris. The city would be buzzing with the gossip: a troupe of rustics had charmed the court. Society would flock to see this pastoral sensation. But word-of-mouth died quickly too: a butterfly. A week or so and they would be forgotten, drowned out by the whispers of the King's latest amour, or the new broadsheet detailing the sinister doings at the Turkish court. They had to act quickly.

Brother Louis, irritated at being removed even temporarily from his position as master planner, returned to be their gadfly. Jocular about their success, he was even more anxious to draw profit from his new investment. He heard the news of Armande with disquiet, but Molière refused even to talk about it. Under Louis' urging, Molière returned to work. The brief holiday was over. First the theater had to be inspected and new scenes made. The scraps of canvas they had carried with them through the south, ripped and tarnished with years of country dirt, would not do for Paris. Even La Grange admitted this, though he groaned at the speed with which money was being spent. The costumes must be worked over too. Some could be salvaged, but most must be made anew: they expected a rich show, these Parisians. As their new theater stood in the Palace grounds, they were served by workmen from the Royal Household who looked down their noses at provincials, and dragged their feet and their brushes. Louis swore at them in three languages.

Molière seized a brush himself, and daubed in clouds to decorate a hanging border. Madeleine busied herself with the costumes, thread in mouth, her bosom stuck with needles, moving among the seamstresses checking and chiding. Armande was nowhere to be seen. Madeleine said she had gone to live with friends. It was easiest to believe her.

Besides, Racine was in Paris. He sought out Molière at the theater and they hugged each other with joy. The fat man was full of his own good news. "I've finally done it!" he crowed. "They're playing my *Medea* at the Hôtel de Bourgogne!" He seized a golden laurel wreath from the rack of costumes Madeleine was working on, and draped it drunkenly over one eye. Strutting to center stage he adopted the posture of a Roman emperor, hand in coat, finger pointing commandingly to the canvas skies. *"Iacta est alea,"* he boomed; "The die is cast. The Church is definitely not for me. Over there, at Port Royal," and his thumb gestured vaguely in the direction of the austere seminary where he had been educated, "they're probably saying Masses for my soul."

He insisted that Molière should accompany him to the first performance; and Molière was only too willing, in spite of the demands on his time. Disdaining a coach, they walked to the theater arm in arm. The play was well advertised, but Molière was surprised not to see Racine's name on the bills. Racine shuffled his feet and looked abashed.

"Yes, they talked to me about that. They don't often do new plays, you see. At least new plays by unknown authors. Their public doesn't like them. So they're just billing it 'by an anonymous gentleman.' When it's a success, of course, they'll tell everybody it was by me. They promised me that."

It was the first time Molière had been in the theater for many years. He remembered vividly his first visit with Madeleine; he had been back once or twice when business had brought him on fleeting trips to Paris. But what a change! It was, if possible, more somber than ever, a tomb for dead language, not a theater. The hangings were black with the deposit of ages, as though dust had floated from the actors' voices and settled there. It was old, old, old. The richness of the curtains had mellowed to an autumnal glow. Patina made lepers of the gilded cherubs. Even the liveried footmen were old; they shuffled on to light the candles with a dogged air, as if performing one last act of piety before they died. The very tapers seemed to be a burden.

Racine, exercising his privilege as author, took Molière backstage, to watch from the wings. Half of Paris seemed to have the same privilege. It was all they could do to find room. There seemed to be as many spectators on the stage as in the pit. They filled every inch of space, bulging the canvas perilously and leaving no room for the actors to pass. They even spilled out onto the stage itself, forming an arc across the width of it. "It's not a theater at all," whispered Racine indignantly. "It's a salon! They've all come to see their friends!"

By judicious application of knees and elbows the two fought their way through the crowd till only one rank separated them from the stage. Racine was for advancing further, when an exquisite in the front row turned round and commanded them not to push.

"Sir," said Racine with enormous dignity, "I am the author of this play."

The exquisite lifted one eyebrow.

"Sir, I am the Comte de Modène."

For once, Racine was left speechless.

They were reduced to watching the play in fragments, over shoulders and through hat-plumes. It was no comfort that all around them were in the same position. What most annoyed Racine was that his play seemed to be the object of least interest there, an undesirable interruption of the flow of conversation. From time to time the spectators would turn their lackluster eyes to the stage, observe the characters for a moment, and then turn back to their neighbors with an air of duty done to discuss the latest news from Spain or Flanders, the doings of the King, the mode in hats . . . anything but *Medea.*

Not, as Racine grumbled afterwards, that there was anything to talk about there. To start with, it was a wonder that
the actors reached the stage at all. Several times the action was
delayed while the entering character forced his way through
the crowd. The actors were used to this, and not the least
discomposed. On the contrary, Montfleury, who played Jason,
made every entrance a royal progress, pausing to acknowledge
his particular friends. At least when he finally condescended to
perform he could be heard. Probably, thought Molière, he
could be heard in the market several streets away. All the
delicacy of the verse was lost. It was worse than Racine's own
reading. The booming voice, coming down on each syllable like
a foot squashing a flea, drove all sense from the lines and
turned them into a combination of meaningless noises. Before
each major speech Montfleury would stride to center, pause and
take an attitude; only when he was assured of the attention of
the inner circle, and his cronies on the fringes, would he deign
to begin. Nor were the others much better. Mlle. des Oeillets,
who played Medea, was too portly for the part. In addition, she
was clearly more concerned with some unseen admirer in the pit
than with her deceiving husband on stage. They were not seeing
a play; they were seeing a play dismembered, cut into as many
parts as Medea's little brother, with the actors all playing in
different directions. Medea's agonizing over her planned murder
of her children was so lackadaisical that no one could find it in
his heart to care whether she killed them or not—except that
the sooner she made up her mind the sooner the play would be
over.

There was one saving grace: a boy who played one of
Medea's children. He had no lines, but an angel's face. Whenever he appeared there was a lull in the conversation in the
wings. The ladies particularly ogled him with a connoisseur's
appreciation. Molière, too, was interested, though for more professional reasons. For this boy, clearly, the play was something
real, something to be taken seriously. As his mother towered

above him, voice vibrating, chest heaving in an ecstasy of tragic
passion, he stood perfectly still and looked at her with innocent
and trusting eyes. It was his unaffected stance, and not the torrent of his mother's words, that made apparent the monstrous
thing she was about to do. He did not posture, either because
he was too young to have learnt how, or because instinct taught
him his way was more effective. His simplicity and extraordinary
beauty won the hearts even of that blasé audience and stole the
scene. Medea, becoming aware of this, whisked him behind
her voluminous skirts and delivered the rest of her tirade into
the air.

"*He'll* never act here again," said Racine gloomily.

"Who is he?"

"Michel Baron, and far too good for them. Shows them all
up." Molière had never seen him so disheartened. The tragedy
wound to its predictable conclusion and they fought their way
out with the crowd. A circle of flatterers had gathered round
Montfleury, who leaned against the wall mopping his brow with
a perfumed handkerchief, an allegorical figure of Exhaustion.
Mlle. des Oiellets, the last line spoken, galloped into the pit and
her admirer's open arms. No one spoke to Racine. What was an
author after all? They came thick as autumn leaves these days,
when everyone in Paris seemed to be writing plays.

"I'll tear it up," said Racine. "It was a disaster. No one's
ever going to have to suffer through that again."

No, argued Molière, the play was not bad. It was the performance that had been abominable. He had been charmed by
the language when Racine had first read it to him, on his sick-
bed in the south; he had thought the play thin then. It did not
seem so to him now. In performance, it became clearer what
Racine was doing. The very lack of incident was an advantage.
He had taken a situation and reduced it to its bare essentials,
allowing the audience to concentrate on what was important.
Molière said as much. "But these people drowned it. They're still
acting as if this were a century ago. All that fustian, all that

bombast. You're Jean Racine, not Alexandre Hardy. Your lines cry out to be read with delicacy. You write for violins, and they play them with trumpets."

Racine brightened perceptibly, though he was still adamant about his play. "But I'm working on a new one," he promised. "And this will be really exciting. I've taken the story from the Greeks again. It's about Antigone."

He mused.

"Pity I can't write an *Oedipus*. But they'd never take it in this day and age. Our sensibilities have grown so delicate. You can't write about incest, not any more."

Then he reached across and seized Molière by the arm.

"Will you do it? I've had enough of these people. Do it simply, the way you think it ought to be. No pomp. No plumes. No heroics. Just good verse, sensibly spoken."

Molière was flattered, and said so. They parted in the best of spirits. Racine had already forgotten the day's fiasco and was bubbling with enthusiasm for their new plan. Molière went back to work. Did he really want to do a Racine play? He was far from sure. But he was not so deeply in that he could not retract if he had to. Besides, there was a great deal in what Racine said. A new kind of tragedy, a tragedy for our time . . . a new kind of acting. Well, it would bear thinking about.

But there were other distractions. Paris itself invited him, and the city was a spectacle not to be missed. There was change in the air. The King was coming into his own. Mazarin was old and feeble, resigned to handing over the offices of state to the appointed ruler. A new age was coming, the Parisians promised each other, an age of gaiety and freedom and light. Even the streets showed it. There seemed to be building going on wherever Molière looked.

He stood on the Pont-Neuf with Madeleine, near the spot where they had first met. Together they looked downstream. The boats were still the same, and the mudflats, and the houses leaning perilously across the water. There was some sort of fête in progress, a water tournament. Skiffs were steering at one another; in each stood a man, balancing precariously with a padded pole, trying to knock his opponents into the river. Applause drifted up from the banks as splashes marked success and failure. Barges were moored by the quayside, crammed with those who had come to pass an idle day. The change lay beyond. It was the skyline that was changing, crumbling, sprouting up into new forms. On the right stretched the gardens of the Tuileries, whose blaze of floral color they could dimly see; whose trees and hedges were trimmed and cajoled into scroll-like shapes, whose flowers were drilled with the mathematical precision of an army on parade, art defying nature. On the left, the Tour de Nesle was being pulled down. They could see the scaffolding overgrowing it, and the tiny figures swarming over the old stone. They could hear the occasional crash as a block of masonry was prised loose and descended into the water, sending up a shower as it hit the river. It was more than the destruction of a monument, it was the end of an age. The tower was as encrusted with legend as with moss. Romance and mystery had seeped into it, gapping the stones as the slow years passed. Paris had whispered the stories with awe, and crossed itself as it passed by. They told still of the queen who had had her lovers brought there, two every night; of how she had devoured them like a spider, and how, in the morning, their discarded bodies would be found floating in the Seine. And now the tower was coming down. The wind would soon blow cleanly through the gap, and some new, gracious building would arise to take its place. Their first theater had been down there somewhere, near the tower; part of their history was going too.

"It's a whole new world," said Madeleine, "and we're part of it, you and I."

Arm in arm they strolled through the city. Everywhere it was the same. Patched plaster and verminous old beams came down, cool gray stone went up. New streets elbowed the huddle of ancient buildings aside. New squares were carved out of the center of the city, symmetrical and orderly. Paris was picked up, shaken and dusted as though preparing for some celestial inspection. Some resented it; the rabble of the streets, for instance, who found themselves driven from their immemorial haunts like cockroaches before a broom. It was a safer town to live in. There were rumors that the King's financial ministers, who had to find the money for their master to spend, were alarmed by this extravagance. They played La Grange to the King's creative whims, admiring the beauty but deploring the expense. But if they expostulated, it was to no purpose. As if in defiance, the King mapped out a whole new square, the Place Vendôme, with a statue of himself in the middle, on horseback. It was to be the most beautiful square in the world.

All this Molière and Madeleine enjoyed, when they could steal an hour to see it. But daylight walks were rare pleasures, pilfered from their precious working time. At night Paris relapsed into mystery. Each month seemed to bring a new ordinance to light the streets, but the rule of the Sun King was limited to daytime. All his urging could produce only a few sputtering lanterns, which went out, or were stolen, before a few hours had passed.

As they worked, they talked. Molière and Madeleine rediscovered the companionship they had once enjoyed. He found he could talk freely of Armande now; of his infatuation, his disillusion, his new peace of mind. "It will never happen again," he said. "You can be sure of that. I have all I want now." He talked of his plans and ideas; of the thoughts Racine had put into his head of a new kind of tragedy, a new kind of acting . . . "but that's all in the future. It will take time, and work. But we'll show them!"

Paris was as eager to see them as they to see Paris. The theater was made ready at last, and the plays went well, there was no doubt of that. It worried Molière that he was still able to offer only country fare. With his actors helping, he had remembered and rewritten a few plays. They had the charm of novelty, and the fashionable public, hanging on the coattails of the court, had to like what the King approved. But all knew it could not last. He desperately needed a Paris subject, something that would reach these people on their own level and talk to them in their own words, as his earlier work had touched the country folk. But to find time to write . . . that was the abiding problem.

He knew he had arrived when an invitation was brought to him one day. They were in the middle of a rehearsal, and Molière was in his shirtsleeves, hot and tired. The flunkey handed him the card on stage, sniffing audibly at the noise and confusion. The company crowded round while he read it.

"It's an invitation to a salon. From Mlle. de. Scudèry. What does she want with me? It's impossible, I can't go. I'm far too busy."

"But Molière, you must!" Madeleine was aghast. "Think what this means to us! An invitation from the most important hostess in Paris! They've accepted you; you belong to Paris now. If you refuse, we might as well close our doors."

The rest of the company added their urgings to hers, and he bowed before the protest. It irked him to spend time in random social intercourse when he was needed in a thousand other places. But if it was a matter of business. . . . "Oh, all right. I'll go, for form's sake. But I won't stay long, and I won't enjoy it."

They dressed him with as much care as if they were sending an ambassador to the Russian court. The most fashionable clothes were borrowed from the wardrobe, his wig was curled and a chair hired; Madeleine was determined that he should arrive in style. He submitted to these attentions with bad grace, protesting that they wanted to see him, and not his clothes. Once again, he was unanimously overruled. When the day came the company turned out *en masse* to see him off, and he made a rude gesture at them as the chair bore him into the busy street. As he jogged along he forced himself into a better frame of mind. He owed it to himself and his friends to be polite. And they obviously wanted him. It might not be so bad, after all.

The chair stopped, and he descended with a flourish. He

rapped on the door, and it was opened by a portly little man who swayed as he walked and wore a permanent painted smile. His clothes were immaculate, his face shining; he was so obviously not a servant that Molière looked around curiously, wondering what had happened to the establishment, and whether it was the latest fancy of the grand to answer their own doors.

The portly man, sensing his bewilderment, smiled more widely still and bowed from the waist.

"I," he said, "am Mercury."

"I beg your pardon?"

A lift of eyebrows at his gaucherie.

"The messenger of the gods. I fetch. I summon. I give welcome. I conduct you to Olympus."

"I am flattered by your kindness," said Molière, recovering rapidly. "But if I return to my friends and tell them I was met by Mercury, they will think I am insane. You have, perhaps, another name in ordinary life?"

Mercury blinked nervously, and his smile flickered. "Paul Pellisson," he said finally, as if surrendering a secret of state. "An old friend, I am glad to say, of our hostess. And here," he went on with less confidence, as if the intrusion of normality had been too much for him, "here is Vesta. My wife," he translated.

Madame Pellisson was nothing if not vestal. She was an arid woman, thin-boned, long-nosed, wig askew. She limped a little on her left foot. Her voice was a high, whining drawl, and when she spoke it was to her husband, though she looked at Molière.

"Is this . . . ?"

"It is, my love."

"I am sure our fellow guests will be agog to see a man who has already made so much stir in the capital. Though Paris being what it is, anything passes for a sensation nowadays. Bring him, my dearest."

"At once, loving heart."

Molière made a face behind her back. He hated her on sight. She talked as though she were a surgeon performing an operation, with the French language as her victim. As they preceded him down the corridor her back became a hedgehog's, radiating disdain. Her husband, matching his step to hers, contrasted his softness to her angularity, and quivered as he padded down the hall.

There was a ripple of guests in the passage, but it was clear there was a vortex elsewhere tugging them towards some central point. This house was a honeycomb of tiny rooms. Through each door there were people, and a surge of talk, muted yet overwhelming in its totality, like a forest gossiping. The other guests stared curiously at Molière but never left their conversation. No one, Molière noticed, was listening. They would pause for a while when their part in the symphony was done, but only to gather strength for a new onslaught. And they never looked at each other. Each looked over his immediate partner's shoulder, searching for someone more interesting in the far corner of the room. Someone they were fated never to find. Molière had a sudden, definite premonition of Hell. Hades, he thought, not Olympus. A new Tantalus, a new Sisyphus, damned to an eternity of frustration. Or a whole party of Ixions, bound to one huge revolving wheel.

The conceit so charmed him that he chuckled aloud, and shocked Pellisson by his coarseness.

"Hush! We are almost in the Presence. Preserve holy silence."

They entered a large room, the center of the vortex. As in any storm, the eye was still. The scurrying and whispering had coalesced into a circle of chairs arranged about a central figure. She was reading from a large book, pouncing on the words like a kite on its prey. Her face was radiant with ecstasy, her eyes half-closed as if in a trance. The book was not necessary. She knew the words by heart, and, from time to time, would turn over a handful of pages in a token gesture. Around her every face was rapt, mute, adoring. The very tapestries on the walls seemed to listen, and the crystals of the chandelier, clinking in the sluggish air, applauded.

Only a fool or a hero could have interrupted such a scene,

and Molière, at that moment, was both. "Who is that?" he whispered to Mercury, who stood inhaling rapturously at his elbow.

Mercury gulped, and shot him a look of ungodly pain. Vesta became even more rigid, and her eyebrows shot up with such force that her wig slipped further out of true.

Either the whisper had been louder than he intended or any noise, in that charmed silence, would have sounded like a gunshot. The faces nearest to him turned in shock, and there were muttered hushings.

Mercury was torn between embarrassment at the offense and his prescribed duties as interpreter. The smile grew strained, and out of one corner of his mouth he said "Juno."

"What?"

"Juno," repeated Mercury in despair. "Our hostess. Mlle. de Scudèry. She is reading from her novel." No mere novel, his tone implied, but holy writ.

But the spell was broken. The fine voice faltered and slid to an ungraceful halt in midsentence. The soulful eyes opened, the book slammed shut and Juno rose to her feet.

"My reading must end there for today," she intoned. "It seems that we have other . . . distractions."

There were cries of "No, no!" from the audience, and angry looks at Molière. Pellisson shuffled his feet and, still smiling, did his best to appear invisible. He failed.

"Who is this gentleman?"

Pellisson reluctantly performed his mercurial function.

"Ah, the actor from the country. Then," she smiled graciously but imperiously round the circle, "we forgive you."

"We may forgive you," called a pale and intense young acolyte, "but God never will!"

"Hush, my dear friend, you are too partial," cooed Juno, delighted. "I am sure that what M. Molière has to tell us is of more value than my poor composition."

And she silenced the clamor of protest by sweeping forward to take Molière's hand and lead him into the circle.

But now there was no circle. It had shattered, as at a ballet master's signal. Its members had formed little groups of their own, and the sussuration recommenced. Mlle. de Scudéry led him from group to group and made introductions. After the first few names he gave up in hopeless confusion. Fortunately there were a few faces he recognized. Some were from court; they smiled and bowed and said vaguely appropriate things. Montfleury was there, holding a minor court of his own. They bowed to each other with mutual antagonism.

"I think you already know our Jupiter?" said his hostess.

The thunderer, thought Molière. How appropriate.

"I have frequently admired M. Montfleury's performances," he said. "Offstage as well as on."

There was some indrawing of breath at this, but the tragedian chose to take it as a compliment.

"You hit the truth, my young friend. Life at its highest level is art. Why should we make a distinction? We prepare ourselves for our performances on the stage. We choose the finest words, the most graceful movements; we charm, we move, we please. Why should we do less in our daily discourse? That is the function of gatherings like this. Our hostess," a bow, "has made a ballet of society." He tapped Molière's chest with his cane, a gesture which Molière found peculiarly offensive. "And so there are moves to be learnt, my friend. A discipline which one must accept. An elegance to which one must aspire. You will learn these things, perhaps, if you arrive in your profession."

"I thought, sir, that by being in Paris on the order of the King, I had arrived."

"Paris!" Montfleury rolled his eyes in disgust. "Paris, dear sir, is the provinces nowadays. We spend some time here, of course. But only in the waiting-room. If you ever go to Versailles, my friend, then you will know you have arrived. Then you will know what grace and refinement truly are."

"It seems," said Molière, trying to be civil, "that I must spend my life continually waiting to be called to some higher place."

Montfleury drew back on his heels, looked him up and down

and laughed. "I fear, my friend, that you are probably right." And he moved off with his sycophants, his way smoothed with the oil of laughter. Paul Pellisson was moving after him, but Molière seized his arm as he passed.

"If you dislike Paris so much, what must you think of the provinces?"

A look of alarm shot into Pellisson's eyes.

"My dear fellow, we prefer not to think of them."

"Oh yes, the country!" His hostess was at his elbow again. "Tell us of your life before you came here. We would be *so* interested."

And again, as if by magic, the circle reformed, with Molière this time in the center. He was about to speak when his hostess interrupted him.

"Now you are one of us," and her eyes flashed round the room, daring the audience to deny it, "we must give you a name. What shall it be?"

"Vulcan, of course," came a voice from the crowd, with laughter.

"Vulcan by all means. Perfect. Now, Vulcan, tell us about the country."

Faced with an audience he was happier. These people must be human, after all. Merely eccentric. He felt ill at ease in such a group. They were not his kind. He could not begin to grapple with the way they talked, their smiles, their whispers, their affectations. But they seemed to have accepted him, though they had a peculiar way of showing it. He had a name among them now; if this was their game, he would play it. Besides, did he not have a right to such acceptance? With his own theater in the capital of France, an actor by the royal command? Versailles, well, that was another thing. He would worry about that by and by. But for the moment he would tell his story, and show them that he could talk as well as they.

He talked about the country, and the circle gradually widened. He talked of his rites of passage in Paris, of the yearning to write and its disastrous consequences. Over his financial difficulties he skipped lightly and humorously. As his hearers remained attentive, he took them with him to the Midi; told of the people he had met there, how they thought and talked, caricatured a few of them, delicately, for amusement. Then he brought them back to Paris and told of his company's hopes and fears, their elation at their triumph. It surprised him that he could now speak of his country struggles with affection, how vividly he could recall the slower tongues and warmer faces of the south; how time and success had erased the dreariness and heartache and left only happy memories. He was carried away. With apologies to Montfleury, he ventured on some of his own theories of tragedy, the thoughts that had been running through his head for the last few weeks. The old heroic ways, he argued, were done; the times were changing and the stage should change with them.

Just as he was warming into his peroration, there came an imperious rapping on the door. He came back abruptly to himself, and found his audience deserting him. Some rose, all began to whisper. Paul Pellisson resumed his function, waddled to the hallway and disappeared from sight.

There was a small commotion in the hall outside—a succession of grunts and curses, the sound of wood on wood. As Molière waited wondering, the doors were flung open and, through the avenue that cleft the crowd, a chair was carried bodily into the room. The porters plodded stolidly across the carpet, looking neither to left nor right; they might have been crossing a public street. Pellisson fluttered round them helplessly, imploring them to spare the furniture. At last, directly under the great chandelier, they responded to a word from their passenger and delicately lowered the poles to the floor. The guests swarmed around the new attraction, and Molière was deserted.

"Who is she?"

He drew a look of pity for his ignorance.

"You don't know? Madame de Rambouillet."

"Is she a goddess too?"

"A *dea ex machina*, now. She hasn't walked for ten years."

Madame de Rambouillet. Of course he had heard of her. The original learned lady. Even in the provinces her salons had been famous. Once she had been the most sought-after hostess of her time. She had caused a scandal by receiving her guests in bed, sipping chocolate. The church, the stage, the state had come running to be shocked. She had made and ruined reputations, and helped to control a kingdom. And now she was a little old lady, centuries old, with a smeared face and a crooked wig, carried about like so much lumber.

The crowd poured forth to pay homage, and Molière found himself alone with Montfleury. The tragedian belched and squinted at him.

"Young man, you're more of a fool than I suspected. So you've come here to reform us, have you? Up from the country with straw still sticking in your hair, and you have the effrontery to tell us—me!—how we should play tragedy."

"That's not what I meant," argued Molière seriously. "There's a place for you and your style. There always will be. But the writers are changing. Look at Racine, and how he writes. Compare him with Corneille, with Rotrou. You ruin him by playing him in the old manner."

"Racine? Never heard of him."

"You played in his *Medea*."

"Oh, *that*!" Montfleury was grandly contemptuous. "Never again. Racine is a clerk, a popinjay who thinks he can write poetry. He nearly ruined us. Well, go your way. Never say I didn't warn you."

He stumped off, having shown, for the first time since Molière had known him, something akin to real emotion.

It was to be his day for warnings. The crowd around the old lady had thinned, and she was looking for fresh prey. A bony finger crooked and a thin voice, surprisingly impressive, commanded, "I do not know that gentleman. Bring him to me."

There were plenty of willing hands to push him forward. He

bent over the wrinkled hand that was extended to him and kissed it. It was ring-encrusted, and smelt bad; the smell of death round the corner, of unwashed old age. But the eyes were still bright, and looked at him with sardonic amusement.

"M. Molière, eh? A mummer, as I understand."

He was dignified. It would not do to be rude to her. Besides, she reminded him of his grandmother.

"I am an actor, Madame, at the pleasure of the King."

"Hmmph! And what do you act in? Tragedies?"

"Principally, Madame."

"Don't lie to me, boy. Country farces are more in your line, are they not?"

He flushed.

"It's true, Madame, that we began with such things. But in the city . . ."

"Poof! The city likes anything, so long as it's not more than a week old. Let me give you some advice, young man. Or are you too proud to take it?"

"From you, no, Madame." He meant it.

She leaned closer, and her thin hand tightened on his arm.

"This is Paris, in this room. For better or worse. They decide what is good, what is bad, what is indifferent. And they are tigers, young man. Beware of them. Drop your guard and they'll eat you alive."

She bent closer still, and the smell of her breath was in Molière's face. What had once been a beautiful woman mumbled into his ear through blackened teeth, and spittle fell upon the ruffles of his throat.

"I was queen here once. I was their Juno. I knew them all, made them all. They couldn't raise a finger or say a word without me. And now look. As soon as I've gone they'll tear me to pieces. Oh, they pretend to love me. But see them sniggering behind their hands."

Her voice grew uncomfortably strident, and Molière knew they were being watched.

"It's my own fault, I suppose. I must suffer for it. But watch them. Watch them. And never tell them anything about yourself."

She released his arm, and tapped her porter on the shoulder. With a lurch and a scuffle the terrible old woman was gone. The last Molière saw of her was her head ducking to avoid the door, but still retaining its dignity. The discarded idol was being returned to its niche.

With her going the room lightened, and the chatter once again grew brisk. Molière had no desire to resume his discourse on the theater. It was time to make his excuses and depart.

As he crossed to the door, hoping to slip out unobtrusively in the wake of Madame, the voice of his hostess stopped him short. She had emerged from another room—hiding, perhaps? —and now, safe from her predecessor, stood in the midst of her cronies.

"You are not leaving, Vulcan? I have many things still to ask you."

He sighed and resigned himself. If he was to be one of this circle he must play his part.

"Vulcan is ever at Juno's service."

"I have a question that I am sure only you can answer."

"I will do my humble best."

"I am sure it lies well within your province. My bailiff tells me he is having trouble feeding my pigs. What do you advise?"

The insult was blatant. Molière flushed, stammered, drew himself upright. The room was deathly quiet. So this was why he had been asked. He had made a fool of himself again. Flattering himself that these people were interested in his art, his plays, his theories. No, he was a sideshow, a village idiot brought into the drawing room for their delectation. It was the court performance all over again; the same sea of malicious faces. Suddenly the significance of his nickname struck him. Vulcan, the butt of the gods. The crippled cupbearer limping round Olympus, striving to please and being laughed at for his pains.

"Did you not hear me, Vulcan? What am I to do about my pigs?"

He thought he was going to choke, but somehow the words came out.

"It would not be seemly in me, Mademoiselle, to tell you how to treat your guests."

Turning on his heel, he walked home in a blind fury.

PART FOUR

Tournament and Chase

THE BLACK MOOD WAS ON HIM for days. What right had these people to laugh at him? They had no wit, no talent, no manners. Because they had inherited a plot of land and a fancy shield, or their great-great-grandfather lent his money or his wife to the King, they thought they could condescend to him, insult him, treat him like dirt. When he knew in his heart of hearts that his little finger was worth more than all their titles, all their rich estates. If he had spent all these years being insulted by farmers and peasants merely to come to Paris and be insulted by the aristocracy, then his life had no meaning. But there had to be a meaning. There was an aristocracy of intellect, which ranked beside that of birth. No. Which transcended it.

To each man his appointed place, he had thought once. Now, this seemed the braying of an imbecile. If that was his appointed place he did not like it, would not suffer it. What mattered was what you built with your own hands, your own mind, your own sweat. He had not come so far to be turned away from the door now. He would show them who he was. He would show them he was to be feared. Then they would accept him as one of them. They would not dare to do anything else.

Work was the only answer. He was glad that Armande was gone. She would only have distracted him, one way or another, and Madeleine did not. Madeleine was there to comfort and advise; she made no claims on him any longer, she asked for nothing; she was simply there. But Armande . . . he dreamt of her sometimes. Or of Madeleine's head on Armande's body, smiling at him, kindly, welcoming; and then it changed, and the head became that of a devil.

One thing at least he had learned from that sordid afternoon. It was what the old lady had said, her parting gift of advice. "Never tell them anything about yourself." How true that was. All through his life, when he had been open, he had been wounded. With Madeleine. With Joseph. With Armande. And now with those people in the salon . . . what a fool he had been. He had given them material for gossip that would last them for a month. Well, he would never make such a fool of himself again. There would be a new Molière, a private man. He would think his thoughts, and he would live for himself. No one had any claims on him now. There would be nothing but his work. There he would show the world how he felt. But in no other way.

Like every crisis in his life, this called for a gesture. His eye lighted on the diary, the repository of his occasional thoughts. He opened it and ripped out the closely written pages. There were not many; life had been too full to be recorded. But the man who was in those scribbled notes he did not want the world to see again. In future, it would all be in his head. When next he saw La Grange, he tossed the diary to him casually, and told him he could have it for a ledger. "Part of it was spoiled. I tore those pages out, and threw them away. But there's some use in it yet." La Grange, who never threw anything away, thanked him for the gift, and treasured it assiduously.

"What are you writing?" asked Madeleine.

"A play."

She ruffled his hair. "Don't be boorish, dear. What sort of play?"

"A comedy."

She made a face. "Don't snap at me. I won't bother you again."

"No, come back." He slipped an arm around her waist as she made to leave. "It's nearly finished. Read it."

She took the manuscript and settled herself on the couch. The room was quiet for an hour. Molière lay back, eyes closed, and let some of the rancor ebb out of him. The anger, the resentment, the frustration were all on paper now. He did not need to feel them any longer.

Madeleine laid down the last sheet. He noticed, with a flash of irritation, that she had, as usual, piled the pages in reverse order. Every time she read a play of his he had to go through the stack again and turn them the right way round.

"Why haven't you shown me this before?"

It was a justifiable question. It was the first time he had written anything without her at his shoulder.

"This was something different. What do you think?"

"We can't play it."

He was on his feet. "Why not? Isn't it a good play?"

"A splendid play. A brilliant play. The best you have ever written. It's what you've been looking for ever since we came here. A Paris subject. But we still can't play it."

"Why not?"

"Do you have to ask? Because you aren't inventing characters any more. These people are real. They exist. Oh, you've changed the names and tried to hide it. But they'll know. And they'll drive us out of business."

He was silent. What she said was perfectly true. He had told her little of the humiliation of that horrible afternoon, but she had found out most of it from others, and guessed the rest. It must be all over Paris by now: the baiting of the bumpkin, the barnstormer in the lions' den.

Madeleine picked up the manuscript again. "Even the title! As soon as we post it they'll know what it's about. *The Affected Young Ladies.* You'll be crucified in every salon. We might as well pack and go back to Uzès."

He was dogged. "This play, or no other. What right have they to set themselves up as judges? What right? They do nothing, produce nothing. It's so easy to be a critic. All you need is a loud voice and the right jargon. So let them suffer a little! Let them look in the mirror and see themselves! Their airs, their affectations . . . their confounded smugness! I have a right to be heard too."

They argued for the best part of the day. Molière grew firmer with each new objection that Madeleine raised. His personal sense of outrage had been pushed into the background. When he had begun the play, it had been to relieve his mind. He had to do something; this was the only way he knew to revenge himself on his persecutors. Then the play had begun, as it always did, to take on a substance of its own; to exist independently, to grow by itself on the pages, as though his hand were an unconscious instrument, a necessary mechanism by which the work must come to life. As though it had been writing him, and not he it. Looking at it objectively now, he could see, without conceit, that it was a brilliant comic idea. Two young women who were the embodiment of preciosity, who could not think a simple thought or use plain language; who lived in the rarefied world of Mlle. de Scudèry's novels, where every thought was a conceit, every sentiment a literary artifice. And to confront them with two products of the gross world they despised— servants masquerading as gentlemen—and by the small deception to expose and mock the greater. To strip away the mask of pretension. To show that smart society wore its own disguises, no less than Pantaloon and the learned Doctor, and to argue that the wearing of the mask obscured, all too surely, the wearer's vision.

Against such persistence Madeleine had no remedy but to call a meeting of the company. It was held; the play was read. There was no laughter, only grave silence. And the verdict was Madeleine's. A masterpiece, but too dangerous.

Molière pushed back his chair. Madeleine reached across the table and caught his arm. "Don't take it too hard. We'll keep it. Some day it might be possible. But not yet."

He ignored her. Surveying the room, he asked a simple question. "If I do this play, how many of you are with me? Those who are not may leave the room, and this company."

A concerted gasp went up from the assembled actors. Could this be Molière? He who had always argued so strongly for the group decision? Was he now to set himself above it?

"I know what you are thinking," he said. "I cannot blame you, and I have no explanation. I only know that this must be. It is up to you now. Make your choice."

There was a long pause. Then, red-faced and ashamed, Garcin rose from the table and left the room. Molière watched him go with regret. He could not find it in his heart to blame him. He had had a rough enough life; he could not be expected to endanger it now. Well, let him go. He was a good boy, and could easily find employment elsewhere.

Garcin was followed by three others. Molière waited awhile longer, and looked round at the handful remaining.

"Thank you. That will be all for this morning."

"We're with you, Molière, as usual," said the Marquise. "But what can you do now? Do your play, if you can cast it."

Cast it. That was the problem. With his company four short, what could he do? He would, of course, play the leading role himself. This was taken for granted by everybody. It was a tribute not only to his acting ability, which was considerable, but to the fact that he composed for himself. He wrote the way he talked. Familiar with his own voice by now, its powers and its failings, he could compensate where necessary in the writing. By splitting up a line, he could give himself a pause for breath. The catch in his throat, which he had hoped would vanish with

time, had in fact become more obtrusive. He often found himself wheezing on the stage, unable to pronounce the next elusive
syllable. But when the script was his own, he could turn the
hazard to comic account. The more he stammered, the more
the audience laughed, and he could usually contrive to introduce some piece of business while he fought to catch his breath.
Madeleine worried over this, and fussed over him in a motherly
way. "It's this damp Paris air," she said. "You were better in
the south." It was true that Paris seemed continually cold. The
gray stone of the palace made perpetual winter. No wonder
Louis spent so much time at Versailles. In the unheated theater
the actors were continually chilled. The courtiers were used to
it—or at least were sufficiently accomplished performers themselves never to reveal discomfort. It took stamina to live at court.
Most of all to be King. His Majesty lived a life without
warmth. The Sun King dined off gold, as kings must; and by
the time it had been served to him with all the ramifications of
protocol, the food was already gelid on the plate. All his life
the King had never had a hot meal.

For himself, Molière laughed off Madeleine's fears. Work
kept him warm. There was no time to be sick. The new play
would be more demanding than ever, and he could use the
cough—which was nothing, after all—to particularly good
advantage. But what about the others? He needed two more
good men. Any he tried to hire would raise the same objections
as those who had left, and he was not anxious to have news of
his play leak out before it opened. The company would be loyal
and silent; he could not vouch for any newcomers.

He was in his room late one night pondering the question,
and almost convinced that he would have to give up his obses-
sion after all, when there was a knock at his door. He opened
it and found Louis and La Grange standing there. They both
looked unusually diffident. La Grange, for once, spoke first.

"We know what trouble you're having, and we thought we'd
like to help. You see, I . . . Louis . . . Louis and I . . ."

He looked appealingly at Louis beside him. Louis stepped into the breach.

"What he's trying to say is, why don't we act for you? We're here; we have the time. And nobody's likely to scare us away."

Molière threw back his head and let out a long roll of laughter.

"Why, that's wonderful of you. But it's just not possible." He pulled himself together as he saw their indignant faces. "I mean, how could you? You've acted a little, Louis, but that was years ago. And La Grange has never acted at all."

"And what's more," said La Grange, "I don't want to. I'll hate it. But if it's to help you, I'll try anything. I've been with you long enough; you know I've watched all the rehearsals, almost every performance. I think I can do it."

"Of course he can," bellowed Louis, recovering his confidence. "Look at him, man. He doesn't need to act. Look at those legs! Look at that moustache! You only have to push him on the stage and he'll be a sensation."

"But what about you?"

"I," said Louis, with sublime assurance, "can do anything." Like all ridiculous ideas, the more Molière thought about it the more reasonable it sounded. Why not try? It was this or nothing.

"All right. I think we can do it. But you'll have to work like slaves."

"We will," they assured him. And they did.

They all did. *The Affected Young Ladies* was demanding. Louis took to it like a duck to water, a fact which annoyed Molière not a little. Why had he had to serve so arduous an apprenticeship when this little pipsqueak learned so naturally? It was infuriating. La Grange was another matter. As soon as he walked on the stage he lost all coordination of his limbs. The memory that retained whole pages of accounts faltered over a simple half-line. He had to be taught how to stand, how to walk, how to speak. Molière spent hours in private coaching, going over the part word by word; when he was tired or had other work to do, Madeleine took over from him. "Don't be too hard on him," she said. "It reminds me very much of how we first taught you."

There were other things to take up his time. Racine was constantly in the theater. His new play was finished, and, as he had promised, Molière's company was allowed first sight of it. They soon discovered that Racine was a worrier. Molière began to have a sneaking sympathy for the Hôtel de Bourgogne. *The House of Thebes* was read by the company, and Molière pronounced it not quite ready. It was a good subject.

Racine had taken the story of the doomed house of Oedipus and watered it down to suit the taste of his time. Incest was ruled out; the tragedy was a crisscross of love affairs, none of which ended happily. But Molière was not yet convinced that it would play. The language, as always, was beautiful. But was it strong enough? Would the ordinary public understand it? He made a long list of suggested changes, and Racine tore it up and threw it in his face. *The House of Thebes* was holy writ for him. Every word was wrung out of his soul; to lose even one was like sacrificing a finger. Molière pointed out that several couplets were redundant and ought to be omitted. Racine countered with four or five arguments why the couplets should exist, demonstrated their necessity to the structure of the work, and showed how they revealed fine shades of feeling that were essential to his conception of the characters. If Molière won a quarter of these arguments he thought himself successful. He staged a trial rehearsal, letting the actors walk through with their parts. It went well until Racine discovered that two lines had been cut without his knowledge. He went off in a blazing temper, and would not speak to Molière for days. Molière, privately, was not wholly displeased, but when he found out that Racine had made the round of their mutual acquaintances complaining of conspiracy and pouring all manner of charges on his head, he wished he had not done it. *The House of Thebes* was allowed to lapse. It was just as well. They needed all their efforts for the comedy.

In spite of their attempts at secrecy, by the time *The Affected Young Ladies* opened all Paris knew about it. The wildest rumors were circulating: that it was a veiled caricature of the Academy; that it preached license and immorality; that it caricatured a prominent hostess, in the manner of old Aristophanes, by name. The last rumor was the favorite, the name of the lady in question varying according to the informant's particular prejudices. Molière was worried that the play would be stale before it had even opened, or that the public would be disappointed when they found him naming no names. Louis, who had spread some of the rumors himself, was noisily optimistic. "It's bound to work," he crowed. "You've written the perfect play for Paris. They can write in their own names. If the cap fits, let them wear it!" And he went back with gusto to his new profession as actor, strutting about the stage, gesturing and snarling with inexhaustible vitality.

In the end they were both right.

The opening performance was a triumph. Never in its wildest dreams had the company imagined a day like this. The benches were packed for hours before the raising of the curtain. All Paris had sent servants to hold places. Three or four fights broke out in the auditorium, and had to be quelled by the Palace guards. Two benches and a quantity of candle-sconces were broken. One elderly dowager broke all precedent by arriving two hours early herself and sitting doggedly through the uproar, claiming that in a matter of scandal she did not trust her servants. When one more person crammed into the building would have brought the walls tumbling down, Molière gave the signal for the curtain to rise. Though he had long ceased to be a devout man, he prayed a little then; and La Grange, in the wings opposite, gave him a sweaty wave of encouragement.

First came a curtain-raiser, a short farce that was received by the audience with undisguised impatience. This was not what they had come to see. Recognizing the inevitable, the actors gave up all pretence of performing and gabbled through their lines. "It's a madhouse!" whispered Louis as he crossed upstage of Molière in the middle of a scene. "They'll tear the place down!" Sure enough, an ominous chant began to be heard, and stamping feet, and clapping of hands. "*The Young Ladies! The Young Ladies!*" Molière knew when he was beaten. Stepping to the front of the stage he raised his arms for silence. It was instant and absolute. He held the pause as long as he dared and then made a characteristic grimace. Instantly the audience was on his side. He held them in his hand and played with them.

"My lords, ladies and gentlemen . . . it seems that you are trying to tell me something."

Laughter.

"We had hoped to offer you a full entertainment by commencing with a little farce. But if it is your will that we proceed with the main play ..."

"It is! It is!"

He talked to them a little longer . . . oh, so humble. But there was method in it. The curtain fell at his back, and behind it a minor miracle was occurring. The setting for the farce was whisked into the flies. Sweating stagehands did in seconds what they had previously done in minutes. Actors and actresses, forgetful of modesty, climbed into new costumes that were tossed to them from the wings. La Grange, hopping desperately on one foot, cried "The other shoe! The other shoe!" God damn you all to Hell, the other shoe!" They had never heard him so blasphemous before. And then Molière, having teased the audience as long as he dared, and whipped its impatience till it was a great beast lunging for his throat, stepped through the opening and gave the signal.

Knock, knock, knock.

Like three slaps in a rival's face with an open glove. Like three blows struck by the challenger on the shield outside the ogre's castle. Like three blasts on the trumpet at the Day of Judgment. *The Affected Young Ladies* had begun.

It was an immediate, extravagant, hysterical success. When they gathered on the stage afterwards, numbed by the applause that came washing through the curtains after they had fallen for the fifteenth time, they did not know which to talk of first. Molière's performance, of course. As Mascarille, the leading impersonator, he had outdone himself; he had been superb. The precise blend of coarseness and mock-refinement. The glib way in which he tossed off fashionable phrases, his eye closing in a half-wink as if to insinuate that a gentility so easily aped was worth very little. The girls, with their preposterous talk: the air of gravity with which they had complicated the plainest statements, their delight in their own conceits. Even Louis and La Grange had come off brilliantly. Louis, of course, was not really acting. Those who knew him saw that he was only continuing his everyday performance. For Louis the curtain only descended when he went to sleep. Not that La Grange had been acting any more than Louis. He was his usual offstage self, stuffy, nervous, pompous, over-precise. Molière had simply used these qualities and built them into the play. On the stage La Grange gave a superbly comic performance of himself.

But it was the play, all agreed, that had worked for them. All knew where the credit should go. They were flushed with the sense of having been a perfectly integrated group gathered together to perform a masterpiece; they came up to Molière one by one and apologized for ever having doubted him. And how the audience had taken it! Every joke, every allusion: how many times had they had to stop, while the laughter cascaded about their ears?

"I was wrong," said Madeleine, embracing Molière joyously. "Paris knows how to laugh at itself." And Louis was happy, because he had been proved right; and La Grange was happy, because he could foresee a long string of golden days at the ticket window.

And Molière was exhausted, and empty, and indifferent to the shouts and plaudits, and went home to sleep till noon.

By common consent, the company did not attend morning

rehearsal. It was taken for granted that such a triumph deserved
a breathing space. There was no need any longer for notices or
announcements. They lived as one, thought as one. Molière
knew that, when he arrived, the theater would be dark and
deserted. This was how he liked it best. He had come to the
point where the performance itself was dissatisfying to him. It
was the preparation, the act of creation, that he enjoyed. He
liked nothing better than to stand on the deserted stage, this
empty box that could, at a touch of a hand, produce wonders.
He liked to go over the last day's performance in his mind, to
recreate it word by word and move by move; to emend, to
improve, to modify. In his mind, there were already groupings
that could be rearranged for a happier effect, an entrance that
had been one beat too slow. He looked forward, too, to walking
round the front of the building; to seeing, in the shelter of the
colonnades, the lines of people already forming, long before
the ticket window opened. To enjoying, in advance, the second
triumph they would have that day, and for many days thereafter.

There were no lines, no people. Inside and out the theater
was blank, anonymous. As if yesterday's success had never been.

Molière was alarmed, confused, unable to understand. Had
he possibly mistaken the day? Could it be the Sabbath, when it
was anathema to play? How could he have been so stupid? But,
as he listened, the sounds of workaday Paris came to his ears.
The vendors in the streets, the carts rumbling. No bells to call
the people in to Mass. All was as usual, excepting here. War, or
plague? Impossible. Nothing could have happened so fast. He
would have had due warning, at home or in the streets.

When he saw the playbills announcing *The Affected Young
Ladies* with CANCELLED scrawled across them in a firm official
hand, he felt like a man who walks into a churchyard and sees
his own grave.

A cough broke the silence. In a corner of the colonnade,
half-hidden behind a pillar, a man had been watching him. His
clothes were dim, his manner noncommittal; clearly an official
of some sort. His mouth was pursed against some casual

imprudence—drawn so tight, in fact, that there seemed to be some powerful suction operating from inside, against which he had to struggle to pronounce the shortest syllable.

"M. Molière?" A step forward, a bow. Courteous at least. Molière acknowledged his name.

"I am commanded to deliver you this order, sir."

It was a fair thing, written in an ornate official script, sealed and ribboned. Molière had never seen a death sentence so elegantly composed. It came as no real shock to him, for he had known what it would contain since he saw the additions to his playbills. It was signed by a high official of the court, and declared that all performances of "the comedy entitled *The Affected Young Ladies*" were prohibited until future notice.

"Why?" he raged in his impotence. "Why?"

The messenger was nervous at any suggestion that he might be asked to commit himself.

"I regret, sir, that I am empowered to give no information on that point. I was charged simply with delivering the document."

He bowed again, formally, and went his way. Then, at the end of the colonnade, he stopped, looked around him with an expression that could only be described as furtive, and returned.

Molière regarded him dully. "Well?"

"Permit me to observe, sir . . . solely in my capacity as a private citizen. . . ."

"Get on with it, man."

The officer's voice sank to a conspiratorial whisper.

"I attended the performance last night, sir. I found the comedy very entertaining. Very humorous indeed."

And with that he fled.

When the actors arrived, they found Molière sitting on the steps, the document at his feet where he had dropped it, his head in his hands. Louis was furious, and started tearing the offending playbills from the walls. Madeleine was clearly trying to restrain herself from saying "I told you so." The others gathered in groups and discussed the disaster. From the sidelong glances that they threw at Molière, it was clear that he was being blamed.

Only La Grange was philosophical.

"It was bound to happen," he argued. "You can't make some of the most influential people in Paris smart and hope to get away with it. They have influence. They've used it. It's up to you now. Show them you have influence too."

"How?"

"See the King. Go over their heads. Appeal to him, personally. He'll be sympathetic. If not—well, we've nothing to lose."

"I can't." He was suddenly frightened. "I don't know how to deal with kings. They were right, those people. I'm just an ignorant lout from the country. I thought I was so clever. Thought I could stand up to them. And they reach out their little finger and squash me."

"You pleased the King before."

"I was acting then."

"Act now. The suppliant's part. Swallow your pride, take your hat in your hand, and move him."

"Louis must do it."

"Louis won't," said Louis, who had torn down all the play-bills he could find and was muttering among the debris. "I'm no use at that kind of negotiation. Backstairs, yes. Plotting over the tavern table. Slipping bribes into a gentleman's hand when he pretends he isn't looking. But not this. It's not my level."

"You have to go," said Madeleine. "We all depend on you."

And so he went like a whipped dog that comes skulking in at the door to find if he has been forgiven. Responsibility, he thought, will there never be an end to it? Will there never be any security? Never a time when I can relax, and write, and be happy?

In the end, it was surprisingly easy. Perhaps they had not thought that he would try. At any rate, there was no attempt to circumvent him, or steer him into the yawning maw of the palace bureaucracy. He sent in his name, and won permission to attend in the waiting room at the King's next levée. Armed with foreknowledge, he took good care to be there early. The room was crowded with petitioners, rich and poor, commoner and noble: King Louis made a great show of democracy. By dint of kicking and shoving he won a place in the front rank, and saw the solemn procession of officials that attended the King's first waking moments. They filed before him with the royal shirt, the royal chocolate, the royal chamberpot—the last in chased silver, carried like a chalice to serve its function in the mysteries behind the closed bedroom door. Then the inner circle of the court, the swaggering, arrogant nobles, whose privilege it was to observe the monarch putting on his breeches and who would have cut off an arm rather than miss this elevating spectacle for a single morning.

Finally, with much pomp and a great thumping of stewards' wands, the King emerged. He had slept well, and was inclined to be jocular. Looking around the crowd, he acknowledged a bow here, a curtsy there. Some faces he passed by without a glint of recognition, and in these cases the luckless recipients of his inattention tried to make themselves invisible and slunk out of the door. If their petitions were inscribed in diamonds upon cloth of gold, they would not be noticed now.

And then the King passed by Molière and saw him; and he smiled. He was truly called the Sun King. At that smile, Molière was warmed. His spirits rose again. There was a perceptible murmur of respect from those around him, and they pressed forward as if by touching him they could attract the royal favor to themselves.

Greatly daring, Molière stepped out of line and knelt before his ruler. Unconsciously, he fell into a theatrical posture: a shade more flamboyant than etiquette demanded, his body a shade too studiously arranged, his whole aspect pleading for attention.

There was a long silence, in which his heart leaped. What had happened? Had he done something wrong? Had the King walked by and left him kneeling? He did not dare raise his head to look, but felt the hot flush of humiliation steal over him again.

And then, by the grace of God, the King was still there; and the King laughed.

"By Our Lady, M. Molière! When you pounce out at me like that, you make me feel that I am on a stage, and have forgotten my lines!"

The whole room was laughing now. It was clearly the best joke anyone had ever heard.

Molière was on his feet now, stammering his carefully prepared speech. Before he had said half a dozen words, a crooked finger cautioned him to silence.

"I understand," said King Louis, "that you have offended a number of my good subjects."

Molière was unprepared for a dialogue. Forgetting his argument, he improvised, gave vent to his suspicions, named names. Again the royal finger hushed him.

"Be discreet, sir. The first rule of court gossip is to leave as much as possible to the imagination."

Laughter again. Molière fought to keep his dignity.

"I shall be discreet, Your Majesty, and brief. By Your Majesty's gracious permission, I am allowed to play here. I ask only that I may continue my art without interruption." And he held up the offending document for the King to see.

Louis brushed it aside.

"I know, I know." He looked round at his courtiers. "All my subjects seem to be so damnably eloquent. Which do you think I should offend?" Then his eyes returned to Molière, and he smiled again. "Very well, actor. You may perform your play. Let them talk about each other. It will stop them talking about me."

Molière was on his knees again, babbling his gratitude. But the procession had already passed, and the stewards hustled him out because he was taking up too much room.

La Grange was triumphant.

"It's the best possible publicity we could have had. Everyone will come to see us now! We'll be able to charge double prices!"

He went off, beaming, to arrange it.

Louis was impressed.

"I wouldn't have thought you could do it. I must have taught you more than I knew. Well," he crowed, "that'll show them. Nothing's going to stop us now."

Madeleine was not so certain.

"This won't be the last time," she said. "They'll try again. We mustn't fool ourselves. Don't you see how chancy it all is? Suppose the King had been in a bad mood? Suppose he'd even eaten something that disagreed with him. We might all be in prison."

But they laughed at her, and went about their proper business.

Madeleine, as usual, was right: only this time, it would not be a matter of intrigue but of outright war. And it would begin, like all wars, with a bombardment.

But even Madeleine did not claim foresight. There was a lull between, a happy time. La Grange spoke sternly to Molière about his financial responsibilities, and argued that, while some people were fair game and it was permissible to provoke them a little, it would not do to make a habit of it. Molière was only too happy to agree. He had had enough trouble for a while. Thank God it had ended happily. Time now to take things quietly, to bask a little in the sun. He promised to be good, and to provoke no one. Amenability, it seemed, was general. Shortly after Molière's visit, great news had come from court. The King was to be married. Perhaps it was this that had put Louis in such good humor. France had been growing restive, sighing for a queen. There had been too much gossip, too many whispers of the royal liaisons. Pardonable, of course, in one so young, but the time had come to settle down, and ensure the continuity of the line. It was known that the royal advisors had long been urging a suitable match. Suddenly, and so far as could be seen, happily, the King had agreed. France breathed again, and sat back to celebrate. The actors caught the mood of the times. No one wanted controversy. Molière took to his desk again and worked up an old Italian play that was guaranteed to please.

The only person who was not delighted was Racine, who chose this moment to appear with a new version of his tragedy. The period of waiting had softened him. He was now prepared to accept Molière's changes, or rather had worked himself round to the point where he believed he had initiated them himself. He arrived in a forgiving mood, all smiles, and at once turned sullen when they put him off. Molière and his companions tried to make him see reason. "I know you want to see your play performed," said Molière. "So do I. But not yet. Six months ago the public might have been ready for it. Now it's not. The people want happy things, not Greek horrors. And if we do it as we want to, it will mean a fight. An open challenge to the Hôtel de Bourgogne. A new way of playing tragedy. We've just had one battle, and I'm not sure I'm ready for another."

Racine was unconvinced, and talked offensively of the light value of an actor's promise. In the end they persuaded him. Do it now, they said, and we'll have no audience. A good play keeps. The longer we wait the stronger it will be. So Racine went off, still muttering, and Molière returned happily to his pen and *Sganarelle*.

It was generally agreed that neither the wedding nor the play could have gone better. May was rainless, by royal command. Boats jammed the Seine, fireworks colored the night skies and tinted the pinnacles of Notre Dame, and Louis married his Spanish princess amid universal rejoicing. Paris was *en fête*, and Molière was part of it. His play was given for the first time at the celebrations. The royal couple attended, and the King, forgetful of his own protocol, laughed to split his sides. This time no one was offended except an obscure Paris librarian, who earned brief notoriety by insisting that the central figure of the comedy was a satirical attack on him. His acquaintances pointed out that this could not be so. Molière had written about an imaginary cuckold, whereas it was common knowledge that the librarian was a cuckold in earnest. The affair subsided into ridicule, and no more was heard from him.

A few days afterwards the bombardment began.

After the celebration of the marriage, Paris had gone back to its working clothes. The city was sated with enjoyment, tired and cross. The people in the streets were irritable; they scurried past with a frown, as if indignant over time lost. Limp flags and streamers floated down the Seine. The city had a dirty, disgruntled look, like a child that has been up too late at a party. Even the gossip was starting again. Paris had a myriad tongues, and could not hold them still for long. The subject was still the King. A new scandal: even during the marriage ceremonies, it was said, he had been more attentive to his sister-in-law than his new Queen. Not that one could blame her, poor lady, for reciprocating any attentions that might come her way. She had few enough from her husband, who pursued the young men of court with as much zeal as his brother did the ladies. But at that point prudence hushed the talk, for such behavior was a capital offense, and even to talk about it dangerous. Fortunate for Monsieur that he was above the law. Paris licked its lips and watched, the great *voyeur*, in salacious anticipation. In the salons the erudite talked of Jupiter and Ganymede and found safety in mythology. And there were some in the salons, too, who looked not at the court but at the theater, and smiled like cats, awaiting what they knew would happen.

The company did not share the general malaise. As usual, they were too busy. *Sganarelle* played to packed houses, and Molière had picked up his work with Racine again. He was also writing a new play of his own. The subject was a mystery. He resisted all attempts to probe. Even Madeleine could not find out what it was. Oblique investigations he turned aside with a smile; direct questions met only with a finger to the lips and "Wait and see!"

They were rehearsing in the forenoon when the noise began. Ordinary noises they were used to. Paris was never quiet, and the building that housed their theater stuck out awkwardly across the narrow streets so that traffic perpetually washed round its sides like jetsam on a reef. Since their first great success, there were few days when the public did not clamor round the building. They crowded the window, spilled out into the street and annoyed the coachdrivers and draymen still further; they intruded backstage for a sight of the actors, so that several times a day the seats had to be cleared of trespassers. No one minded this. It was part of the air the actors breathed, a visible sign of success. Molière had long since grown accustomed to it. He no longer objected when the Marquise flirted with her admirers—a new one every day, it seemed—in the parterre between scenes of the rehearsal, or when Louis conducted his business negotiations in the foyer. The stage alone was sacrosanct. This he insisted on. Any visitor who intruded there, however high his rank, was urged unceremoniously to leave. It was the magic ring where they created their own silence and worked in peace.

On this day, the magic was abruptly broken. There was only a little noise at first, a muffled thumping that made the actors pause in mid-speech and look at one another questioningly. The chandeliers rattled, and a single crystal drop was shaken loose and tinkled to the stage at Molière's feet.

"The skies are weeping," said a wit. "Are we so bad?"

They laughed, but not for long. The noise redoubled in volume, culminating in a series of thunderous crashes that made them look instinctively for cover. A storm had broken loose inside the building. The chandeliers were all swaying drunkenly now, and somewhere in the recesses of the theater they could hear bricks falling, and the crash of breaking glass. A closer crash, a scream, and the Marquise came running from the dressing-room, her face anguished.

"My costumes! My costumes! They've ruined my beautiful costumes!"

They stared at her aghast. Her hair was snow white. She shook her head violently and they spluttered in the cloud of dust. It was plaster.

"An earthquake!" coughed La Grange. "Outside, everybody!" Dreading what they might see, they ran through the foyer and out into the street. Once in the open air they pulled up short. There was no storm, no earthquake. The disaster was local and man-made. While they had been rehearsing a web of scaffolding had crept up the theater's façade. It was alive with workmen, masons and carpenters hammering and sawing. On the roof above the dressing-rooms a gang attacked the slates with hammers. Others were prising stones from the walls. Even as they watched, a cornerstone gave way and brought a pile of rubble cascading into the street. The air was full of dust and curses.

Purple with fury, Molière rushed at the nearest workman and tore the heavy hammer from his hands. The lout stared at him in surprise, as if a gnat had bitten him; then, placing one huge hand on the playwright's chest, he sent him staggering back against the wall.

"What do you think you're doing?"

"What are you doing?" yelled Molière. "Have you all gone mad?"

He was like a man berserk, running among the workmen, tugging at their shoulders, trying to prise the tools from their hands, ordering, imploring them to stop. They took not a scrap of notice.

"Nothing to do with us, mate," said a great ox of a fellow with greasy hair tumbling about his eyes. "We got our orders. Talk to the foreman, if you got any complaints."

They found the foreman on the far side of the building, supervising the demolition of a pillar. They already had the ropes and tackle fastened, and a team of horses stood ready along the street to take up the strain when the word was given. With one eye on the column and the other on the men who hung round it prying it loose from its foundations, the foreman had no inclination to answer questions.

"Players? I don't know about no players. All I know is, this building's to come down, see? Widening the road, I reckon. Been on the list for months, this has. Whoa, mates! Take the strain; easy now!" His men hauled out the last brick from the base. "Stand clear, lads! Let her come slow!"

Come she did, but not slow. With a rending crash the column fell in one piece, bringing half the awning with it. A precarious caryatid, deprived of her support, dangled aimlessly from the parapet. Molière seized the foreman's shoulder again. A flying splinter of masonry had cut him over the eye, and sent blood streaming down his face. He did not notice it. The horses were already dragging the shattered column down the street.

"This is incredible. There must be some mistake."

The foreman, less preoccupied, looked at him with a not unkindly eye. Molière was caked with dust, with which the blood had mingled to grotesque effect. His hands were shaking and his mouth working in fruitless rage; but some trace of his stage clothes could still be seen, and the foreman began to suspect that he might be speaking to a gentleman. Safer to take no chances. He tugged at his forelock and produced a grubby piece of paper.

"No mistake, sir. This is orders. Look for yourself. From the King's Architect in person. Been on our list for months, like I said, sir. Should have got to it long since, but we been busy, very busy. Deal of building going on these days."

Molière stared at the paper dumbly. The words swam before his eyes, and he had to hold his head in his hands to make sense of them. It was an order, sure enough, dated from before his occupancy of the building. The whole structure to be demolished and the ground to be levelled off.

"But didn't they tell you . . . didn't they say we had our theater here?"

Only an actor, said the foreman's face. His manner underwent a rapid change.

"Don't know anything about that. Place was empty, so far as I knew. Out of the way now. We got work to do here." He marched across the street to give more orders.

"But everything we have is in there! Our scenery! Our costumes! Everything!"

"Better get them out quick then, mate, hadn't you? Look alive, boys! We want this front down by nightfall!"

They marched in a body to the King's Architect's office, looking like tramps, scarecrows, revolutionaries. The architect was in but not inclined to see them. They disregarded this, and forced their way through the scandalized clerks to where M. Ratabon sat over his plans and instruments. He heard them out—he had to—but was no more helpful than the foreman had been, and hardly more civil.

"Of course I'm sorry that you've been inconvenienced, M. . . . Molière, is it?" he said, peering at them severely over his spectacles. "But we had no instructions that the building was currently in use. If we had, you would have been served due notice."

"But the King gave us the building himself! He must have known!"

The spectacles grew frosty and the voice more stern.

"I should advise you not to talk like that. It is, to say the least, in bad taste. Almost treasonable. His Majesty has a thousand claims on his attention. Do you expect him to remember every detail? Think yourself lucky to have had the place for so long."

Molière controlled himself with an effort.

"For us, sir, it is not a detail. It is our whole livelihood. We have no place to play now. Not even anywhere to store our things. Your error, sir, has beggared us."

Ratabon by now was equally angry. "It was no error, M. Molière. The building of which you had the temporary use is nothing. An eyesore. A nuisance. See here." His voice warmed a little as he turned to his plans. "See how it broke the flow of traffic. How it destroyed the symmetry. And see what we plan to do with it. An ornamental fountain here. And here, a mall. . . ."

"Damn your fountain and your mall!" Molière swept the plan to the floor, and a scattering of quill pens with it. Ratabon leaped in alarm, and began to back towards the door. He clearly thought he was dealing with a madman. Molière continued to advance upon him.

"The building, yes, that is yours, I suppose. There has been some mistake. Yours or someone else's. I shall find out. If it is yours, you will pay for it." He spat this out with such ferocity that Ratabon, retreating in terror, tripped over a stool and fell sprawling on the floor. His spectacles were broken, and he groped for them blindly. "But what's inside is ours. We must take our things out, can't you see that? If we lose them we're beggars. God damn you, man, have you no humanity?"

Ratabon, still groping, squeezed behind a desk to shield himself from the menace of this assault. His hands flapped helplessly. A spreading stain on his breeches displayed the measure of his terror.

"If you don't call your men off I'll . . . I'll . . . God help me," said Molière, collapsing on a stool himself and dropping his head in his hands, "I don't know what I'll do."

Seeing him break down, Ratabon took new courage. He pulled himself to his feet, and his voice rose to a squeak of fury.

"Get out of this office, do you hear me? Get out! If you or your companions ever come here again, I'll call the King's Guard and have you arrested. As for your rags, your geegaws, get them out as best you can. I have important work to do. I don't intend to hold it up for a pack of painted ruffians and prostitutes. Get out, do you hear?"

He ran at them, supported by a number of his clerks, and would have done them or himself some injury if Molière and his companions had not already gone.

They had to wait till nightfall to get back into the theater. The workmen had already started ripping out the seats and loges, but mercifully the stage and dressing-rooms were still intact. They worked all night by lantern-light, salvaging what they could. Some of the costumes had been ruined by dust. There were rents in the scenery, and not one chandelier remained unbroken. All that was still useful they stored in baskets, in sheds belonging to some friends nearby, and in a makeshift shelter they patched up out of old lumber and canvas in a corner of the gardens. Then, still filthy and their eyes hollow from lack of sleep, they held a counsel of war.

There was only one thing to be done. Molière must go to the King again.

This time, his enemies must have been better prepared. It took him four days. He asked permission to attend the levée and was refused, contemptuously, by a chamberlain who eyed his haggard face and third-best dress and told him to be about his business. Then he sought interviews with various nobles he knew to be close to the King who had attended his performances and laughed at them, made love to his actresses and would, he thought, be sympathetic. No use. They were either not in residence or too busy to see him. One of them did not even recognize his name. Finally, he used Louis Béjart's method, bribery, and found a sufficiency of servants who were venal enough to pass him up the chain of command and sneak him past the higher officers who had denied him access earlier, until he found himself ushered into a tiny room where the King sat writing at a table. A whisper in his ear reminded him that he had a bare five minutes to make his plea.

For one awful moment he thought that Louis had forgotten him, too. The King stared at him with no recognition in his eyes, and looked angrily round to order him to be removed. Then he remembered, and spoke to him, though with less warmth than at their last meeting. The King was a man distracted. His fingers picked at the gold ring on his right hand. A mass of papers lay upon the table. He looked as tired as Moliére felt. An officious secretary beside him prepared another document for his attention.

"M. Molière, is it not? You constantly thrust yourself upon us."

Molière was miserably conscious that he cut a poor figure. His court clothes had been mislaid in their hasty evacuation. His head was splitting with fatigue, and he had not had time to prepare a speech. He coughed from the dust that seemed to have settled in his lungs, and the King frowned ominously.

"Don't stand there spitting, man. What do you want?"

"A theater, sire."

"Hell's teeth, man, did we not give you a theater? What more would you have from us? Do you know what you cost our treasury—you, and the painters, and the poets, and the music-makers? Read these" and he slapped the pile of papers on the table "and you may find out. Oh, how they complain against you. M. Molière, you and your kind. We try to make our Paris a Helicon, a place of beauty, a joy to the world, a new Byzantium. And they talk to us of livres and pistoles!"

At least, thought Molière, he's not angry with me. The King had been meeting with his financiers again.

"You did give us a theater, sire. It has been taken from us by the order of your architect. Your order, sire." Grievance and the need for haste made him bold.

"We gave no such order. What do you mean?"

Molière told the whole story, heedless of his five-minute limitation, blind to the secretary whose eyebrows rose reprovingly as the tale went on and on. He spared no detail, stressing the extent of their plight and their present homeless state. Louis' frown grew more menacing, and his fingers began to drum upon the table. As Molière was warming to a climax he cut him short.

"Spare us the rest, M. Molière. We are no child at school, that you need to spell out every word for us. As for this present business, there is nothing to be done for the moment. We may have given such orders. If so, we have forgotten them. There is more weighty business to distract our mind."

He rose impatiently.

"We shall look into it. Remember that," he snapped at the secretary, who made an obsequious note. "You shall have a theater again, when a suitable hall becomes available."

"But sire, what are we to do now?"

"Now? As best you can. As we all must."

He turned away. The audience was over. Hands were already plucking at Molière's sleeve. He stood his ground, desperate.

"But sire . . ."

Louis rounded on him with a face like thunder.

"What would you have us do, little man? Build you a theater with our own hands? You have our word. That is enough."

Molière bowed. He doubted it. But there was no more to be done. As he backed out of the room a courtier pushed past him and whispered something in the King's ear. As the door closed behind him he thought he heard, "The Queen can wait."

"We have his word," grumbled La Grange, when he took the news home. "Much good that did us last time." In the end, as it turned out, things might have been a great deal worse. They became nomads again, this time in the city instead of in the fields. They played where they could, by invitation, in the great houses of the capital. Once or twice they were invited back to court. Molière took heart at this, saying that it showed the King was thinking of them, but his colleagues were derisive, calling it a token, nothing more. When the King could call them at his pleasure, why should he pay to house them permanently? "No," said La Grange, as they set up their stage in the same hall in the Louvre where they had made their debut, "this is the closest we'll ever get to the Palace again." Molière, his mouth full of nails, nodded, and reflected that his career seemed always to be traveling in circles.

The return to the scene of their triumph, and her disgrace, awoke memories of Armande. It was months since he had heard of her; he had grown used to thinking of himself as a man without attachments, for Madeleine had become a part of himself. How was Armande, he wondered, what was she doing? Certainly not acting in any of the other Paris houses. Could she have forgotten the theater and settled down to a quiet life with some new man, keeping his house, fathering his children? He doubted it. No, she would come back some day. She would have to, when the pull became too strong. As for him, he held fast to his promise. He would never go to her.

The company found other patrons also. They suffered the inevitable mockery, for Paris found it amusing that a troupe of actors should have their theater pulled down around their ears. A favorite joke was that Molière's constant hiccuping had weakened the fabric of the building. He gritted his teeth and bore it; it was no time to be truculent. But when the city had done laughing and realized that it could no longer see the players who were the funniest in the capital, it offered a kind of pity. Molière had many enemies, and it was from them that he now profited. His company became a pawn in the social game. To champion him was to deprecate his rivals; to give his company houseroom, an assurance that the things he had said, the criticisms he had made, were right.

They lived from hand to mouth. There was little money in it, and the constant moves were exhausting. Their days fell into a familiar pattern. In the morning, arrival at the servants' door, their scenery reduced to a minimum and strapped on a cart, their costumes in bundles on their backs. Then the preparation of the hall under the eyes of a supercilious majordomo, whose chief concern was that they should not steal the silver or the tapestries. This done, they were banished below stairs to eat in the same room as the household staff but at a separate table. Even the newest, grubbiest, most overworked and underprivileged page boy considered the actors to be beneath him. And then the summons, and, for an hour or two, the joy of recreating their own world. Finally, the applause done, the dismal chore of dismantling and repacking, with the unwilling help of footmen who yawned in their faces, cursed them and would rather have been in bed. And there was still a long walk home before they could sleep themselves and be up again to do the same next day.

Hard though it was, they were working and glad of it. They played before some of the most illustrious men of France: for Fouquet, Minister of Finances, who was constantly chiding the

King for his expenditure while spending vast sums of his own; for Marshal Daumont, the Duc de Roqueleure, the Comte de Vaillac, the Duc de Mercoeur. It was at the latter's house that Molière saw the King again.

They had arrived as usual in the morning, and their stage was set. The Duc de Mercoeur was a generous man, more sympathetic than most of their patrons. Instead of banishing them to the servants' quarters he had allowed them a table at the banquet which was to precede their play. It was a small table, true, and cramped into a distant corner; but at least they were waited on like gentlemen, and felt that they had returned to the civilized world. It was clear from the beginning that this was no ordinary occasion. The servants were flurried, and inclined to duck into corners and whisper among themselves. The musicians fingered their instruments nervously and kept glancing at the clock. "They're expecting somebody important," said La Grange. "Is it the King?"

"Impossible," said Molière. He had surveyed the layout of the room, and knew about such things. There was no chair of state, no spot marked out in splendid isolation. Nor, apart from the air of anticipation, was there anything unusual in the behavior of the guests. They were finely dressed, but not as for a royal visit; even a suspicion of the King's presence would have brought them out like peacocks. It was a normal dinner at the Hôtel de Mercoeur. The company sat down again at table and speculated idly on what the special attraction might be.

At last the perspiring majordomo gave the signal. The orchestra struck up the latest air by Lully. At the far end of the hall the double doors were flung open and the formal entry of the guests began. In the center was a man distinguished only by his dress. He wore plain gray, as to a bourgeois churchgoing. This was enough to single him out from the silks and ruffles of the rest. But his face, too, set him apart. It was laughing, excited, a sight of sheer joy which offset his spreading corpulence and made him handsome. Molière jumped to his feet. "Look! It is the King!"

There was a horrified gasp from the wall, and a steward hurried forward white-faced.

"You maniac! Do you want to have us all punished?"

Molière was pushed into his seat again, protesting.

"But it is the King! Do you think I don't know him? Even without his robes? Why is he dressed like that?"

The steward rolled his eyes to heaven and prayed to be delivered from the imbecility of actors. "The gentleman you are so rudely pointing to . . ." Molière blushed and dropped his hand to his side, "is a private gentleman. No one else. Remember that. If he should condescend to speak with you," his manner indicated that such a thing was ludicrously improbable, "it is his desire to be addressed simply as 'Monsieur.' If you forget that, God help you."

"I see," said Molière, though he did not. He looked at the guests again. "Who is the lady with him?"

Monsieur's companion was a lovely thing. A young girl, all in white; a face as glowing as that of the man beside her, yet with a touch of . . . was it apprehension? A mass of golden hair; and above all, an air of sweet innocence that marked her out from the other guests no less than her escort's drab attire did him.

The steward turned a bland face to Molière, and his eye relaxed into a wink.

"There is no lady with him."

"Oh," said Molière. Now he understood.

Louis Béjart had his own methods of seeking information. He ran downstairs, and had the whole story in five minutes. The girl was Louise de la Vallière, a lady-in-waiting at court. Apparently she was as innocent as she looked. The King's sister-in-law, flattered but alarmed by his undiplomatic approaches, had used the girl as go-between and pretended to the world at large that it was the attendant that the King was really interested in. Accepting the deceit, he had become infatuated in earnest. Louise de la Vallière became the recipient of his attentions. She had protested unavailingly, and tried to withdraw from court; he would not permit it. Finally she had yielded to the magnetism of the man, forgotten all propriety and consented to be seen with him in public. But only on occasions like this. The whole household had been sworn to strictest silence—which meant that it would be at least six hours before all Paris knew of it.

The play went particularly well that night. Much wine was drunk and the tension evaporated. By the time the performance began the King was in high good humor, Louise was laughing and relaxed, and the other guests enveloped in the general bonhomie. Molière knew that he had played his best, and was not surprised when after the company had bowed their adieux, Monsieur in gray beckoned him over.

"You do not know who I am, do you?"

"Monsieur," said Molière, playing the game, "I have never seen you before in my life."

"Good, good! But I have seen you, Molière, often. And it seems to us . . . to me . . . that you have not been fairly treated."

"Monsieur?"

"You were promised a new theater, were you not? And the promise has not been fulfilled. Well, well. Kings are not like other men, Molière. In matters of state and," his lips tightened, "in their private lives they have burdens to bear which may make them forgetful."

Molière agreed that this was undoubtedly true.

"But seeing you here tonight has reminded us . . . me . . . that someone has been remiss. I have some influence at court. Not nearly so much as I should like"—enormous laughter at this—"but a little. You shall have your new theater. See to it." This breach of incognito was directed at a man whom Molière recognized without difficulty as Fouquet.

There was a muttered consultation, in which Molière caught only the word "expense."

"Don't talk to me of expense, man," cried Monsieur in gray. "If I can't afford it out of my own pocket then you may. God knows you're rich enough."

Fouquet smiled resignedly and vanished. Molière was overcome.

"I shall never be able to thank your M . . ."

The smiles froze on the faces of the guests, and warned him in time.

". . . most generous kindness," he concluded, inelegantly but safely. There was a ripple of laughter. He bowed and turned away.

"I see you're learning tact at last, Molière. But there is one thing more." Monsieur was beckoning to him again. "Promises have been made to you and not kept; but you are a little guilty too. You have not kept faith with us."

How so, Molière wanted to know.

"I well remember your first appearance in Paris. The only good thing in your dreary tragedy was a young actress . . . I do not know her name. Why have you not shown her to us since? I do not see her here tonight."

Sick at heart, Molière knew what was coming.

"You mean . . . ?"

"Do not play games with me, Molière! You know perfectly well who I mean. An exquisite girl. A charming thing, who to my inexperienced eyes at least was one of the prettiest sights of Paris."

"I remember."

"What sort of behavior is this, then? Are you some market huckster, to lure the customers with your best goods and then hide them out of sight? Bring her back, do you hear me? When you get your new theater, bring her back."

"If you wish."

"I do wish, sir. I want the stages of my city to be filled with beauty, no less than the court." His arm tightened round the fair-haired girl, and Molière was forgotten.

"We play a strange game," he said on the way home. "We work ourselves to the bone to learn our trade; we starve, we humiliate ourselves, we suffer. And in the end we become good at it. Does that matter? Not a jot. What makes the difference, in the end, is who the King takes into his bed."

"No matter, dear," said Madeleine. "We do the best we can."

"At any rate," said La Grange, "I hope this new girl lasts."

They had their new theater, in undisputed possession. It was in the Palais Royal, and more sumptuous than the last. They fell on it like exiles returning home after a long sea voyage. New costumes were made, new scenery painted; and a deputation went to call on Armande.

Molière had put it off as long as he dared, and in the end did not go himself. He did not know what he could say. A formal letter had been written, signed by him in the name of the company, inviting Armande to return. La Grange took it; Madeleine accompanied him, on Molière's urging. She had gone with bad grace. "What will happen to you now?" she had said to him ruefully. "What will happen to us? Without her you were happy. Now it will start all over again."

"What should I do, then?" he replied. "How can we disobey? Don't worry. There's nothing between us now. She will be an actress in the company, nothing more. Our lives will go on as they did." But Madeleine did not believe him.

Waiting for their return, he filled in the hours by putting the finishing touches to his new play. It had been nearly done when they were faced with their forced move. Since then it had languished in drawers and cupboards, unread and untouched. Coming back to it after months, he rediscovered it with pleasure. Yes, it had held up well; the respite had been good for him, perhaps, for he could look at it objectively, as though it had been submitted to him by someone else. He had kept his secret well. His fellows knew that he was writing something; they unanimously assumed that it was another farce in the Italian manner.

So much the better. They would be all the more surprised. It was not a farce. He ruminated over the title. *Don Garcia of Navarre, or, The Jealous Prince.* If pressed he could not have said exactly what it was. A tragedy, but not in form; a comedy, but like no comedy that had ever been written. It had a pathos, a wistfulness, a sense of desperation at the end. The hero was a man in love. Common enough. There were none of the usual obstacles to thwart him. No angry fathers threatening with their sticks, no difference in station, no accidents of fortune, none of the usual tricks by which stage love was blighted. The Prince's only obstacle was himself. He was beloved in turn, but could never bring himself to trust his own good fortune. His nature held him back. He was a pessimist, a cynic, who saw the rose and sought to find the canker. The play had a happy ending, sure enough. Molière had tried to avoid it, but his commercial sense warned him that he must not try the audience too far. He could not break every tradition at once. Well, the ignorant would swallow it. As for the intelligent public, they would know at once the sort of play it really was. A study of a man who was too sensitive for his own good. Who looked into his own mind, and did not like what he saw.

What to call it, then? It must have a label. Slowly he took up his pen and squeezed in between the title and the opening line "A Heroic Comedy." That would do, for want of anything better. Ridiculous, in any case, to try to classify it. It was original; it was unique; it was himself on paper, though he did not recognize himself.

The embassy returned empty-handed.

"She wants to talk to you," said La Grange. "We did our best, but she won't listen to us. You'll have to go yourself."

"I will not."

"You must."

"What does she want of me, then?"

"Who knows?" said La Grange. "That's all she would say to us. Tell him, if he wants me, he must come himself. You have to go."

"I'll go, then. Tomorrow."

"Take care, Molière," said Madeleine.

Armande had bought herself a house at Meudon. With whose money, he could only guess. If she had a new protector, he was discreet. There could have been no gossip about her in the neighborhood; he had to inquire five or six times to find out where she lived, and even then his informant was not sure; he thought Molière must mean the quiet lady who lived alone and talked to no one. The door was open when he arrived, and after he had called her name, a voice from upstairs asked him to ascend.

She was sitting in her bedroom, sewing. Everything about her was neat and orderly. The floor was scrubbed and polished, the hangings of good quality. A pile of logs lay in the fireplace unlit, for though late summer was sliding into autumn it was still warm. There were pictures on the walls, of ordinary scenes: A bird in flight, a hay wain, a girl on a swing. She looked up demurely when he entered, but did not rise. Motioning him to a chair she continued with her work.

"So you have come at last."

"It was not my choice."

"I know it."

A long silence, broken only by the ticking of the clock in the next room.

"Why did you want me to come?"

"I made a promise, Molière; don't you remember? I swore that I would never come to you. You would have to come to me."

"Does it mean so much to you, to win?"

"Everything."

He crossed his legs uncomfortably.

"You know why I am here, then."

"Yes. La Grange told me. I read the letter. You have decided that you need me again."

"I have been told that I must have you again."

"I know that too."

Another pause. Molière rose abruptly and strode to the window, speaking without looking at her, gazing out.

"Your one appearance seems to be remembered here. I said that I would never come to you. I would not be here now if I were a free agent. But when the King insists, we must all break our promises."

"Suppose I do not choose to come back?"

"Who knows? The King will be angry, if he remembers. And that is the sort of thing he chooses to remember. We lose our theater again. We start from scratch. I can't do it. None of us can. There's no more time for new beginnings."

"Could this not be a new beginning?"

He turned. She had laid her work aside, and was looking at him directly for the first time since he had entered the room.

"For you as an actress, yes. As my—as anything more personal, no. I have forgotten that. I was in love with you once. That does not interest me any longer. What I am offering is a professional relationship, no more."

"That is not what I am suggesting."

He was angry. "My God, what do you want of me? I humble myself, I come here to apologize—"

"I have not heard you apologizing."

"Very well, then, I do. I may have been wrong. Hasty. I tried to make you something else than what you were. I saw you as a woman. I forgot you were a child."

"I am a woman now."

She was. He saw that. She still had her incredible youthfulness—what right had she to laugh at passing time when his hair was turning gray?—but the fragility had gone. She did not rant or scream at him. She was harder, more self-possessed. And there was something in her eyes he did not like.

She crossed to a small bureau and took a paper from it.

"I have learned many things from you, though you may not believe it. You taught me to be methodical, to think ahead, to plan. I have been thinking for months of what I would do when you came back to me. I always knew you would, you see. We need each other, you and I . . . professionally."

He said nothing.

"So here I have a list of my demands."

"Read them. I'm listening."

"One. That I have first choice of roles."

"But Madeleine and the Marquise . . ."

"Are too old. Ours is a cruel business. Yes or no?"

"Agreed." She was right, he thought, though he hated her for it. Madeleine was still superb; she had a supple voice, a grace of movement, but the public wanted youth and freshness. There were already some parts that Madeleine could no longer play. As for the Marquise, she was almost grotesque. She had become so affected during their stay in Paris that the public now greeted her with friendly derision. It would not be long before it ceased to be friendly.

"Two. I have a full share of the profits of the company."

"Agreed." This was only reasonable. She would be worth it.

"Three." She stopped and looked at him, then tossed her head defiantly and went on. "I am to become your wife."

"Never!"

"Ah, that horrifies you. Why? Am I so ugly? So undesirable?"

"You know that's not true. But all that is over between us. I see you as an actress, nothing more. An excellent one, I admit that. One I can write my best for. But marriage—it's out of the question. Could you marry a man who has no feelings for you?"

"We could reawaken those feelings, perhaps," she said softly. Then, as she saw the look on his face, "Well, perhaps we could not. Does it matter? Listen to me, Molière. We need make no pretenses, you and I. You need me. You have to have me. I need you, or someone like you; and there is no one like you, I'll admit that on my own account."

"But we would be working together—"

"That is not enough!" Her eyes flashed. "I want a station in life, an honest name, respectability. Don't laugh! It may sound strange, coming from me. But I've had the other thing. I've had enough of the other thing. It brought me this . . ." She indicated the room and its furnishings. "But it doesn't last. If I came back to you now, without marriage, you know what they'd all say? He's sorry for his cast-off mistress, he's found her a job again. And then, in a few years . . . if the King's humor changes and you find you can get along without me, where would I be? Thrown out again, like the last time. On my own. And older. Aren't you frightened of growing old?"

"Yes."

"Well, so am I. And with more reason. You have something. It may not seem much to you, but it's a lot to me. I have a pretty face, a pair of legs, a voice. That's all. And there's not much in the world for people like me. You think I'm cynical and heartless. But I have to fight for what I can get."

He let her finish, then crossed to her chair and stood looking down at her. She thought he was going to strike her, and flinched away. He did not. When he spoke, his voice was surprisingly calm.

"Very well. You have made your conditions. I shall now make mine. You want me to marry you. I will, if you insist on it. If that is the only way you will come back to us. But it will be a marriage in name only. I will not sleep with you or live with you. You may have my name, but not my bed or my company. You will not make a fool of me in public. Oh, don't worry, I'm not asking for fidelity, I know you far too well. But when you deceive me, let it be done discreetly. I promise to do the same for you. You shall have my protection while I am alive, my worldly goods, if any, when I am dead. You will work hard, and do everything that is required of you. That is what our relationship must be; no more, no less. Agreed?"

"Agreed."

He walked to the door. The sun had almost set, and neither of them had thought to light a candle. Her face was a white blur in the darkness, and in the room adjoining the clock struck eight.

"You will report for rehearsal tomorrow morning. I shall arrange for another share in the theater, for your use, as my wife, but in my name. A lawyer will draw up the marriage contract, and the ceremony will take place as soon as possible. Goodnight, Armande."

"Goodnight, Molière."

She sat in silence for a long time after the echo of his footsteps had died away on the stairs. Then she rose, lit a candle, and, a quiet smile upon her lips, began to pack.

"You will marry her, then?" said Madeleine.

"I have no choice. It is the only way she will come back. I do not want to. It is for the company."

"For the company. Yes, of course. I understand."

"Why did she go?" fumed Molière. "And where has she gone? Just when I needed her most."

"What did you expect?" said Louis. "She wouldn't stay here now. Not with you married to Armande."

"But what difference does it make? It's a marriage in name only. Nothing's changed. If she could live with Armande before, why can't she now? Has she no gratitude? I took her back."

"You took her back," said Louis. "You poor fool."

"What do you mean?"

"Are you really so blind? Could any man be so selfish? She took you back, don't you see it? Oh, I admit she had me fooled as well, that day she came to the rehearsal. She's never given a better performance in her life."

Molière felt himself growing cold. "What are you saying?"

"Only this. She wasn't starving. She needed work like you need another ear. I took the trouble to investigate, which is more than you ever did."

"Investigate what?"

"She had money enough. She wasn't rich, but she could look

after herself. She came back for your sake, you lunatic. Because she couldn't bear to be away from you any longer. Because she thought you needed her. Which God knows you did."

"But ... why didn't she tell me?"

"And humiliate herself even further than she did? You were still crazy about Armande then, you would probably have laughed in her face. No, that was the only way she could do it. By giving you an opportunity to be generous, and noble, and forgiving. Sometimes I hate you, Molière."

"So that's why she came?"

"And that's why she stayed. In the hope that you'd forget Armande in time, and remember her again. She was in love with you, don't you understand that? In love with you. And then you came half to your senses and threw Armande out. You should have seen Madeleine then. You would have, if you'd had eyes. But all you did was treat her like a big sister. She wanted to marry you. And you turned her into a family Mother Superior, weeping on her shoulder when things went wrong, and ignoring her when they didn't. And still she hung on. Hoping. Then, just when she was beginning to think you'd remember she was a woman, you turn round and marry Armande. No wonder she's walked out. I would have stuck a knife in your back."

"But ..." Molière stammered ". . . I didn't want to. I didn't mean to hurt her. It was the King . . . the company . . ."

"One of these days," said Louis brutally, "you may realize there are more important things than the company. Good night, Molière. Pleasant dreams."

So Armande came back, and Molière, after forty years, became a married man. The ceremony was a quiet one, with only a few of the company attending, out of duty. Louis did not come, and there was no word from Madeleine. Molière took a glass of wine with the priest, for form's sake, and then signaled to Armande that it was time to go home. She obeyed him, surprised but docile; she was learning her part. He was silent in the carriage, and sat alone in the front room while she prepared for bed. Then, with the air of a man going to his execution, he went to her. She saw him standing in the door-way, contemplating her.

"What is it, Molière? Why do you look so strange?"

He flung her on the bed and tore off her nightdress, strangling her cry with a brutal hand. Coldly, methodically he took her, in all the remembered postures of love, till he was spent and she exhausted, trembling half with fright and half with pleasure. He drew himself off her, reached down and flung her nightgown in her face.

"That is for what you have done to me," he said, "to show you that I learn my lessons well. Now you may keep to your room and sleep in peace. I swear before God I will never touch you again as long as I live."

He was alone now. His solitude before had been pretense; he had imagined he could cut himself away at will from human contact, from the little pulls and ties of everyday affection; from the need that each man has to unburden his soul to another. But now he saw, cruelly and clearly, that he had never truly been alone till now. In the background, in the corner, waiting to be spoken to, cherishing the carelessly flung word, the nod of casual affection, there had always been Madeleine. She had, by being, grown into a part of him; she was the furniture of his life, needed but never noticed till gone away. And at this moment, when he needed her so desperately, she had vanished; and in her place was this automaton, this jeweled doll, this varnished husk that was his wife, Armande. When he turned to *Don Garcia* again, he knew at last why he had written it, and who his hero was; and he revised it with a bitter pen, letting seep into the narrative the poison that corroded his own soul. Don Garcia. The man who trusted no one, and ended by destroying himself.

Yet, on the surface, all was harmony and peace. Armande made her return to the company. When they addressed each other, it was always with formal courtesy. She was punctual at rehearsals, was properly docile in her husband's presence, and addressed the other actors with respect. They warmed towards her when they saw she had lost none of her old skill. Indeed, she seemed touched with genius. Before, her acting, good though it was, had seemed the instinctive virtuosity of a brilliant child. Now she performed with discipline and iron self-control. On the stage all seemed natural and effortless, but they knew how long she spent preparing every word and gesture, and respected her for it. Molière was impressed, and secretly surprised. He had expected more temperament from her. The storms, had he but known it, were to come later.

They opened the new theater with *Don Garcia*. For the second time Molière had to force a play on his colleagues. It was *The Affected Young Ladies* all over again, but this time it was not the repercussions that they feared, it was the play. They could not understand it.

"Heroic comedy?" grumbled La Grange. "What sort of thing is that? What does it mean? It's neither one thing nor the other."

"All that philosophizing," said Louis. "What audience will ever stand for it? They come to us to be entertained. If they want to be bored, they can go to the Bourgogne."

But Molière gave them to understand that, as long as he was head of the company, his word was law. He compelled them, but failed to convince them. They rehearsed half-heartedly, and Louis in particular parodied his lines in a way that Molière found offensive. Nevertheless, he thought the play would carry it.

It did not. *Don Garcia*, at its opening performance, was a failure. He knew how complete when his friends and patrons among the audience came round to offer their customary congratulations. A play, he thought, should be like a slap in the face; it should shock, provoke, excite. If it merely earned the meaningless clichés, it had failed. And as they moved before him murmuring how elegant the verse was, and how they had admired that novel thought in Act Two, he grew more and more depressed, and when the theater had emptied went out to get drunk.

At least his visitors had been polite. The general public was openly derisive. He had the playbills taken down, revived an Italian comedy, and threw the script into a drawer. The company muttered among themselves, saying that this was a bad omen for the opening of the new theater, and in the town they were beginning to say that Molière had lost his touch.

Don Garcia had one other unlooked-for result. It almost cost him his friendship with Racine. The tragedian had been present at the first performance. Molière had seen him from the stage, leaning in rapt attention over the edge of his loge, apparently enthralled. The sight encouraged him; it was a welcome contrast to the yawns, squeaks and rustlings that filled the rest of the house. A bored audience is a noisy beast. He had been surprised, therefore, when Racine did not come round afterwards; he was even more surprised when his friend burst into the theater the morning after, interrupting the rehearsal and assailing Molière with shouts of fury.

Molière's head was still thick with the last night's drinking. He was depressed by the aura of failure and the knowing looks on the faces of his actors, and his temper was not at its best. He stalked down to the front of the stage and bellowed back at Racine.

"Are you mad? We're working. Go away."

This only provoked Racine to greater fury. He stamped in rage, and brandished his stick in the air.

"Thief! Plagiarist! Traitor!"

Molière leapt into the parterre and accosted him. They faced each other with a bench between them. On the stage the actors gathered to watch the fun.

"What are you talking about?"

"My play! My tragedy! What do you think?"

Molière was flabbergasted. "What about your tragedy?"

"Oh, you were clever! Putting me off, always postponing it . . . next week, next month, next year, wait till the audience is ready, wait till the public's mood has changed—and all the time you were pilfering from it! Stealing it for your own!"

"Will you stop dancing about!" Molière seized him and propelled him to a bench. The fat man struggled limply, then succumbed. He stared up at Molière with big, watery eyes.

"How could you do this to me? How?"

"Listen," said Molière, "I don't know what you're accusing me of. How could I have stolen your tragedy? My play was about a prince in Spain. Yours was about a king in Greece. The characters are different. The stories are different. The moods are different. I don't need to steal from anyone. I write my own."

"And much good it seems to have done you," snapped Racine. "Oh, I know they'd pass for different works. But I know. And you'd know, if you only had the honesty to admit it."

Hauling a script of his *House of Thebes* from his pocket, he began to read. "Listen to that. You'll say you had forgotten it, perhaps. Give me your Prince's soliloquy in Act Two."

To appease him, Molière recited. As he did so, the uneasy conviction grew on him that Racine was partly right. There was no obvious borrowing. He could not be accused of that. But the structure of the verse, the balance of the thought; the way his characters, in their introspective moments, questioned and analyzed; the influence was clearly there.

"My friend." He wondered how he could be most tactful. "In a sense, everything you say is true. But believe me, I was unconscious of it. I tried to write a play that would be different from anything I had ever done before. It was too different, clearly. Now I see why. I learned more from you than I realized."

"So you admit it!"

"I admit nothing. At least, not what you mean. I took from you, but not with intent. Your thoughts, your feelings, your attitudes—they had become so much a part of me that I took them for my own. Forgive me. It's a kind of a tribute, after all."

Racine was beginning to come round. What a curse it was, thought Molière, this writing. Did he never have an original thought? Was he simply a sponge, to absorb the work of others, reshape it and present it as his own? When he wrote a farce, it was Italian. When he wrote *The Affected Young Ladies,* he had simply versified the gossip of the salons. Those lines that caused such great offense had all been said before, in earnest, by others. And now this: a play he thought so serious and profound, the expression of his own true self, was merely another borrowing and he had not even known it. Where am I in all this, he thought; what am I? Is there really a man called Molière, and does he think and walk and reason? What am I here for, what am I doing, what have I done?

"Stage my play," snapped Racine. "Now. Let them see the real thing, not a pale imitation."

"But, . . ." He was about to say that the time was not yet ripe, his company was not ready, nor was he; after the failure of *Don Garcia* he would have to write more comedies, win the public round again, prepare them. But how could he say all that now? Well, he could temporize. Put *The House of Thebes* into rehearsal; that would appease Racine as long as he saw something going forward. Plead the difficulty of the work, the problems of training his actors in a new style; hold off as long as possible.

"Agreed. We shall begin rehearsals tomorrow."

Suddenly Racine was all smiles. They were friends again. Laughing, happy, he flung his arm round Molière's shoulders and escorted him back to the stage.

"Till tomorrow!"

"Till tomorrow" said Molière. Tonight, he thought. I must start a new comedy.

He wrote furiously, for the need was urgent. The new house was expensive, and there were debts to be paid. Worse, the audiences were falling off. Paris battened on his failure. The word was out that he had lost the knack, his brilliance was fading. Well, he would show them.

The new comedy was finished in four days. During that time, he hardly slept. His daylight hours were spent rehearsing and performing. Coming back to *The House of Thebes* after so long an interval, he found problems enough, without needing to invent them. Racine wrote in a new and subtle style. When the actors threw themselves into the old heroic postures, it looked and sounded absurd. Discarding his earlier production scheme, he began afresh. He sought new movements and postures, and cut down the action to the bone to match the spareness of the verse. It was not easy, for himself or for the actors. He strove to make them feel the delicate cadences, to avoid the odd false stress and overemphasis; to see how little they could do, and still be effective. The company did not like it. They foresaw another debacle, like *Don Garcia*. It took him all his time to cajole them.

They liked his comedy, however. All, that is, except Armande. When he read the scripts to them, she showed her first sign of rebellion since her return.

"I will not play in this."

"As you please. It is your choice. But tell me why not."

"It makes me look ridiculous."

"I cannot see that."

It was true. If it made anyone ridiculous, it was himself; for he had written a play about himself. There were two prospective husbands in it, with divergent views about the nature of women. One preached severity, the other kindness and tolerance. It was the kindly one who found himself loved and respected. The tyrant—a part Molière had destined for himself—was covered with ridicule. It was called *The School for Husbands*.

"It makes you ridiculous, then. And I suffer by association. We are married now, and everybody knows it. When you write a comedy about marriage, what do you think the world will say?"

"I don't care what they say, as long as they laugh."

"Let them laugh. But not at me."

Nothing they could say would make her change her mind. She would not do it. Molière did not really care. The play was good enough without her. He could put a weaker actress in the part, cut it down somewhat, so that the focus was off her, and on him . . . yes, it would manage well enough. Armande could continue to play her other roles. She would come round, when she saw his triumph.

A triumph it was, so great that he was moved to write another on the same theme, *The School for Wives*. Armande held out at first, claiming that this was as great a travesty of her as the other. In the end she yielded, as Molière had known she would. She could not resist the applause. And in a part that had been written for her, and about her, she was wonderful. She played an ingenue brought up by her guardian in total ignorance. This way, he hoped, she would be faithful when she married him, for she would never know enough to deceive him. He was doomed to disappointment. Coquetry, according to the play, was natural in women. It required no knowledge of the world to cheat, lie and deceive. It was an instinct. So Armande won her young lover and the old man, Molière, shuffled off in melancholy defeat. Paris roared with laughter, and none more heartily than those of the inner circle, who knew how close the play was to truth, and lost no time in initiating their friends.

"How can he make such a spectacle of himself?" they wondered.

"The man must be completely callous."

Molière was not callous, only resigned. His marriage meant nothing to him. It was a sham, a pretense. Why should he not make dramatic capital out of it? He felt no bitterness, but only a strange, sad joy; he had learned that he could only write his best when he was writing about himself. In *Don Garcia* he had done this, but with another's voice. In his plays of marriage, the voice was his own, and Paris, fickle Paris, flocked to hear it.

Molière was fashionable again. The invitations poured in. Commands. He could not afford to ignore them. He was at once the public's master and the lowest of its servants. For two hours, in the theater, he was in control. They laughed, gasped, applauded, at his dictation. The rest of the time the roles were reversed. A great lord planned a fête at his castle on the Loire. A play was needed, several plays. Who would write them, who perform in them but Molière? A speech was needed for a triumphal entry. Whose pen should compose it but Molière's? The King sought diversion and commanded a ballet. Who should shape the plot but Molière?

He found most of the work trivial and disgusting. But it filled his time. La Grange remonstrated with him when he complained.

"You're unhappy when you can't work, unhappy when you can. Won't you ever be satisfied?"

He could not fully explain. There was no one near who could understand him now. There was so much to be done, so many plays waiting to be written, if people would only listen to them, if he only had the skill. The ancients, he recalled, had said that a man's most significant work was done at forty years. He was past this now. How many years were left? He could not guess. Sometimes, when his cough racked him agonizingly in the privacy of his room, he thought he would die tomorrow. At others, when he bestrode the stage in the mastery of his art, he felt immortal. But every moment must be put to use. He had no time to be merely fashionable. He was a toy, he felt, a manikin to make the public laugh. They would use him till he broke, then tire of him.

What irked him most was the amount of time he had to spend away from Paris. For these command performances, everything had to stop. Rehearsals for Racine's play were abandoned, occasioning another angry meeting. Racine accused him of devoting himself to frivolities. Molière had pleaded necessity.

"How can I refuse? If I don't do as they ask, I'll have no theater, and then you'll never see your play."

They were at Vaux, performing for Fouquet. The Minister of Finance had become a French Lucullus; his name had become a byword for sumptuous entertainments. Each new show outdid the last. There were rumors that the King had eyed this extravagance askance and wondered audibly whether it was paid for by Fouquet himself or by the Treasury. On this occasion there would be six thousand guests to dine, as usual, off silver and gold. In the evening they would watch the customary spectacles, and these Molière had been commanded to provide.

He sat gloomily in Fouquet's garden, on the great sweep of the lawn, rehearsing. The invitation had found him more than usually pressed. There had been no time to work with a full company. Half-derisively, half-proud of his own dexterity, he had dashed off a piece that could be done by two actors. A young man, hurrying to see his lady love, is assailed by bores who hold him back and distract him. That was all. It did not matter in which order the scenes were played. Armande was to speak the prologue. Molière would play all seven of the interruptors. In this way, the rest of the company could be left at peace.

When the tiny group had arrived at Vaux, Fouquet had been angry, suspecting an insult.

"Only three of you, M. Molière? Is this all you think my entertainment is worth?"

Molière had turned off his resentment wittily enough.

"Not at all. I bring you my best actress, and my seven best actors. Molière himself, in seven roles."

Fouquet eyed Armande lasciviously.

"As usual, you have perfect taste." And taking her by the arm, he led her off to inspect the chateau.

But even with so simple a play, the rehearsals seemed endless. For the prologue, he had thought of the device of having Armande emerge from a giant shell, dressed as a Naiad. Mechanical tricks were sure to please an audience. The monstrous thing had been made to his instructions, but in too much haste. It was not functioning properly, and had given endless trouble since they started rehearsals.

"Try it again," shouted Molière. A gang of sweating workmen hauled the shell out of sight behind the avenue of pines. "Now this time try to get it right. You pull on the red lines first. And when the shell is up against the fountain, and not before, pull the blue line. That will open it."

The musicians, responding to his nod, struck up for the eighth time that morning. Lurching through the opening, the shell trundled crabwise across the lawn, fouled its own ropes and stuck.

"Let me out!" cried Armande, entombed in a mountain of paint and plaster. "I'm suffocating!"

The shell vibrated as she hammered from inside; the lid gave two inches and then stuck irremediably. Molière flopped onto the lawn and buried his head in his hands. Fouquet, who had strolled by to study progress, found the contretemps diverting.

"I see you have the oyster, M. Molière. It only remains to extricate the pearl. Oh, by the way," he glanced down at some notes in his hand, "we have some special fireworks in honor of the King. You will have to shorten your entertainment by half an hour."

"But—" Foolish though this diversion was, it was his work, and he ran to its defense. Cut some of his lines for a firework display? Half an hour? Ridiculous. Two whole episodes would have to go.

It was no use protesting. Fouquet had already moved on, and was feeding sweetmeats to Armande through the crack in the shell. It seemed to appease her.

"Didn't I tell you it would be like this?"

One of the musicians had laid aside his violin, left the orchestra and come to Molière's side. He sweated in the morning sun.

"You don't remember me, I see. Dear, dear," he sighed in an affected way, "how easily we forget a favor. I doubt you would be here now, if it wasn't for me."

His manner of waving his hands struck a chord in Molière's memory. He often forgot a face, but never a gesture. It was a ghost from the past, his distant relative, the man in black, his advocate at that fateful family tribunal so long ago. Groping, his memory found a name. "Michel . . . Michel Mazuel. How are you?"

"As you see me." The smooth face was rumpled now, and the black had grown rusty. "I've been fortunate enough, I suppose. There has always been work. They grew tired of my compositions, but they always need violinists. And I took care not to make any enemies." He glanced quizzically at Molière. "But I should not talk about that subject to an expert. And how are you? What do you think of all this?" His gesture included the park, the restive musicians tuning their instruments and waiting, the workmen prising Armande out of her absurd prison. "Now you have it, does it make you happy?"

"No."

"Far be it from me, dear boy, to say I told you so. How vividly I remember that day! Never have I seen disbelief more obviously written on a human face. You listened to me, but you didn't trust me. However, you saw that it was policy to have me on your side. A pity you haven't had more policy since."

He picked a blade of grass from the immaculate lawn and sucked it between yellow teeth. A bee buzzed idly past him, pursuing its serene course through the human commotion.

"Young men are all the same. They think there is such a thing as Art. A vision, a goddess. I did once, too. But it does not take long to discover the truth. As I told you then, there is no art, only merchandise."

"I still don't believe you. Any more than I did then."

"How can you say that? Look at you now. You write a play to order. So many verses at so much a line. No, says the customer, that's too much, give me a little less, please. Yes, sir, of course, sir, I'll chop off half an hour, sir; will that suit you better, sir? Thank you, sir, *good* morning. Always smiling, because you're afraid the customer might take his business somewhere else."

There a shout of triumph from the huddle by the fountain. Like an enormous walnut the shell split in half, and Armande emerged, more a Fury than a Naiad.

"I spit on your shell," she shouted to Molière," and I detest your play. I shall come back when you promise me this thing is working." She stalked off in search of consolation. There were many willing to offer it.

Molière turned to reply to Mazuel, but he had already gone; he was back in his place in the orchestra, where he ducked his head to Molière and smiled derisively. It's still not true, thought Molière. All this is only part of it. The game you have to play. But people will learn to listen to me. They're starting to listen now. And one day I shall write a play that speaks the truth. They will listen and wonder; and then we'll see who was right.

In the end, both the shell and the play opened successfully. The King came, the guests were delighted with Molière's inventions and his multiple appearances, and they left Vaux exhausted but richer. They did not stay for the fireworks. Talking to La Grange later, Molière wished he had. The news had preceded them back to the capital.

"But how could you have missed it?" said La Grange. "All Paris is talking about it. Things are changing, mark my words."

Apparently Fouquet had gone too far. The fireworks had been mostly in honor of the King, as he had said. But the final setpiece, topping all the others, had been Fouquet's own motto, *Quo non ascendem?* To what heights may I not rise? This, blazoned in reds and yellows on the night sky, had fired Louis' wrath. The word was that Fouquet had been arrested. His affairs were being investigated; he was charged with peculation of state funds.

A cold breeze blew across Paris, and many shivered, the actors amongst them.

"There'll be a change," said La Grange. "I can feel it coming. The King is growing older and more careful. If he starts to economize it will affect us all."

But if there was a change, there was as yet no outward sign of it. Summer succeeded summer, with the same fêtes, the same balls, the same gaiety. And Molière's company received the ultimate honor, the longed-for invitation to Versailles.

This time Molière did not dare to stint. Nor did he want to. He had been waiting for this chance. It was a clear sign of royal protection. Whatever had happened to him in the past, his star was rising now. At Versailles he would be safe from criticism and impertinences. Anything he said there would have, to all intents and purposes, the stamp of royal approval. So it was time for him to take the offensive. His enemies had done their worst, and he had survived. The moment had come to declare open war on them. No more trivialities. Michel Mazuel, he thought, I hope you're there to watch me.

He called his entertainment an impromptu. Never had an impromtu been more carefully rehearsed. The actors were to appear under their own names, as if meeting for a rehearsal, not giving a performance. Molière would conduct this rehearsal in his own person, as he always did. And in the course of instructing his company he would contrive to burlesque every well-known mannerism of the actors of the Hôtel de Bourgogne.

It was a brilliant idea, brilliantly written, and the company rejoiced in it. It was just as well; their enthusiasm gave them the stamina to endure the daily nightmare of working at Versailles. It was impossible for them to lodge anywhere in the immediate vicinity of the palace. When the King moved to Versailles, all France seemed to move with him; the palace was packed from cellar to garret. Rooms that in Paris would have been considered unfit for a maidservant were fought over tooth and nail by the highest in the land. Duels had been waged over a few square feet of space. Most of the rooms had no heat, no water and little light; the fortunate invited had to walk miles for a meal. When it was hot they sweltered, when it rained they soaked in misery, for the household staff, who could spend months designing a fountain or laying out a walk, had no time to spare for leaking roofs. And yet they came. An invitation to Versailles meant that one had arrived, that one officially existed. To refuse would have been suicide.

It was a three-hour journey from Paris, so Molière and his friends were forced to find accommodation in the neighborhood, as close to the palace as they could get. Every morning they would make the journey in—on horseback if they could, on foot if they could not, for horses and carriages were at a premium too—and rehearsed behind locked doors until every gesture was a work of art and every sentence shone. Racine came with them, reconciled, for Molière had explained that this was part of a grand design.

"First we make the Hôtel de Bourgogne ridiculous. We show them up for the posturing fools they are. Then, we do your play. As it should be done, decently, properly, with restraint and dignity. Believe me, it will be a new beginning. The tragic stage will never be the same again."

It went off even better than they dared to hope. Molière's burlesque was accurate enough to please the cognoscenti, and sufficiently malicious to entertain the court. Montfleury and his associates were easy targets. The comedians ridiculed their stance, their gait, their private mannerisms; and when Molière delivered one speech in a deadly parody of the standard rolling tragic voice, the play was held up for ten minutes by laughter and applause.

None of the Hôtel de Bourgogne troupe was officially present. They must have had good informants, however. It was immediately after this that the rumors started. Molière first heard of them, ironically, from his father. It was typical that the old man should die with a remonstrance.

He had seen almost nothing of his family since his return to Paris. His brother Jean occasionally, his father never. There had been no desire, on either side, for a meeting. From what he heard, his father followed his fortunes with mixed feelings. He was happy at his son's success, and impressed that he had made closer contact with royalty than anyone in the family before him. On the other hand, the feuds and scandals in which Jean-Baptiste seemed to be constantly imbroiled saddened and frightened him; they bore out his worst fears that the theater was a scapegrace life and its practitioners gaudy charlatans who met, more often than not, with disaster. Nor had he ever truly forgiven his son for breaking his promise. None of the family had been present at the wedding with Armande. It was just as well.

When the word came that the old man was dying, Molière went like a dutiful son to the bedside. His brothers and sisters greeted him with mixed suspicion and awe. They admired his courage, and basked in the reflected glory of his adventures in high society, but were nervous of a returning prodigal who might demand a share of the inheritance. He reassured them. "What would I do with this business now? If I ever knew anything about it, I have forgotten. I would be as inept in your work-rooms, I assure you, as you would on my stage. So let us be at peace, and talk no more of money."

After this, they were much more pleased to see him.

He was led upstairs to where his father lay in a troubled sleep. A priest sat by the bed, waiting. Molière bent over and studied the wan, unshaven face, almost smothered by pillows. Strange that he could ever have been afraid of him. There was a smell of sickness and decay in the room; it was cruelly hot, and quiet.

"Do not disturb him," said the priest. "He has made his peace with God."

The old man's eyes opened, and he coughed, leaving a string of spittle on the bedclothes. He lay quiet for a while, staring at the shadows on the wall, then shifted his eyes to the bedhangings made by his workmen to his own design, and a faint glow of animation crept into his face. Another fit of coughing. It hurt him, and he moved to ease the pain. In doing so, he saw who was sitting at his bedside.

"Jean-Baptiste?"

"Yes, father."

"So you've come home, have you? It's about time."

"They told me you were . . . ill. If I'd known I would have come before."

"No you wouldn't. You wouldn't be here now, if you hadn't thought I'd already be dead."

The priest made soothing noises from the corner. His eyes fixed on the ceiling, the old man rambled on.

"You've been a great disappointment to me, Jean-Baptiste. I always had great hopes for you. We could have worked well together. We could have built a name, a house, that people would point to with pride. But no, you had to go your way. You chose the life you wanted, and what have you gained from it? Nothing solid, nothing that will last . . . when you die, who will remember you? Nobody!"

It was almost over. The words subsided to a fitful murmuring, the breath grew jagged and the eyelids fell.

"But that's all . . . over and done with, no remedy now. No going back . . . no going back."

"I think you should leave, my son," said the priest.

But at that moment some memory crept into the old man's mind and jerked his body into ghastly animation. He sat up violently and pointed a trembling hand at his son. The priest crossed himself.

"But this other thing . . . no, that can't be true. No son of mine could do a thing like that. Could you? Could you?" Weaker now, he dropped his head back on the pillow. "Tell me that is a lie, and I forgive you all the rest. Tell me it isn't true, and I shall die happy."

"What isn't true, father?"

He had to lean close to catch the words, no louder than a breath.

"These things they are saying . . . about your wife . . . they aren't true? Are they? Are they?"

Molière had no idea what he was talking about. What rumor had the old man heard about Armande? What particular piece of gossip out of so many? No matter. He had lied once for his own sake. He could lie again for his father's.

He put his mouth to the old man's ear and said very slowly and distinctly:

"I know what you mean, father. And I swear to you it is not true. Just more gossip, invented by my enemies."

His father's face relaxed.

"I'm glad to hear it. I knew it could not be so. Even you . . . if you had. . . ." He raised himself again, and for a spasm became the formidable figure of years past. "If it were true I'd . . . I'd . . ." Then the fit took him, and he concluded his sentence to the angels. The room was already echoing with Latin as Molière left.

His brother was waiting on the stairs, and took his arm. "I heard what the old man said. It worried him a lot, you know." He glanced round furtively, and winked at Molière. "Is it true, though, really? You can tell me."

Molière jerked the offensive hand away.

"I don't know what you're talking about. Leave me alone, or I'll kick you downstairs."

It was thus that Jean-Baptiste Poquelin finally parted from his family.

What had his father meant? The words burned in his memory as he walked home. At the first opportunity he asked La Grange.

"What are they saying about Armande?"

The simple question produced a terrifyingly disproportionate response. La Grange had been entering figures in the huge leatherbound ledger that had become part of his person. His hand jerked, the column was ruined, and his pen scrawled a line from one side of the page to the other.

"Oh my God, you've heard it. We tried to keep it from you. We didn't know whether you'd heard or not. We thought you might have done and were ignoring it."

Molière was at a loss. "I know there's talk. I don't know what about."

La Grange mopped his brow. "Don't ask me. I can't tell you. Forget it. It's not worth bothering about."

"Tell me, man! Do you think I don't know my dear wife? I only want to find out what particular tidbit she's thrown to the public this time. I assure you it won't shock me."

"It will."

His tone and manner convinced Molière that he was serious. Crossing the room in a stride he seized his friend by the shoulders and shook him violently.

"Tell me, man. I have a right to know what it is."

The words came out in a disconnected babble.

"It's those devils at the Hôtel de Bourgogne. You should never have provoked them, Molière. Nothing's too filthy for them, if it serves their purpose. They started it. It's been going around for days, weeks. No one dared to tell you. We thought—as long as you were busy enough—perhaps you mightn't hear it, it would all die down before—they're saying that Armande—"

"Armande what? In God's name, spit it out!"

There passed across La Grange's face the same look, half-furtive, half-fascinated, that Molière had seen his brother wear.

"That Armande—that Madeleine—" He gulped, then poured the rest out in one breath, like the last wine gurgling out of a bottle.

"That Armande's not Madeleine's sister. That she's her daughter. Her daughter by you. That's what they—" He broke off abruptly as Molière's hand struck him across the face. Reeling back, he stared disbelievingly at the blood dripping from his mouth.

"How dare you say a thing like that? It's foul! It's blasphemous!"

"I never said it. You asked me. I'm only repeating . . ."

"Who said it, then? Who?"

"Everybody, now. It's all over Paris. Montfleury even wrote a letter to the King—"

He said no more, for Molière had rushed from the room.

Where was Madeleine? She could disprove this monstrous thing, this foul obscenity. He would take her to a lawyer, to a justice, have her testimony, serve a writ on his slanderers. How dare they do this to him? How could they sink so low? Was he so dangerous an enemy that they had to accuse him of incest to get rid of him? To paint him as a monster, begetting a new mistress on the old? Well, he would settle them. He would have the dates produced in court, show that it could not possibly be true. . . .

God have mercy. It just possibly could be true. His mind raced back through the years, remembering old dates and places. When Armande joined the company, how old had she been? Did he know? He did not. She had told him her age, but she had lied about it at least once. Even now he did not know how old she was. And a few years before that—what had they been doing? It was when they first left Paris for the south. Those miserable, grimy early years of traveling. What had Madeleine been doing then? Oh God, it all came back to him. Those frequent absences, the journeys back and forth to Paris. On her mother's business, so she said. Yes, and he knew that, he had been with her. Only once, said the devil in his mind, only once. What about the other times? At least one had been long enough to . . . bear a child, to put it out to nurse . . . and then, when it was old enough. . .

No! No!

Is that why Madeleine had not returned when he and Armande became lovers? Was it horror that kept her away, revulsion at what she had brought to pass, and not jealousy? Did she need time to learn to wear a mask, to cover her foulness with hypocrisy? How could she do it? How?

No, it was impossible. Louis would have known. Madeleine's mother would have known. The child was hers.

Or was it? She had always been a close-mouthed bitch. And old. How old? Too old, surely, to have children when Armande was born. Forty-five, fifty, perhaps. Why had he never thought of it before? The more he counted dates, the less probable it seemed that the same woman could have brought forth Madeleine and Armande.

But Louis would have known. And Louis, for all his sophistication in the world of business and intrigue, was transparent in personal matters. He could never have carried on the deceit all these years, even for his sister's sake, even for the family reputation. . . .

But need he have known? He had been abroad, on his travels. Armande was already grown when he came back. It could have been a secret from him too. Only three people need have known the truth. Madeleine, her mother, and Armande.

Oh God.

Into his mind, unbidden, crowding, came images of Armande as he had first known her. Not the woman, the seductress, the company whore, but the child; the pretty child following him round the theater and asking, so timidly, to be allowed to help in any way she could. How had he thought of her then? As a daughter, how else? How vividly it all came back. That night in the dressing room when he caught her with the boy . . . what was his name? When he had been so angry. Why? Why had he run from her when she offered herself to him? Was it anger born of lost illusions, or something deeper, a subconscious voice admonishing him that this must not be?

He did not go to find Madeleine. Instead, he locked himself in his room for three days and nights. He did not eat, or drink, or sleep. Afterwards, when sanity returned, he could not remember how the time had passed. He could recall a little: pacing the floor, engaged in an endless monologue; praying, cursing, asking whether he should make an end of himself.

And the word that rose in his mind was self. Louis had told him often enough that he was selfish, but he had never believed it till now. Madeleine had told him so, Armande. And they were right and he was wrong. For all these years he had shut himself away, guarding his own thoughts, his own aims, his own desires. And the only person to whom he had been able to give himself was an extension of himself, the child of his own flesh.

In his delirium, he told himself that he had known this all along. He was a monster, a thing defiled. And yet there was a fearful pleasure in it too. When he was in her body he had known it. When he was spending himself he was not yielding himself, because it was still in him, in his own flesh. And as he now stood naked in his room, he looked down at himself and saw himself grown hard, excited at the thought of her.

His mistress, his love, his daughter.

Madeleine came. They fetched her from the place where she had gone, and told her; and she came in anguish, beating on the door until he answered. He knew it was she, even before she spoke. They conversed with the impenetrable oak between them.

"Do you hear me, Molière?"

"I hear you."

"You must come out, my dear. You must eat and rest."

"Come out for what? To have them make a mockery of me? Call me a fiend, a devil?"

"I know what they say—"

"You knew it long ago. Why did you never tell me?"

"We wanted to keep it from you. We did not want you to be hurt. These stories, these slanders . . . you always take them too much to heart. They will pass, as the others have done."

"Madeleine, listen to me." His mouth was pressed against the door, his body forcing it as though he could reach through the wood and touch her. "This slander. Swear to me it is not true."

A sharp intake of breath from the other side.

"You need to ask me that!"

"I must be sure. Swear to me that she is not my daughter."

He could hear her crying.

"Could I deceive you? Have you so little faith in me? I swear it, Molière! Before God, I swear it!"

And out of the turmoil of his soul he answered. "You swear it. But you would be bound to swear it, whatever the truth was. How shall I ever know? God, how shall I ever know?"

"Can you not trust me, after all these years?"

"Not any more," he cried out in the loneliness of his despair. "Not any more."

And then there was an emptiness outside the door, and he heard her footsteps going down the stairs. He called to her, but the only answer was a door banging in the distance.

They had to break in, in the end. They found him in a coma, with a face so terrible that the pious crossed themselves. It was Madeleine who nursed him back. Madeleine and Racine, as he had done before. When Molière woke up and saw the fat face peering into his, and felt the warm soup trickling into his mouth, he felt strangely at peace, as though ten years had slipped away.

"Why are you both so good to me, after all the trouble I have been to you?"

"Because we love you. Because we need you. Because, whatever may happen to us, we are all part of each other now."

"I'm sorry, Madeleine."

"You need not be. But, Molière, stop torturing yourself. There are some things in this world we must take on trust. And if we cannot trust each other, you and I, after all these years, then we are finished."

It was enough, for the present. But even as she spoke, he knew that the doubt would keep alive, to plague him; and he knew too, with a flicker of revulsion at himself, that it did not really matter.

"I shall leave her."

Racine and Madeleine spoke together. "No. That is what you must not do."

"But how can I—"

"You have to stay with her. If you leave her now, the whole world will think you guilty. They'll destroy you."

"Am I to go on living a lie, then?"

"Yes. If you will. For all our sakes."

"Remember," said Racine, "it's the work that counts. You can't lose everything you've fought for. Nothing else is worth bothering about. Go and see the King. Make an issue of it. He'll support you, there's no doubt of that."

"Jean Racine, you are a very wise man."

"Jean-Baptiste Poquelin Molière, you are far too sensitive a one. I often wonder how you managed to survive this far."

"Go back to Armande," said Madeleine. "And I shall go away again. For the new reasons, and the old ones. You will not want to see me."

Armande had been well schooled, and went out of her way to say nothing to provoke him. She came the nearest she had been for years to tenderness. Stroking her husband's aching head, she spoke to him much as Racine had done.

"Molière, you think too much. We could show you all the proof you liked—certificates of birth, sworn testimony from mid-wives, a signed deposition by the Archangel Gabriel himself. And you would still never be quite sure, would you?"

"No," he answered dully.

"Well, my dear," she said, kissing him on the forehead, "we must do the best we can. Goodbye for now, Don Garcia."

"I can't do your play now, you know," said Molière. Racine was honestly surprised. "Why not?"

Molière laughed bitterly. "Have you thought of the subject? The house of Oedipus. A whole family raised in incest."

"Please—" said Racine in alarm.

"Oh, don't worry. I'm not going to rant and rave again. But have you thought what people will say? 'Oh yes, we saw *The School for Husbands* and *The School for Wives*. Now here's another play about his marriage!' "

Racine was earnest. "And I say to you exactly what I said about Armande. You have to brave it out. The play must be done." When Molière raised his eyebrows quizzically, he went on, "Not so much for my sake. Though Lord knows I want it done, after all these years, and not put off yet another time. No, be bold about it. Go on as before, and take the whole matter to the King."

Louis was preoccupied. Colbert, his new Minister of Finances, had been plaguing him again. Sometimes he regretted losing Fouquet. "I'd rather be robbed by a pleasant thief," he used to say, "than made rich by a bore." He received Molière with bitter raillery.

"Are you aware, M. Molière, that in the last two years we have spent more time with you than with our generals?"

"Your generals, sire, have their own weapons to fight their enemies. I have none. I can only borrow power from others."

Louis laughed. "So long as it is only power you want to borrow. If it were money, Colbert would have you arrested. What do you want with us?"

"Protection, sire, against unwarrantable slander." He poured out his story, and Louis nodded sagely.

"This is no news to us. There was a letter . . . well, no matter. We shall say it is not true."

The condesension in his voice offended Molière. Forgetting where he was, he spoke more sharply than he intended.

"It *is* not true, sire."

"God's wounds, man, is this a court of law? It does not concern us whether it is true or not. We do not wish you to be hurt, because you are amusing to us. There are few witty men around us. Therefore we shall say it is not true."

"But sire—"

"M. Molière, you grow tedious. Truth and falsehood are as we decide. Now go away and fight your little battles, and leave us to our big ones."

There was no more he could do. It was a hollow victory. Even the King, then. Was expediency the only god? Were things only true or false because they suited someone's turn? Not that he had any right to criticize. He was living a lie with Armande; a sham marriage, for the sake of appearances. More and more it was unclear to him where the theater left off and life began.

Against all his inclinations, he threw himself into the rehearsals for Racine's play. After a while the problems began to engross him again. The medicine was working, as Racine had known it would. Neither of them dared to prophesy how it would be received. Molière cautioned his friend that it would probably be booed, for the wrong reasons. "Let's see it, that's all," said Racine. "We can worry about the audience later." Molière's worst problem, as it turned out, was Racine himself.

As the rehearsals moved into their final stages, he could not keep away from the theater. He was insuppressible, and seemed to be everywhere at once: offering suggestions to the actors, criticizing the choice of costumes, and arguing violently with Molière's ideas from the darkness of the auditorium. "You write the play," Molière shouted at him furiously, "and I'll put it on the stage. Agreed?" The daily conflicts between them were a source of amusement to the actors, and daily bets were made on who would win.

The first performance came, and Molière's worst fears were justified. After all the gossip, the play had a sensational appeal. People flocked to see it, and vied with each other in identifying the characters with members of Molière's family. He had told himself that he would have to face this, and did his best not to let it depress him. But after so much effort, the performance seemed flat. Had he been wrong to take away so much, to hold his actors down? It was Molière himself who received the final insult. As he stepped forward to take his bow, some anonymous spectator tossed two sous on the stage at his feet, and a voice called "Better pick them up, Molière. That's how much acting you've given us tonight."

He wanted to take *The House of Thebes* off after the first night, but Racine persuaded him to give it one more chance. He was glad he did so, for he found that the people kept coming, even when the novelty and sensation had worn off. The simplicity appealed to them; they were actually prepared to enjoy the play on its own merits. After a dozen performances, the author and the actor congratulated each other. They had achieved a success—qualified, perhaps, but the interest was there. The public had been shown that there were other ways of playing tragedy besides the style of the Hôtel de Bourgogne.

Racine had another play ready, and it was agreed that this should go into production immediately. Molière was as excited as Racine now. After so many disappointments, at least one of his dreams would be fulfilled. The new tragedy had another Greek subject; it was called *Alexander*, and dealt with the exploits of the world conqueror in India. It went into rehearsal for the next season. Molière was relieved to find Racine less temperamental. After the first few days he stopped coming, and Molière, interpreting this as a sign of confidence, poured all his energies into the play. They would have an even greater success this time.

Alexander opened at the Palais Royal to general approval. It opened at the Hôtel de Bourgogne three days later.

Molière could not believe his ears when he heard of it. Racing to Racine's lodging, he demanded an explanation. The tragedian was shamefaced but determined, and pouted like a child.

"I know what you think of me," he said, "and you're right. But what could I do? You have a name already, Molière. I wanted one for myself. We're none of us getting younger."

And so it all came out. The insidious agents of the older troupe had done their work. They had seen *The House of Thebes* and been impressed by it, impressed enough to forget that they had once staged Racine and dismissed him as a failure. They had made concrete offers to produce his next play. Racine was tempted, but loyal at first to Molière. This pleased them, for it now allowed them to do two things at once—perform a play that they wanted and move against an enemy they hated. They protested fervently that there was no question of his breaking any promise already made. They merely wanted to do the play themselves. It had taken little urging to get him to agree. After all, why should he not? They had not told him they would present their version in direct competition. And now the harm was done; there was no question which was the more popular. The great names still charmed the public; it was the Bourgogne that the people went to, in the end. Racine was made.

"I'm sorry, Molière," he said. "But I've always told you that the work is the most important thing. Nothing must stand in the way of that."

"I wish," said Molière, "that you would examine your own conscience as carefully as you make your characters examine theirs. What a tragedy that would be!"

They never spoke to each other again. In a way, Racine's defection hurt Molière more than Madeleine's. When personal ties had failed him he had been strengthened by this professional bond, by the knowledge that the two of them were working, in their different ways, towards the same goal. And now this too had gone. He felt isolated now, and increasingly bitter towards a world that would say one thing, and do another.

PART FIVE

Finale

As usual, his bitterness boiled over onto paper and formed itself into a play. It was the only release that he had now. Work became a drug and an escape. The scandal about Madeleine and Armande ceased to torment him, though the King's edict had not laid it to rest. From time to time it still arose to plague him. He found, to his surprise, that he could be tolerant, and discuss the matter with an indifference that amazed those about him, as though it were some other man in question. A play was circulating in the city—it had been performed several times, in private houses—in which the leading characters were himself and Armande, thinly disguised. The dialogue was a pastiche of his own, not unwitty, twisted into lewd suggestions and double meanings. He asked for a copy, and read it. When he had finished he tossed it aside without rancor and remarked that he doubted whether it would last a season.

This was a new Molière, and one they were not certain if they liked. Armande found his polite indifference troublesome. She would have preferred either rage or melancholy; she was well equipped to deal with the extremes, having practiced them so successfully herself. Mere tolerance irked her, and she began increasingly to forget her promises and divert herself in other ways. Molière was still unruffled. No scandal, no gossip could disturb his lofty serenity. The victim had become the judge. He watched and waited; they did not know that he was planning to pass sentence.

They were invited to Versailles again. In spite of the increasing pressure from his ministers, Louis was determined to surpass himself. The palace would be transformed into a magic island, a fairyland where all would be enchanted. Ostensibly, the fête was in honor of the Queen. In reality, as everyone including the Queen knew, it was to celebrate the birth of a child, irrefutable proof of the King's conquest of the lovely, timid, virginal Louise. Louis' happiness, they said, had made him overbold. Anne, the Queen Mother, disapproved violently and publicly of her son's behavior. The Queen had her party of friends and sympathizers. Colbert, who had drastically purged the court of overpaid idlers, argued that this one celebration would cost the King all he had saved in over two years. Louis was deaf to all these arguments. His word was still law. The festival would take place as planned.

The moralists were scandalized but society cheered. None cheered louder than Molière's company, who forgot the physical discomfort of Versailles, and remembered only the lights, the brilliant company, the acclaim and prestige. Molière was commanded to produce a series of tableaux and a new comedy. The tableaux were easy. He could devise such things in his sleep. Of the play he was less certain. He knew what it would say, but as yet had only the haziest notions of character and plot. Of one thing he was confident; at Versailles he could say what he liked. The King's support was evident by now. This did not mean protection from attack. Nothing would still the yapping of his rivals. But what could they do worse than they had done already? With the King behind him he could write as he wanted and face the consequences. This time there would be no compromise.

The struggles of the past few years, the broken faith, the loss of friendship, had soured him more than his closest acquaintances could guess. Paris was a jungle. The old lady in the salon had been right. You had to fight with every weapon if you wished to stay alive. Eat or be eaten. He had no family, no friends except La Grange. Madeleine was gone, Armande a shadow on the horizon of his mind. Racine was gone. His work was merciless, and every play was haunted by the phantom of failure. He must always cater to the mob, the mass of stupid faces. . . . Very well, then. This time he would show them.

He needed an image, a point of focus that would show this brilliant, cruel, bedevilled society what he thought of it. No, what it was: its true face. He roughed out several plots, but impatiently discarded them. It must be something extraordinary, simple but strong; an image drawn from the familiar world that could be rent asunder and inverted to show old habits in a harsh new light.

Not an Italian plot this time. His purpose was too serious for that. Nothing from Terence either, though the old Roman had served him well enough in the past. No borrowing. He would admit no partner to this work, even one who had been dead for centuries.

Where?

Into the corner of his mind there crept a memory. He tried to grasp it but it laughed at him and escaped. Some old humiliation; something that had seared him at the time, and whose scar he still faintly bore. Too faintly. He could not recollect it, though he wrestled with it nightly. In vain he used the timeworn dodge of immersing himself in something else, so that the memory would spring out like a mouse from a wall that imagined itself unobserved. Nothing would come. The weeks were passing, and he had only the tableaux to show—so monumental in their expensive stupidity that he could not see how even the court could relish them. But they would.

Then, one day, walking by the river, he heard a single low bell ring for Mass. There was a washerwoman squatting by the quay. Her face, half-shadowed in a mass of greasy hair, half-vivid in the slanting shaft of sunlight, recalled to him, incongruously, an aspect and an attitude. Into his mind there came a revenant, an unkempt priest with filthy fingernails leaning across a banister and snarling at him. And the same priest later in a different guise, in lawn and lace, his hands bedecked in rings, his hair pomaded, rejoicing in his triumph.

He thrust some coins into the washerwoman's hand, and ran home to write his play. He finished it in two days.

"What's it called?" asked La Grange.

"*Tartuffe*, or *The Impostor*."

"Ah," said La Grange." An Italian comedy."

Molière smiled, and let him think so.

The fête began peaceably enough. Whatever quarrels Louis had with his immediate family had been laid aside, or were at least in abeyance. Louise de la Vallière was discreetly present, in a plain white gown which denied her recent motherhood. The King was unusually attentive towards his wife, and Anne the Queen Mother smiled serenely. Even Colbert abandoned his accounts and tried to be amiable, reflecting that his project for the manufacture of tapestries and the proposed tax reforms could wait till later. If this occasion led to amity, it was worth it; though he shuddered when he saw Molière's preparations for the tableaux, and calculated how many minor officials he would have to dismiss to pay for them.

Molière had devised a beast show. Things exotic were in fashion, and the more grotesque the better. He was an old hand at the game now, and knew how to play his effects. Start with something commonplace, even a little dull. Let them grumble and complain of disappointment. Then, bang—the sensation, the novelty. It would seem all the better by contrast. So, for the first entry, he had devised a procession of cooks. His whole company entered in procession, accompanied by as many supernumeraries as the palace staff could spare. Some carried torches and candelabra. Others held great platters heaped with false fruit, plaster roasts and boars' heads of papier mâché. They sang as they marched, and paid homage to Louis and his Queen in verses whose banality still made Molière wince. On such occasions, however, any departure from the conventional sentiments was suspect. Louis liked to be reassured that his subjects loved him.

Then the surprise. The cooks pirouetted, huzza'ed, raised their torches and tossed their chef's hats high. On to the lawn rode Molière and Armande, he perched high on an elephant, she clinging grimly to a camel. The beasts were led down to the royal spectators. Molière held his breath and prayed. A fanfare rang out, and—wonder of wonders—the two beasts kneeled on cue. He gingerly removed one hand and wiped his brow. He had been nervous about the camel. It had bitten, just before their entry, an overcurious page boy and a careless player of the counterbass.

Now, with Armande smiling seraphically between the humps, it was a sensation. A court wit improvised a poetic tribute to the beast and its rider, which began

> *The shaggy camel hollowed out its back*
> *The better to receive her lovely form*

and went on to insinuate that Armande had made other, less decorous concessions in regard to the camel. The poem was well received around the court, and was popular for three days, particularly among the ladies.

There were other animals, equally docile, all improbable. A white bear roared inside a gilded cage. An ostrich strutted disdainfully by. A rhinoceros snorted noisily. Then Molière dismounted gratefully and, feigning to be Orpheus, made a pretty speech in which he pointed out that these beasts represented the far corners of the earth, all equally subservient to His Majesty's pleasure. He was well applauded, and behind the arbor, when the trumpets had sounded retreat, acknowledged the congratulations of his actors.

"The King's well pleased," said Colbert, who had come behind for a closer look at Armande. "If your play goes as well, you'll be the talk of the country." Someone coughed a respectful warning, and he stepped aside just in time to avoid the defecations of the elephant.

The Pleasures of the Enchanted Isle wound on their languorous way. In the mornings no one stirred; no one, that is, of any consequence. Only the army of gardeners and cleaners, moving across the lawns with silent care, removing the debris of pleasure, the empty bottles, picked bones and discarded fans; smoothing out, without comment, the depressions in the grass where bodies had lain, trimming branches broken in amorous chase, removing litter from the fountains, raking, cleaning, tidying, admonishing Nature that, like the human denizens of this world, it must respond to symmetry and order. By noon there was a blush of young girls on the terrace, and young men recovered from the last night's conquest and ready for the next, anxious to escort them. By midafternoon the festivities had begun. A concert, perhaps; an orchestra ranked on the terrace steps or under silken awnings in the park, tinkling and harmonious. Or a tournament, reviving the glories of medieval chivalry, with combatants jousting decorously with toy lances and vying for the favors of the Queen, who, high in a pasteboard castle, threw wreaths and jeweled trinkets to the victors. Then, with the coming of evening, all went in to dine: an endless succession of rich courses, each served with some allegorical device and more of the eternal music. Out on the lawns again, some belching, some staggering, some already moving towards an embrace. The fountains radiant with colored light, a sparkle of fireworks in the sky; ballet dancers on a stage above the water, grottoes wrought like Scylla and Charybidis or Circe's cave; masks, grotesque, jeweled, beautiful, looming through the darkness, that might conceal a lover or—if you were unlucky—a wife. The richness and the grandeur and nobility of France were poured across the park like pearls upon a green silk tablecloth. When the last illumination sputtered to its end, and the musicians scrubbed their red-rimmed eyes and put away their instruments, the night subsided into sighs and whispered assignations, the furtive music of illicit, tolerated pleasure.

Life was an enchanted island, in which there was nothing sober, nothing lasting, nothing serious. King Louis the enchanter had struck them with his wand. For what they did today, no one would hold them responsible tomorrow.

So it went, until the fourth day.

Since his successful opening, there had been speculation about Molière's play. All knew the title; few knew more, though this did not stop them guessing. There were rumors that he was planning something disagreeably moral—"a purge," said somebody, "after four day's feasting." But these were discounted. All knew how Molière's detractors loved gossip. Most had participated in it. Others, nearer to the truth, said it was a play with a priest in it. Well, why not? He had had his fun with doctors in the past, and men of law, and country squires; priests were no less amusing. No one questioned how these rumors got about, who spread them, where they started. It was the Paris air that crept into men's minds, extracted their most secret thoughts and spread them to the winds. Molière was deaf to all hints and entreaties. Worse, he had sworn his company to silence. It would cost them their places, if they let it leak out.

He wondered that they had accepted it so lightly. Were all his actors stupid? Did even La Grange's astute brain fail to perceive what the play was about? It seemed to have meant nothing to them. All through rehearsals, they had accepted it as just another farce. So much the better. They would play it without nervousness, with more conviction. Or had he been too subtle? No, he did not think so. There would be some, at least, who would hear and understand.

The audience sat down to *Tartuffe* in contented satiety, waiting to be politely amused.

It began quietly, even tamely. The scene was a wealthy Parisian household, dominated, it appeared, by one Tartuffe. This Tartuffe was the religious adviser to the family ("I told you so," whispered the knowing ones to their friends) and Orgon, the paterfamilias, was under his spell. His wife and children were derisive while he lavished praise on Tartuffe's head. A few in the audience began to yawn, and some were already predicting the plot. It was to be a moral play, after all. The daughter—or perhaps the wife—would engage in some escapade, and be brought to heel with Tartuffe's assistance. Or perhaps the girl had a lover who was not rich enough, or lowly born; and Tartuffe would disguise himself to help her out. Yes, of course, that was it. Was it not called *The Impostor*? The same old plot, the same old characters. After such a splendid beginning, they had hoped for better from Molière.

Where was Tartuffe, anyway? Why did he not appear? What sort of way was this to write a play, to talk so much about a character and keep him hidden? After all this rhetoric, he could only be an anticlimax. When the first act ended and the violins struck up, the audience were glad to talk of other things. Some of them left their seats, and drifted away.

Act Two. The setting was unchanged. More of the same, no doubt. This was the slowest plot that Molière had ever written. Perhaps it was true, what people were saying—that he was losing his hold, the sparkle had gone out of him. Still, he was the King's favorite. It was best to be polite and applaud.

Wait! Who was this, striding onto the stage so forcefully? Tartuffe himself. What a singular fellow he was. Dressed all in black, with his hair plastered lankly over his eyes, and a cry of hair shirts and scourges. After so long a wait, his appearance came like an explosion. From that moment, he dominated the play. Complete silence wrapped the audience, as they waited to see what he would do.

This was no ordinary schemer, surely. A man of God—so he described himself—with a missal always ready in his hand, and a flow of pious phrases on his lips. He would not soil himself with amorous intrigue. No, it was going to be a sermon after all. The peccant son and daughter would be brought back to the bosom of their family by sage words and biblical advice.

How dreary. One would have thought that Molière would have had better taste.

But, as they watched the plot unfold, the conviction began to dawn on them that it was not going to be the sort of play they expected.

Little by little, Tartuffe revealed himself as a monster. His piety was a masquerade, his prayers a fraud. Under the guise of the religious devotee there lay a greedy lecher. How his actions betrayed the protestations of his words! When he counseled the servant-girl to veil her bosom with a kerchief, his hand cupped automatically, as if he would caress what he claimed to despise. As his power increased he became more open. Having the house, he coveted its occupants as well. Foolhardy in his success, he attempted to seduce Orgon's wife. But Orgon, by a trick, had been forewarned. He hid beneath the table at their assignation, and overheard his wife's virtue, and his protégé's perfidy. What a confrontation that was! Orgon, angered by his own humiliation, perceiving how far his blindness had led him astray, banishing Tartuffe from his house. And Tartuffe going—no, Tartuffe not going; Tartuffe halting at the door and turning like a monstrous black spider to announce that he would not leave the house, for it was his; that Orgon, in his dementia, had signed away all his worldly goods.

In a brilliant invention, Molière had refused to use the customary finale, in which the cast lined up to receive their applause, the fiddles shrilled and the audience remembered that it was only, after all, a play. Instead, Orgon and his family left the stage and made their exit through the audience; a long slow exit, while Tartuffe howled in triumphant laughter from the stage and, as the curtain fell, took handfuls of golden coins and tossed them in the air. That was the last the audience saw of him, malevolent, loathsome, revelling in a golden shower.

There was a long silence. No one in the audience dared to

move or speak. It was as if they had been shattered by what they had just seen, and did not dare move out into the dark for fear Tartuffe would get them.

Only one man laughed. A laugh of sheer delight, that spiralled high into the air and cracked the silence; and the whispering began, and the laughter stopped abruptly. His Majesty Louis XIV, King by the Grace of God, had realized that for the first time in his life he was laughing by himself.

The whispers spread through Paris by the morning. No one who had seen the play remained untouched by it.

It made no difference whether you had seen it or not. Everyone knew what it was about. Any chance acquaintance met in passing in the street would take you by the shoulder and explain what it had been about. Everyone saw the inner meaning. Everyone had his own key.

It was a play against the Jesuits who followed their faith in luxury and ease. It was a play against the Jansenists, who were dedicated to austerity. It was against the Pope, because it showed the hypocrisy of conventional religion; it was against the King, because it showed the rottenness of French society. It was against the home, it was against the rights of fatherhood, against the church, against the law. Each man had his own interpretation. All agreed on one thing only. It was a mockery of all the laws of decency. A travesty, an outrage, that should never have been permitted. A play whose author should be pelted through the streets. Above the tumult there rose, stronger and stronger, a recurrent, sinister refrain.

Blasphemy. Blasphemy. Blasphemy.

The choir concluded the polished perfection of the psalm; the last notes of the organ rumbled into silence, and the Archbishop of Paris mounted the steps into the pulpit. He climbed slowly and carefully, for all eyes were upon him; it was important that he should not stumble.

"*In nomine patris, et filii, et spiritus sancti, amen.*"

He surveyed his congregation. The Cathedral was packed to

the doors, as was every church in Paris that day. In all his days, he had never had so huge or so attentive an audience. Clearing his throat, he began to speak.

"Since, by the grace of His Holiness the Pope, I have been your Archbishop, I have on many occasions been moved to speak to you about the sins that beset our realm. The sin of wrath, and even as I speak, war has come once more upon us. The sin of envy, which turns the Faith against itself and has made division between us, creating diverse sects—I would almost say, heresies, where we should be united under God; the sin of covetousness, which has made many among you cast eyes on what should be the Church's, and appropriate to your vanities that which should be spent to the greater glory and honor of Our Lord. On these things, I say, I have talked to you before. Never enough; and you will hear me speak such words again, I promise you.

"But not today. For now there has happened something so gross, so shameful, so blasphemous, that were I to keep silent I should be failing in my high office; yes, I would deserve to be led through the streets of Paris behind a cart, and to be scourged, and have my robes rent from me.

"Of all the evils our fair city holds, I tell you there is none greater than this, these actors, as they call themselves; these apes and mockers, as I call them, these caterpillars of the state, in whom all lies and vanities are one, these agents of the devil, who by their tricks, their paintings and disguises seduce the souls of simple men, and send them down to Hell. Oh, often have I seen this, my children; yet never dared to speak of it before, for they have had protection from high places. Yes, from the highest in the land. Not out of malice, or of spite against our Mother Church, but because there is no heart so noble, no estate so strong as to be proof against their lures and wiles. For they are Antichrist; and those who in their mistaken kindness have supported them have unwittingly cherished a serpent in their bosoms. And the serpent now has reared its head to strike.

"Time was, my children, when the stage performed God's
work; when priests and holy monks thought it no shame to play
the parts of saints and martyrs, and by so doing to reveal God's
work more clearly to the people. But those days are past, my
children. The stage has fallen into the hands of the godless.
Where are those old plays now? You will not see them any
more. Rather trumpery, and lies, and amorous deceits; the
glorification of sin; vice painted in fair colors.

"Too long have we suffered this in silence. But when the
enemy attacks us openly, before the highest in the land, then
we must suffer it no longer, but strike back with all the power
we may. And that power is great, my children; and though it
bide its time, the wrath will come, and the godless shall go
down in darkness.

"From time immemorial, wise men have counseled us to
avoid these shows, these abominations. Even before the coming
of Our Lord; yes, in the days of darkness, when the light of
truth shone but fitfully, there were those who had eyes to see.
Let me recall to you the words of Seneca the philosopher. Yes,
he who was minister to a proud and bloody tyrant; he who
oppressed the poor, and the meek, and the humble; he who
saw the followers of Christ cast daily to the wild beasts in the
pit. Even he could say that when he went to a show, a spectacle,
he stood among his fellows and felt defiled. Should we, who
have been shown the truth, see with a dimmer light? Should we
not rather rise and drive out the impostors from our land?

"This week there has been shown to us a play that would
pretend to divert us and make us laugh. I shall not dignify this
play by naming it; you all know whereof I speak. It shows one
who claims to be a man of God; who lies and steals and forni-
cates; who is seen, at the end, laughing in the triumph of his
foul desires. And I say to you, that laughter comes straight
from the pit of Hell. I say to you, that this play is an affront,
deliberate, direct, to every man and woman who has taken holy
vows; to myself as to the humblest priest in the smallest village

of France; to the Holy Father in Rome; to the whole state of God's church.

"And so I say to you that this play is anathema, a cursed thing. That he who wrote it and those who act in it are men who do the devil's work. That they, and all who see this play hereafter, or read it, or have acquaintance with it in any form, have no rights within the Church. As your Archbishop, by the powers invested in me by the Church of Rome, I excommunicate all such. They shall have no right of sanctuary or holy water; they shall have no right of Christian burial, but lie like dogs in an unhallowed grave.

"*In nomine patris, et filii, et spiritus sancti, amen.*"

It was midnight when they came for Molière. He heard the clank of soldiers in the street outside and knew what it must be. When they knocked at the door he was already cloaked, and waiting for them hat in hand. There was no one for him to trouble with farewells. They marched in silence through the cobbled streets. When he asked diffidently where they were taking him, the captain said only, "You'll see." He did not ask again.

They went down to the quayside and embarked. It was a short trip, to a watergate he did not know. The oars splashed softly, and they steered by muffled light. It was raining hard, and pitch black outside the circle of the lantern. The boat changed course several times, and he no longer even knew which bank of the river they were making for. Then the boat scraped against the steps and he was hauled roughly ashore. "Follow me," said a sentry. He walked behind him in the torchlight. There was no other escort. He could have run away, if he had known where he was or where to run to; if he had wanted to.

They walked through a labyrinth of corridors, up and down steps, through door after door. At last they came to a long tapestried wall. His escort pulled the hangings aside and revealed an unpretentious door.

"Where am I being taken?"

"No questions."

"But . . ."

"No talking. Get inside."

The door closed firmly behind him and he found himself in a large room. If this is a prison, he thought, the cells are spacious enough. A candle burned at the far end and showed a bed, a table. He moved towards it; at least he could sleep. Then he saw a figure on the bed, a face that, without its wig, looked curiously young and defenseless. It turned towards him and spoke.

"Good evening, M. Molière," said Louis, King of France.

He was so dumbfounded that he forgot to kneel. The figure in the bed seemed not to notice.

"I am sorry to have summoned you in this manner. You were frightened, no doubt, and thought of prisons, and inquisitions, and all sorts of horrors. Well, not yet. Never, I hope."

The candle spluttered, and he was nothing but a white luminosity against the dark.

"I am sorry, too, not to be able to receive you in more comfort. You see now how Kings must live. And I am so petrified with etiquette that I would not even know how to ask you to sit down."

"It is enough for me to stand, sire. How many of the greatest men in France would give their fortunes to be in my place now?"

"How many would have dared to put themselves in your place now? Molière, Molière, do you know what you have done to me?"

He was silent. After a while, the King continued:

"You know how people look upon your play? What the Archbishop said this morning? Of course you do. He said it very loudly. Do you know why he said it? No, you can have no idea.

"I will be King in my own realm, Molière. Since I was old enough to think I have been sure of this. Years ago, when I

was a child, I lay in another room in this palace and pretended
to be asleep; and I felt the stinking breath of the mob in my
face as they passed through to look at me, and make sure the
ministers had not stolen me away. I have never forgotten that
night. It seemed endless. How I hated them. It was not me
they were interested in. I was a pawn, an emblem. That room
was bricked up when I came to manhood. No one will ever
enter it again.

"And I decided then that when I became King, I would
rule in fact, not in name. I endured the plotting of my ministers,
the urging of my mother. I made a marriage that I did not
want . . . and waited . . . and waited."

"But you do rule, sire." He plucked up courage to move a
little nearer. "France has never been so powerful. You are the
greatest king that she has ever had."

"You think so? I wish it were true. I try to make it so. But
if I am to be King, I shall be King over all. I accept no opposition from any man . . . or priest."

"Sire?"

"Or priest, I said. However rich his vestments, however many
jewels he wears in his miter. I will not share my kingdom,
Molière. Not with the Pope himself.

"This is my one remaining quarrel now. The lords and barons
have been brought to heel . . . for a time. I have to thank my
father for that, at least. As God's anointed king, I am head of
the Church in France. But they would tell me—yes, that fellow
in the pulpit, who dislikes you so much—that I am not the head
in fact. That I must bow across the mountains. Take my
instructions from Saint Peter's, like a verger who must tug his
forelock to the priest.

"So now do you see what you have done to me? Given them
ammunition to fight. Shown them that I support the godless,
the blasphemers. That I am not fit to be in charge."

"Sire, that was not the intention of my play. I—"

"I know perfectly well what your intention was. Do you take
me for a fool? You looked at the world and found it full of

hypocrites. So you drew us a glorious example. A hypocrite to end all hypocrites. How do you think your audience liked that? You were showing them themselves. You might as well have walked out and slapped them in the face."

"But how can the Church believe—"

"The Church believes what suits its purpose. Unfortunately for both of us, this suits it very well."

"Then will you not support me, sire? Since you agree with what I meant to do—"

A weary wave of the hand interrupted him.

"Believe me, it is with infinite regret that I say I cannot. Not this time. It would be fatal. We are much of an age, you and I, are we not? We both look older. We work too hard. But we have matured together. Ten years ago I would have supported you without the slightest hesitation, just as I would have taken a new mistress and told the world to go to the devil. Ten years ago, you only wanted to make people laugh. Now you want to teach us. So much the better for you. You've learnt responsibility. So have I, unfortunately. And responsibility means that you can't always do what you want. . . .

"If I opposed the Archbishop and let your play go forward, I should be throwing myself to my enemies. All I've worked for, all the good I've done would be lost. I have to sacrifice the smaller good to the greater. It is unjust to you, but I hope you understand."

"I shall try."

"Mother Church, unfortunately, is a more powerful enemy than the Hôtel de Bourgogne. And the older it grows, the more stubborn it gets. Don't worry. You'll write other plays."

"Never so good."

"Probably not. Keep it. Times may change."

His hand reached for the bellrope on the wall.

"Now you had better go. You've been here far too long. It was rash of me to invite you here at all. I've no doubt that the four or five people who have been peeping through the cracks in the paneling will make up all sorts of lurid tales about us. At least I'm powerful enough to take care of that."

Molière was groping for the door in the dark when the King called him back.

"One more thing, if you would be so kind. There is a jug of chocolate on the little table over there . . . would you pour some, and bring it to me? Thank you." He grimaced. "Cold as usual. Your father made the hangings for this bed, you know," he added inconsequentially. "Goodnight, Molière. And be careful."

Within five minutes Molière felt the cold night air and the rain upon his face. He shook his head bewilderedly and started on the long walk home.

"The trouble with you," said La Grange "is that you're too honest." Molière had reported the last night's conversation to him. There was no reason why he should not; he had not been sworn to secrecy. That had not been necessary. Who would believe him if he spoke of it?

La Grange believed him, and found grounds for hope.

"Of course the King won't do anything about it. What is there in it for him? He's right. If he supports the play, his enemies will use it against him. If he could turn it to his own advantage, though—" he riffled through the pages "—if it were for the King and against the Church . . . what do you think he'd do then, eh?"

"I've told you," said Molière, "it's not against the Church. It's not for or against anybody."

"That's what I mean," replied La Grange. "You're too honest. A few minor changes, and I think we've got it. As it is, Orgon and his family are crushed. There's nothing left for them at the end. How do you think the King likes that? It's as good as accusing him of licensing robbery. Write a new ending. Show the King intervening, setting everything right again. I swear he'd support us then."

"Go away," said Molière wearily, "and leave me alone. I'm tired of fighting, and compromising, and adapting, and making concessions . . . a little change here, a little alteration there, and before I know it, it's not my play any longer. I won't change a word, do you hear? I said what had to be said. It's done its work. I don't care if nobody ever sees it again."

"What a pity," said La Grange. "After all this talk we only need put up the name and we'd be sold out for the rest of the season. Strange, isn't it, how good excommunication is for business?"

The next day brought visitors. Molière had said he wanted to be left alone, but La Grange ushered them in defiantly. "If you won't listen to me," he whispered, "you might to them."

They were surprising visitors for the Palais Royal. La Grange made unnecessary introductions.

"M. Montdory, of the Théâtre du Marais. M. Montfleury, M. Brécourt, of the Hôtel de Bourgogne. M. Molière."

It was Brécourt who acted as the spokesman, a dapper man with long nervous hands.

"You are surprised to see us here, M. Molière. We are not exactly easy in our minds at being here. But we felt we had to come."

Molière looked at him and said nothing.

"There has been . . . unpleasantness between us in the past. Well, it is better not to speak of that. There have been faults— on both sides." Montdory smiled. Montfleury flushed and gazed at the floor, admitting nothing. Brecourt went on more forcefully:

"But this present crisis which you have, er, precipitated affects us all more deeply than you may think. The Church has been at war with us for a long time. I do not need to tell you that. Oh yes, in theory we are free and equal citizens. We have as many rights by law as the pastry cook or the ostler or the law clerk. But in practice we are a race apart, despised, humiliated. The Church even denies us Christian burial when it can.

"So the Archbishop's pronouncement is a threat to us all. We may not agree with what you have written—"

"We do not," wheezed Montfleury.

"—but we have common interests, after all. This ban on you is bad for all of us. If we let it pass unchallenged there will be more bans, more censorship; in the end there will be no theaters at all."

"What do you want me to do?"

"Make changes. Compromise. Find some way to make your play acceptable, so that the King will support it. He can override the Archbishop if he wishes. As it is he does not dare. You have not given him the chance."

"I wish I could help you," said Molière. "But it's too late. I can't change it now."

"Is there nothing we can say to persuade you?"

"Nothing. I'm sorry. Good morning, gentlemen."

They left resentfully. Montfleury turned at the door.

"Young man, I have always disliked you. Now I despise you. This *Tartuffe* of yours is vicious trash. Nevertheless, you ought to listen to what my colleagues say. There is a bond between us, once we have succumbed to this madness of the theater. You talk of honesty and integrity. We are the only honest people. We admit we're playing a part. They," his gesture indicated with supreme contempt the world at large, "do just the same, but never admit it. Save the honest people, Molière. Change your play."

"I like to think," said Molière, "that my honesty goes somewhat deeper. Good morning, M. Montfleury."

The tragedian puffed at him, and waddled down the stairs.

La Grange was torn between ecstacy and outrage. "Do you know what you've done?" he demanded. "Made Montfleury apologize! For that fat old fool, coming here was like going down on his knees to kiss your hand. And then you had to turn him down! This could have been the finest thing for the players in Paris since . . . since . . . I don't know when. No more bickering and fighting. A united front. An end to the quarrels. Molière, Molière, how can you be so selfish?"

"My dear La Grange," replied Molière, "you should read your history. Oh yes, they're united now, perhaps, against a common enemy. It always happens. But if I gave in to them, we'd be at one another's throats again in three weeks. I'd be burlesqueing them, and they'd be traducing me. It's not worth it."

But La Grange still had his highest card to play.

Two days later, in the evening, came a low rap at the door. When Molière opened it, Madeleine stood there.

"La Grange sent you," he said.

She nodded.

"He asked me to come. I would have done so anyway."

She entered without being asked, laid down her hat and looked round the room.

"Nothing's changed, has it? A little more untidy, perhaps. Is there no one to look after you now?"

He was impatient with her.

"If you've come to ask me to change my play, you're wasting your time."

"That's what I have come for." He made an angry movement. "But hear me out. I know why you don't want to, and you're right."

"Then why—"

"For your sake. Not the King's, not the players', but for yours. You've always said, haven't you, that the work was the most important thing? That everything else had to be sacrificed for that? I've always let you persuade me, at whatever cost. You must listen to your own arguments now. You have two choices, it seems to me. Keep it as you write it; keep your cherished integrity; and have it lost for ever. Change it ever so slightly, make it more acceptable; get them to lift the ban; and share it with the people who ought to see it."

"It won't be the same."

"Nearly the same. Better half Molière than no Molière at all. Come now. Are you satisfied with only one audience?"

He smiled for the first time in days. "Not really. But I swore I'd never change it."

"And I swore I'd never come back here. Come now. If I can break an oath, you can."

"You always see things clearly, Madeleine."

"Come then." She was at home again, as if she had never left. "Pick up your pen and write."

They worked all night. When they had finished it was as much hers as his. She suggested changes and additions and he fought them. Little by little she wore him down, making him perceive the sense of what she said. In the first part of the play they increased the importance of the love plot, making it more like a conventional comedy. The character of Tartuffe was left alone, though in the new context the anger that had begotten him was less blatant. What he was doing, what he stood for, crept more subtly on the consciousness. Molière was forced to admit her cleverness. The way it stood now, you could not realize what you were seeing until it was all over; and even then, you could not quite believe it.

"You can't expect to cure the patient in one dose," said Madeleine. "He'll simply vomit it up, and be angry with you. You have to purge him by degrees."

It was the new ending that he really objected to. Madeleine had taken up La Grange's suggestion. To soften the blow, the family must be rescued at the end. An emissary from the King must come. Let him announce that His Omniscient Majesty had seen the whole proceedings from afar; that he would let no harm fall on his subjects; that Tartuffe would go to prison, and Orgon's property be restored.

"It's ridiculous," protested Molière. "It's like one of those gods in the Greek plays that pop out of the sky and solve everyone's problems because the author's too lazy to work out a proper solution. It's imbecilic. I'll have nothing to do with it."

"Of course it is," said Madeleine, "don't you see? That's the whole point. It's so ridiculous that anyone with half a mind will see it's no real ending to the play. The Tartuffes always win in this world. But it's exactly what you need to win the King's support. He'll love it. And don't tell me it's beneath your dignity, because you've done it before. Look at the way you ended *Don Garcia*."

"I didn't feel so strongly about *Don Garcia*. Anyway, what you're suggesting is positively blasphemous. It puts Louis on a level with God Almighty."

"I dare say he'll think that God is flattered by the comparison. Write it."

He wrote it. La Grange was given the new manuscript and rejoiced. "No time to lose," he said. "Let's take it to the King."

But the god peculiar to dramatists, the god who pounces from his machine to rearrange lives, had not yet finished with La Grange. The King was not in Paris. He was no longer in France. War had broken out in the Low Countries. The French army had crossed the border, and Louis had gone with them to add luster to the campaign.

If Louis still had any interest in his Spanish wife it was as a means of acquiring property. When she had married, her father, determined not to yield any of his territory to France, had insisted that she renounce all rights of succession, in return for a dowry of five thousand gold crowns. At the time this had suited Louis well. He needed money, and had enough land. Now things had changed. He saw himself as an empire-builder. There was a new king on the Spanish throne now, and, to make matters worse, the promised dowry had never been paid. Louis therefore insisted on his right, through his wife, to the Spanish possessions in the North. It made no difference that Maria Theresa was the child of a first marriage and that the offspring of the second, by Spanish law, took precedence. His ministers could settle that; what else were advisors for? And, to be sure, they found ample precedents in lawbooks and history.

There was no legal obstacle. Nor would the Spaniards put up much of a fight. It would be a safe war, the only sort that Louis cared to engage in. What could he lose? There would be enormous prestige for him; his army would earn its keep for once, instead of eating its expensive head off in the provinces; and it would get him out of the capital, where it was increasingly uncomfortable for him to be. So the King had gone campaigning, with his silken tent, his cooks, his butlers and a retinue that made a sizeable army of its own.

"How shall we reach him?" wondered La Grange.

"There's nothing for it," said Molière. "We must go to Flanders, and do a little campaigning for ourselves."

To this Madeleine had strong objections. "Not you, Molière. It's a long, hard journey. You're not fit for it. It would kill you."

It was true. He had been looking haggard lately, and coughing more.

"La Grange must go. He's the only one we can trust. You will go, won't you?"

Of course he would. The journey would not be too bad, he said, and he was used to roughing it. He should be back within a week. Say at the most ten days. There was no doubt of their success. Let them announce *Tartuffe* for that time. The Archbishop would be angry, but he could not impose punishment in advance. Long before the day of performance came, he would be back with the royal permission.

They saw him off in a coach, primly grasping his bags and bundles, with a metal box that contained his treasured ledger bouncing on his knee. He was an inveterate recordkeeper. Everything that happened to the company was of interest to him; he would not miss this chance of recording his adventures and impressions. His moustache curled with pride, and he was as happy as a child going on a visit to the country.

"Goodbye," they called to him as the coach rolled out of the inn yard. "Come back safely!"

"In a week!" he shouted back at them. And before the coach had even reached the highway his pen was out and the fat ledger spread upon his knees as he dabbed at the ink-horn hung round his neck and wrote, in careful script: *First Day. Departure from Paris.*

The week passed, and there was no sign of him.

The eighth day, the ninth; no word, no message. The company was growing anxious. Since the announcement of *Tartuffe* the theater had been besieged. Though threat of excommunication still hung over their heads, the people, it seemed, were prepared to defy the devil. Louis would have been pleased. The public knew which way the wind was blowing. They realized that this was more than a play. It was a tussle between Church and State, and they had a shrewd idea which would win.

The tenth day. Nothing.

"What shall we do?" said Madeleine.

"We'll have to cancel. What else?" Molière shrugged his shoulders in resignation. "If we play *Tartuffe* today, La Grange will find us in prison when he comes back. If he ever does come back."

"We'll have to play something else, then."

"They won't like it."

They waited till the last moment, in the hope that La Grange might yet come panting into the theater with the precious permission in his hand. The theater had been full for two hours before the performance, and a crowd almost as large again waited in the street outside. On the fringe of the mob were files of soldiers, ominously attentive.

"What shall we do?" muttered Du Croisy. He was in his Tartuffe costume, but his wig still hung limply in his hand. He was afraid that if he put it on his head soldiers would burst through the door and arrest him. They were already fifteen minutes late. Through the curtain came that most menacing of noises, the rumble of an impatient audience.

"Do something," said Madeleine. "They're starting to stamp."

They were. It began in the balconies and through the whole theater; it was like an army of giants on the march.

Molière flapped his arms in despair.

"Go and change your costumes. We'll give them *School for Wives*."

He lifted the corner of the curtain and walked out before the audience, raising his hands in an appeal for silence. There was no need. The stamping stopped as soon as they saw him, and the whole theater was as quiet as death.

"Ladies and gentlemen, you have honored us with your presence to see a new comedy, *Tartuffe*; a comedy which at its first performance found favor with many, but—I swear with no intention of ours—offended some." A half-wink to the audience, and a rapid gesture with his right hand, as though he were crossing himself. They loved it. There was a sustained burst of applause, and a shout of "Don't worry, Molière. We're on your side."

"He's doing it," whispered Madeleine, with her ear pressed to the curtain. "He's winning them over."

"Unfortunately," his voice broke with nervousness. The laughter stopped abruptly, and the silence returned, total and menacing. "Unfortunately circumstances have arisen which prevent us from keeping our promise to you and presenting *Tartuffe* here today. Instead we offer you *The School for Wives*, a comedy—"

He was allowed to go no further. A turnip cannoned through the air and hit the curtain just behind his head. Another missile caught him on the forehead and made him stagger. He put his hand to his face and found it covered with egg. Something else hit him on the ear, more painfully, and the stickiness turned red and became blood. The audience was like a wild beast crouched to strike. Half-anticipating such a disappointment, they had come armed. From under the benches came the refuse of the Paris streets, rotting fish, fruit, stones, the filth of animals. Molière stood helpless, pleading as the volley crashed round him and the cry went up.

Tar-tuffe! Tar-tuffe! Tar-tuffe!

"Get him away, for God's sake!" cried Du Croisy. "They'll kill him!"

Still protesting, Molière was dragged off the stage. In full stage costume, the actors ran for their lives. Outside, in the street, the soldiers watched the crowd make a shambles of the theater. It seemed that they would not be called upon to make an arrest after all. What was going on now was none of their business.

Safe behind locked doors, Madeleine bathed Molière's wounds.

"I have to go back," he protested. "They'll tear the theater apart."

"Better it than you. In God's name, where is La Grange?"

La Grange, at that moment, had not even reached the King. The exhilaration of his journey had faded abruptly on the second day when, after waiting for some hours at Amiens, he was cursorily informed that he could expect to travel no farther by coach.

"Why not?"

"There's a war, haven't you heard? Anyone who tries to take a coach through there will have it torn to pieces."

"But I thought the Spaniards weren't putting up a fight?"

The innkeeper laughed coarsely. "Who's talking about the Spaniards? It's our boys I'm frightened of."

La Grange was desperate. "How am I to get there, then?"

The innkeeper looked at him curiously.

"There's still horses. I suppose you can ride."

"I can always learn," said La Grange, in sudden terror.

"Well, we'll see what we can do. How much money do you have?" Not enough, apparently; the cost of hiring horses in Amiens had risen alarmingly, in direct proportion to his need. After much argument and dubious head-shakings the innkeeper consented to take his bags and his watch in earnest of future payment. He cast envious eyes on the metalbound box, too, but

La Grange opened it and showed him there was only a ledger inside.

"What are you, anyway?" asked the innkeeper curiously. "Some kind of scholar?"

"A man of business," said La Grange cautiously.

Man of business, thought the innkeeper, not much; not after what you've just paid for that horse. "All right, man of business, let's see how well you ride. Hoo-up!" And La Grange found himself hoisted ignominiously astride a scraggy beast whose back was studded with more protuberances than the laws of nature allowed. With some experiment, and after backing the animal twice against a wall, he trotted off, with the innkeeper's voice still resounding as he passed over the hill out of sight, listing the extra charges he could expect to face if he should graze a flank or bark a leg.

It was the most ghastly journey he had ever taken in his life. After a while he learned how to give the beast some semblance of rapid forward motion; for a long time after that, he wished that he had not. Bumping, bouncing, his hat lost to a hanging tree and his legs bruised with contact against walls and fences, in constant terror of falling off, he covered the slow miles from Amiens to Arras where he had last heard that the army was. He was unable to go very far each day. As he drew nearer to the scene of fighting, he found that every horse had been commandeered. Not only was it impossible to find a fresh mount, but he was in constant danger of losing the one he had. He took to sleeping in the stable by its side. Not that he would have known what to do if a thief or an inquisitive officer appeared; he had no pistol. But by good fortune the military did not trouble him, and any prospective thieves were put off by his desperate appearance. He had not shaved since he left Paris. His wig was gone, his clothes were torn and filthy; he clung with increasing fervor to his box, the last link with the peaceful, civilized life he had led—how many years ago was it? Long, long in the past; he could not remember a time when he had not been on this horse.

The army was not at Arras. No one seemed to have heard of it. He was advised to go on to Lens.

At Lens, he was told that the troops had only recently passed through. "No fight in these Spaniards," said his informant gleefully. "They run away as soon as they set eyes on us. It's all our boys can do to keep up with them."

I wish something would hold them up a little, thought La Grange, forcing his aching body back into the saddle.

At last he caught up with them, not far from Lille. He reined in on a little wooded hill, and saw the soldiers spread out in the valley below. Tying the horse to a tree he sat down to watch and draw breath. He had never seen a battle before; never thought that it would look like this. It was a show, a stately dance, a ballet. All over the valley grew the uniforms, yellow and green, purple and gold, a flag occasionally blowing among them, and horsemen wheeling and curvetting through the ranks. They marched in order, keeping tight formation, as if there were nothing more deadly in the fields beyond than partridges and foxes. Then the shooting started. Plumes of smoke rose from the surrounding hills, and some of the pretty figures toppled over and lay still. The rest marched on unperturbed. The noise of the cannon, to La Grange's ear, sounded no more frightening than the popping of fireworks at Versailles. Then, out of the corner of his eye, he saw an object moving in his direction. Someone was playing *petanque*. Slowly, lazily, it rolled across the valley at his feet. The cannonball grew closer, and immense. He recognized the awful force of it, and ducked in time as it whistled past and smacked into the trees beyond. When he had stopped praying and risen to his feet he found that a tree had been uprooted, and his horse was gone.

He never knew how he finished the journey. On foot, in the dark, through streams and marsh and brambles; through a farmyard once, alarming the cows, who ran at him, while a dog howled somewhere in the distance and the farmer called his wife to bring a musket. Finally, as he sat beneath a broken signpost not knowing where to go or where he was, a lumbering provision wagon emerged out of the dawn and picked him up; he entered the encampment royally, between two sides of beef.

They laughed at him when he sought access to the King, thinking him a madman. He sympathized; he knew how he must look. But give up now he could not. Summoning his last reserves of strength and remembering all that Molière had taught him, he drew himself up to his full height. The guards were startled by the lordly tones that issued from the mask of mud and grime. The arrogance of the voice, the assured insolence of the posture, belied the scarecrow appearance.

"You dogs! Have I gone through all this to be held up now? To ride without rest from Paris, to have my horse shot under me. . . . Take me to the King, you scoundrels, or I'll see the flesh whipped off your bones. His Majesty will not be pleased, I promise you, when he finds out why his messenger was delayed. His messenger," and La Grange's voice sank to a conspiratorial whisper, while he tapped his beloved box significantly, "from Mlle. de la Vallière."

"You realize," said Louis, not unpleasantly, "that we could have you whipped, or hanged, or both."

La Grange gulped and said nothing. He realized it all too well.

"To do all this," said Louis, "for a play? You must love your Molière very dearly."

"I would give my life for him," replied La Grange, thinking that he might well have to.

"Well, we have read it," said Louis, "and approved the changes. It is not unflattering to us. So be it. Devotion must be rewarded. We give you our permission."

"But the Archbishop—" worried someone in his retinue.

"The Archbishop is not here to preach at us. Neither, we trust, is anybody else. It will be good for him. It will show him who is master. After what we have accomplished here, will any man dare to oppose us now?"

He snapped his fingers, and documents were thrust into La Grange's hand.

"Go back to Paris, Monsieur. A carriage will be found for you, and horses. Put on your play, and tell them we have won a great victory."

"A great victory," exulted Madeleine. "Nothing can stop us now. Brother, go and make the announcements. See that our bills go up on every wall in Paris. We shall play *Tartuffe* tomorrow night. La Grange—" But La Grange was on his stomach, sound asleep.

Tartuffe played for forty-three nights in succession. No play in Paris had ever run so long. The company could never understand why Molière seemed so little pleased, or why, after the third week, he surrendered his part in it to Louis, and though he watched every night from the wings, never stayed to see the ending.

The theater was dying. Everybody said so, though few could agree on the reason why.

It was politics, they said. The war had turned sour. Louis, excited by his easy Flemish conquests, had let victory go to his head. There was other Spanish territory to the east, that bordered on Burgundy. It was to be had for the picking; why should he not take it? The armies marched across France again. Besançon yielded, and Dôle fell after a siege of only four days. Anthems sounded in the capital, and Louis entered Paris under huge effigies of himself dressed in the likeness of a Roman emperor.

No, said the other powers. France would soon be on the Rhine, and such proximity was dangerous. England moved, and Holland, and Sweden; while Louis chattered angrily of cabals and conspiracies, the powers around him came to an accord and stopped him in his tracks. He was forced to give back half of what he had taken.

Like a boy who has been slapped for stealing apples, Louis burned to justify himself. Were they laughing at him? They would see. Off went the invincible army again. It was Holland this time. Once more they cheered him in the streets of Paris. Bonfires were kindled nightly in celebration, and when the message came that the army had reached Amsterdam the bells rang in every church in France. Then the dour Dutch broke the dykes and let the waters loose, and the invincibles stopped, impotent. Once more the kings of Europe formed a coalition, and took their unruly brother to task. Louis was forced to sign an angry peace.

With all that money going on the war, the players asked, how could people spare any for the theater? It was impossible. Louis was forcing them out of their livelihood. Why didn't he stay in France where he belonged?

No, said others, it was not the cost; it was the fear. Louis, persecuted, feeling himself demeaned, had grown withdrawn and defensive. His spies were out, sniffing for insults to his glory and slights on his prestige. It was not safe to write freely any more. Look at Racine and that new play of his, about the Emperor Nero and his cruelties. You'd think that would be safe. But no! There had been rumors that Louis was offended, thinking that an attack on any monarch, however long departed, was an attack on him. What an opening that had been! The actors could not make themselves heard above the booing, and they had to drop the curtain twice in the first act for fear of violence. Racine's rivals had been behind it; they had packed the house. But there were whispers that the real trouble had come from the King's men.

Still others, more loyal, had a different story. To talk of censorship and suspicion was ridiculous. Louis had no need of such things; what had he to fear? No, it was simply that his interests had taken a different turn. Ballet was the thing now. At last France had discovered the ultimate art; it abolished the tyranny of words, and replaced them by the voiceless perfection of the human body; for the metrical trammels of the Alex-

andrine it substituted the infinite variety of music. Look at
Lully, and his meteoric rise in the court. It was Lully, Lully,
Lully at Versailles now; the day of the playwrights was done.
They had to learn, literally, to dance to a different tune.

The playwrights themselves said this was false. These ballets
were a passing whim, a toy, a temporary fashion. The trouble
was that the King was turning pious. He changed his habits
with his mistresses and it was bad luck for all of them that he
had fallen into the hands of a god-fearing woman. Her name
was the Marquise de Maintenon; by serving as foster-mother
to a number of the King's bastards, she had drawn the royal
attention on herself. He had courted her, and, incredibly, she
had refused. This unheard of maneuver had riveted the King's
attention. He was besotted with her, they said, but the more
he pleaded the tighter she clung to her virtue. The cynics
muttered that it could not last, and nicknamed her de Main-
tenant, "the lady of the moment." Louis was merely intrigued
by the novelty of a refusal, they said. It would all be over in a
month, they said. Yet the month became a year, and the year
several; and Louis, though he kept other mistresses, fell more
and more under the woman's sober spell. The court grumbled,
and foresaw a day when chastity would be fashionable.

Molière's company succumbed to the general feeling of
gloom. They took their tone from their leader, and after the
Tartuffe fight something seemed to have gone out of him. He
still wrote, but most of his plays were strange, bitter things that
the public did not like and the actors did not understand. It
was *Don Garcia* all over again. The distaste for life, the weari-
ness, the failure to acknowledge any satisfaction, any joy; and
the happy eccentrics who had once skipped across his stage now
seemed vicious and perverted caricatures. The public shuddered
at them; they reminded them of things they would rather
forget.

When he did write farces, as the actors urged him to—there
were still mouths to be fed and wages to be paid—he seemed
to have lost his lightness. All the old tricks were there, the old

inventions; but they were the old tricks, and the public had grown tired of them. The critics did not help. With them, at least, Molière had grown fashionable, for it was a cardinal article of their belief that if a thought could be understood by the vulgar it was not worth uttering. Therefore the less the public frequented him the more he was exalted by the savants; and, by the same token, they condemned his farces, complaining that he was reverting to rusticity in his dotage.

From time to time a commission came from court. Louis had not entirely forgotten him. But they were always for a ballet, or an interlude. He was no longer his own master; they would not risk another *Tartuffe* at Versailles. He complained that he had become a writer of pamphlets and broadsheets. They would throw him an idea from time to time and ask him to work it up; like the time the King was displeased by the ill manners of the Turkish ambassador, and, through Colbert, commanded him to write a ballet satirizing Turks, and a play to go with it. Molière said it was the first time he had ever written a play backwards.

There were mostly new faces about him now; young faces, which pretended respect but had no sympathy for him. Little Louis Béjart had bustled into his grave. The Marquise, still fluttering the rags of her charm, had deserted to another company. Armande was a total stranger to him now. They were still married, in name; but they no longer saw each other except when accident or royal command threw them together.

The last time he saw her was at Versailles. It had excited him to be asked there again, and when he learned that he was to work on a piece dealing with the Cupid and Psyche story something of the old enthusiasm came into his eyes. It died again, however, when he found that he was merely to be one of several writers; that he was to provide only a synopsis and a fragment of the dialogue; and that Lully, the insufferable Lully with his airs and graces and his ever-twirling baton would be in charge. Lully saw the whole piece in terms of music, and regarded Molière as a hack, a necessary nuisance

Armande, of course, played Psyche. She was ageless; she looked scarcely older than when he had first met her. Cupid was a young god from the Hôtel de Bourgogne, whom Molière looked at with failing recognition.

"I have seen you before, M. Baron, have I not?"

"I once played Medea's son, sir, in the play by your friend Racine."

"Of course. How stupid of me. We prophesied great things for you then, Monsieur. And I hear our prophecies have been fulfilled. I regret that I have not had more time to watch you at work."

Baron bowed impeccably.

"Indeed, M. Molière. I should have thought that you would have had a great deal of time to go to the theater now."

Molière swallowed this. Then, seeing Baron and Armande staring at each other with mutual admiration, he said:

"May I leave my wife in your care, sir? I have other business that I must attend to."

Baron bowed again.

"Indeed you may, sir. Pray do not let us detain you. It's bad to remain too long in the night air . . . at your age."

He watched them stroll off arm in arm across the lawn, and almost shouted after them "Watch out! She's Circe, immortal, indestructible; she'll destroy you as she did me, and two hundred years from now, when we're both rotting in our graves, she'll still be walking on these lawns smiling, coquetting, luring . . ." And then he thought why bother, let him find out for himself; and out of spite he stayed up all night at rehearsal, though the air was damp and made his cough worse.

He was so ill that Madeleine told him he must not act again.

"Go down to the south. You were happy there. The sun will warm you, and you'll come back well again."

He would not go. He had to cling to what he had. It was not much, but he had made it with the labor of his hands and mind; if he relaxed his hold someone would take it from him, it would be gone.

The doctors came and bled him. He felt worse than he had before.

He took the only remedy he knew, and made a play about it. He thought that the old sympathetic magic would work, that the cough would pass on to the paper, as his anger and resentment always had, and leave him whole again. *The Imaginary Invalid*. A play about a man in love with sickness, surrounded by potions and clysters and ointments . . . there were comic doctors in it, and the actors thought them grossly exaggerated. He thought he had drawn them from life.

The public thought his performance was exaggerated too. No hypochondriac would ever look like that. Those staring eyes, the trembling lips; the cough which seemed to break up his thin frame and leave him shaking; was this a comedy? No, it was too real, too ugly. Poor Molière, they said. He's already forgotten how to write. Now he's forgotten how to act, too. "Molière has never had enough breath to finish a line," said his enemies. "But this is taking it too far."

He took his bow on the fourth night and went to the dressing room. There was a noise, a cry, and they found him lying on the floor.

When they carried him home they knew that he was dying. Madeleine sat on one side of the bed and La Grange on the other. The doctors had been sent for, but he would not let them in.

"They'd kill me," he said. "Out of ignorance or out of spite. No, let me be. La Grange, you must take rehearsal in the morning. I'll be ready for the performance."

"You must rest," said La Grange. "Rest for a long time. You've earned it."

"Rest?" said Molière. He was growing feverish. "Rest is not for you and me. You have to keep busy, or you die."

He slept for a little. Madeleine wept quietly, her gray hair falling round her face.

Then his eyes opened, and he said quietly:

"Madeleine, my dear, why did we never marry?"

She stroked his forehead.

"We were always far too busy, my dear."

"Where is the script, La Grange? There are some lines I need to change for tomorrow. It would be funnier if—"

The last cough took him and stilled him. Madeleine reached forward and pulled the sheet over his eyes.

"He never wrote his tragedy."

"He wrote it," said La Grange. "He died."

He took his ledger out of its metal box, and carefully inscribed the irreducible debit, the hour and minute of his death.

The man of business turned actor, and the mistress who had been wife and mother, sat on either side of the bed, looking not at him or at each other, but back into the past, and into the future.

There was silence in the room.

AUTHOR'S POSTSCRIPT

This is a novel, not a biography, and though the principal characters are firmly based on history, I have taken the novelist's liberty of adapting names, dates and incidents. Students of the period will know that Jean-Baptiste could not have taken Madeleine to see, in 1643, a play that was not written until 1645; that Racine did not write a *Medea* (though he might have done); and that in many cases, I have preferred the legends to the facts. But in the case of a man like Molière, the legends are usually more truthful.

For one liberty I make no apology: that I have made Madeleine outlive Molière. It is what they both would have wanted.